Killing
Suki Flood

Rob Leininger

Novels by Rob Leininger
robleininger.com

THE GUMSHOE SERIES
Gumshoe (Nominated for a Shamus Award for Best PI Novel of 2016)
Gumshoe for Two
Gumshoe on the Loose
Gumshoe Rock
Gumshoe in the Dark ("Diabolically entertaining"—Publishers Weekly)
Gumshoe Gone
Gumshoe Outlaw (pub date to be announced)

THRILLERS
Killing Suki Flood
Richter Ten
Sunspot
Maxwell's Demon

OTHER NOVELS
The Tenderfoot
January Cold Kill
Nicholas Phree and the Emerald of Bool *
Olongapo Liberty   (R rated)**

*   laugh-out-loud funny, for adults who are still young at heart, who remember the good old stories that really took you away. For ages 10 to 110.

** The way it *really* was to go on liberty in the Navy during the Vietnam War. This one is not for the squeamish. Even the tattoos are ugly. A trip down Memory Lane for "old salts."

Rob Leininger

Killing Suki Flood

In memory of my brother, Sandy.
1953 — 1977

1

New Mexico, 1986

Trouble.

Frank Limosin knew the girl was going to be trouble the moment he saw her. She was perched on the rear deck of a bright red Trans Am in the barren New Mexico desert ten hard miles from the nearest highway, wearing hot-pink shorts and a Day-Glo lemon top.

Good-looking girl showing a lot of skin in a skimpy little outfit and the first thing he thinks is *trouble*? That told Frank more than he wanted to know about how old and fusty he'd become, but also had something to do with $77,000 in unmarked bills he'd stashed behind a fake panel in one of the camper's cabinets.

The past few days had been interesting enough. The last thing he wanted was a big change of plans.

Now, this.

The girl was leaning back on her arms, legs dangling off the back of the car, high-heel sandals swinging loose off her toes, not a worry in the world. Nineteen years old, give or take—legs a mile long, a strapless top looping over her breasts, held up by hope and a prayer.

He stared as he drew near, not so distracted that he didn't slow for a dry wash—an eighteen-inch dip and a bump that could bust an axle if a truck banged over it fast enough. From sixty feet away the girl looked like one of those unreal Pepsi girls he'd seen on TV: smooth and sleek, belly tight, hips slender, not one gram out of place. A real piece of work.

"Aw, shit," Frank said.

And right in his path, that was the cherry on this sundae, her car was partly blocking *his* goddamn road. Not his, really, couldn't call it that. It wasn't his, and it certainly wasn't a road, just a dirt and gravel washboard that took off from Highway 401, nine miles southwest of Quiode. The barely-visible trail rambled into the De Baca Mountains, out where vultures glide the empty blue sky and sometimes strip the carcass of a stray cow, or a person who'd run completely out of luck.

Dust drifted past the hood of Frank's truck as he slowed. The girl, smooth young skin tanned a nice honey color, slid off the back of the Tranny and stood with her thumb out, smiling, looking at him. Her other hand clutched a map.

Funny.

Frank didn't like it.

The Trans Am's left rear tire was flat. Frank checked it out as he drew near—expensive new car, fancy wire wheels, car slumped to the left, pretty girl not wearing much—a surreal tableau out here in the empty desert that stank of trouble.

Ambush? The girl might be a decoy. Frank scanned the desert all around.

This couldn't be a trap. No one came this way more than once a month. He saw nothing threatening within a half mile, just dry scrub not two feet high, needlegrass, knotweed, rocks—an impossible place to stage an ambush. He figured the melodrama of the past few days had worked on him too long, addled his brain. After nine hundred miles of checking his rearview mirror for cops, he needed a break. Still, he couldn't shake that brooding sense of trouble.

He leaned across the bench seat and rolled down the passenger-side window, spoke to her through the width of the cab.

"Trouble?" Might as well find out.

She blew a bubble. Late afternoon sun blazed off her pale corn-silk hair, tied back in a ponytail. Big green guileless eyes the color of old Coke bottles. Small, upturned nose. A shiner mottled her left eye, a bruise the color of mustard and mud.

"What I did was I turned left instead of right," she said.

Frank closed one eye. "Huh?"

"Sixteen miles from Imogene, except it was s'posed to be sixteen miles the *other* side of Imogene, not this side."

"Try to make sense."

"I am." She blew another bubble. "Hell, I was tired and it was dark and I don't read maps real good."

"You're lost."

Her eyes narrowed to slits. "I am *not* lost. I'm just not where I expected to be."

"Which is?"

"Santa Verti."

"Christ, you're lost."

"Lost means you don't know where you are, right?"

"Pretty much."

She stuck the map through the open window and pointed to an emptiness southwest of a town called Imogene. "Well, I figured it out and I'm right here, right?"

"Nope. Other side of the highway. Over here." He tapped a spot on the map several inches farther north and east.

"Well, hell," she said, pouting. "Which way's north?"

Frank pointed over his left shoulder. "That way."

"Dammit. Sun sets in the east, right?"

"West."

"Did I say east? I meant west."

Frank sighed. "How long've you been here, anyway?"

"Since morning, just before it got light. Tire's flat."

"I see that. Got a spare?"

"Sure. In the trunk."

"Why don't you change it?" Hell, why bother asking? He knew why. Her silver dangly earrings spoke volumes. She wouldn't know a carburetor from a tin whistle.

"I don't know how. I figured somebody would come along in a while, so I waited."

"You could wait out here a month and not see anyone."

She shrugged. "Guess I got lucky, huh?"

"That's no way to stay alive out here, girl."

She gave him a blank look. "You gonna help me with the tire or what?"

Reluctantly he switched off the engine and climbed out. His back felt slow, tight. He'd been driving since first light that morning and most of the afternoon, mile after mile running beneath the wheels of his truck. Trying to get more distance between himself and the police.

He came around the front of the old 1975 one-ton Ford.

The girl took one look at him and backed up a step. Frank was used to it, pretty much expected it, especially out here where if she screamed no one would hear a thing. He weighed two twenty-five and stood five foot eight. Wide shoulders, big arms. In two-inch heels the girl was two inches taller than he was, so they were of a size—except she'd be lucky to tip the scales at more than a hundred twenty-five pounds. Frank's neck was almost as big as her waist.

His face was craggy, unshaven, eyes dark beneath a heavy brow. His hair was graying, lopped off in a bristly crew cut. His left index finger was just a stub, the first two phalanges sheared off.

She sized him up, maybe wondering if she could outrun him if she had to. Not in those heels, Frank decided, but her legs were long and lean—slender, like a deer's. Frank was fifty-four years old, not as nimble as he'd once been. In good shoes she could probably leave him in the dust, sad to say. In those dumb-ass heels, it would be an interesting scramble.

"Peace," he said. "I'm sort of a tank, I know, but I'm a friendly tank."

She continued to look at him. "God, I hope so."

"You thirsty?"

"Yeah." Still wary.

Frank went around to the back of the camper, a twelve-year-old Caveman he'd picked up for eight hundred bucks and loaded on the back of the used Ford pickup he'd bought in Palmdale, California, just two days ago. He'd used the name Steve Hayden, paid with cash, and driven off with temporary plates. Using one alias or another was already starting to become a habit.

He opened the camper door. "Beer okay?"

"Anything. I'm dry."

He dug a Budweiser out of a chest filled with ice and handed it to her. She popped the top, spit out her gum, threw her head back and drank like a construction worker. Frank took the opportunity to look. Firm breasts, nicely rounded globes, a good handful each. No sign of a tan line anywhere around that tiny yellow top, lot of skin showing, so she might be the same color all over up there. Took her just thirty seconds to empty the can.

It was mid-July. Even though they were over four thousand feet above sea level in the De Baca foothills, the temperature must've topped out at over a hundred that day. Not much breeze, either. Frank squinted at the mountains across the valley, tinged blue in the hazy distance, miles beyond Highway 401.

It was still damn hot. She'd been here at least nine or ten hours, maybe more. If he'd come this way three days later he would've come across a Trans Am and a corpse.

"Another?" Frank asked.

The girl nodded.

It took her a little longer to empty this one, throat working, neck arched. He watched as bead of sweat rolled down her neck, over her collarbone, disappeared between her breasts.

"Again?"

She shook her head. "Better not. Another of those and I'd be on my butt. You got anything else?"

"Coke."

She nodded. "Yes, thanks. If it's not too much trouble."

"No trouble." He rooted around in the ice chest, hauled out a dripping can of Coke and handed it to her, suppressed a frown. He'd brought along three cases of beer and a couple of six-packs of Coke for the bourbon. Girl kept on like this, though, she was going to put a crimp in his drinking plans. She'd already screwed up his schedule, such as it was. He wanted to reach camp before it got dark, and it was still way the hell up in the De Bacas over a rocky trail that was only going to get worse, a *lot* worse, which was why he'd bought a truck with four-wheel drive.

She spent a full minute downing the Coke, beginning to slow.

"Another?"

"Thanks, not right now. You must think I'm a pig, huh?"

"Nope, just parched. Let's see about that tire."

She wobbled across the rubble-strewn dirt to the Trans Am and popped its trunk. Bright yellow flames were painted along both sides of the car's body. Twin chrome mufflers poked out the back, one of them hanging loose, almost dragging on the ground.

"How fast you come up this road, anyway?" Frank asked. The girl had pink sparkly polish on her toenails. Cute.

"I dunno. Thirty, maybe thirty-five."

At least. Fifteen would be too fast. She'd hit that dry wash in the dark, launched herself, come down hard, ripped off a muffler and blown a tire. Way the hell out in the hot summer desert. Stupid. Frank peered into the trunk.

Spare tire. Scissors jack. Lug wrench. A bottle of Pennzoil, rags, a gallon of gas. Duffel bag in a corner. Everything she'd needed to get going again, but she was too dumb to figure out how. Frank didn't like dumb. He poked the spare tire. It was full, didn't have much give to it.

"Spare tire's okay," he said.

"Uh-huh." She waited, arms folded across her chest.

"You want to haul it outta there?"

She frowned. "Me?"

"Yeah, you."

"It's dirty. You got a bad back, mister?"

"Frank. Frank Wiley."

She smiled. "Like the coyote, huh?"

"Kinda. Just one word, though. W-I-L-E-Y."

She scratched her belly. "Oh."

"You got a name, or should I just call you 'hey you'?"

"Suki."

"Come again?"

"Suki. S-U-K-I. Erickson."

Jesus. Bubblegum name for a bubblegum girl.

"Well, Suki, my back's fine, thanks. Now, if you'll haul that tire outta there, you can get started."

She gave him a narrow look. "Me?"

"That's right."

"You . . . you're not gonna help me?"

"I'll give you all the help you need. Which is to say, I'm gonna tell you how to change a tire."

She stared at him, wide-eyed. "You gotta be kidding."

"Nope." He got a beer and sat on a rock with a sigh, fifteen feet from the car's flat tire, late afternoon sun hot on his shoulders.

"The tire," he said, wagging a finger at her.

She banged the trunk down and climbed up on it. Frank watched appreciatively as her muscles flexed. No Einstein, but she was sure a work of art. Flat belly, shorts so short he could see the tendons of her inner thighs, up near her crotch.

"See," Frank said, "if I change that tire for you—"

"I don't wanna hear it."

"—next time this happens you'll be as helpless as you are now."

"Be prepared, all that crap?"

"Being prepared never hurt anyone, Suki."

"Think I'll just wait for the next Good Sami . . . Samarian to come along. Thanks anyway."

"That's Samaritan."

She rolled her eyes. "Whatever."

"Could be a while." Frank stood up.

"C'mon, Frank." Suki slid off the car. "Be nice, huh? All it is is a tire."

It was more than that, a hell of a lot more, but all the finer points of the situation were sailing right over her head. "Pretty doesn't pay the bills, Suki."

"*Huh*?" Her eyes widened.

"And pretty doesn't get your tire changed when you're all alone in the desert, either."

She stamped a foot. "I'm *not* all alone, you jerk."

"Look around. Imagine how it'll look after I'm gone." Frank trudged back to his truck and opened the driver's-side door.

"Hey!"

"What?"

"You can't just *leave* me here." She lurched toward him in her heels. He decided he could probably catch her if he wanted to. Which he didn't.

"You don't want help," he said, "that's your business."

"I want *help*, not, like, *instructions*."

"Give a man a fish and you feed him for a day. Teach him to fish and he'll eat for a lifetime."

"What? *Fish*?"

"Nothin'. Forget it. See you around." He got behind the wheel and banged the door shut.

She stared at him.

He started the engine, put it in gear, inched forward.

"Okay!" she cried. "*Okay,* dammit, tell me what to do."

Frank switched off the engine and pocketed the key. "What you do first is get out the spare."

Suki staggered back to the Trans Am and opened the trunk. She glared at him, then wrestled the tire out while Frank made himself comfortable on the rock again.

"Ouch, *dammit*!" Suki clutched her hand.

"What?"

"I broke a nail, that's what."

"Life is full of traumatic events."

She shot him a baleful look. "*Now* what?" She stuck the nail in her mouth.

"Get the jack out."

She looked in the trunk. "That's this, right?" She pulled out the jack, wrinkled her nose at it. "It's dirty." She shoved a wisp of hair out of her eyes, leaving a grease mark on her forehead. Frank smiled.

"That's it. Before you get going you better block both tires on the other side of the car with rocks so it won't roll on you."

She sighed. "How do I do that?"

He pointed out a few rocks, showed her how to use them.

"Okay, *now* what?" she asked when she was finished.

"There's a handle for the jack in the trunk. Get it."

"What's it look like?"

Well, shit. This was taking too long. He wouldn't get up into the De Bacas before it was full dark. He pointed out the handle to her.

He crouched by the flat tire and explained how to position the jack. He backed off a few feet and watched as she planted her elbows in the dirt, back arched, and positioned the jack. Her shorts rode up, exposing an inch of nicely rounded rump the same golden shade as the rest of her. Frank wondered if she had any tan lines on her at all.

"Is this all right?" she asked.

He crouched beside her. "Little farther to the left. You've got to catch that heavy lip of metal there."

She shoved the jack over two inches. "Now what?"

"Put the end of the handle on the end of that shaft there and turn it. Clockwise."

She sat on her heels, knees splayed out, and cranked the handle around a few times. The car groaned, began to lift.

"It's workin'," she said, surprised.

"How 'bout that." Frank sat on the rock again, watched her work for a minute. "Okay, that's enough for now. Too high and you'll have trouble getting the lug nuts off. Where'd you get the shiner?"

"None of your business. What's a lug nut?"

"Those six things holding the tire on. Maybe you walked into a door."

"Maybe I did. How'd you lose the finger?"

He looked at the stub. "Had it resting in a hydraulic lift when my partner hit the switch."

"Smart. Hurt much?"

"Nope. Felt terrific."

Suki stood up. "*Now* what?"

"There's a lug wrench in the trunk."

She peered into the trunk. "What's it look like?"

"There's not a lot left in there. Take a guess."

"This?" she held up a heavy chrome object, shaped like a cross.

"Bingo."

She stared at him. "Bingo? Seriously?"

"See, what we're trying to do here is get the bad tire off and put the good tire on."

"No shit. And what do you mean *we*? I'm doin' all the work."

He ignored that. "Think of it as a bunch of little tasks. You just have to know what they are. Do 'em all in the right order without skipping any and you've changed a tire. It's a lot like life."

"What're you? Like a poet or a phili . . . philot . . . a philozer or something? She whipped her ponytail back in an angry gesture.

The modern high school education in action. *Philosophe*r had one too many syllables, wouldn't fit in her mouth.

"There's four different-sized sockets on that wrench. See which one fits the lug nuts."

She crouched in front of the tire. Frank admired the long, lean stretch of her thighs with a sigh. He hadn't looked at a girl in a long time, *really* looked, certainly not a girl like this.

Suki tried a few sockets, found the right one. She pushed it on a lug and gave it an experimental twist—the wrong way.

"Counterclockwise," Frank said. "In America, off is just about always counterclockwise, except for water faucets."

She shot him an angry look, then twisted the wrench. Nothing.

Harder, the muscles in her arms and shoulders standing out. Her arms were slender—strong, but not strong enough.

"Shit," she said.

"Problem?"

"I can't turn it." Frustration filled her voice, a heated kettle, beginning to steam. "You want to fuckin' help out here a minute?"

"You pick up that language at home or at church?"

"I'm old enough to say whatever I want."

"How old's that?"

"None of your business."

He shrugged. "Fine. Nineteen?"

"You gonna help me with this, or *what*?"

"See, I do that and you're right back where you started. You get a flat out somewhere all alone and can't get the lug nuts off, you're in the same fix as you are now."

"I can't turn the sonofabitch!" she yelled. She looked good, mad. Corded and wiry, sort of like a cat.

"Relax," he said. "We'll figure something out."

Her eyes glittered. "All those muscles you got and you won't goddamn help or nuthin'?"

"You need more leverage. You could tie a stick to the crossbar. That'd do it."

"God, I don't believe this shit!"

"Not many of 'em around, though. Sticks, I mean. Another thing you could try is putting a rock under the part of the wrench that's sticking straight out and crunching down on one side of the crossbar, see if you can get all your weight into it."

"Hell," Suki muttered.

"Might be kinda tricky, though. I never had to do anything like that myself. And you'll need different-sized rocks to get all the nuts. Guess that'll take a while, but there's plenty of rocks around here."

He pointed out a likely specimen, watched with interest as she squatted next to it, lifted it with a grunt, hugged it to her belly as she staggered over to the car and let it drop.

Frank stood a few feet away. He told her how to place the rock, describing its purpose. She put both hands on one end of the wrench and pushed down on it tentatively.

"Harder."

She glared at him, then lunged on the wrench, grunting, hair dancing, and the lug nut racked over a few degrees.

"That oughta do it," Frank said. "Grease monkeys grind those bastards on too damn hard with pneumatic wrenches."

"Tell me somethin' I don't know."

"Anyway, you might be able to get it now without the rock. Give it a try."

She crouched over the lug wrench and lifted on one side, pushed down on the other. Muscles stood out in her shoulders and arms. She looked good like that. Working out in a gym in that outfit, she would have every woman in the place ready to tar and feather her and run her out the door.

Lord, she made him feel old.

The nut spun a quarter turn. "Got it," she said.

"Another Coke?"

She nodded.

"Keep at it," he said encouragingly. "Try the next one."

Inside the camper he looked out and watched her for a while. She was getting the hang of it, lean torso bent over, straining, and he heard the squeal of metal as another lug nut came loose.

At the rate Suki was going, it'd take her another half hour to get it done, maybe more, but at least she was doing it. Frank didn't like helpless, and he didn't like dumb. Which was a riot, with cops all over California looking for him—wrong state, which wasn't *too* bad —but maybe the FBI, which wasn't good. Hard to get much dumber than that, he supposed, except by letting a cute little number like Suki walk all over him just because she looked like someone's wet dream.

Hell with it. He had thirty-five years on her and it'd been a long time since his palms had gotten sweaty over some girl, no matter how finely tuned she was. A very long time . . . years before Fanny had died. Fanny and Frank; he still liked the sound of that. He was too old for Suki. She was an ornament—nice to look at, nothing more.

He came back out, handed her another Coke. "Tell me again how you ended up out here."

"I already said."

"I'm not all that bright. Run it by me again."

She swept hair out of her eyes. Doing a good job of greasing her face as she did it. Frank smiled.

"I was headed for my cousin's place, out near Santa Verti. Cora told me to turn left off the highway when I got sixteen miles from Imogene. That's what I goddamn did, and here I am."

"Where'd you come from?"

"Shreveport . . . Louisiana."

"You get the black eye there?"

"I told you, that's none of your business."

"Touchy subject, huh?"

She hunched over the last lug and leaned into it. Getting better at it too, Frank noted with satisfaction.

"So, what she meant was the *other* side of Imogene," Suki said, ending the sentence with a grunt. "Which means I turned the wrong direction as well as the wrong place. Right instead of left, or maybe left instead of right. Got it?"

"Not entirely. Anyway, left and right are kinda relative. Better if you used north and south, east and west."

"It was dark out."

"Right. Good thing Columbus set sail in the morning. Where would we be now if he hadn't?"

"Very funny. *Now* what?"

She had the lug nuts off, scattered in the dirt. Messy. It grated on Frank's nerves.

"Looks like that tire might come off now."

She crouched down, tugged on it. "Nope."

"Maybe if you jack the car up higher, get the weight off that tire. I saw that done in a movie once."

She glowered at him, squatted by the jack again and began cranking. Slowly, the Trans Am lifted. The tire tottered and fell off. Suki jumped back with a squawk and fell on her rump.

"Okay," Frank said. "That's high enough."

"You're really enjoying this, aren't you?" She stood up, slapping dirt off her rear.

"Beats the hell out of TV."

Suki stared at the tire. "Now what?"

"The bad tire's off. What d'you think?"

"Put the good tire on?"

"There you go. See, you can do this."

She struggled with the spare, a wide, heavy Goodyear, grunting, puffing, arms trembling with effort as she tried to lift it onto the lugs.

"It won't go on."

"That new tire isn't flat. You'll have to jack the car up a little bit higher to get it on."

Suki glared at the tire, biting her lip. "Perfect."

"After you get it settled on the lugs, put a nut on partway to hold it while you find the other nuts you've scattered all over hell and gone in the dirt."

While she did that, Frank observed—in what he hoped was a suitably detached and clinical manner—the way in which her nipples pocked the fabric of her thin cotton top. She had to know what effect she had on men and counted on it, used it a thousand times. Wasn't working this time, and she was angry, mouth tight as she spun a lug nut on with her fingers. Which was fine with Frank.

Thirty years ago his heart would've lurched into arrhythmia just looking at her. Thirty years ago he would've given her the world for a smile. Now ... now she was good to look at, gave him pretty good range for his fantasies, not that they were all that heated these days, but he couldn't imagine things getting past the fantasy stage. That's how old he'd gotten, and he supposed it was a damned shame.

He explained how to tighten the lugs to seat the wheel properly. She cranked them on tight, then lowered the car onto its new tire. Old tire in the trunk, and all the rest of it.

She banged the lid down. "Done." She dusted her hands, a smug, satisfied look on her streaky, glistening face.

"Good work." Frank was almost sorry the show was over, but he had to get going. The sun had gone behind a western projection of the De Baca's, a ridge called the Devil's Spine, spreading a ruddy glow over the mountains to the east.

"Another one for the road? How 'bout an apple?"

"Thanks." She came around the rear of the camper and accepted a Granny Smith and another Coke, then trailed along after him as he ambled to the cab of his truck and got behind the wheel.

"Just want you to know you're a real creep, Frank," she said. "But thanks anyway."

"Anytime."

He started the engine and she stepped back. He gave her a last look, smiled, and said, "See you."

She lifted her Coke in farewell and he took off, past the fiery Trans Am, up into the darkening foothills of the De Baca Mountains.

2

The plan was off schedule, not that there was much of a schedule or that there was much of a plan. But Suki had seen him, and that wasn't good. She'd sure as hell recognize him if she saw his face on television, wanted by the police, and she knew he was headed up into the De Bacas.

All he'd wanted to do was to fade into the landscape with five bottles of Jack Daniel's, three cases of beer, enough steak and chicken, corn, fruit, and canned goods to outlast the booze, and five or six Stephen King novels that he intended to read fast and loose and partly drunk. Only way to read King.

Lay low for a week or two, as they say.

Maybe by then he'd come up with another plan—maybe a way to get to Rio, something like that. Seventy-seven thousand dollars might last quite a while in Rio, if he lived like a native and not like some hotshot who thought he was big-time and could afford a girl on each arm. The pot wasn't *that* sweet. He couldn't blow much of it on the ladies, or on anything else for that matter.

Right now, all he wanted was to get up to that spot between Cable Peak and that other mountain—its name had somehow slipped through the cracks of his memory; happened a lot lately—where a natural spring bubbled up year round. Hell to get to, but that made it all the more likely he'd have the place all to himself the whole two weeks, or however long it took him to work his way through five fifths of good sour mash without regretting the experience too much.

The road angled left, climbed steeply, and Frank Limosin looked out over the valley below where long shadows covered the land. He'd gained considerable altitude in the mile and a half since he'd left Suki. Down there, looking small, she opened the door of the Trans Am and got in. He stopped the truck and watched, racing the engine a bit to let it cool.

Damn good-looking girl, Suki. But dumb.

Well, maybe not dumb, but goddamned unprepared, like so many kids were these days. Tearing around without any comprehension of reality. They watched television then got their toy cars stuck way out in the hot empty desert.

What the country needed was another good war, not like Vietnam or that dumbass Grenada thing back in '83, but a good one with bad guys and a clear-cut objective—like rousting Nazis in World War II. Shake these spoiled brats up, give them some direction. Except he had the feeling that kids with blue mohawks and earrings would roll over and die before they marched off to war to protect their freedom.

The Trans Am went crossways in the road, backed up, moved forward again. Even this far away he could hear the deep-throated beat of its engine. It crawled forward, stopped. He heard a roar as Suki gunned the engine. And then it died.

He waited.

Waited, then Suki got out, slammed the door, kicked the side of the car, pounded the hood with a fist, and walked away a few paces and stared down at the ground.

"Aw shit," Frank said.

And there she was again, sitting on the rear deck of the Tranny, legs drawn up, forehead resting on her knees, small and vulnerable and alone in the desert.

"I will be," Frank said, enunciating each word with terrible precision, "a miserable . . . son . . . of . . . a . . . *bitch*!"

He jammed the truck into reverse and backed to a wide spot he'd just passed, got it turned around, and began rumbling back down the trail.

• • •

Suki looked up as he drew near. Slid off the car and stood there, waiting.

"What's the deal?" he asked.

"Son of a bitch is dead."

He turned off the engine and got out. "Dead how?"

"Dead dead. How the hell would I know?"

How indeed?

About to open the door of the Trans Am, he glanced up and saw a dark sheen covering the road fifty feet away. Oil. Lots of it.

Shit again.

Frank headed for the oil, Suki trailing awkwardly in her desert survival gear. He crouched and dipped a finger in a smear. Fresh.

"What do you know about this?" he asked.

"It's oil, huh?"

"Yeah. Little more refined than the stuff they pump in Texas."

She gave him a blank look. "Well, I don't know." She bit her lip. "You think it's from my car?"

He walked back, took a look underneath. Yep. Oil pan was torn all to shit under there. His fault, of course. He should've known she would do more damage than to just blow a tire and rip off a muffler.

She'd frozen the engine. Gunned it as it was dying and turned sixty-five hundred dollars' worth of fine machinery into scrap metal.

But what did you expect? She was a golden, glorious girl with brains of sawdust and air. An oil pressure light blazing red on her instrument panel wouldn't mean squat to her.

Frank hit the ignition to see if it was terminal. The starter motor had a go at it but couldn't budge it. Nice. He pulled the key out.

The sky was clear, not a cloud anywhere. When night came the temperature would drop into the fifties. It wouldn't kill her, dressed the way she was, but she'd be very uncomfortable. And that wasn't the point, really. The problem was, she was going to die out here if he left her, period, like a poodle with a rhinestone collar lost in the Everglades. When he came back this way a few weeks from now, he would find her lying on the trunk of her petrified car with vultures standing on her exposed ribs, eyes gone, tongue ripped out.

So what he had to do was drive her to the nearest town—Quiode. Ten lousy miles to the highway, nine more to one of the smallest wide spots in the road in all of New Mexico.

"It's bad, huh?" Suki asked.

"It's done." He got out, slammed the door.

"Yeah, well, *now* what, Mr. Frank Wiley?" The sun was below the horizon, temperature into the seventies. She shivered, more from her predicament than the cooling day.

"Now I drive you into town."

"What town?"

"Quiode."

"Charming. I went through there this morning in the dark."

"Grab your stuff, let's go."

She opened the trunk of the Tranny, took out a duffel bag. Black nylon with maroon trim, NIKE on the side with the swoosh. Not a big bag, but it looked full.

"You want to change into something a little less obvious?" Frank asked.

"What do you mean, obvious?"

"You dressed like that might turn a few heads where we're going. The place isn't much."

"That's life. Bet they're just sick, the Charleston goin' out of style like that."

He smiled, then shrugged. "That all you're bringing?"

"Yeah."

"Okay, let's move it."

She climbed into the truck and sat near the passenger side door with her legs stretched out, duffel bag on the floor tucked under her calves. Frank eased the truck around the dead Trans Am and bumped across the small gorge in the road that had killed it.

"Wait!" Suki yelped.

He hit the brakes, skidded the truck on the loose dirt. "What?"

"I forgot somethin'. Just a sec." She grabbed her bag and scrambled out the door. Gone.

"Aw, shit," Frank said.

He watched in the side mirror as she made her way back to the car in the twilight, lifted the trunk, hauled something out. Opened a door and leaned in. Came back out, backed away twenty feet. Stood and fumbled a few seconds with something.

A lighter flared. She dropped it. Flames leapt up, gold in the gathering dark, hot, running swiftly for the car. Frank's jaw dropped. Suki came toward him, hurrying.

The atmosphere was mildly explosive in the Trans Am when the flames hit it. The windows blew out and it jumped an inch off the ground, then began burning merrily, rosy flames spewing out the windows, black smoke curling into the sky.

Suki dumped her duffel bag on the floor and climbed in, shut the door. "Ready."

"Sweet Jesus, wha'd you do *that* for?"

"I believe in cremation."

"Sonofabitch." He stared at the flames a moment longer, then looked over at Suki. Her face was dark in the gloom, unreadable. "Sonofabitch," he said again.

"We gonna go, or what, Frank?"

What else? Piss on the flames? He pulled away. A few minutes later the gas tank blew, the sound rolling over them and across the valley.

•   •   •

She was quiet. Maybe pensive, but Frank didn't want to give her too much credit. Might not be much of anything going on upstairs in that sawdust mill of hers.

"Married?" he asked.

"Hell, no."

"Boyfriend give you that shiner?"

"Who says I got a boyfriend?"

"That his car back there?"

She stared at him. "Maybe."

"Guy gives you a black eye, gets his car trashed, something like that?"

"Fulla questions, aren't you?"

"Just trying to figure out what happened back there."

"Well, don't."

"Want to at least tell me how old you are?"

"What's it matter? You worried I'm jailbait?"

"I don't like surprises, that's all." Frank got a tennis ball from the seat beside him and began to squeeze it rhythmically, hard, muscles flexing in his right forearm.

She stared at his fist. "I'll be nineteen the first week of October. Happy now?"

"Relieved." At least she wasn't seventeen, or less. Seventeen and he might drop her off at the highway, let someone else take over.

Suki fell silent and he just drove, down the rocky slope with its endless loops and rises and dips, feeling the weight of the camper in the bed of the truck, wondering if Suki was crazy or what the story was. Somewhere below in the growing dark was Route 401. Behind them lay a smoking ruin.

"You got a heater in this thing?" Suki asked.

"Yeah." He hit the fan, shoved the temperature lever to the right. "You got any more clothing in that bag of yours?"

"It's fulla toys."

"Huh?"

"For my cousin's kids. Cody and Gretchen. Toys. Teddy bears, stuff like that."

"Christ, that all? You don't have any other clothes with you?"

"Nope."

"Really came prepared, didn't you?"

"Don't start with me again. I didn't plan on gettin' stuck out there an'—"

"Left Shreveport in a hell of a hurry, didn't you?"

"Who says?"

"Just figures. You grab a duffel bag full of toys and haul ass, not bothering to pack anything when Mr. Wonderful got in a shot at your eye. Makes sense."

"Smart-ass. I didn't grab the bag and run. It was in the trunk for a week. And if it makes you feel any smarter, yes he hit me. Asshole son of a bitch."

"Now we're gettin' somewhere."

"Where?"

He stared at her. "Where what?"

"Where're we gettin'? What's it to you, anyway, Frank?"

"Hell, I don't know. Christ, you always this hard to get along with?"

"Mostly."

"Figures. So what you're wearing is all you've got?"

"This's it."

"Fantastic. Hope they let you on the bus."

• • •

They reached the highway. Frank turned right and drove fifty-five all the way to Quiode. A sign marked the limits of the town:

QUIODE

POP. 33 ELEVATION 3988

The place was dark, quiet. A one-pump Texaco station built in the fifties, two bars—Blue Bottle and Ernie's Tavern—some sort of all-purpose drugstore cum hardware store cum food market standing next to an ancient Laundromat boarded up with weathered plywood. And Belinda's Café, the only bright spot in town.

A motel sat at the east end of Quiode—cracked adobe, four tiny, faceless units featuring queen-size beds and TV. The Siesta Motel, with a red vacancy sign illuminated by a dirt-encrusted bulb.

Belinda's was blue and red neon, a blaze of fluorescent lighting that punched a hole in the night. The bars sported Coors, Bud, and Miller signs. A couple of rangy-looking pickup trucks languished in front of the Blue Bottle. The rest of the town was dark. A dog crossed the street and disappeared between Ernie's Tavern and Mason's all-purpose whatever. Suspended from wires overhead in the middle of the street, a melancholy yellow light winked on and off.

"Lovely," Suki said in a low voice.

Frank drove past Belinda's and pulled up in front of the Siesta. Behind them, a low-slung car with a big V-8 engine rumbled slowly by on the street.

"Guess this'll have to do," Frank said.

Suki opened her door. "I hope this place doesn't have a bunch of roaches. I hate goddamn roaches."

The motel was squat, umber, and dark—gloomy beneath rustling cottonwoods and mulberrys. Shaggy tangled shrubs spilled over the walkway in front. The office door was locked. Frank pressed a button on the door frame. Inside, a buzzer sounded faintly.

"I'm hungry." Suki gazed longingly at Belinda's Café with drooping eyelids.

"Let's get you a place to stay first."

A porch light came on. Frank felt someone staring at them from somewhere inside. Ten or fifteen seconds later the door opened and a man with hunched shoulders and hanging jowls peered out. Six foot two. Endless liver spots. At least eighty-five years old.

"Room?"

"Yeah," Frank said.

"Single queen-size do ya?" He had a smoker's phlegmy voice. A garlicky aura filled the air around him.

"It's for her. I'm not staying."

The man looked Suki up and down, slowly. "You alone?"

"Yeah."

Another look, gaunt, fixed mostly on her breasts. A gray tongue licked cyanotic lips. He blinked. "C'mon in, then."

Frank turned to Suki. "You got money?"

"Some."

"What I mean is, enough?"

"I guess so, sure."

"Want me to stick around a while?"

"Maybe a few minutes. My skin's crawling."

"Okay."

They went inside. The proprietor—Mr. Drummond he told them his name was, Earl Drummond—was on his last legs. Suki was probably the best thing he'd seen in thirty years. While she signed the register he leaned partway over the counter, trying to peer down her top, eyes fluttering in their leaky old sockets, drinking so deeply of the vision of her that Frank thought Drummond's heart might cough out an embolus that would drift up into his brain, and that'd be that. Frank had come across Suki, saved her from scavengers, and already another old buzzard was pecking away at her.

Drummond's eyes wandered, landed on Frank's finger. "Used to live on a farm," Frank offered. "Sonofabitchin' pig bit it off, big six-hundred-pound sow." Suki looked over at him.

"That'll be fifteen dollar," Drummond said when Suki shoved the register back toward him. He went into a coughing fit that sounded as if it might be his last.

Suki produced a twenty from the waistband of her shorts, handed it to him, got change and a key.

"Room one-oh-two," Drummond said, eyes suddenly sly.

Suki gave him a curious look. "One-oh-two?" The place only had four units.

"First floor, room two," Drummond said with a cackle, then went into a wheezing fit that sent him reeling through the door behind the counter and into a room where a television was playing, some used-car dealer trying to make an honest buck. Drummond hawked loudly, spat into something.

Suki rolled her eyes. "Unbelievable. Let's get outta here."

They stepped out into the night, temperature down to sixty-five. Two cats screeched nearby. Suki shivered.

Frank pushed three twenties into her hand.

She shook her head. "No, I'm okay."

"Take it."

She looked into his eyes. "Yeah, thanks."

"You gonna be all right?"

"I guess. Once I get a little food in me."

"Okay." He didn't know what more to say. Belinda's Café was a hundred feet away. He didn't want to see inside Suki's room, a naked twenty-five-watt bulb illuminating a saggy bed, peeling wallpaper. "See you around, Suki."

"Sure."

"Try not to blow anything else up, okay?"

"Yeah, okay. Uh, Frank?"

"What?"

"You hungry?"

"Not very."

She gave him a look, almost hurt, then turned away, duffel bag in one hand. "See you." She began walking toward Belinda's.

He watched her go, hips swaying in silhouette against the light of the café. Nice walk. Gorgeous legs.

He shook his head and climbed back into his truck.

Now what?

Back into the hills? He didn't relish the thought of trying to reach camp in the dark. Couple of serious slopes on the way up that'd be bad enough in daylight. Maybe he'd just drive back to where Suki's car was probably still smoking and crash for the night in the camper, far off the highway where cops never go.

And what he could do before that, come to think of it, is get a start on the booze in one of the bars in Quiode, just to take the edge off the evening. All the unexpected changes in his plans had wound him up pretty tight.

He drove two hundred feet to the Blue Bottle Bar, other side of Belinda's café, glanced at Suki sitting at the counter as he went by. He parked his rig in a pool of darkness beside the bar. No one would be looking for him here, this far from L.A.—at least not for a while, but why take the chance?

•   •   •

In the Siesta Motel, Earl Drummond squinted at what the girl with the big-city hooters had inscribed in his register:

s. arksun
60 gan stret
Srepor, lu

He shook his head at this ciphertext, rubbed his grizzled old cheeks, and clumped back to his bathroom to spit.

•   •   •

Frank locked up tight. Quiode didn't look like a big crime area, but with all that money back in the camper he wanted to play it safe. The two pickup trucks still stood out front, and a muscle car—a dark, aging Oldsmobile Toronado with the kind of custom-mounted air scoop on the hood he hadn't seen in a while, vinyl roof ripped all to hell, scabrous gray primer. Brutish machinery. A Bad Boy's car. The sound of the throbbing, slow-moving horsepower Frank had heard as he and Suki pulled up in front of the Siesta Motel passed through his mind again. Might've been the Olds.

The Blue Bottle was saving a bundle on electricity. Coming in from the night, Frank almost had to let his eyes adjust to the gloom. A glowing Heineken sign the size of a license plate was perched atop the cash register. At the end of the bar, a blue and yellow neon sign read HIRAM WALKER SCHNAPPS. A poisonous blue-green glow emanated from the well beneath the bar. The jukebox was inky glass, its cord trailing cobralike on the floor. The place was like a crypt in the Caverns of the Dead.

A couple of cowboy-rancher types with big mustaches and dark, inhospitable faces sat at a table against a back wall, nursing beers. Belonged to the pickups outside, Frank guessed. At the bar sat two hard cases who were probably with the muscle car.

Frank ordered a double Daniel's, took it to a dim corner where no one would get a good look at him—which was dumb, he thought. He was big and wide, as memorable as an earthquake. It wasn't as if the barkeep or Drummond couldn't finger him if anyone came by asking.

Have to catch Drummond pretty soon though; he wouldn't be around much longer. It wasn't terribly smart, sitting here. Running into Suki had already done more than enough damage to his plans, and here he was, doing more.

The bartender was in his forties, balding, dozing off and jerking awake—ticking, it seemed, like some sort of strange clock. The two old ranchers were downing their beers quietly, sullen and serious.

The Bad Boys had their heads together at the bar, talking in low voices. Suddenly they stood up, one of them tossing a handful of change onto the bar. They came shuffling over in Frank's direction.

Uh-oh.

One skinny, the other with muscles, both in jeans, dirty T-shirts, tattoos on their arms. The big one sported a buzz cut that gave him a dangerous, retarded look.

The skinny one's dark eyes reflected points of light. He held out a lighter and a picture. Flicked his Bic and said, "Seen this girl around anywhere in the last day or two, dude?"

It was Suki.

Shit.

3

"Nope," Frank said.

The skinny one snapped off the lighter. "Let's split."

They walked out, both in boots, looking like funhouse images of each other. In her high-heel sandals, Suki wouldn't be able to outrun either one.

"Son of a bitch," Frank muttered.

There were more vultures circling her than flies on horse turds. Wasn't his fight, though. Wasn't any goddamn reason at all why he couldn't sit right here, drink his drink, let the world do whatever the hell it was going to do. People were starving in Ethiopia and he had a bunch of steaks on ice in his truck outside and there wasn't a damn thing he could do to make those two facts come out right either. Suki had her problems; Frank had plenty of his own. His plate was full as it was, and besides, he didn't owe her a thing. Not one damn thing.

Bloody hell.

He stood up, downed his drink and went out into the night. The two hardcases were halfway to Belinda's. They hadn't spotted Suki yet, but Frank thought things would liven up any moment now. That pair wasn't tracking Suki down to tell her her mom missed her.

He crouched behind the muscle car, still figuring it for the one the two toughs were driving, and peered over its flaking, air-scooped hood at Belinda's. He didn't want to make some sort of a big deal out of this, but he wasn't sure how to avoid it. What he didn't need was a big scene, a dozen people getting a good look at his face. On general principles, he let air out of the Toronado's front and rear tires, left side. He crouched at the driver's side where the thugs couldn't see him. He'd feel pretty dumb if the car turned out not to be theirs, but if it was, it seemed like a good idea to limit their mobility.

Yep, they'd made her. They drew back into the shadows by the door, partly hidden by a truck that looked like a local fuel-oil hauler. Skinny had a few words with Muscles, then he trotted around back.

Okay, good, they'd split up—which made sense. Belinda's had two entrances, one on either side. No way to tell which door Suki would come out, and if they took her quick, before she could holler, they might make a clean job of it. Made Frank's job easier, though.

He shuffled toward the café, hands stuffed in his pockets, head down. The town was quiet, not a breath of wind. Gravel crunched beneath his shoes. Wasn't his fight and here he was, playing Sir Galahad like some twenty-two-year-old feebleminded schmuck.

He went around the front of the stubby oil truck, GUMP'S FUEL & HEATING on its doors in black letters. Muscles was hanging around by the door of the café, looking in, waiting.

"Got the time?" Frank asked, slurring his speech.

Muscles shook his head. "Ain't got no watch."

"That your buddy comin'?" Frank pointed.

Muscles turned to look. Frank kicked him in the groin. Muscles staggered back, doubled over. Frank dropped him with a fist to the side of his head.

Rubbed his knuckles. Been a while since he'd last used them that way, twenty years at least. Hurt like hell. Maybe he'd busted one, or at least sprained something.

Muscles was sprawled on his side, legs loose. The town was still quiet. An owl hooted in a tree behind Belinda's. The highway was empty; the yellow glow of the caution light pulsed in the trees. Frank took a ten-dollar bill from his wallet and went into the café, moving fast. Four people were inside: an old man and his wife picking at their food, sour-faced and silent; the Gump's oil man in greasy blue coveralls giving Suki looks; and Suki, sitting there half naked, legs lanky and tan, wearing those dumb-ass sandals. Frank dropped the bill on the counter next to her plate and grabbed her arm.

"C'mon."

"What? *Hey!*"

He hauled her to her feet, pulled her toward the door he'd just come in. She snagged her duffel bag as she stumbled after him.

"What're you *doin'*, Frank?" she asked around a bite of burger. "I didn't hardly get started yet."

"Don't talk with your mouth full."

His hand was big on her arm. No arguing with that. She went outside with him.

Frank rolled Muscles over with a foot. "Know this guy?"

Suki paled.

"C'mon. Let's move it. His pal's on the other side of the building." Frank drew her toward the Blue Bottle at a half run.

She trotted along—and broke a heel.

Of course.

Hobbled around looking for the useless sonofabitch until Frank pushed her into the shadows behind the Blue Bottle and told her to get lost.

Frank looked back at Belinda's. Skinny was coming fast, arms pumping. Frank glanced around, spotted an old push broom leaning against the Blue Bottle by a barrel of trash. He grabbed it.

Skinny had a knife. He'd seen Suki run behind the bar and he wanted to go after her, but Frank was in the way.

"Move it, fucker," Skinny snarled.

Frank held the broom in both hands, handle pointed at the skinny shit.

"Who the fuck're you?" Skinny said.

"Ed Sullivan. Who're you?"

Skinny smiled, missing two front teeth. He tossed the knife from hand to hand, showing Frank he knew what he was doing. His feet kicked up a pale mist of dust as his legs scissored black shadows over the ground. The blade wasn't long, but it looked long enough. Sharp enough, too.

"How 'bout I whittle some of that beef off you, old man?" Skinny said.

"How about I ram this poker up your kazoo till your ears ring?"

"Give it your best shot." Skinny danced around, swinging the blade. Frank drove the broom handle straight out several times, short hard jabs, connected with Skinny's belly on the fourth try. Skinny folded up and fell to one side, retching. Might've been good with a knife, given a log to whittle, but he wasn't all that good on his feet.

Frank grabbed Skinny's knife and jogged cautiously around the back of the bar, calling Suki's name.

"Over here, Frank."

"C'mon, let's get outta here."

She came hopping out of the darkness, yellow Day-Glo boobs bobbing up and down half an inch. Jesus H. Christ.

He unlocked the truck and she piled in with her duffel, scooted over. He started the engine and backed out into the street. Muscles was up, lumbering toward them, hunched partway over his nuts.

Frank roared off. A minute later the truck topped a rise and the lights of Quiode disappeared behind them.

"Spill it," Frank said.

"Spill what?"

"What the hell you think? Those two were looking for you, showing your picture around. What was that all about? You knew the big one. Small one, too, I bet."

She stayed silent, considering. "Mote and Jersey," she said after they'd gone another half mile.

"Huh?"

"Those two. Big one was Mote, small one was Jersey."

He waited.

She sighed. "They're friends of Mink's."

Like that explained it, like he knew who the hell Mink was. Real good name for a dumb-shit hoodlum though. He looked in the mirror. No lights behind them, so maybe he'd flattened the tires on the right vehicle after all. Frank kept it at fifty-five and waited for her to talk.

Kept on waiting.

Nope, she just sat there, sunk into a cloud of silence thick enough to chew. "Who the hell's Mink?" Frank asked.

"Mink's the guy whose car had a bummer of a day."

"Same guy that gave you that shiner?"

"Yeah."

"Mink a nickname or what?"

"Yeah."

He waited. Nothing. He pulled the truck to the side of the road, hung a U-turn, headed back toward Quiode.

"What're you *doin'*?" Suki yelped.

"Maybe Mutt and Jeff'll talk to me."

"Mote and Jersey. Don't be a jerk, Frank." She reached over and switched off the ignition.

The truck lunged. Frank stomped on the clutch and they coasted to a stop in the middle of the empty road.

He doused the headlights. The night got big and dark around them, full of stars. He left the parking lights on, dash lights glowing in the cab. "You got guys chasing you, showing your picture around, carrying knives. What's the story?"

She bit her lip.

"C'mon."

"Nobody drives Mink's car," she said in a low voice. "Nobody *touches* Mink's precious goddamn car except Mink, understand? He's nuts about that stupid car. He hit me and I grabbed his car, because nobody touches *me*, either."

"All this is about a car?"

"Yeah."

"A stupid goddamn *car*?"

"And a black eye, Frank. Don't forget the eye. That's why I took the car."

Frank stared at her in the glow of the dash lights. "So who're Mutt and Jeff?"

"Mink's . . . friends."

"Must be a real prince, friends like that."

"Can we get goin' now?"

"In a minute. So, this Mutt and Jeff were chasing around the country looking for you, right?"

"I guess."

"You didn't know they were after you?"

"No."

"They came all the way from Louisiana?"

"Guess so."

"Those two must be bloodhounds, trailing after you six or seven hundred miles like that."

"This is a stupid place to sit and talk. Turn around and let's get going. I'll tell you what I know."

Made sense. He got them rolling away from Quiode again.

"There might be more than just Mote and Jersey after me," Suki said.

"That right?"

"Mink's got lotsa friends."

"So what you're sayin' is Mutt and Jeff got lucky, that there's a whole army of Mink's buddies out looking for you?"

"Could be. I don't know how many and I don't know how hard it'd be to keep after me—car like that, hair like this."

"Girl like you, dressed like that."

She looked at him. "Guess so. And I'd told him about my cousin here in New Mexico. Maybe he remembered."

Frank didn't respond to that.

A minute of silence went by, then Suki said, "We were gonna get married."

"Who? You and this Mink guy?"

"Yeah. We picked a date back in March. Well, Mink did. It was gonna be the eighth of September."

"How old is this guy?"

"Thirty-four."

"Like 'em older, huh?"

"Whatever. That all the hell right with you, Frank?"

"Fine. So what we've got here is your basic domestic squabble, right? Guy pops you in the eye and you take off with his car. Gears of love all filled with grit."

"Mink loves his car, not me. Mink doesn't love anybody. I don't think he can."

"Nice. And you were gonna marry this guy?"

"I didn't know him back in March like I do now. As far as I was concerned the marriage was off. I was just waiting for a chance to take off."

They rode in silence for a few more miles, then Frank slowed at the place where they'd come out of the hills an hour earlier. Paved road for a quarter mile, leading to an abandoned gravel pit, then dirt and rocks after that, a track winding into the hills that soon faded into the kind of disuse only the most serious of outdoorsmen ever bother to follow.

He pulled to the side of the road, stopped the truck and switched off the lights.

"Now what?" he asked.

She looked at him. "Hell, I dunno."

"Next town in this direction is Imogene. About sixteen miles. I guess you'd know that, though."

"They would find me there too." A hard note of fear was back in her voice.

"Possible," Frank said. Likely, actually. Imogene was bigger than Quiode, but it had less than two hundred people and only one motel.

"Where were you goin' up there?" Suki gestured at the De Bacas.

The hills were black against the stars. No moon was out.

"Place I know. I was hopin' to have it all to myself."

Softly, she said. "I wouldn't be any trouble, Frank."

"You gotta be kidding. You've already been a bad year's worth."

"I mean, now. Anymore." Her voice was pleading. "If you take me up there, that'll be the end of these guys."

"How about you go on back to whatzizname, Mink? Get things straightened out. Tell 'im you're sorry. Christ, what kind of a name is Mink, anyway?"

"I killed his car, Frank. He'd kill me."

Knowledge of the inevitable filled Frank, but he fought it anyway. Not his problem, this business with Mink. None of it had anything to do with him. He could take her back to Quiode, dump her off in Imogene, boot her ass out right here.

Sure he could—like pigs could fly. "Shit," he said.

She smiled hopefully. "That mean yes?"

"It means shit—exactly like it sounds. Don't try to read between the lines when someone says 'shit'."

"Lights comin', Frank. Behind us."

Yep. Mile, mile and a half back. Could be the muscle car. This thing was turning into a circus. He turned the engine over, kicked up gravel pulling onto the side road, lights off, banging over potholes and broken asphalt. Hard to move fast in the dark, but Frank pushed it. They were a quarter mile up the road, partly hidden by a gravel pile, when the car tore by on the highway. Doing a hundred miles an hour, easy.

"That's gotta be them," Suki said.

"Which means they're not in Quiode anymore, right?" He looked at her. "You've still got that motel room back there."

"They might come back. Or their friends. Really, Frank, I won't be a problem if you take me up wherever you're goin', I *promise*."

"Aw . . . shit."

•   •   •

Forty minutes later they passed the Trans Am, still smoldering in the lights of the pickup.

"Nice work," Frank said.

"Thanks."

Then up the hillside, grinding over rocks, spinning tires on loose gravel, up into the switchbacks that took them high enough to see where the highway lay dark and empty below. This was a part of the world not many people had any use for. No wonder they exploded the first atomic bomb out here.

"Mind if I have a look in that bag of yours?" Frank asked.

"I already told you what's in it."

"Humor me. I've got a problem with the way things've been going this evening. I'm gettin' tired of surprises."

She picked the bag up, unzipped it, pulled out a stuffed rabbit and shoved it into his arms.

"Here. Don't get it pregnant, okay?" She held up a rubber duck, squeezed it, quacked it in his face.

He shoved the rabbit back at her. "Who the hell's Mink? And don't tell me he's the guy that owns that car, either. I mean, what's this guy do? What is he?"

"He's an asshole."

He gave her a quick look and she said, "He's just some . . . I dunno. Corporate executive kind of guy, I guess. Owns his own company. Some kinda telecommunicationing or marketing thing, something like that."

"Guy like that'd have insurance on his car, right?"

"Might, yeah."

"So when his car is found, the insurance company'll pay up and he'll just buy another one and that'll be that. You'll be off the hook with this guy, right?"

"Mink isn't like that."

"Like what?"

"Reasonable. He's a son of a bitch. Keeps comin' at you, like the Terminator or something. I've seen him do it before. Nobody gets the best of Mink."

"Terminator? What the hell's a terminator?"

"You didn't see the movie? Arnold Schwarzenegger?"

"Arnold who? I haven't been to a movie in twenty years."

"Figures. You're into what? Baseball? Boxing? Cockfights maybe?"

"Reading. Keeping life simple." Riding around with seventy-seven thousand bucks squirreled away in my camper and a bunch of cops trying to figure out where I've gone. Getting into knife fights while trying to lay the hell low. Stuff like that. Just your basic shit.

"Reading?" Amazement in her voice.

"Yeah, as in books. You've heard about books?"

"Jesus." She shook her head. "Go figure. You really look like some kinda big-time reader to me."

"So we've got this CEO called Mink who's maybe psychotic, has a real bad temper, and has a bunch of guys out looking for you."

"Yeah." Defiantly.

"That your story?"

"Yeah. Like it?"

"Shit," Frank said.

4

She hadn't wanted to tell him the rest of it, get him any more riled than he already was. If she'd told Frank what Mink was really all about and what she'd done to him, Frank might've just dumped her at the highway and taken off. Hard to tell.

So she kept her bag tucked carefully under her legs and went over her story in the dark, searching for holes as the truck bounced along. It had plenty of holes, but nothing she couldn't patch up, or so she hoped. Frank wasn't dumb.

Her eyes burned, but she was still too wired about everything that had happened that evening to think about sleep yet. She hadn't slept much in the past two days. She'd driven Mink's Trans Am across Texas the previous day and much of the night, catching a few cramped hours of sleep at rest stops along the highway. Her sleep had been disturbed by the windy snarl of passing trucks and by dreams of Mink—Mink coming for her, smiling, his eyes glowing like hot coals. By the time she'd reached New Mexico her eyelids were heavy, her mind numbed by fatigue. She'd crash-landed the car a little before daybreak, then dozed a few minutes at a time during the day, waiting for someone to come along, until Frank did.

"What d'you do?" she asked. If she got him talking about himself, maybe he wouldn't pester her with so many questions about her past, questions for which she might not have ready answers. "For work, I mean."

"Drive a truck," he said.

"Yeah? What kind?"

"Big rig. Standard eighteen-wheeler."

"Fun?"

"Lotsa laughs, sure."

"I mean really."

"Twenty-five, thirty years ago it was a kick. Now it's just a way to make a buck. I guess you get tired of anything you do that long, except maybe for habits you oughta give up. Like drinking."

"Yeah? You drink a lot?"

"I've done my share. Still do, I guess."

"Married?"

He shook his head. "Used to be. My wife passed away four years ago. Her name was Fanny."

"I'm sorry. Miss her?"

"Yeah."

"Where're you from?"

"California."

"This a vacation, or what?"

He wasn't used to anyone asking so many questions. "No, I'm meeting these guys up here in this garden spot to cut some big business deal. I've got this nice Eye-talian suit back in the camper and—"

"Hey, you don't have to get nasty. I was just askin'."

"Yeah, a vacation." His voice was tight. "Sometimes I just want to be alone. Been that way a lot since Fanny died."

"How'd you find out about this place up here?"

He shifted into low, four-wheel drive, and took a creek bed at one mile an hour. The creek was bone dry. "I stumbled across it a couple years ago, just out looking. Four wheelin'. I sorta like the desert. These days if you want to get away, I mean really get the hell away, you have to go out looking in places you figure people aren't likely to go. Chews up a bunch of gas and tires, but you see country that way that others don't."

"Like this?" She gripped the arm rest as the truck heeled over sharply, engine racing, wheels spewing dust that turned to bloody mist in the taillights.

"Like this," Frank said.

The headlights played over a rocky moonscape tilted at a dangerous angle, darkness and big boulders all around, stars bright in the black night sky.

"How much farther we goin'?" Suki asked.

"Six, seven miles."

"Jesus. Like this?"

"You ain't seen nothin' yet."

"Super. How 'bout we stop somewhere, go the rest of the way

when it gets light?"

He sucked on a knuckle. "Naw. That's what I was gonna do after I left you at the motel, but the hell with it. Now I just want to get there."

"Hurt your hand?"

"Maybe popped a knuckle against Mutt's head back there in Quiode."

She laughed. "Mote."

"What's it matter?"

"Guess it doesn't, really."

He was pretty rough around the edges. A good man behind that crusty façade of his, and dangerously savvy. What she'd told him was mostly true, just that she'd left out the two best parts, which left her story kinda thin. He probably wasn't buying the whole thing, but she couldn't think of any way to flesh it out without risking getting caught in a lie, so she just left it alone. So far they'd been mostly lies of omission, which was bad enough, but manageable.

He was strangely attractive. She tried to figure out why, big wide moose that he was. She didn't come up with much. He'd saved her, twice, but that didn't seem to have anything to do with it. He'd looked her over pretty well, but hadn't come on to her. Aware, but polite; that was nice. She felt good about the way she looked. It turned her off, though, when guys, even nice-looking guys, started panting and trying to talk her into bed two minutes after they'd met her. That had happened a lot. Until Mink came along.

So here she was, bouncing along in this truck, feeling a little something for Frank, a little looseness in her loins. Crazy. Maybe it was the way he'd made her change that tire, sort of treated her like she was a real person. He was at least six or seven years older than her father . . .

Dear old dad. She wondered if her mother was still pushing the ineffectual little shit around. Big brassy bitch married to this bony little twerp way out in Des Moines, where in the best of all possible worlds a nuclear warhead would wipe it all away so people could start over, or walk away from it and just let it be.

Suki couldn't imagine anyone pushing Frank Wiley around, and that included Mote and Jersey. From the shadows she'd seen what he'd done to Jersey. Very quick and neat. Whatever he'd done to Mote must've been quick, too.

Mink could take him down, though. Jesus, wasn't Mink one of the world's all-time horrors? She could just see him in that big old house in Shreveport where they'd set up the last operation, Mink silhouetted against the misty morning light coming through those tall French doors, performing those exotic moves of his in a deadly kind of slow motion, all controlled and silent. Like he wasn't really real, like he was on film or something, with the sound turned off. Like Bruce Lee, in the movies—

"You hungry?"

Frank's voice startled her. "Huh?"

"Hungry?"

"Oh. Yeah, a little. Didn't get much dinner, did I?"

"Want another apple?"

"Maybe when we get up to where we're goin'."

"Be another couple of hours."

"That's all right."

He shrugged, shifted into second as they rolled over the crest of a hill and down into the blackest kind of black she'd ever seen in her life. End-of-the-world black.

Not even Mink could find her here. She hoped.

•   •   •

They got there at one-twenty in the morning. Half a dozen big cottonwoods grew on a low rise fifty yards away, pale rustling ghosts in the glare of the headlights. Frank found a level patch and parked. When he doused the lights, colored spots floated in the emptiness in front of her eyes.

"Dark," she said quietly.

"Camper's got lights." The dome light blazed as he opened his door and got out. Cold mountain air swirled into the cab.

She climbed out. Dark mountains blotted out the stars all around. Overhead, they were brighter than she'd ever seen in her life. Frank opened the camper and went in. A few seconds later a little overhead light came on. He straddled a big pair of Igloo ninety-four-quart ice chests that must have weighed two hundred pounds each.

Suki shivered. "Got somethin' like a shirt I can borrow?"

"Just a sec."

He backed out, dragging the first chest with him, and set it in the darkness beside the camper with a grunt. After he'd done the same with the second, he went back inside and pulled a flannel shirt out of a drawer.

She stepped up into the camper and put the shirt on. The sleeves weren't too bad, just needed a little rolling, but the rest of it was a joke, like wearing a tent. Warm, though, wrapped around her almost double.

"Thanks." She gazed around. "This thing got a bathroom, by the way?"

He opened a cabinet, handed her a roll of toilet paper and a flashlight. "Out there. Just keep away from the trees."

"Wonderful."

She went outside, hobbled thirty yards in her broken heels before saying, "Screw it," in a low voice. She squatted in the cold amid a pile of rocks. Dry grass brushed her thighs.

"Remind me never to do this again," she said softly. The camper glowed like a jack-o-lantern in the night, Frank in there, banging things around. The winking red and green lights of an airliner passed almost soundlessly overhead. Something howled in the hills—dog, coyote, werewolf. Something.

Goose bumps stood out on her arms.

She got to her feet and staggered back, found Frank staring uncertainly at the bed above the cab.

"Problem?" she asked.

"You tell me."

"Only got that one bed, huh?"

"I wasn't expecting company."

"Got room enough up there for two?"

He met her gaze. "I'm not sure that's a good idea, Suki."

"Fine. Got another?"

He stared at the bed for a moment with the corner of his mouth sucked in thoughtfully. "It's a double. I'm pretty big, though."

"Hell with it," she said, extricating herself from his shirt, kicking off her shoes. "*I'm* not. Anyway, it's all we've got and I trust you. And I'm exhausted. I wouldn't be a whole lot of fun anyway."

She tossed her duffel bag onto the bed, climbed up in her shorts and top and slid into the coolness of heavy flannel sheets, felt the camper jostle as Frank went out into the night.

When he came back she was almost asleep. She heard the quiet rustle of clothing, felt him struggle into the bed beside her and knew he was trying not to accidentally touch her. The old sweetheart.

And then she was asleep.

5

Jersey spat on the floor of the car between his feet, a thin mixture of puke and blood. He'd discovered that at a hundred fifteen miles an hour it wasn't real smart to spit out the roaring darkness of a window. His gut throbbed where Suki's ape had rammed him with that broom handle.

Son of a bitch stole his knife, too. Black Mantis butterfly knife with a four-inch blade. Fuck. It'd been his favorite. Patches of hair were missing from his forearms where he'd tested the keenness of its edge.

Mote was still complaining about his balls, telling Jersey his head was sort of ringing.

"Shut up," Jersey said.

"I got this headache, Jers."

"Just shut the fuck up." Jersey leaned over and let more watery gruel dribble from his lips to the floor. The ache in his belly wasn't going to go away anytime soon.

They topped a rise. The lights of Imogene showed ahead, maybe half a mile.

"Shit," Jersey said. "Missed 'em."

"Couldn'ta," Mote said. "They couldn'ta made it here that fast in that big old camper."

"Slow the fuck down. You sure they took off in a pickup with a camper, Mote? You *sure?*"

"Sure, I'm sure, Jers. I seen it."

Jersey wasn't sure, couldn't really trust Mote, whose name he figured derived from the size of his brain. But Jersey had been curled up on the ground when the girl and her gorilla had taken off, losing his dinner and four dollars' worth of rye. He hadn't seen a thing, which he sure as shit didn't want to have to explain to Mink. Or to Mink's crazy-bitch mother.

If Suki and the guy she was with were in a truck with a camper—and even Mote could probably identify a camper—then they probably couldn't have reached Imogene ahead of the Toronado, even though Mote wasn't noted for that sort of analysis. But he might be right. It had taken them only six or seven minutes to get the Olds over to the Texaco station a hundred feet away, driver's side tires flapping, and fill both tires with air. Good thing it was one of those old places where you could still do that.

Seven minutes, eight tops. Jersey wasn't much on math, but it stood to reason that at about a hundred fifteen miles an hour over a twenty-five mile stretch they'd have caught up to a goddamn camper sooner or later.

Jesus, would Mink ever be pissed. And getting Mink pissed was something you never wanted to do.

Imogene was bigger than Quiode. Maybe a hundred fifty, two hundred people, two gas stations, a restaurant, one of those old Sears catalogue stores, grain and hardware, Gump's Fuel with a couple of big black tanks out back, a fair-sized market, sheriff's substation, post office, houses scattered up and down the street among the business establishments. It didn't have a traffic light. Like Quiode, it was dark and empty, just a few blots of neon and another flashing yellow light to keep people from blasting through at eighty miles an hour.

Mote cruised the main drag slowly, Jersey checking both sides of the street for the camper.

"What color you say it was again?"

"Kinda white," Mote said. "Bluish stripes, I think."

Kinda. Blu-*ish*. Shit. "You think?"

"It was dark, Jers."

Jersey looked at Mote. Great big anaconda arms, not two grams of brain. Like one of those brontosaurs in those books his grandpa used to read to him when he was a kid. Jersey'd liked the pictures.

At least Mote's description of the truck hadn't changed. When Mote's descriptions got to wandering, you knew you were in deep shit.

Nothing in Imogene. Couple of old campers off a few side streets, but the colors were wrong and the hoods of the trucks they were on were cold. Jersey went into the two restaurants and showed the girl's picture around. Nothing. But if they'd come through, they would've been idiots to stop.

Still, Jersey was feeling fairly comfortable with the idea that they'd never made it as far as Imogene. What he wasn't comfortable with was the idea that they might've gone up some side trail, let the Toronado go wailing on by on the highway, then doubled back to

Quiode and headed out east, maybe gone on down to Roswell. If so, the game was more than likely over.

Either way, it was time to report in. Past time, he saw nervously. Should have done it before leaving Quiode, but if he'd done that, the girl and the gorilla would've for sure made it to Imogene and beyond before Mote and Jersey got there, and then where would they be?

He found a pay phone, made the collect call to Shreveport.

The Bitch, Mrs. Voorhees, answered the phone. She was coordinating the search. Mink's mother, Charlotte Voorhees, was a tummy-tucked, chin-lifted, nose-jobbed horror. It hadn't helped any either—she still looked like a disease. He could just see her there at her big rosewood desk, light shadowing her small, deep-set eyes, thin lips puckered around a Vantage cigarette like the asshole of a pig.

"Tell me," she said.

Tell me. Not "hello" or "Mrs. Voorhees," or even "Yeah?" but *Tell me*, like she was flying on coke or something, even though she'd put a live rat up her nose before she vacuumed a line of nose candy. A space case, but dangerous as quicksand—like her boy. If the pay wasn't so damned good, Jersey'd go find something else to do. But where else could a guy with an eighth-grade education make $60,000 a year, tax free, and have a nice expense account?

"This's Jersey, ma'am," he said. "We found her."

"You *did?*" The sound of a tarantula. "Where. *Where?*"

"Quiode."

"Where's *that?*" She made it sound like where the fuck's that, but Charlotte Voorhees would never let so foul a word slip past her lips. She was much too much a lady for that.

"Twenty-five miles northeast of Imogene. Still in New Mexico. Ma'am."

Paper rustled. "Okay, okay, I've got it."

Jersey closed his eyes. "Mote and me're in Imogene now."

"Why? You've got her, haven't you?"

"Not exactly."

Cold silence. "What do you mean by that, Jersey?"

God, he hated it when she spoke his name. She rarely did so when she was happy, and when Charlotte Voorhees was unhappy you could taste her bile in your throat.

"She's with some great big guy now. Must weigh over two hundred and forty pounds. Old guy, sort of. Probably about fifty. They . . . uh, they got away, ma'am."

More silence. Then her voice, like embers snapping in a fire: "Mink is *not* going to like—"

"We've got 'em boxed, Mrs. Voorhees," he said quickly. "At least, we will if you can get Benny and Isaac to cover the road from Quiode out to Highway Two-eighty-five. We chased 'em from Quiode to Imogene and didn't see 'em, so they gotta be somewhere back along the road. You get Four-oh-one north outta Quiode cut off real quick and we've got 'em. Ma'am," he added respectfully.

"Elaborate," she said.

He did, editing madly as he went. Mote had been sucker-punched by this big dude and Suki'd run off with the guy. The guy had a gun—a necessary lie. Jersey'd seen 'em take off in a white camper with blue stripes, another lie. He told her about the two flat tires.

"Truck color?" Mrs. Voorhees snapped.

"Uh, kinda beige, maybe cream." At least that's what Mote had told him. Jersey's breath came a little faster.

"What make?"

"Chevy, I think." Which was pure fiction.

"You think?"

"It was dark, ma'am. Real dark."

"No license number, I suppose."

"No, ma'am."

"Okay, Jersey. Now listen carefully to me. Are you listening very carefully, Jersey?"

"Yes, ma'am."

"I want you and Mote to stay right there in Imogene and watch the road from Quiode. I want you to do nothing but watch the road, do you understand?"

"Yes, ma—"

"If you see them, call me. Then follow them, and if you can, I want you to capture the girl. If you can't, then I want you to continue tailing her. If you let her slip through your fingers again, Jersey, I'll have your feet flayed and soaked in alcohol. Do you understand?"

Jersey trembled. "Yes, Mrs. Voorhees."

"Can you see the road from where you are right now?"

"Yes, ma'am."

"What's the number of the phone you're calling from?"

He read it off to her.

"Be watchful," Charlotte said. "Be sure to answer if I call." She hung up.

Jersey wiped sweat from his upper lip with the shoulder of his shirt. "Motherfucker," he whispered.

•   •   •

"Simon?"

"Yes, Mother." It was late, late and quiet, but Simon had been awake, imagining. His imagination was well developed, and it often gave him great pleasure. As now.

"Can you talk, dear?"

Simon Voorhees, alias Mink, alias forty-three other names at last count and increasing at the rate of roughly eight or ten a year, looked around his private room in Stanford Medical Center's dermatology unit.

"I'm alone."

"Jersey found her, but he let her slip away."

Mink sat up straighter in bed. "Where? When?"

"Southern middle region of New Mexico, maybe an hour ago. Between the towns of Quiode and Imogene." She told Simon what Jersey had told her, and what she'd told Jersey, including the business about flaying his feet. Already, Benny and Isaac were moving, blocking the road from Quiode out to Highway 285.

"I want that bitch alive, Mother." His voice was calm, almost conversational. What he felt was less human than rage. Rage was a human emotion. Enraged, a person's thoughts are impaired, but Simon Voorhees was never, never impaired.

"I know, darling. You'll have her."

Mink wanted to tear the bandage off his forehead and rub madly, but he let the itching continue. As he suffered, so would that vile little whore suffer, but exponentially. And when he could do nothing to increase her suffering, she would die.

Charlotte Voorhees said, "How's the graft taking, dear?"

"It's too early yet to tell."

"Dr. Pinnell is one of the best in the country."

"*Find* her, Mother."

"We will, darling. We will."

"How are things coming along in Reno?" He didn't really care, not with Suki still free, but it seemed as if he should ask.

"Very well. Daniel's got the paperwork completed. We're fully licensed now. Banks are being most cooperative, as always."

"Good." He didn't care.

"Sleep now, dear. We'll have her soon."

Mink hung up, gazed around the room with its private bath, curtains, IV stand, colorless décor, medical stink and sterile hush.

Suki'd put him here, he thought. Amazement fed the fires of his hatred. She'd taken him by surprise, and Simon Voorhees didn't like surprises. They shook that sense of invulnerability he'd thought was inseparable from the rest of him.

Steamy little sugar-candy bitch from Des Moines. He closed his eyes and visualized her, stretched out naked, immobilized, a single glowing coal lying on that tight little tummy of hers in a place where the light was dim and he could see the fever of its fire. Screams, flesh searing as the coal ate its way slowly down into her guts. In a place where no one could hear her agonized shrieks. He wanted to *hear* her die.

One single coal. He would give her one place on which to focus all her pain. Such a wonderfully Oriental way to die, so very Zen.

The image soothed him, made him hard, but he didn't think she would die in quite that way. It would be too fast.

Much too fast for Suki Flood.

6

Sleep wouldn't come. Frank stared up at the darkness; pure clean, interstellar black. Could be a zillion miles up there instead of ending only eighteen inches above his head.

Suki breathed slowly, deeply. Just like Fanny had, years ago.

Frank had wanted Fanny to quit smoking, he just hadn't been able to really get on her case about it. Nagging would have only made their time together unbearable, and he hadn't wanted that. He wasn't too smart about relationships, but he'd known that much.

So she'd killed herself, or so it seemed. Frank had no idea why. Smoking was an addiction he didn't understand, particularly in doctors, nurses, even chemotherapists. People who knew the risks, saw what terrible damage smoking caused to—hell, to *other* people's lungs.

Until you'd felt that on-again, off-again pain—and let it settle a few years to be certain it'd metastasized nicely—and then had the X-rays taken and discovered beyond all doubt that those coffin nails—SURGEON GENERAL'S WARNING—had finally gotten their hooks in deep, cancer was something that Wouldn't Happen to You.

No way, Jose. All that professional medical knowledge of what happened to other people made you immune. You were different, special. Cancer sticks might kill those other poor bastards out there who didn't have that rabbit's foot of Special Knowledge, but for you those butts were just like candy. Yessiree. Just like chocolate, and they didn't even make you fat.

The depth of his bitterness was a stake through his heart, and he rolled over on his side to dislodge it, away from Suki.

Seventy-seven thousand dollars. What would Fanny have thought about that?

He slept.

. . .

He came awake with sunshine boring straight through a window into his left eye. Better than coffee, that blood-red haze filling his entire brain. His hand throbbed.

He'd slept fewer than four goddamn hours, but he was up. He turned his head. Suki's fluorescent yellow top was hanging from a roof vent handle over the bed.

Jesus.

He got up stealthily, still dressed in jeans, and pushed his feet into his shoes. Went outside carrying his shirt, socks, the roll of TP, a book, and a toilet seat on an aluminum frame. He set the seat up out of sight of the camper, over a hole from which he'd removed a good-sized rock, and began the day's business with a Stephen King novel cradled in his hands, morning sun already warm on his shoulders.

. . .

Halfway through the first chapter he packed it in, replaced the rock, checked back in the camper. Suki was still flaked out, glossy hair spread over her duffel, which she was using as a pillow, same as when he'd left. Only six-thirty; she hadn't even slept five hours yet.

So he made breakfast: eggs and bacon, even coffee. If the noise and the smells didn't wake her, nothing would.

But they didn't, so he figured her for dead, except that the covers were lifting at slow, regular intervals.

He stared at her top, hanging where she'd left it. When the hell'd she do *that*?

He opened windows in the camper, got a breeze moving through, and left the door open while he went outside and set up a folding chair in the sun on the east side. He got an apple from one of the ice chests and sat down with the King novel as the day heated up. It was too early to be hitting the sour mash; he would have to read sober for a while.

Three hours went by. Suki was still dead to the world.

The sun was beginning to cook. Frank climbed on top of the camper and unfurled a big roll of canvas he'd stowed away up there, hung it off the rails on either side. He staked it to the ground, shading the camper from the heavy beat of the sun. If the pounding of the hammer didn't wake her, nothing would.

But it didn't, so Frank said the hell with it and grabbed a towel and his book and marched off toward the smilax shrubs and cottonwoods in the distance, to the place where the spring burbled out of the ground, cool and eternal.

• • •

Suki stretched. She rolled onto her side and looked around the empty camper.

Swinging her legs over the side of the bunk, she clambered down and stood rubbing her breasts absently, scratching underside itches. She didn't hear Frank anywhere around, but even so she reached up and grabbed her yellow top from where it was hanging.

He must've seen it. What had he thought? She smiled, imagining his consternation.

She stepped into it, pulled it up past her hips and over her boobs, staring in surprise at the breakfast things lying where he'd left them. She hadn't heard a thing. She glanced at the stove, her eyes passing over the printed operating instructions without really coming to rest. She couldn't figure out how to use it, so she went outside.

Frank wasn't in sight, but he had to be around somewhere. He'd spread a big canvas tarp over the camper to keep it cool. Crude, but effective. She found an apple in one of the ice chests and took it inside.

A radio was mounted in a nook. Car radio: AM-FM. She turned it on, got a low roar of static. FM wasn't picking up anything so she switched to AM, found a station playing some old Ventures tune: "Walk, Don't Run."

It made her feel less like she was out in the wilderness, which gave her the eerie feeling that Mink was closer too, but she left it on anyway and began checking out the digs.

Wasn't much to see. Tiny refrigerator, which didn't work and was packed with room temperature cans of Bud. Bed over the cab. Small booth with green seats and a white Formica table. Stove. Counters. Cabinets all over hell and gone, scarred and gouged. Tiny wardrobe. A stainless steel sink, stained.

She felt suddenly jumpy, wondering where Frank had gone. She switched off the radio, grabbed the apple, and went outside to look for him.

•   •   •

He'd stuck King face down on a rock and was sitting there with his eyes closed, sun on his shoulders, the cool water of the spring up to about his armpits.

Ninety minutes he'd been there. Keep this up and he'd shrivel up like a prune, but it felt good on his hemorrhoids, which weren't much but weren't quite nothing, either. Now that he was out of the trucking business for good, maybe they wouldn't get any worse. Doc Schneider, the old shit, had told him last year he'd ream him a new asshole in another ten years if he kept driving a big rig. "Right about here, Frank," he'd said, grinning that hideous nicotine grin of his, pressing a cold finger into a spot on Frank's left side. Another unfathomable smoker; it wasn't likely he'd last long enough to ream a new exit hole in Frank's side, even if Frank needed one.

In Rio, if Frank made it that far, he wouldn't be burning diesel, jamming gears. And if he got caught, packed off to prison for the good of the country, he wouldn't have to worry about hemorrhoids there, either.

"Hi."

He opened his eyes, felt a fluttery feeling around his balls. Suki was standing on the bank, smiling, chomping on an apple, dressed in that skimpy top she hadn't been wearing in bed this morning. Good legs, rising up into hot-pink shorts. She even had her silver dangly earrings on, and here he was, wearing nothing but this cool, crystalline pool of water.

"Hi yourself." He crossed his legs and created a bit of turbulence to ripple the water's surface.

She gazed down at the pool. Six feet wide, maybe twelve long, jammed in among granite boulders. Almost five feet deep at its deepest point. Undisturbed, you could see the bottom like you were looking through glass.

She'd let her hair down. It spilled over her shoulders and halfway down her back in a cascade of sunlit silver. Hell of a sight.

"Nice," she said. "Last place the circus out there hasn't found yet, huh?"

"People've been here. Not many, but a few. I've seen signs. Most people who come way up here don't leave much behind, though."

"Great place for skinny-dippin'." Her eyes took in his jeans and underwear and shirt, drying on a rock where he'd laid them out after washing.

"Uh, yeah," Frank said uncomfortably. "Look—"

Suki dipped a toe. The flex of her calf gave her leg an exquisite look. "Not bad. It looks colder."

"What I maybe oughta do is slip into something—"

She stepped down gracefully into the pool, from one rock to another until she reached the sandy bottom. Six feet from him she sat on a ledge with water lapping at the level of her collarbones. She shucked off her top.

Frank swallowed.

She leaned back, eyes closed, face turned up to the sun, and sighed. Her nipples hovered a few inches beneath the surface.

Frank wasn't sure what to say, so he didn't say anything. Every so often Suki took a bite of the apple, eyes closed, as if this were the kind of thing she did every day.

Frank had trouble filling his lungs. The day felt quieter than before, his breathing louder.

"What's with the tennis ball?" Suki asked, setting the apple core on a rock. She began washing her top, scrubbing it beneath the water.

"Huh?"

"In the truck. Last night. You were squeezing a tennis ball most of the way into that town. Quiode. And then after we left."

"Oh. I dunno. Habit, I guess."

"Habit?"

"Now, yeah. Eight or nine years back I started losing strength in my right hand. Doc gave me a few shots, vitamins or something, said it was something to do with my nerves and told me to exercise the grip, get more sleep. Whatever it was, it got better. Now it's just something I do. Here, have a look."

He held up his arms.

She stared at them. "Yeah. So what?"

"Right forearm's bigger than the left, see? Not a lot, but a little."

"Yeah, I guess." She laid her boob holder out on a rock in the sun. "How'd Fanny die? If it's none of my business, just say and I'll shut up."

"Lung cancer. Cigarettes."

Suki stripped off her shorts and underwear, began rubbing them together in the water. Hot pink flashing against a bit of creamy ribbed cotton. "What'd she do?"

"Hah?" His response was airless, not real swift, either.

"For work. Housewife, or did she work?"

"She was a nurse."

"Yeah? That's good."

"It was, yeah."

"How's the knuckle this morning?"

"Better."

"You planning on shaving today?"

He rubbed the heavy stubble on his face, more salt now than pepper. "I didn't bring a razor."

"Figures. Got any soap?"

"What kind?"

"Like for washing clothes." She gestured at his, drying on the rock.

"This here's our drinking water. Get it soapy and it'd be two days before we could drink it again."

"Oh."

Just as he was beginning to feel almost comfortable with her, sitting there chatting in the nude, she stood up and spread the rest of her things out on a rock, water just at her knees. His breath caught at the sight of her. Her nipples were bumped out from the cold. Tiny thatch of pale golden hair, mostly shaved off. Not a tan line on her. It seemed as if he ought to look away, but he couldn't.

"Where're you from?" he asked, voice unsteady.

She sank back into the water. "You mean originally? Like where I grew up?"

He nodded.

"Des Moines," she said.

"Yeah. Been there lotsa times."

"Drivin' a truck?"

"Uh-huh."

"Ugly, ain't it?"

He gave her a look. "Depends on your point of view."

"Like if you've been drivin' a long time and hafta take a leak, it looks pretty good. Otherwise not, right?"

"I take it you don't care much for Des Moines."

"Place sucks, Frank. I couldn't get out fast enough. The highest place in the state was when a gopher popped up in our backyard."

"So you hooked up with this guy, Mink."

Her eyes lit on his face, green, flashing. "Got it all figured out now, don'tcha?"

"I've been around."

She closed her eyes, leaned her head back, face to the sun. In the light, Frank could see the tiniest of flaws in her skin, mostly around her eyes. Too much sun, but she was still young and like all kids her age she was never going to grow old, never going to get wrinkled, never going to die.

Had he ever been that young, that certain of his immortality? Not since his football days. He'd been an all-state tackle on the Webber High football team in Northern California where he'd grown up. Sometimes a center. He'd been big then, too. Two hundred fourteen solid pounds as a senior, seventeen years old. He'd run over a lot of guys in his day. Back then, he couldn't imagine someday growing old, dying.

Dying? Christ, he was going to be seventeen forever, and with a perpetual hard-on, too.

But life didn't give a shit if you dealt with reality or not. The years passed and you learned that the mountains were going to outlive you by a hundred million years and grass was going to grow on your grave. All you got was a flicker of life, then it was gone.

Tell that to a kid, though. Like Suki—a flower, just beginning to bloom. She'd look at him like his skull was full of Jell-O.

He glanced at his watch, a big waterproof Casio Fanny had given him one Christmas. It was a few minutes past noon, time to begin drinking, which was one of the reasons he'd come up here in the first place. That, and to figure out what he was going to do when he left. Two of those mutually exclusive objectives that make life so interesting.

"I've got a stack of books in the camper," he said. "If you want something to read. Stephen King."

"No, thanks." She ducked her head under, came out with hair plastered to her head, dripping.

"Rather watch television?" he said.

Her eyes grew wary.

It seemed to be a closed subject, so he dropped it. "You hungry?"

"Yeah."

"Turn your back and I'll get up outta here, go make us a couple of sandwiches."

"You're a hell of a prude, Frank."

"Yeah? Turn anyway."

She smiled. Turned slowly and gazed off toward the west where a gap in the mountains showed a blue expanse of space, a wedge-shaped view of washed-out blue-gray peaks far in the distance.

He got up, dripping, his back turned to her, and reached for his shorts.

"That a bullet hole?" she asked.

She was looking at him. He'd never felt so naked in his life—or so old and out of shape.

"Thought I told you to keep your head turned."

"Nope. You said turn, didn't say anything about keepin' turned."

Jesus. He hurried into his shorts.

She climbed out of the water, shook water from her arms and legs. "That a bullet hole?" she asked again, wringing out her hair, staring at the cicatrix on his shoulder.

"Old bullet wound, yeah."

"Where'd you get it? I never saw one before."

"Korea."

"Korea?"

"Yeah, Korea. Ever heard of it?"

"Sure. How'd you get shot over *there?*"

"We fought a war there, remember? Long time ago."

"We did?" Giving him an incredulous look.

Christ. He was into his jeans now, feeling a little more comfortable. They'd dried hot and stiff in the sun. Suki stepped into her panties, facing him, as unconcerned with her nakedness as a child of two, breasts perched high on her chest, full and round, hair spread over her shoulders in ropy tangles.

"Tell me about it," she said.

"What? The Korean War or the bullet wound?"

"Both."

"Maybe later sometime."

By the time he'd put on his shirt, socks, and shoes, Suki was in her shorts and top again.

What struck Frank as funny, just before they went back to the camper, was that neither he nor Suki had mentioned the big Ruger .357 Magnum he'd left lying on a rock within easy reach the entire time they'd been there, now in his left hand.

7

The phone rang. It was the Bitch.

"Yes, ma'am," Jersey said. A couple of hayseed kids went by at the side of the highway, one walking, the other keeping pace on a bicycle. A blond cocker trotted along behind, tongue lolling.

"Have you been watching the highway, Jersey?" Charlotte Voorhees asked.

"Yes, ma'am."

"You haven't seen the girl?"

If I had, I would've phoned, you skinny old fuck, Jersey thought. "No, ma'am," he said, standing in the ungodly heat near a Conoco station at the east end of town, sweat trickling down his back. Rory's Conoco. Mote sat in the Olds, sucking on a bottle of Orange Crush, feet up on the dash. The radio was playing hillbilly music. On the rear bumper was a faded sticker that Jersey thought was a kick: HERE'S HOPE! JESUS CARES FOR YOU. Bugs chirred hotly in the weeds. In the distance, the highway shimmered beneath the blazing sun.

"Listen to me, Jersey," Charlotte said. "Are you listening *very* carefully, Jersey?"

"Yes, ma'am." Like talking to a leech or something. Bitch could suck your soul right through the wires.

"You'll need two cars. Possibly a truck. I want one of you to stay in Imogene and continue to watch the highway for the girl. The other, preferably you, Jersey, must search for her between Imogene and Quiode."

"Where we gonna get a truck?" Silence. "Uh, ma'am."

"*Rent* one, Jersey."

"I don't think this place's got any place to rent a truck, Mrs. Voorhees. Ma'am. I didn't see anything like that around here. Place ain't all that big, an'—"

"Maybe from one of the locals, Jersey? A private transaction, perhaps?"

"Oh. I guess. Yeah."

"Do you suppose you could manage that, Jersey?"

"Yeah, sure. Ma'am. I kin try."

"You've got enough money?"

One thing they had was plenty of money. Hang around Mink and you had plenty of the green.

"Yes, ma'am."

"Then why don't you ask around, Jersey? See what you can find. People in small towns often jump at the chance to pick up a little extra money."

She was so deadly patient, explaining every little thing, like she was talking to a kid or something. Her and Mink, so fuckin' superior, like no one else didn't know shit.

"Yes, ma'am."

"Let me know."

"Yes, ma'am."

She hung up. Didn't even say good-bye.

Bitch.

•   •   •

Simon Voorhees practiced killing Suki Flood, over and over, experimenting with one idea and another, filling himself with her richly imagined suffering. He lay perfectly still on his bed, a tiny smile lifting the corners of his thin lips. Not a cruel smile though, but one that reassured the nurses drifting in and out of his room on silent, crepe-soled shoes. When Simon was amused, his smile was quite pleasant. He was thought to be one of the better patients at SMC.

Dr. Ernest Pinnell came in, pale blue eyes questing.

"How's the patient?"

"Bored." He wasn't, really, but under the circumstances it would be expected.

"There's television."

"Television is for children, Doctor."

"Children?"

Simon's empty gray eyes locked on Pinnell's. "Children of the mind, Doctor. Children of the soul. Television is the womb of strangling mediocrity."

Pinnell's eyebrows lifted. "Something from the library, then?"

"Spinoza, if you have anything. If not, then Kafka might be an interesting diversion."

Pinnell's eyebrows lifted another improbable notch. "I'll have a nurse's aide look into it. Perhaps we can locate something suitably enriching."

Pinnell changed Mink's bandage himself this time. "Looking good," he said, eyes never shifting down to look directly into Simon's. He stared only at the place on Simon's forehead where the graft had removed Suki's vile word:

CROK

"Terrific," Mink said. He'd tell his mother.

Pinnell's eyes crinkled in a smile. "No more wild parties after this, eh, Mr. Voorhees?"

"How long before I can leave, Doctor?"

"Well, we want to be certain the graft takes, don't we? A few more days should do it. If everything looks good, we'll try for Saturday. How's that?"

"Good."

"Fine." Pinnell scribbled something on Simon's chart then left the room, humming something that sounded suspiciously like an old Sousa march. His stride was a march, too, the corridors of the hospital his parade ground.

Mink returned to Suki's pain.

8

Darkness came to the hills. Frank was pleasantly lit, but he hadn't gotten as far into the booze as he'd intended back when he'd been motoring through Arizona. Suki had distracted him, puttering around all afternoon in that skimpy little outfit of hers.

He hadn't done much thinking about his personal situation, either. He wasn't sure if Rio was the place to go, or if he should try someplace that didn't sound so full of bugs. He didn't know why he thought Rio was infested, but the image refused to go away. Brazil was jungle, maybe that was it. Jungles were full of bugs, including venomous Brazilian wandering spiders the size of his hand. He'd never been to South America, never been south of Corpus Christi, Texas. Rio was probably too exotic for him. What the hell would he do in Rio anyway?

He hadn't managed to get very much further into the book, either, Suki prancing around just inside his field of vision. Not prancing, really, but there, moving around. His mind was active, conjuring up images of her tits, the way they'd looked with water sparkling on them in the sun.

Young tits, full and round, perfectly formed.

Jesus.

So he'd pissed away the entire day, taken a dip that afternoon—alone—that'd removed whatever little buzz he'd managed to acquire to that point, napped a couple of hours, went over in his mind the things that had happened that had brought Suki up into the mountains with him, said "shit" fifty or so times just to keep it fluid, and now the sun was nothing but a dying purple glow in the sky through a low place in the mountains to the west.

They sat out in the gathering gloom, Suki on the big red cooler, leaning back against the side of the camper, Frank comfortably hunkered in a folding nylon chair, letting the night slip down around them. Not saying much.

"Nice," she said after a while.

"What?"

"This. Up here. It's so quiet."

"Ain't it, though?"

"I've never seen anything like it. I've only been up here one day, and I think I could stay forever."

"Without television?"

A bristly little pause, then, "Yeah, I might last a day or two without the tube, Frank. You never know."

"Sorry. Cheap shot."

"So I'd rather watch TV than read. So what?"

"So nothing. I didn't mean anything. Forget it."

She didn't reply, but he could feel her sitting there in the dark, steaming. Funny how you could feel another person's anger, like heat. Fanny had been like that. Every once in a while she'd get worked up about something and bang pans around in the kitchen, radiating her displeasure like an oven.

Suki cooled off after a few minutes. "You hungry?" she asked.

He was. It was almost nine-thirty and they hadn't gotten around to eating yet. "Yeah. You feeling domestic?"

"What's that mean?"

"Can you cook?"

"Sure—if you teach me how to use that stove in there. I never used one like that before."

"Nothin' to it. But I think tonight we oughta barbecue. I've got steaks that need eating."

"Barbecue? You better do it then, Frank. All I ever do is catch things on fire."

"Like cars?"

She laughed, a bright, happy sound in the night. She was still pleased with the way she'd fried Mink's car.

Frank lit a Coleman lantern and hung it from a bracket outside the open door of the camper. Suki unwrapped a couple of steaks from one of the coolers while Frank squirted starter fluid on some charcoal briquettes and set them ablaze.

"Got some fresh corn we can cook, too," he said.

"I'll do it, if—"

"Yeah, yeah. If I show you how to use the stove, right?"

"Right."

Thirty minutes later they were sitting under the stars in the quiet of the night, eating, each with a beer. Frank had turned the lantern low and hung it inside the camper. Only a dim glow spilled outside. Overhead, the Milky Way was a ghostly band of white.

"Tell me about Korea," Suki said.

"Not much to tell."

"Gettin' shot isn't much, huh?"

"I was walking along and suddenly I was lying in a rice paddy with mud in my mouth. One moment you're all right, the next hundredth of a second you're down, numb, not really even wondering what the hell happened. Just there."

She absorbed that in silence for a while. "How old were you?"

"Nineteen."

"Almost like me now," she said quietly.

"Almost like you now."

"What happened then?"

"Took them two days to get me to a hospital. Medic kept me pumped so full of morphine I hardly knew my name."

"Freaky," she said.

Freaky. Yeah, freaky. Thought he was going to die; that's freaky, in the parlance of the young. During moments of painful consciousness he'd had words with a God he'd barely known existed.

Please, God, don't let it be over yet.

Freaky. At nineteen he'd lost his immortality.

"Gettin' cold out here," she said.

"You could put on that shirt I gave you last night."

"Think I'll just turn in instead. I'm beat."

"Suit yourself."

"I don't guess you'd have toothpaste and a toothbrush anywhere inside, huh?"

"Try the drawer next to the sink."

"Mind if I use 'em?"

"Nope."

Frank sat alone with his thoughts, black night all around, but now everything was wandering, nothing sitting still inside his skull. Suki, Mutt and Jeff, some guy called Mink. Seventy-seven thousand dollars concealed in his camper. Fanny gone. A bullet wound he hadn't given any thought to in ten or fifteen years that'd earned him a Purple Heart.

What you gonna do, Frank?

Christ, I dunno.

How 'bout Rio? Thought you said Rio was the place.

It's fulla bugs.

You don't know squat, Frank. Stick you in Madrid instead of Rio and you wouldn't know the difference for a month.

I know. That's the problem.

How'd you get into this mess, anyway?

Long story.

He got up, went inside. Bright lemon boob-holder slung over the vent handle again. He stared at it, turned the valve on the Coleman lantern. It sputtered, went out slowly.

Life just never was what he thought it'd be.

• • •

He wore his underwear to bed, aftertaste of Colgate in his mouth. He felt cumbersome, trying to work his way under the covers without touching her.

Fanny, up there in the dark, smoking, wanting to talk, waiting to see how close he'll get to this girl.

Forgive me, Fanny, not tonight. I'm all talked out.

Okay, Frank. Whatever you say.

He closed his eyes, tried not to think about the girl lying topless beside him, inches away, tried not to think of money or the FBI or pictures of himself in the L.A. *Times* or on TV or maybe on a post office wall. Tried not to think of anything.

Might as well try to turn a hurricane by spitting into the wind.

She was eighteen years old. Eighteen. He had a daughter in Spokane nine years older than that. Fairly worthless kid of twenty-seven with three spoiled screamers of her own and a pudgy husband who managed a 7-Eleven. Debra Limosin, now Debra Speth. Never even graduated from high school because she was so smart, knew so much more than her old man.

And Robert Limosin. Bobby. Twenty-five now, couple years of college at U.C. Davis, and still the kid couldn't find his ass with both hands and a candle. A clerk at some men's store in San Francisco. Frank couldn't even remember the name of the place. Gerardo's or Gregorios's or some such shit.

Suki's hand found his arm, slipped down and took his hand, pulled it toward her and placed it on her breast.

Soft, but firm. Warm. He could feel the nipple against his palm, a hard little nub. Good handful, just like he'd thought.

Jesus.

"Suki, I don't—"

Her lips sealed his. He was startled, didn't know her face had been so close.

She backed away a few inches and her voice came at him, kind of husky in the dark. "What you're gonna do now is give me a big lecture of some kind, right? Talk me to death?"

"I just don't . . . You don't have to do this." He was having trouble getting air into his lungs.

"No shit, Frank."

"I'm old enough—"

"Yeah, yeah, to be my father, that what you're gonna say? Think that matters?"

"Christ, Suki, I'm three *times* your age."

"So what?"

So what? He wasn't sure what. Just seemed as if it oughta *what*, that was all. She should be with a kid her own age.

"It doesn't mean anything, Frank. Here, look at you for chrissake. You're all tensed up."

She pulled his hand down to the flat of her belly, held it lightly against her while moving it around. God, she was soft, hard too; a medley of textures. Up across her rib cage, down past her navel. His fingertips lightly brushed pubic hair trimmed short.

Jesus Christ, she didn't have a stitch on.

"You gettin' the idea, Frank? Touch me." She turned loose of his hand.

No way. He couldn't do this.

Her hands found him, gently. He shuddered.

"Christ, Suki . . ."

"Don't tell me you don't want to," she whispered, breath warm in his ear.

In his state, that would have been too obvious a lie. It was just as well he didn't have enough air left in him to say much of anything.

Her hand guided his again. Down between her legs, into a silky wetness.

"Leave your hand right there," she said. She began to tug off his undershorts.

Oh, Christ, Fanny! Please understand. I don't want you to think that I—

Shut up, Frank, you silly old foof!

He smiled then, just for an instant. She'd called him an old foof a million times. Which meant old fart and they both knew it, and it was true, too, but foof was Fanny's word, and her saying it meant everything was all right.

Jesus. Thank you, Fanny.

Suki pressed herself against him.

•   •   •

"Frank?"

"Yeah?" He was on his back. He lifted his head an inch. Suki'd been quiet, lying on her side, one arm flung across his chest, breasts pressing into his side. He'd thought she was asleep.

"That gun you got . . ."

"What about it?"

"What's it for?" Drowsily.

"A guy'd have to be nuts to come all the way up to a place like this without some kind of protection."

"Thought so. You sure got a lot of booze up here."

"I'd planned on doin' some drinking."

"Figured that, too. Frank?"

"Yeah?"

"I think I broke a nail on your back. Didn't hurt you, did I?"

He smiled, waited half a minute. "Go to sleep, Suki."

But she already was, too warm and soft and young to really be lying next to this run-down old foof in the starlit darkness of the De Bacas way out in the lost empty nothingness of New Mexico. But she was.

She was.

9

Darkness flowed sluggishly around Jersey's truck, a rattly old Dodge he'd picked up for twenty-five dollars a day from some old geezer seventy years old who'd farted loudly and moistly eight or ten times while Jersey'd been negotiating with him.

Ed Farley, widower, and his dog Belle. Jersey'd found the bucolic duo sitting out on a screened-in porch watching Imogene's sparse traffic churn up short-lived dust devils in the street.

The truck didn't have a clock. It didn't even have dash or dome lights that worked, so Jersey didn't know what time it was and couldn't tell how fast he was going.

He guessed it was maybe midnight, maybe a little after, and he thought he was doing about forty-five. When the truck got moving much faster than that it had one hell of a shimmy.

Jersey's head nodded. The Dodge's right wheels went off the road, onto the gravel shoulder, and Jersey snapped his head around, eyes burning, got the truck back on the road.

Fuck this.

He'd been up how many hours now? Since the morning of the day that big dude had dropped him in Quiode. His fogged brain added it up: thirty-five hours. Before then he'd only got six hours' sleep as Mote drove them across Texas. He was running on fear—which he'd managed to sublimate into dedication to his employers. Fear of Charlotte Voorhees, which was really fear of Mink, Charlotte's baby boy. But even Jersey's fear was beginning to wear a bit thin as fatigue set in.

He'd been up every little dirt track and side trail from Imogene to within nine or ten miles of Quiode. Benny and Isaac were doing the same from Quiode all the way out to Highway 285. The task was just about hopeless, but they were keeping at it anyway. If Suki got past them now, they'd never pick up her trail again.

Jersey wondered if Mote was awake in Imogene. Probably not. He and Mote should get a room in Imogene and trade off watching the road, catch up on some sleep. But that'd cost them a whole day and the Bitch wouldn't go for that. The Bitch was rabid about catching Suki Flood.

For the thousandth time he wondered exactly what Mink and Charlotte did to get so much money, but in his exhausted state the thought wouldn't stick. Something illegal, he was sure of that. He was just one of Mink's messenger boys. He and the others followed orders, which were always simple and specific, part of some larger scheme. But he didn't know what that scheme was, what Mink and the Bitch did to get so much money, enough to toss around hundred dollar bills like it was confetti or wads of junk mail.

A paved road appeared off to the right. Jersey slammed on the brakes and still had to back up a ways to make the turn. His lights swept over a gravel pit that looked as if it hadn't been used in years. He went slowly, almost letting the old truck idle along, peering into darkness on either side.

Nothing.

The asphalt was cracked, chunks of it scattered around, and even that gave out after a quarter mile. Beyond, a dirt road of sorts ran out past the reach of his lights.

Nope. Wasn't gonna go out there. Not tonight.

He thought about going back to Imogene and trying to get a room. Probably too late for that, though. Anyway, it was fifteen, sixteen miles from here, and he was dog-ass tired.

Jersey switched off the engine, parked right there in the middle of the road where the asphalt left off. He curled up on the seat of Ed Farley's truck with a greasy denim jacket pulled over his shoulders, knees cramped into the gear shift, and was dead asleep in four and a half seconds.

World-record time.

•   •   •

Jersey came awake when a hawk landed on the hood of Farley's truck and flapped its wings. Christ, maybe it was an eagle. Whatever it was, it was a big sonofabitch. Sounded like a fuckin' helicopter.

Jersey pounded the horn and the sonofabitch flew off like he'd shot it in the ass with rock salt.

Nine-fifteen, sun already high in the east. Jersey got out of the truck with a groan, legs stiff, and took a long leak against a splintery fence post, eyes following the scrabbly dirt road he'd seen the night before. It looped over a little rise and disappeared. Farther on, the foothills rose up into barren, rocky mountains.

Beautiful New Mexico. All Gila monsters and dust.

He walked a short way up the road, looking around like an Apache or something, checking out the dirt, and found the tracks of some rig that'd been through since at least the last rain. Christ only knew how long ago that'd been; probably sometime before Nixon was president.

Now what?

He saw Charlotte Voorhees's face, black-widow eyes staring at him like shiny agates. *Go up the road, Jersey*, she said.

Yeah, he'd go up the road. If for no other reason than to say he'd done it. Fucking thing might show up on a map.

He got in the truck and started out, pounding the rusty old Dodge over bumps and through washes, up the slopes of hills covered with hackberry shrubs, needlegrass and sandbur. He was miles from the highway and just about to hang it up when something ahead caught his eye. He roared around a curve and down a slope and was staring at a burned-out wreck in the road ahead when a dip and a bump launched him into the air, engine whining. When he came down, two of Farley's balding Firestones blew out with the sound of farting elephants. Jersey's head slammed against the roof and he bit his tongue when he came down.

"Sonothabith!" he yelled, tasting blood.

The Dodge slewed sideways in the road, came to rest canted like a leaking sloop. Jersey hopped out, kicked the door shut, and checked the truck's tires. Both rear tires were flat.

"Mother*fucker!*" he said, drawing air from deep within his diaphragm, letting the curse resonate, rubbing his head, sucking on his wounded tongue.

Took him three minutes to get around to looking at the wreck in the road. Farley's truck didn't have a spare, not that one would have done him any good when what he needed now was two.

Jersey stared at the burned-out ruin. A Trans Am. With Louisiana plates. Mink's plates.

Oh, Christ, Jersey thought.

Not that it meant Suki and the guy she was with were up in the hills ahead, or that they were in goddamn New Mexico any longer. Mink's Trans Am wasn't even warm, at least not from the fire that'd destroyed it.

Not much left to see. Just a stinking ashy ruin, seats burned up, dashboard mostly gone, glass blown out. Tires were burned up too—which figured.

The day was heating up.

Not a damn thing he could do here, so he started walking down the trail, back the way he'd come. Ten or twelve miles to the highway, and his stomach was already beginning to rumble. Fourteen hundred and seventy-three dollars in his pockets, and not a HoJo in sight.

This was not going to be his best day ever.

10

Frank was gone. Again.

He couldn't relax, just cuddle up with her and sleep an extra hour. He wasn't the cuddly type. Well, he was and he wasn't—just wasn't the type to think he was. And he wasn't the type to sleep in, either, had to be up and doing something. Probably a little shook up about last night, too. Her and him, her so much younger. Suki smiled, knew it bothered him some.

She stretched, feeling the good tightness of muscles that had been properly used, legs still a little bit rubbery.

She got out of bed, went outside naked and looked around, didn't see Frank anywhere. Probably at the spring, soaking. After what they'd done last night, he probably needed it, the sweet old thing.

She smiled, felt deliciously naughty.

Inside, she turned on the radio. It was 10:02. She'd slept pretty late. Keep this up and Frank would think she was a pig for sure. The news was on, some story about disarmament talks in Geneva with the Soviet Union. She turned it down low so it wouldn't bother Frank if he was out there somewhere reading.

She put on underwear and slipped her feet into the thongs he'd given her yesterday. Better than her busted sandals, but not much. Size eleven men's on her size nine feet.

". . . still searching for Frank Limosin, who left his partner stranded at a truck stop outside Bakersfield Monday morning and disappeared with a load of ball bearings valued at over half a million dollars. Limosin is described as five foot eight, two hundred thirty

pounds, fifty-four years old. As yet, the truck he was driving has not
been found. The search has been expanded to include eight counties
in central and southern California. The highway patrol has—"

Suki went outside to pee, topless, thongs flapping. Shivers went through her as the morning sun caressed her body.

Came back. Still no Frank, so she rummaged through cabinets, looking for something to eat. On the radio, The Byrds were singing "Mr. Tambourine Man." Old music, but she liked the sound of it.

She had a good eye for checking things out. Living with Mink had given her that. Mink was good at stashing stuff in weird places, the slippery shit. Charlotte too. Even so, Suki almost missed the fake ash cabinet over the sink where Frank kept the hard stuff, five bottles of Jack Daniel's.

It was sort of crude, but, hell, she hadn't been expecting anything like it.

The cabinet wasn't quite as deep as the one next to it. Curious. It took her a while to figure out that the vertical brace to the left wasn't really a brace. She pried it out, slid the rear panel to the left, reached in and took out a small navy blue nylon bag.

She unzipped it, looked inside. Stared, mouth open at the sight of all the money.

Beneath the money was a driver's license and other wallet-sized items. California gun permit, Sears credit card, Texaco and Chevron and Visa. The license had Frank's picture on it.

Frank, she thought. You sneaky old son of a bitch!

All the cards were made out in the name of Frank Somebody. Not Wiley, though.

L-I-M-O . . . She pieced it out slowly, painfully, straining to pronounce the letters, say them aloud.

Li-MO-sin. Li-mo-SIN. LIM-o-sin.

Not Wiley.

Limosin. She'd heard a name like that before, somewhere. Not long ago, either.

Something clicked in her memory and she stared at the radio in surprise, where Frank Zappa and the Mothers of Invention were singing "Jelly Roll Gum Drop." Right there. Something about a Frank Limosin. Something about a truck stop and money. Lots of money.

Jesus. Frank told her he drove trucks.

Heart pounding, she zipped the bag shut and shoved it back where she'd found it, slid the panel back in place, and put the vertical brace in place. And the booze.

She hurried outside and looked around. No Frank. Good.

Went back inside, tried to think. No wonder he'd wanted to be alone, and to drink. He didn't seem like the criminal type. She knew criminals, and he wasn't one.

She didn't feel unsafe, way out here in the middle of nowhere with Frank. Not after being around Mink awhile, and not after finding all that money, either. Frank wouldn't hurt her. Frank and Mink—Christ, there was no comparison.

This was weird, really weird.

At 11:00 a.m. the newscast was repeated, word for word, and this time Suki heard the whole thing.

•   •   •

He'd never get used to this. Never. Suki gliding up to him in the pool like an otter, wrapping her arms around his neck, letting her breasts glide teasingly over his chest. Him just sitting there stupidly in his Levi's, Suki smiling, laughing at him with her eyes.

He still felt too old for this, didn't know what to do with his hands when she was around.

Last night had a dreamlike quality to it, and this afternoon felt the same—Suki showing up in thongs and a few square inches of cream-colored bikini underwear that emphasized the slender firmness of her hips. No top, skin glowing, a perky little grin on her face. She'd handed him a beer and stepped down into the water, closed her eyes and sighed. After a while she'd stripped off the underwear, glided over, wrapped her arms around his neck and said, "So, Frank, what's new?"

Never get used to that. Not in a million years.

She slid away, climbed out on a rock, and began to comb out her hair with her fingers.

Water glistened on her skin. Frank couldn't keep his eyes off her, couldn't believe he'd made love to this young beauty the night before.

"What're you gonna do?" she asked. "After this vacation of yours is over, I mean."

Frank shrugged. "Go back to drivin' a rig, I guess. It's what I do." Which, of course, he could never do again, but he wasn't about to get her tangled up in what he'd done.

"Ever think about doin' something else?"

"Like what?"

"Like anything. You said drivin' a truck was just a way to make money. That all you want?"

"What else is there?"

"I don't know. Bein' happy?"

"Driving trucks is all I know, Suki," he said uncomfortably, wondering at the turn the conversation had taken. "Tell me, is that your real name? Suki?"

"Why?"

"Just sounds . . . I don't know, unusual."

Her emerald eyes watched him. "My real name is Anne. So what?"

"So nothing." Anne.

"After I left home, I called myself Suki. I didn't want to be Anne anymore. I'd had enough of bein' Anne."

"You ran away from home?"

"Sorta. I left when Mink came along."

"Looking for a thrill?"

"Lookin' not to die. Lookin' not to wake up some day and find myself old and fat and shrill like my ma, married to some scaredy-cat wimp who'd kiss my feet just to avoid a fight."

Lot of bitterness there, Frank thought, not just in her words but in the way she'd said them. Under that sunny hide was a toughness that had come from doing more than watching television and baking herself at the beach, teasing the boys with her body while numbing her brain with rock music.

Some sort of semiarticulate common sense operating there, even if she couldn't change a tire or read a map.

"Why'd you go with him?" Frank asked.

"Mink? He was . . . I dunno. Fun, I guess. Flashy, exciting. He treated me real nice, at first. Seemed to care how I was feeling. Talked to me. Mink can be pretty much whatever he wants—but mostly what he wants, I found out, is to hurt people, as much as he can."

Her head was thrown back, face catching the sun. She could be a Playmate, wouldn't even need an airbrush. An easy awareness of her body showed in her movements.

It was almighty damn confusing.

"You change your name legally?" he asked.

"Uh-uh."

"So your driver's license still has you as Anne?"

"I don't have a license, never did. Forget about Anne. My name's Suki, period. Anne is someone who died."

"You drove all the way from Shreveport in a red Trans Am without a license?"

"Yeah." She grinned at him. "In those shorts and that top, I was pretty safe. I know how to smile and act ditzy, Frank. If some cop pulled me over I'd just look for my purse and then start cryin' when I couldn't find it. I'd tell him I must've lost it at the last place I stopped to eat. Just look kinda dumb and sexy and lost, sniffle a lot. I can cry real good. Anyway, after the first hour I wasn't driving all that fast. Maybe sixty, sixty-five."

And it'd work, too. Suki could melt hearts like chocolate on a tin roof in July. Unless she got herself pulled over by a woman cop whose reaction, when presented with so fluffy a confection, might be rather less sympathetic than a man's.

"These guys, Mutt and Jeff—"

She grinned. "Mote an' Jersey."

"Whatever. Names like that, who can remember? Anyway, it still seems pretty crazy. Them out chasing you like that."

"That's Mink for you. Son of a bitch is worse than crazy, he's goddamn insane. Really. I'm not kidding."

"Even so," he said. "All the way from Louisiana?"

She sat up. "You're pretty smart, Frank. Been around and seen a lot, but there's something you've never seen, I can tell. You haven't never seen anyone like Mink."

"I've known some pretty damn rotten bastards in my day." He wondered why he felt so defensive about it.

A strange look was in her eyes, something that gave Frank an uneasy feeling. "Not like Mink," she said softly.

"Christ, all this over a goddamn *car*?"

She stared into his eyes, chewing on her lower lip. "Can I trust you, Frank?"

"What d'you think?"

"Tell you what. Maybe we could trade—I dunno. Secrets, maybe. You tell me one of yours, I'll tell you one of mine."

"What makes you think I've got any secrets?"

"*Every*body's got secrets, Frank."

"Got something you want to get off your chest?" He spoke without thinking, then grimaced at his words. Too late.

She glanced down at herself. "Nope. Can't spare it." She grinned at him.

"Like hell you can't."

She wrinkled her nose and climbed down off the rock, slid back into the water. "Mink's got another reason for chasing me. More than just the car."

"Yeah? What's that?"

"I left real early in the morning." She paused, thinking. "Last Tuesday, like about three o'clock, before it got light. Mink and me were up late the night before. I made dinner for just the two of us." She gave Frank a searching look. "I can cook, really. Not just corn, either."

"I believe you."

"Anyway, it was some kind of Cajun casserole thing Mink likes. Catfish, lotsa spices. I didn't really want to do it, and I was pissed off at Mink for some reason, so I told him I wasn't his slave and I wasn't gonna make it for him. So he hit me—the son of a bitch. Gave me this eye. So what I did was I put some of Mink's mother's Sec—"

"Mink's mother?"

"I didn't mention her? Charlotte Voorhees? That's Mink's real name, Voorhees. The two of them are close. I mean *real* close. *Weird* close, actually. Simon's his real name, but he likes people callin' him Mink."

"Guy sounds like a real winner."

"Mink's mother is a bitch like you wouldn't believe."

"It happens."

"Actually, she's his stepmother, ever since he was like two years old. His real mother died when he was born. His father ran away when Mink was four. Just took off—not that I blame him any, married to someone like Charlotte. He probably sneaked off late one night and never looked back. Charlotte raised Mink after that, alone.

"Anyway, I put some of her Seconal in Mink's food. She can't hardly sleep without it. The two of us were alone 'cause Charlotte had a headache and went to bed early. Didn't even watch Johnny Carson like she usually does. So I emptied six or seven pills into Mink's plate and stirred it in, along with extra pepper an' stuff. It really knocked him out."

"I bet."

She looked pleased with herself. Frank waited, gazing at her as this latest image of Suki-Anne Erickson unfolded. At least Erickson was the name she'd given him day before yesterday. He wasn't sure it wouldn't change again.

Suki shrugged. "Before I took off, I got this bottle of India ink and a needle and I tattooed his forehead. Guess he didn't like that very much."

"You did *what?*"

"Tattooed his forehead. He steals from old people, Frank, that's how he makes his money. So I tattooed 'crook' right on his forehead. C-R-O-K, crook. And then I took his goddamn car and split."

Frank just stared at her.

"Now you," Suki said.

Frank was still a little dazed. "Now me what?"

"Your turn. I told you a secret. Now you tell me one."

Frank rummaged through his memory, sorting, discarding, searching for something with a little bite to it that didn't give away too much.

"Back about twenty years ago in El Paso, I came out of a bar, don't remember what it was called, and this guy was across the street, knocking some woman around in a parking lot. So I ran over and slapped him."

"Slapped him?" Her lips twisted into a frown.

"Yeah. Openhanded, hard. Really rang the guy's bell. He landed on the ground, eyes rolled up in his head like I'd hit him with a billy club or something."

"Hmmph," she said, disappointed.

"I took off. Didn't know how bad I'd hurt him, but I go kinda crazy when I see guys beating up on women. No one ever found out it was me. Next morning I was on my way to Albuquerque with a big load of El Paso sandstone."

She didn't say big deal, Frank, but it was in her eyes. She climbed out on a rock and sat there a while, quiet. Finally she looked at him and said, "I think my secret's a lot better than yours, Frank. Maybe you don't trust me enough to tell me anything really interesting."

Then she put on her underwear, shoved her feet into the thongs, and clumped off in the direction of the camper.

"Well, shit," Frank said to the empty afternoon. "What'd she want, anyway? Murder?"

11

By the time Jersey pulled into Quiode he was all money and no smile, not even a remnant—which, however, didn't keep him from being civil to Mrs. Voorhees, the Dragon-Bitch of Shreveport. He was sweat-sticky, ripe as a week-old Hell's Angel T-shirt, and his booted feet hurt like the devil.

It had taken him nearly five hours to hike out to Route 401, another two hours to hitch a ride with a pair of Mexicans who'd tried to sell him some grass—successfully, too. Screw Mrs. Voorhees and her crazy-ass boy. What they didn't know wouldn't hurt them, or Jersey.

Jersey's stomach was just a scrap of shriveled flesh inside him. His mouth felt like an acre of Oklahoma dust bowl. The first thing he did when he got to Quiode was to chug three beers at the Blue Bottle Bar, one right after the other. By the time he picked up the phone and made the call, it was five in the afternoon.

"Tell me."

Jersey gripped the phone tighter, like it was her skinny fuckin' neck.

"It's Jersey. I found Mink's car."

"You *did?*" Where?"

He described the place. Wanted to tell her it was six thousand fuckin' miles from the farthest kind of nowhere, but instead managed to pinpoint it within some kind of reason.

"It doesn't appear on my map, Jersey."

"It ain't much of a road, ma'am."

"You say it goes up into some mountains?"

"Yes, ma'am. There's sure a lot of real empty territory up there, though. No tellin' how many places it branches off or if there're other ways out or anything. Shitty—uh, real bad road, ma'am. Truly."

A moment of silence. The Bitch was thinking. Finally she said, "Can you rent a plane somewhere around there, Jersey?"

"A plane, ma'am?"

"You know. Those things with propellers and wings? That kind of a plane."

God, he wanted to kill her. Would've paid good money to put a bullet between her eyes, watch brains mist out the back of her skull and stick to a wall. "To search the hills, ma'am?"

"Yes, Jersey. To search the hills. Something quite small and maneuverable. I'm not pleased with how long it's taking you to find the girl."

"I . . . dunno. Probably nothin' like that in Quiode or Imogene. I could maybe ask around, though."

"Why don't you do that, Jersey?"

Something in the ensuing silence made him ask, "Uh, *now*, ma'am?"

"Yes, Jersey. Now."

Christ. "Just a minute. Ma'am."

He let the phone hang from its cord. Before he left it, he gave it a violent twist so it banged against the wall, *whack, whack, whack.* Muzak.

Jersey went to the bar, waved the bartender over.

"Yeah? Whatcha need?"

"I want to rent an airplane. And a pilot," he added hastily. "You know of anything like that around here?"

The bartender grinned. "You mean like with a propeller and wings, like that?"

Jersey almost vaulted the bar and substituted the Asshole for the Bitch, but he held himself back.

"Yeah, that kinda plane."

"Naw. Not round these parts."

"Someplace else maybe?"

"Chicago. O'Hare. Heard tell they got planes."

"Very funny," Jersey said, still keeping it in. Maybe he would burn the place down before he and Mote left for good. "I mean, around here. Imogene, or someplace else nearby."

The bartender, swarthy, wearing a mustache long enough to chew thoughtfully against his upper lip, said, "Just a minute, Mac," and disappeared into a back room.

Jersey went back to the phone, gave it another spin.

Whack, whack, whack.

The bartender returned. "Roswell," he said. "Got a place in Roswell for sure, but you might give Cap Streeter a try first."

"Streeter? Who's that?"

The bartender grinned. "Cap's got a kind of chicken farm off four-oh-one. Go up east 'bout ten miles, turn left off the highway, go another five, six miles out. He's got this place back in the hills. Can't miss it. Only place out there."

"This Streeter guy's got a plane?"

"Be pretty funny, wouldn't it, me tellin' you t' go all the way out there if he didn't?"

"Figure he'd take us up?"

The bartender's grin widened. "Us? You got crabs, Mac?"

Jersey almost killed him, right there. Instead, he went back and gave the phone a final twist. *Whack, whack, whack.* Went back to the barkeep who might not live another day. "I got a friend wants to go up too. Think this Cap guy'd do it, pay him enough?"

"Christ only knows what Cap would do for money."

Jersey didn't like the sound of that, but he went back to the phone where Charlotte Voorhees was still hanging.

"Ma'am?"

"What was all that terrible *racket*, Jersey?"

"Place is doin' some construction, ma'am. Tearin' out a wall."

A moment of silence. "What about that plane, Jersey?"

"We could rent one for sure in Roswell, but there's a guy here thinks maybe some guy called Streeter might take us up. Cap Streeter, local dude."

"Check it out, Jersey. Get back to me." She hung up.

"Sonofabitch," Jersey snarled. He dialed the Bitch's number again.

"Tell me."

"This's Jersey. Uh, look, Mrs. Voorhees, I'm in Quiode. That truck I rented blew two tires way up in the hills, so I had to walk out. I don't have any wheels. You want to maybe send Benny or Isaac over to pick me up?"

She didn't, he could hear it in her silence. "What I think I'll do, Jersey, is send Benny to Imogene to relieve Mote and then have Mote drive to Quiode. That way we'll keep the road covered at both ends, and you and Mote can go up in the plane first thing in the morning."

Assuming we can goddamn rent one, Jersey thought. "Yes, ma'am," he said.

"Wait where Benny can't miss you, Jersey. When he comes through, tell him where he can find Mote in Imogene. See if you can locate this Streeter person before dark."

"Yes, ma'am."

"I'll be in Reno by three tomorrow afternoon. Phone me there after that time. Daniel will coordinate the search while I'm en route."

"Yes, ma'am."

She hung up.

"Up your wazoo, Bitch," Jersey said, gesturing vulgarly. Oh, but the money was too good to even think about quitting, just too damned good. And he'd never been to Reno before. Twenty-four-hour town, Reno. Could be fun. Be even more fun if he just had the money, none of this aggravation.

• • •

The road to Streeter's ranch shot arrow-straight through a flatland of sage, giant hyssop, and seneco toward the southwest end of a rounded knob of rock that looked just like the tit on that one-tit whore Jersey'd known in Memphis. The one who'd still had a pretty face and good legs and who'd discovered she could charge a kinky clientele a lot more after the operation. Pretty soon she'd gotten so expensive Jersey had to take his business elsewhere.

The road wound past the base of the tit and up into the cleavage, if a single tit can be said to have cleavage. Streeter's ranch lay nestled like a mole against the far side of the hill, out of sight of Route 401. Not many chickens, but the whole yard was covered in dried chicken shit.

The sun was already behind the hills when they got there, the day vaguely purplish. A decrepit-looking Cessna 172 stood in a field of scrabbly hardpan, a quarter mile from the house.

Cap Streeter was sixty-five, but cigarettes, booze, and a touch of Alzheimer's had him looking seventy-five. When he peered at Mote and Jersey through watery eyes and said he'd gladly take them up in his Cessna for ninety bucks a day and gas, Jersey wished he'd never asked. But, too late. It would be exactly like Charlotte Voorhees to get hold of Streeter's number and ask if they'd been there. If she found that he and Mote had gone tearing off to Roswell to get a plane after Streeter'd agreed to take them up, she'd flay his goddamn feet for sure.

He was stuck with it.

"Sure you boys don't wanna drink?" Streeter asked as they were leaving.

"Well, yeah, sure," Mote said. "I'd kinda like—"

"No thanks," Jersey said curtly. All he wanted was to get a room in Quiode, inhale the half lid of Mexicali Gold, and crash—all night long.

"See you boys tomorrah then," Streeter said, rubbing three days' worth of snow-white stubble on his chin.

"Can't wait," Jersey mumbled, turning away. "Can't goddamn wait."

•   •   •

One more day. Mink worked on maintaining his inner calm. He closed his eyes and found that deep place of utter darkness in which Suki screamed. If you lacked such a place, a place over which you were absolute master, you had nothing.

One more day, then he would leave the hospital.

. . . Suki, screaming . . .

And now Mink knew how she would die. Not in the seething maw of fire, but beneath the deliberate, dispassionate, hammering thud of water. And, in the end, he would combine the two. Fire and water, heat and cold . . .

The phone rang. It was his mother, and she had a surprise for him. Two surprises.

"What, Mother?"

"Jersey found your car. The girl left it in the hills in New Mexico. She burned it. It can't be traced, of course, but at least it's a sign that she was there."

Was there. "And the other?"

"You'll see when you arrive in Reno, darling. Daniel arranged it. I'm still in Shreveport of course, but the operation is completely shut down here. We're no longer checking post office boxes, and the accounts have been emptied."

"That's good."

"I'm only staying here to coordinate the search. I expect to be in Reno by three tomorrow afternoon." She gave him the number of the new Citadel Daniel had set up for them in Reno.

Simon didn't write it down. He had that kind of a memory. Charlotte spoke a while longer and then hung up.

Mink went back inside his head, back to where Suki still lay screaming, shrieking, dying . . .

He smiled.

12

It hadn't started out like much, Suki practically sulking in fact, but whatever funk she'd slipped into that afternoon had all but disappeared by nine that evening. The whiskey she'd put down had probably helped. A lot. In no time at all, everything was dandy. Maybe too dandy, Frank thought, but after Suki's immodesty at the pool earlier that day—not to mention what had happened the night before—any prudishness he was still harboring seemed both false and a little too damned late.

After downing her fourth whiskey—which was by no means a precise measure of her blood alcohol level—Suki'd removed her top and gone wheeling around like a minx, not quite making herself obnoxious but nonchalantly flaunting herself, showing herself off, posing in small ways.

Looking good, too, even if her hair was beginning to get a bit ratty. She'd smiled at Frank's discomfiture.

Later, when the sun had gone down and the evening chill had driven her into one of his shirts and a pair of faded Levi's, she'd hit the bottle even harder. While she drank, he'd fixed up a dinner of chicken and beans to help counteract the booze.

His Levi's looked ridiculous on her. Snockered, she'd tried to prove that she could get both legs down one leg of his pants and still pull them up to her waist. Damn near made it too, giggling furiously, golden thighs wedged together.

She was drinking Jacky Dee straight now, eyes blurry, a funny little smile on her lips.

"You believe that?" she said, running her words together like a painter mixing watercolors. "My ma was third runner-up in the Miss Iowa contess back in, shit, I dunno, sixty-two, sixty-three. Sumpin' like that.

"I believe it," Frank said, not even feeling a buzz. One of them had to stay sober. Looked like it was going to be him. He couldn't believe the damage being done to the drinking he'd wanted to do.

"Five four, hunnerd an' ninety pounds now. Looks like a schmoo. You know what a schmoo is, Frank?"

"Yeah."

"Guess you'd know my ma, then, if you saw her." She drank another half-ounce of amber liquid and poured herself another.

"You're gonna get sick."

"No way, Frank. You never saw me drink, didja?"

"I've got an idea how it'll go."

"I kin hol' my likker."

"I see that."

But for the long sweep of her neck and a glimpse of perfectly-formed collarbone, her borrowed clothing hid every lovely curve of her body. The two of them sat inside, heater turned down low, just enough to keep things comfortable. Overhead, the Coleman lantern hissed as it gave off a yellow glow. The world outside belonged to a different universe.

She wagged a finger at him. "You know the def'nishun of a wimp, Frank?"

"Sure."

"My ol' man. That's a wimp. Fin' it right there in the dick-sherry."

He wasn't about to tell her not to talk about her father that way. Guy sounded like a wimp to Frank. Just because he was her father didn't mean he wasn't a wimp, and she was old enough to know.

"Get this," she said. "One day my ol' man comes home from the store, middle of the day. My ma said she was feelin' kinda sick, so she stayed home. Usu'ly worked down at the store with pa. Pa came home, check an' see she's all right. She's all right, all right—fuckin' one of the Miller boys right there on the couch. Kid was like, I don' know, seventeen. Sumpin' like that. Del Miller. Had pimples an' this big cowlick. Tried t' feel me up a coupla times. I wouldn' let him so then he's over't the house, bangin' ma.

"Think my pa did anythin'? Fuck no. Miller kid jumps up with these big scaredy eyes an' ma grabs his arm, throws an old vase at pa, almos' hits him in the face, tells him to get the hell outta there. He got out an' ma just kep' on doin' it with Del. Pa tol' me 'bout it later, whinin' like always, cryin' an' callin' me his li'l baby, over an' over, all sloppy an' stupid. I wuz twelve years ol', like I could fix any of that. How's that for fam'ly, huh?" She grabbed the bottle and poured herself another.

"Better take it easy with that stuff."

"Chill, Frank. I kin han'le it. Ma knows pa'd never leave her, no matter what. She *knows*, know what I mean? Pa owns a feed an' grain store out on southeas' Fourth, up near Saylorville. What I did growin' up was I cleaned out chick pens an' swep' the floors, carried sacks of feet." She looked at him and giggled. "Did I say feet? I meant feed."

"Uh-huh. And you went to school, too."

She gave him a funny look. "Las' year I was Miss Tractor Pull, down at the fairgroun'. All those hayseed bozos, whistlin' and shoutin' when all of us girls came out in bikinis. I hated it, but ma said do it. Firs' prize was three hunner' bucks. She said I could win easy, an' I did. So guess what I did."

"What?"

"I was suppos' t' give a trophy to this sweaty guy in bib overalls just won some dumb event. In my bikini. So I gave it t' some ol' lady in a suit, some kinda judge or sumthin', tol' her t' do it—kiss the sweaty sumbitch for me I tol' her, an' I grabbed some guy's arm an' made him take me on the Ferris wheel 'bout ten times. Thought, fuck'em, they can't take a joke. That was that for Missy Miss Tractor Pull. Had'ta give back mos'a the prize money, too. Boy, was ma ever pissed!"

"Then Mink came along."

"Mink." She sneered. "Yeah, Mink. The son'vabish. He knows how t' dress, though. Nice car, too." She gave Frank a cloudy look, then began to laugh. "BOOM! You see the windows come outta that thing, Frank?"

"I saw. Why'd you leave him, Suki?"

"Who?"

"Mink."

"He's crazy, thass why. Din' I tell you that?"

"You did. Often. Didn't say how, though."

She poured another slug of whiskey, a big one, spilling half. Frank winced, took the bottle away.

Suki leaned forward. "Din' never make love t' me, how's that for crazy?" She downed her drink like it was water.

Frank swirled his drink, same one he'd been nursing for the last two hours. His drinking wasn't making any headway at all. Not one single goddamned inch.

"So I ast him why we never made love. 'We gonna get married, Minky. Why'd you never take me t' bed?' Shit, he don' like me callin' him Minky. All he ever done is get me all dolled up and we'd go out t' dinner in these fancy-ass places. Sometimes I'd cook, but mos'ly we'd go out an' he'd show me off. At home, too. He'd get me wearin' these skimpy li'l outfits, show'n off my tits, 'specially when some of his guys were 'round, tough guys like Mote an' Jersey an' like, Isaac. Like that. Guess showin' me off was all he wannid."

She reached for the bottle, found it gone.

"Gimme li'l more, Frank."

"I think you've had enough."

"Uh-uh. C'mon."

"Nope. Bar's closed."

She looked into his eyes. "Hell, I gotta pee, don' I?"

"Bathroom's outside."

She tried to get up, slipped back down, began to giggle. Frank got behind her. He grabbed her under the arms and hauled her to her feet.

She tried to look back at him. "Jeez, you stron', Fran'."

"Yeah."

"I gotta pee."

He helped her outside. She clung to things—the refrigerator handle, cabinets, the door frame, Frank—as she wobbled along in his oversized thongs, clothes flapping.

"This's far enough," he said when they were a little way from the camper. "You gonna be all right here alone?"

She fumbled at her waist. "Where's the butt'ns on this son'vabish?"

No buttons. He untied the length of cord she'd been using as a belt. The pants dropped suddenly to her knees, his shirt hitting her at mid-thigh.

"You gonna be all right?" he asked again.

She stood there, swaying in his grasp.

"Why don't you pee here?" he suggested patiently.

She nodded. "Yeah. Gotta pee." She seemed confused, didn't quite know what to do next.

"Hell," Frank breathed. He put an arm around her waist and helped her out of his pants.

"Col'," she said.

"Yeah, cold. Let's hurry, huh?" He worked her underwear off with his left hand, holding her upright with his right.

"Now squat," he said. He lowered her to the ground, heard a sudden rush of liquid and looked off into the night. She was beautiful, but human. Probably wouldn't want to go over the details of this evening when she was sober again.

He gathered up her clothes and walked her back to the camper, taking most of her weight. She began to struggle weakly, making noises, and he let her down gently, knowing what was coming next.

She threw up suddenly, a lot of the alcohol she'd recently consumed. Do her good. Keep her from getting even sicker. Might even keep her from upchucking in bed, but Frank didn't want to hope for too much.

He let her go dry, then carried her into the camper, wet a rag and wiped her face. She had a tangly, wretched look, still moving feebly, beginning to go entirely incoherent. He undid the buttons of her shirt, speckled with vomit, got it off her, wiped her down again, and lifted her naked into bed.

He'd never seen her look so vulnerable.

He pulled the covers over her. In seconds she began to snore. He rolled her onto her side, which helped.

"Beautiful," he said softly. Now he'd seen her drink. She wasn't very good at it. He hoped she wouldn't get any worse. Or better, whichever.

He capped the whiskey, put it back in the cabinet. Got King off the countertop and began to read. Couldn't quite remember who'd been killed and how, so he backtracked four or five pages and caught up on the gore, read straight through for a few hours in the light of the Coleman lantern while the night deepened outside and Suki slept, snoring gently.

He felt very protective. It was a feeling he hadn't had in a long time.

Mink. Someone named Simon Voorhees, but preferred the name Mink. Real sweetheart of a guy, sounded like.

How Suki got herself mixed up with a shithead like that was beyond Frank, but she was young. Kids these days got tangled up in all kinds of things. Got in over their heads before they knew what they were doing. From the sounds of it, Suki'd escaped just in time.

Mink and Charlotte Voorhees.

Left Mink with a really bad tattoo, too. Not real smart, but she'd explained her reason for doing so with all the maturity of her years. She'd been pissed at him for hitting her. Enough said?

C-R-O-K. He couldn't say much for her spelling. You couldn't hardly guess what she was trying to write.

Suki's parents sounded like winners too. But, Frank reflected, not all that unusual, really. Just your basic screw-ups, plowing through life. He'd known a few people in his day who'd give the Ericksons a run for their money in the asshole department. He'd even once met a supposed former beauty queen who'd gone to seed early, down in Phoenix, and the world was awash in losers and wimps.

Even had a few dumb-ass jokers on the run from the law, too. All he had to do to find one was look in a mirror.

Jesus.

Thing of it was, he wasn't sorry he'd done it—at least, not yet. But it'd been just four days now; five, since it was after midnight. Two-ten in the morning, in fact.

Suki groaned, rolled over. Her duffel bag slid off the bed, landed on Frank's shoulder and tumbled to the floor. She was quiet again.

He picked it up, looked at it a moment, then unzipped it, feeling a bit crawly inside at the invasion of her privacy.

Took out the stuffed rabbit, the duck, a Nerf football, a goddamned Rubik's Cube, three twenty-dollar bills—the ones he'd given her. Underneath that was a towel over the rest of the stuff. He took it out and stared into the bag at all the money, a great huge wad of it. He blinked.

Ho-ly *shit*.

13

Loose bills lay piled in the bottom of Suki's bag like lettuce in a chef's salad.

Frank's first thought was that she'd found his stash and ripped him off.

He emptied the cabinet over the sink and shoved the false panel aside. His bag was still there with all his money and his papers, just the way he'd left it.

He sat down, hard.

Jesus Christ.

Jesus *H*. Christ.

He tried to think, but his brain had turned to oatmeal. Dazed, he carefully returned his bankroll to its hidey-hole, put the Jack Daniel's back in the closet, and sat down again.

Mostly fifties and hundreds in her bag, a few twenties and a scattering of tens.

Used money, loose, tossed in hastily.

Suddenly he wasn't a bit tired. Suki was asleep, breathing

heavily, out of it.

He upended the bag over the table. The unique musty odor of money filled the confined space. A few big wads slithered to the floor, *plop*. Money even had its own sound. Lord, there was a lot of it. He felt a chill creep up his spine.

He started gathering up the hundreds first, because there seemed to be more of them than anything else. Ten bills to a thousand, a hundred bills makes ten thousand.

He found some string and began tying it up in bundles of ten thousand. He gathered more of it from the floor where it had fallen.

It was a task of no little magnitude. Twenty-six bundles, sixty-four left over. Whatever she'd done, she'd scored big. Bigger than he had. Suddenly Mink's interest in her made a lot more sense.

Then the fifties. A hundred bills makes five grand. He made up five bundles before he realized it was getting light outside. Another eight bundles, twenty-six bills left over, and then he didn't need the lantern any longer. Dawn light tinged the hilltops a pink-orange color.

Twenties: ten bundles, fifty-seven extra. Tens: two bundles with six extra. Even had seventeen fives thrown in. No ones. Frank totaled it up: $355,985.

If that don't beat all, he thought, using another of Fanny's favorite expressions.

"Sheee-it," he said softly.

• • •

The Cessna rattled and wheezed, finally lifted off like an albatross on methamphetamine. Jersey stared at the ground below with glazed eyes, wondering if the last thing he would see would be rocks coming at him at a hundred forty miles an hour. The possibility didn't seem all that remote.

He and Mote sat in back, Cap Streeter in the pilot's seat up front with his dog, Woozer, sitting copilot.

Woozer, a baggy-eyed basset hound with wet, drooly flews, was stolidly indifferent to anything going on around him. He'd gotten his name from his bark, a soggy chuff that was half bark, half howl. Streeter had told them Woozer was hell on prairie dogs, but Jersey believed that like he believed Manson would one day have his feet up on the desk in the Oval Office. The mutt wouldn't give a merry fuck if prairie dogs did laps around him on the front porch, goosed him, and stole his Purina. Sorta liked to fly, though. Every few minutes he'd look outside, blink wetly, and *whoof* a bit, or *wooz*, like he was happy, or maybe he'd inhaled a jowl.

"Okay, now't we's up, what wuzit you boys wanted t' see?" Streeter asked. Stale booze rode his breath.

"Mountains up over that way." Jersey pointed to the left.

The Cessna went into a sudden rolling turn and Mote's eyes bugged out. Jersey's stomach reached his nuts before crawling back up. Woozer howled.

"Wooz likes that," Streeter called back over the unsteady throb of the engine.

"Great," Jersey replied, bile in his throat, wondering how Wooz would taste, skinned and deep-fried, served on a stick.

They'd gotten off fairly late, nearly three in the afternoon, Cap trying to work off the effects of half a case of beer the previous evening. Which wasn't late enough, Jersey'd thought earlier, looking distrustfully at the crate Streeter said he'd take them up in. The plane looked like it was missing parts. He'd said as much to Streeter, trying to sound like he was kidding, and Streeter'd said it was, "quite a few of 'em, which makes the ol' kite lighter." Jersey couldn't tell if the son of a bitch was joking or not.

As they passed over Quiode, Jersey picked out the Siesta Motel where he and Mote had spent the night. They crossed Route 401 at an angle, and a few minutes later Jersey spotted the wreck of the Trans Am and Farley's old pickup truck, six hundred feet below.

"There," he said. "There's the car."

Streeter stood the plane on its left wing and roared in a circle above the blackened hulk, banking at a forty-five degree angle.

Woozer howled.

• • •

Suki came awake like a carp on a riverbank, ninety-five percent dead. Not even the smell of coffee helped. One eyelid rolled up, exposing a bloodshot eye, slid shut again with a quiver as she let out a faint moan.

"Morning," Frank said amiably. Beneath the canvas awning, the interior of the camper was dim with the curtains pulled. Warm, but not unbearably so. Frank kept on with his cooking.

Suki moaned again.

"Four in the afternoon, actually," Frank said. "You've been asleep for something like seventeen hours. Must have a bladder like a ballast tank."

She made another little sound of pain, almost a whimper, and turned toward the wall with the blankets pulled over her head, bare feet hanging out.

"Want a beer?" Frank said.

"Ugh!" She shuddered under the blankets.

"At least you're alive."

"Who says?" She rolled over, groaned again. "Hurts."

"What, your head?"

"Yeah."

"That surprise you?"

She wiped a dewy line of sweat off her upper lip. "Jesus, what're you cookin'?"

"Eggs. Got to use 'em up or they'll go bad. Want some?"

"Don't be disgus—" She saw the money, stacked neatly on the table. She lunged for her duffel bag, but it wasn't there. It was on the floor, empty. Her face, already pale, went white. She propped herself up on an elbow. "What's goin' on?"

He gave her a direct look. "It appears you haven't been entirely honest with me, Miss Suki-Anne."

She got out of bed, still looking drawn, but awake. She put on Frank's thongs and went outside, still naked, moving unsteadily, muscles working in her honey-colored rump.

She came back a few minutes later, pushed past him without a word, and began searching for her underwear. She found them, put them on, climbed into her pink shorts and shrugged into her bright yellow top.

Still not a word, which Frank found amusing. He'd grown accustomed to her wicked comments, but this had stopped her cold. The eggs were done, so he turned off the stove, got a fork, sat at the table, and began to eat right out of the pan, egg and catsup stew, waiting for her to make the first move.

She opened the cabinet over the sink and set bottles of Jack Daniel's on the countertop. His heart began to beat heavier, faster. Christ, what was *this*?

She slid the hidden panel aside and took out his blue nylon bag, tossed it in his lap.

"Guess you haven't been entirely, wonderfully honest with me, either, Mr. Frank Goddamn-Liar Limosin-Wiley." Her eyes gave off sparks. She turned and stormed outside.

Limosin. She knew about the money, even knew his name.

Shit.

He sat there a while with the bag in his hands, wondering how long she'd known.

He took another bite, sighed, got up and went outside. She was standing with her back to the camper. "Now what?" he asked, trying to figure her mood. She was angry, sure, but what else? And how much more did she know?

Her arms were folded, back still turned, afternoon sun blazing on her hair.

She spun around, bleary eyes level with his. "How much was there?" she said, quiet now.

"Where?"

"In my bag."

"Three hundred fifty thousand and change."

Her eyes flickered. "Jesus. How much change?"

"Somewhere around six thousand. You didn't know how much you were carrying around?"

"I left in kind of a hurry. I didn't have time to count it."

"Looks like we both left out a few details when we were trading stories."

"Looks like."

"How long have you known?" he asked. "My name, and about the money?"

"Since yesterday, little before noon. I found the money kinda by accident, and there was something on the radio about you. I didn't know it was you they were talkin' about, till I found your license."

On the radio—way out here. That wasn't good. Up this high, AM might travel quite a distance though. And now Suki knew he was wanted. More trouble.

"Hungry?"

She shook her head. "Not very. You got any aspirin?"

"Tylenol. How about some toast? Dry?"

"Maybe. Lemme try the pills first."

They went inside. Suki hefted several bundles of hundreds—$40,000 worth. She saw his .357 lying on the counter, and he saw her looking at it.

She glanced at him, took the Tylenol he was offering and a cup of water. "I was drunk," she said. "You could've taken off with all of it, left me here."

"Could've, yeah. Still could."

She blinked. "So? Why don't you?"

"Because I'm basically a very honest person, Suki. I want you to understand that."

"That why the cops're after you?"

"It's a long story."

"Usually are, aren't they?"

"Yours too?"

She thought a moment. "Not really. What I did, before giving Mink that tattoo, was I got that week's take out of a small safe Mink kept around. Business Mink's in, ripping off old folks, he likes to deal in cash for rent and stuff so he can't be traced and so he can clear out quick if he has to. The safe was the same kind my pa had at the store, a Fidelity model 40 combination safe. Took me a month to figure out the little clicks and bumps on my pa's safe, but then it wasn't all that hard, even when he took to changing the combination. I didn't take much. Just a little spending money." She held up her hands. "I've got good fingers, might make a pretty good burglar, maybe."

"So you picked Mink's safe, took the money, left him with a bad tattoo, and split?"

"Yeah."

"Anything else?"

"Uh-uh. Just sorta stole his car, but you already know that."

"Gave him another reason to hunt you down, don't you think? Three hundred fifty-six thousand reasons."

"You don't know Mink, Frank. Losing that money'd bother him, sure—but not as much as you'd think. The tattoo is what'd make him go really crazy. Maybe I shouldn't have done the tattoo."

"Maybe not. Too late now. Toast?"

She shook her head. "Uh-uh. Maybe later. Think I'll just go to the pool and soak instead. Try to keep from dyin'. I still don't feel all that wonderful."

"Suit yourself."

She went outside. He had an oblique view of her through a window past the canvas awning as she walked away.

A minute later he heard a sound: an engine laboring in the high mountain air. Went outside to take a look. An old Cessna, a mottled dusty yellow, was coming in at an angle not three hundred feet off the ground, wingtips swaying.

Oh, Jesus.

•   •   •

"There!" Jersey shouted, pointing. "What's that?"

Streeter hung a breathtaking turn so close to the ground that Jersey could see every rock and wildflower below, saw where and how he was going to die, big seventy-foot-tall cottonwoods reaching up to get him.

Woozer howled with pleasure. Shit-for-brains mutt.

Jersey saw a man below, standing next to a dark green trapezoid that soon resolved itself into some kind of a tent. The hood of a truck stuck out from under it.

"That it?" Jersey yelled at Mote. "That the guy's truck?"

"I dunno," Mote said. "Can't see much of it."

Jersey hardly heard him. "That's him, that's the son of a bitch that—" He stopped abruptly.

"That what?" Streeter asked, ears twitching.

"Never mind," Jersey said. "That's him."

"There's the girl," Mote said phlegmatically, as if he were pointing out milk in the dairy section of a supermarket.

Jersey grabbed his shoulder. "Where?"

"There, kinda under them trees."

Jersey saw her then, platinum hair in shadow but still blazing away. Same yellow top and pink shorts he'd seen in Belinda's Café. She was shading her eyes, gazing up at the plane.

"That's her all right." To Cap he said, "How the hell do we get up to this place?"

"Truck, I reckon."

"Shit, I know that. I mean, where's the *road?* How're we supposed to get up here?"

"Beats the hell outta me."

"Can we follow the trail out, see where it goes?"

"Yuh. Give 'er a try. We're gettin' a mite low on the go juice, though." He tapped a dial.

"Let's do it."

The plane straightened out, moving northeast into a high gap where the road, such as it was, came up over a ridge. Just about impossible to see where the truck had come in from up here. An all-but-invisible double track snaked over the rocky ground. They lost sight of it repeatedly as it switchbacked down the mountain. They circled, picked it up again, lost it a dozen times. It was tedious, stomach-wrenching work, but Woozer loved every minute of it.

"We don't go back pretty soon," Streeter said after forty minutes of aerial artistry, "an' you kin pick out which rock you want t' kiss when I pile 'er up. Course, by then your asshole'd be puck'rin' up a dern sight more'n your lips." He grinned, chortling muddily at his own wit.

"Shit," Jersey said. In the hazy distance he could see Mink's fire-gutted car, just a speck of black on the ground. He'd gotten a rough idea of how the trail crawled up into the hills: a big uphill loop to the left as you went past the Tranny, then to the right, over a ridge, down through a washboard canyon. Up again, southwest. Something like that. Mostly what he'd learned was that the girl was up there. El hombre, too. That was huge. That was the ballgame.

"Guess I've seen all I need to," Jersey said. Which wasn't entirely true, but he was starting to feel he'd already used up too many years' worth of luck in Streeter's crappy old plane.

Streeter jinked the plane like he was dodging SAMs. Woozer howled. The plane rumbled toward Quiode, engine coughing every so often, which didn't faze Streeter a bit.

The time was five-fifteen.

• • •

Frank Limosin watched the plane disappear over a ridge. The pilot was a crazy son of a gun, that much was evident, but not much else. He couldn't see who was up there. The plane had circled twice, sunlight glinting off its windows, before flying off more or less back the way it had come. That seemed ominous.

Suki came hobbling over the rocky ground, arms pinwheeling for balance.

"What was that all about?" she asked.

He stared at the now-empty horizon, shading his eyes. "Your guess is as good as mine."

"Someone lookin' for us?"

"Could be."

"Mote an' Jersey?"

"Or maybe a pilot out having fun, showing off."

"You think?" she said hopefully.

"I dunno."

He went into the camper. Suki followed. He said, "If it was those two friends of yours, then—"

"Those two ass-wipes aren't friends of mine, Frank."

"Sorry. Ass-wipes, then. Anyway, if that was them, we'd be smart to clear out, and soon. On the other hand, if we leave and it wasn't them, we'd be leaving a damn nice place to hole up for no reason at all."

She bit a knuckle. "So, what're we gonna do?"

Frank sighed. "Only thing we can, I guess. Clear out, at least for a couple of days."

"I'm makin' trouble for you, aren't I?"

"That's one way of looking at it, yeah."

"What's another?"

"I don't know." Frank looked at his watch. "If we leave now, it'll be about dark by the time we reach the highway. If we push it."

"I got time for a quick soak before we go? I still feel like hell."

"Few minutes wouldn't hurt."

"Wonderful." She squirmed out of her top and handed it to him. "Put this someplace safe for me, huh?"

She gave him a quick peck on the cheek then went out the door.

He stuck his head out. "Hey!"

She turned, striking a nice hipshot pose. "What?"

"Why the hell you do this kind of thing, anyway?" He held out her top, letting it dangle from one hand.

"A present. You like to look, Frank. Don't tell me you don't. Anything else I gave you right now would slow us down too much."

He smiled. "Go soak. And don't forget your head."

"Yeah, yeah. Hey, Frank."

"What?"

"Are the cops really after you, like they said on the radio?"

"Uh-huh."

"I'm sorry, then. About all this."

"Yeah, yeah."

He ducked back inside, looped her top over the vent handle and began thrashing around, putting things away.

14

The plane came sideslipping into the weedy field where they'd taken off, engine throttled back, coughing, and Jersey knew he was going to die. They'd made it this far, found the girl, and now he was going to end up smeared like cheese pizza over a little nothing patch of New Mexico. The landing gear wasn't aligned with the runway, the plane was crabbing awkwardly into a side breeze, and Jersey saw that they were going to flip at sixty-some miles an hour, wrap themselves into a noxious wad of blood and bone and aluminum that would make a page-nine item in a Roswell newspaper.

At the last instant, Streeter did something with his feet and the Cessna slewed left, settling gently into a bumpy roll over the field.

"Shit-fire," Jersey breathed.

Woozer howled. Liked landings too, fuckin' retard.

They paid Streeter in cash, didn't bother thanking him, and roared back to Quiode, Jersey liking the proximity of the ground. In the darkness of the Blue Bottle Bar he dialed the Reno number.

"Tell me," she said.

"It's Jersey, ma—"

"Where have you *been*, Jersey? Do you have *any* idea how late it is?"

"We saw her," he said quickly. "Ma'am."

"*Where*?"

"Way up on a mountain. From the plane. Southwest of Quiode."

"Is she still up there, Jersey?"

"Gotta be. It's a bad fuck—uh, real bad road, ma'am. *Real* bad. That guy's up there with her. Probably take them at least two or three hours to get to the highway from way up there."

"Is there any other way out?"

"I didn't see one, ma'am." And I wouldn't have even if there was one anyway, and up yours very much ma'am. He felt goddamn lucky just to be alive.

"Okay. Listen carefully now, Jersey."

Jersey closed his eyes, waiting for the rest of it. "Yes, ma'am."

"Are you listening *very* carefully, Jersey?"

Red lights shot like tracers through the darkened interior of his brain. "Yes, ma'am."

"What I want you to do, you and Mote and Isaac, is to go up into the mountains, find the girl, and bring her out. Have Benny stay at the road near the highway in case they manage to get past you. Is that perfectly clear, Jersey?"

"Yes, ma'am."

"Don't hurt the girl."

"No, ma'am. How 'bout the guy? Want him messed up any?"

"If you must, but not too much, Jersey. He's not important. Don't do anything that would make it anything but a strictly local matter for the police. You and Mote have made a presence of yourselves in the region."

"Yes, ma'am."

"Do not fail us this time, Jersey."

"No, ma'am."

"Call when you've got her."

"Yes, ma—" But the line was already dead.

"Fuck you and all your kin, ma'am," he said softly. "And your dogs and cats and all their fleas."

. . .

A rock clanged against the wheel well, making the cab of the truck ring like a bell.

"Jeez," Suki said.

The truck heaved, tossing them both several inches in the air, slammed back down. Frank jammed in the clutch.

"Was it this bad comin' up?" Suki asked.

"Yup."

"I didn't notice. Must've had something on my mind."

"Must have. And we were going quite a bit slower."

Afternoon sun slanted into the hills, giving the canyons a gloomy look. Lengthening shadows crawled over the land below, out where Route 401 snaked through the valley. The day was still hot. Suki was back in her pink shorts and yellow top.

"Be fairly dark in another hour or so," Frank said.

"Yeah." She gave him a sidelong look. "Where'd the name Wiley come from, Frank?"

He didn't look at her. He felt uncomfortable with the lies he'd told her. "Wiley's my mother's maiden name."

"Why'd you do it?"

"Do what?" But he knew what she meant.

"Take that truck. Steal stuff. What kind of a truck was it? What'd you do with it, anyway?"

"You writin' a book?"

"Just I'd like to know. That so bad?"

He spun the wheel, avoiding boulders as the truck ground up a twisty slope of loose rock. "Guess not."

"Well?"

"I drove a truck for this company, J. K. Lomax. JKL. They make bearings. One of the bigger manufacturers on the West Coast."

"Bearings?"

"Ball bearings. Roller bearings, needle, lot of special-order stuff. Do a good business in turbine and pump bearings for power plants and municipal water places over much of the western United States."

"Guess there's money in that, huh?"

He gave her a wry look. "Yeah, there's money in it. You take a case of quarter-inch ID ball bearings, thousand bearings to a case, weighs thirty-five point three pounds and takes up about as much room as your average carry-on suitcase. Guess what that box retails for."

"I dunno. Couple thousand bucks?"

"Not bad. Try seventy-five hundred. Hundred cases'd run seven hundred fifty thousand dollars—retail, not wholesale. It'd weigh almost as much as an eighty-two Cadillac."

"Jesus, Frank. You stole that much?"

"More. Hundred twelve cases of assorted-size general-purpose needle and roller bearings, a few dozen big turbine bearings; two hundred fifty special-order rollers for some big farm equipment outfit in Nebraska. Manifest put the shipment at eight hundred forty thousand bucks, wholesale. Retail, it'd go for something like one point four million, give or take."

"How much you get for it?"

"Right around eighty-six thousand."

"That all?"

"I got the price I'd negotiated. Ten cents on the dollar, wholesale, for the stuff they could unload easily. Less on the special-order stuff. Fairly typical black market."

"Why'd you do it?"

He glanced at her. "Enough about me. These sons-a-bitches of Mink's are out looking for you, not me. I want to know why. I want to know what this's really all about."

"I already tole you, Fra—"

The right rear tire blew out with a sharp report.

"Dirtysonofawhore!" Frank yelped.

The truck, which wasn't going very fast, thunked down on its rim and heeled over hard to starboard in a dry wash that descended steeply into a dark saddle of the hills.

Frank got out, glared at the tire, kicked it. "Shit," he said.

"Flat, huh?"

"Just look at the sonofabitch. Ever seen one flatter?"

"Yeah, once. Got a spare?"

He nodded. "Two. One underneath, another one on top of the camper."

"Okay, lemme help."

He stared at her.

She sat on a nearby rock. "First thing you do," she said, "is haul out the spare and the jack. Probably oughta set the emergency brake too."

"Christ," he growled. "Thanks."

"No problem, Frank. I'm pretty good with flat tires. Give you all the help you need, which is to say, I'll tell you how to—"

"Yeah, yeah, yeah."

•   •   •

Jersey'd rented the truck for eighty dollars from some old Indian with the crotch of his jeans sagging down around his knees. A four-wheel-drive, three-quarter-ton Ford pickup. When he'd turned the key, Slim Whitman was singing "Blue Eyes Crying in the Rain" on the radio at nearly full volume.

Jersey had wanted two trucks, but Quiode was a dry well and in Imogene he'd only found the one before he saw that the sun was getting low in the west. Real low.

So he and Mote had piled into the Ford and taken off. Isaac had driven the Toronado. They met Benny a little after seven-thirty at the gravel pit where the road went up into the hills, Benny in the souped-up Chevy Malibu he and Isaac had been driving, cheeseburger juice dribbling from his chin. Benny was a class act all the way, one small rung up the evolutionary ladder from Mote. A pterodactyl, bony, with pale skin and protruding blue eyes.

"Seen anything?" Jersey asked.

Benny shook his head. "Nope."

"Keep watchin'." Isaac left the Toronado there, got in the truck, then Jersey gunned the engine and roared off toward the hills.

Mote sat in the middle, with his big arms and Neanderthal brain, playing pretend cowboy with a snub-nose .38, spinning the cylinder, flipping it in and out, peering down the barrel, snapping it shut with a flick of his wrist. Isaac, a slender black from Detroit whose palms were as pink as Jersey's ex-wife's ass, sat nursing a beer in silence.

Jersey imagined that Isaac's silence was a sign of satisfaction. Whatever happened, Isaac couldn't lose. Isaac was the one who'd gotten them this far, and it wasn't likely Mink or Charlotte would forget that, even if the girl managed to get away. Isaac had been standing guard over the house in Shreveport when the girl ran. He'd tailed her in the Malibu as she left town and followed her all the way to the west side of Dallas before she stopped for gas and he finally had a chance to phone in.

What a commotion then! Everyone scrambling, Charlotte giving orders, Mink out cold, Jersey and Mote and Benny taking off in the Toronado, headed for Dallas like they were sitting astride a bomb.

Isaac had lost the girl somewhere east of Abilene, and for a while it looked as if he'd lost her for good, since she didn't show up for over four hours. But he'd waited just outside Sweetwater and, Jersey thought sourly, gotten lucky as shit because Suki'd finally come rolling along, just about dusk. She'd turned up Highway 84, headed for Lubbock, surprising the hell out of everyone. That night she'd disappeared somewhere around Fort Sumner, New Mexico, sixty miles west of Clovis.

By then the Toronado wasn't far behind, Mrs. Voorhees guiding them. Isaac had waited around and Benny had piled into the Malibu and the two had roared up north on 84 to Santa Rosa, then down 54 to Vaughn, while Mote and Jersey had gone south on 20.

For a while it looked as if Suki'd finally gotten away clean, but then Mote and Jersey had gotten lucky themselves and stumbled across her in Quiode. Just about had her, too—would have, if that big sonofabitch hadn't come along, interfering.

Jersey wanted the sonofabitch, wanted him bad. He still felt the ache in his gut where the bastard had rammed him with the broom handle.

Dust piled up on the corners of the windshield, billowed out behind the truck in a reddish-brown rooster tail.

"Put that goddamn thing away," Jersey said to Mote. It made him nervous, Mote whipping his gun around like that.

"When you gonna give me my bullets?" Mote asked.

"When hell freezes over, or when we see this guy Suki's with, that's when."

"Jeez, Jers."

Isaac snickered.

Jersey looked over at him. "You got your piece, Izzy?"

"Yeah."

"Loaded?"

"What d'you think?"

Mote said, "How come he gets bullets an' I don't?"

"Cause you'd blow your nuts off, fuckin' around like that, that's why. Izzy's got brains. What you got is wood shavings and liberry paste."

"Goddammit, Jers—"

"Christ, cool it, you two," Isaac said. "Jersey didn't mean nothin', Mote. Listen, tell me whatcha think: suppose this big airliner took off somewhere in Ohio and crashed in Canada. Where d'you think they'd bury the survivors, back in the United States or right there in Canada?"

Mote gave him a perplexed look. "How come you're always askin' me shit like that, Iz, huh?"

"No reason. Just passin' the time, bro."

"Shit, I dunno. Canada?"

Jersey laughed.

• • •

The truck was nosed downhill, leaning to the right. The slope made changing the tire a much more difficult task. It had taken Frank ten minutes to block the front tires with rocks so the truck wouldn't slip downhill even though the emergency brake was on, and another fifteen to dig out a flat place with a crowbar for the jack so the truck wouldn't slip off. Suki sat on her rock, watching.

"So," Frank said, "tell me about Mink's operation."

"Whatcha want to know?"

"Everything. We've got these guys after us, I'd like to know what we're up against."

"Scuzzballs, that's what we're up against."

"That's not very helpful, Suki. Tell me about Mink."

"He's the head scuzzball."

He glared at her in the failing light. Her top was a band of glowing yellow. The air was cooling but still warm, rocks all around giving off the day's heat.

"Okay," she said. "All right. What Mink does is he's got this big scam all worked out where he sells phony shares or something to old people. Mostly in phony mutual funds."

"It's been done before." Frank put the wrench over a nut and spun it a quarter turn—*rak*—as easily as if someone had put it on with his fingers.

Suki stared. "Shit—how'd you . . ."

"Huh?"

"Nothin'," she said. "Mink and Charlotte've got a bunch of people who talk on the phone, ten hours a day. Six of 'em, usually."

"Standard boiler-room operation, sounds like." *Rak.*

"Yeah. I heard someone call it that once. Boiler room."

"What's so special about this one?"

"I don't know. Maybe nothing. They make a big pile of money though."

Rak. Another nut spun loose. "What do you think?"

"Maybe the psykill . . . psycolol—"

"Psychology?"

"Yeah. Psy-*chology*. What he does is he scares old folks, but he does it real nice, without scaring them about *him*. He makes 'em wonder if they're doin' the right thing with their money, makes 'em wonder if their money is really safe where it is. Gets 'em worried sick about inflation."

"Charming." *Rak.*

"Listen to this. I heard this kinda thing so many times I sometimes hear it in my sleep." Her voice changed, becoming more confident, more soothing, and, Frank thought, subtly sly, although she probably wasn't aware of it.

" 'Lord, isn't inflation awful, Caroline?' " she said. " 'May I call you Caroline? You sound so much like my own mother, it makes me kinda homesick. Seems like every time you go to the store these days, things cost a little bit more, don't they? Shame, isn't it? . . . Yes, thank God it isn't as bad as it once was, but what with the government printing money like it was going out of style, now that we're not on the gold standard anymore—well, how long can it last? You'd think Congress would *do* something, but it just keeps getting worse. It makes me feel terrible to think that a day might come when innocent people like you might not be able to afford to keep living in their own homes, inflation and taxes eating them up like they are. That's why it's so important for your money to not only be absolutely safe, Caroline, but to *grow*. If the interest on your savings doesn't keep pace with inflation, you'll find that as time goes by—what's that? . . . Your son said the same thing just last week? There, you see. Inflation hurts us all, doesn't it? Why, just last month the power company turned off the electricity to my grandma's house when she couldn't pay her bill. She didn't tell us she was having trouble . . . Yes, we got the power back on, thank goodness, me and my brother, but we sure wouldn't want anything like that to happen to you, would we?' " Suki produced a sad little laugh, perfectly sympathetic, perfectly cold underneath.

Frank stared at her.

In a normal voice she said, "They get to that part of the speech about ten minutes into the call. Before that it's all nice and chatty, talking about this lady's grandchildren and how she likes them to come visit, how her son is a big shot in some company, or maybe a doctor, and the name of her cat. If she's got a cat, then the 'yack'— the person in the boiler room—has a cat too. If she's got a dog, the talker has the same kind of dog. The dog's name is always Buddy. No talk about money in the first five minutes. What they look for is someone who's kinda lonely and has a little money, but not enough to feel real comfortable with how much they've got. Someone who's nervous, maybe a little bit scared.

"After a while, if this person's still listening, they get something like this: 'I'm lucky, Caroline. I've got a really good job with a really good company—good benefits too, which is nice. V. R. Gibbs and Associates. We mostly handle investments for banks and mid-sized corporations, but we have a division that sets up similar accounts for people just like yourself. People who want a good return on their money and have to have absolute safety too.

" 'You're getting how much from your bank? Three and a half percent, four if you're lucky? Well, V. R. Gibbs and Associates—' " Suki looked at Frank and said, "That's what Mink called this phony company he set up in Shreveport. He was good at inventing phony names. In Wichita we were the Cheney Investment Group."

"Uh-huh," Frank said, pulling off the flat, lifting the spare into place, pushing it onto the lugs.

"Anyway. 'Caroline, V. R. Gibbs and Associates pools all its investors' money and invests it in mutual funds. Surely you've heard about mutual funds? . . . Yes, I thought so. Last year the fund earned twenty-six percent interest . . . Yes, that's right. Isn't it wonderful? I had two thousand dollars in it myself. I wish I had more, but, well, my mother was sick last year and I helped her out with the bills. And the year before that the fund earned twenty-four and a half percent, so it's up a little this year. Right now it's doing about the same, maybe a little bit better.

" 'But what's *really* special about V. R. Gibbs, Caroline, is that money invested with us is backed by U.S. Treasury bills earning ten and a half percent. What that means is that no matter *what*, you can't earn less than ten and a half percent, and your money is absolutely safe because treasury bills are absolutely safe, backed by the U.S. government.' "

"Bullshit," Frank said. "They can't invest X dollars in mutual funds *and* also in treasury notes."

"Jesus, Frank, they weren't doing either. But that isn't the point. The point is, a lot of these old fogies don't know treasury bills from toilet paper. It sounds good, that's all. That's all Mink needs, and it's what an awful lot of old people want. They want so much to believe that nothing bad can ever happen to them. Caroline is told that her money is completely safe, making twenty-six percent interest, and that she can have it back in her own bank with just a single phone call anytime she wants, day or night."

"And that crap works?" He began to tighten the lug nuts on the new tire.

She laughed, a soft, clean sound in the twilight. "Yeah, that crap works. Ask me how well."

"How well?"

"I heard Mink and Charlotte talking one day, maybe three weeks ago. In Shreveport they had six yacks bringing in a little over twelve thousand dollars a day. Each. Not all that much, Frank, considering. An operator'd make fifty or sixty calls for every person who sent in money. Sometimes they'd talk to a hundred people and get nothing, then hit two in a row, or three in the next ten. They had little contests, see who had the best day, best week, that kinda thing."

Frank paused. "Six operators, twelve grand a day. Christ, that's about three-fifty, three-sixty grand a week." He gave each of the nuts a final twist with the wrench, then lowered the truck onto its new tire. "Sounds like you got an entire week's worth."

"Uh-huh. Mink told me they got over two million in Shreveport in just six weeks."

"He told you that?"

"He trusted me, sort of. Well, actually, Mink doesn't trust anyone but Charlotte, but he told me how much they'd made. Bragging, kinda."

"Want a beer?"

"Oh, please." She made a puking gesture.

Frank opened a chest, dug a Budweiser out of floating ice for himself. "The FBI never caught on to these assholes?"

"There was a close call once, before I came along. They move around more now. They were in Des Moines, then Seattle, Pittsburgh, Wichita, and Shreveport. After Shreveport it was gonna be Reno. They were about half packed and ready to move when I took off. The yacks were all off on vacation like they do between moves, supposed to get to Reno sometime next week, Monday or Tuesday. Danny goes on ahead, gets everything all set up, the house, bank accounts, all of that. He's this kinda moonfaced guy, about forty, wears these round granny glasses. Some sort of business manager or something for Mink. I guess Mink has to trust Danny, too, sort of."

"I've been to Reno," Frank said.

"Yeah? Anyplace you haven't been?"

"Rio."

"Where's that?"

"Rio? You know, *Rio*. Rio de Janeiro. Brazil."

"Oh, sure. I meant in the United States."

"Lotsa places."

"Name one."

"New York City. Believe it or not, I never made it to the Big Apple."

"The big *what*?"

"Forget it. So what you did was you grabbed Mink's walking around money before they took off for Reno, huh?"

"Guess so. That week's take, anyway."

"What happened to the rest of it, the two million?"

"Every week Mink puts the money somewhere, I don't know where. I think only Charlotte knows. Probably in one of those safe deposit boxes banks've got."

Frank frowned. "Then he's gotta have what? Ten, maybe twenty million dollars floating around somewhere. Maybe more."

"Most of it's in diamonds."

"Diamonds?"

"Danny told me. Back in Seattle, last year. Mink goes to New York City and buys a bunch of diamonds when they move from one place to the next. Doesn't ever keep them around, close by, just keeps 'em in a safe deposit box in some big bank out there in New York—hey, what's that?"

"What's what?"

She stood, pointing. "Down there. Some kind of light."

Frank saw the sweep of distant headlights over the land below, between them and Route 401, moving slowly over the rough, broken country.

"Shit," he said.

"Think maybe it's Mote and Jersey?"

"I'd say it's a possibility we can't ignore." He finished stowing the jack, shoved the flat in back of the camper. They got back in the truck and Frank started the engine.

"Now what?" Suki asked nervously.

He stared straight ahead out the windshield for a moment. "Now I don't know what. Now we wing it, kid."

"Wonderful."

"Yeah, ain't it though?"

15

Frank drove at a crawl in the direction of Route 401. Darkness descended in the De Baca Mountains; a burnt orange glow lay dying across the far horizon, as if all of Southern California were ablaze, seven hundred miles to the west.

Frank wanted to avoid these guys altogether. If they could get past them somehow, that'd be the end of it, no big confrontation, no muss, no fuss, no nasty little knife fights or shots fired in the night. He had to figure on the worst—that Mutt and Jeff had guns and that they would come straight up the trail without getting sidetracked or lost.

The blackness of the night was a mixed blessing. A puny silver crescent hung over the western mountains, illuminating nothing, including the trail they were trying to follow. Frank didn't want to use his headlights and possibly give away their position or the fact that he and Suki were on the move. The trail was a rocky blackness, all but impossible to follow in the dark. Frank couldn't see much of anything to either side. If they stayed on the trail, however, Mutt and Jeff would eventually run across them, assuming they were the ones winding through the foothills below. Every so often a faint wash of light was visible, drawing closer.

"Stay here," Frank said. Letting the truck idle, he got out and walked ahead with the flashlight, searching for a place where he could pull the truck far enough off the trail to hide it.

He went a hundred feet, two hundred, found nothing that looked promising. The seconds seemed to tick by faster, and he felt a sense of urgency begin to build. They were in a box, and its rock walls were closing in on them.

"Nothing?" Suki asked when he got back.

"Nope. We're kinda locked in here."

The darkness was all but complete, smothering.

"Can't we use the lights?" Suki asked. "Just long enough to find a place to hide?"

Six of one, half a dozen of another. Without headlights, they were trading speed for stealth. The Defense Department thought that was a hell of a good idea. Frank put the truck in gear, inching forward. "Let's go up a ways farther and try the flashlight again."

She wiped her palms on her thighs, didn't say anything.

.   .   .

"Know why the moon shines?" Isaac asked Mote.

"Jeez, Iz, c'mon."

"Know why?"

"Sure, the sun, right?" Mote's voice was a whine.

"Yeah. Okay, now suppose it's night and there's a full moon out, bright, and there's an eclipse of the sun over in China where the sun's shining. What color's the moon then, over here?"

"I dunno. Kinda black or sumthin'?"

Jersey cackled.

Mote said, "What's so funny, Jers?"

"Nothing." He slowed the truck, stopped, flicked off the lights and killed the engine.

"What're we doin'? Isaac asked.

"Piss break," Jersey said. "Looks like we're gonna be up in these friggin' hills a long time."

All three piled out into the night's deep silence.

Jersey said, "There were these two guys crossin' a bridge, see, had to take a leak one night." He unzipped his own fly.

"Yeah?" Isaac said.

"Yeah. Coupla black dudes, how's that? Bridge wasn't very high, so these guys pull out their dicks, toss 'em over the side and there's two splashes in the dark. One guy turns to the other and says, 'Cold sonofabitch, ain't it?' and the other guy says, 'Yeah. Deep too.' "

Isaac laughed softly.

Mote said, "What's that suppos' t' mean, Jers?"

Jersey shook his head. "Christ."

"Listen," Isaac said.

"What?"

"Just listen, you two."

They listened. Quiet. A soft susurration of air moving over the land, through the weeds. Rhythmic ticking of the truck's cooling engine. Hiss of white noise in ears deprived of all but the remotest of vibrations.

Mote began to hum.

"What're you, a kazoo?" Jersey said. "Shut up."

Far away, a faint, purring noise.

"There," Isaac said.

"Shush."

Again. In the distance, an engine revved up, faded.

"Sounds like they're movin'," Jersey said.

"Maybe they seen our lights," Isaac suggested.

"Maybe."

"You know where we're going?"

"Yeah, kinda."

"Sure is a dark sonofabitch out here."

"Let's get movin'," Jersey said, touching the grip of the Llama Comanche .38 special he had jammed between his belt and belly. If he'd had it with him back in Quiode that night, that big old bastard with Suki'd be worm chow right now and they wouldn't be way up here in the dark, making like Daniel Fuckin' Boone.

• • •

The truck crept down a rock-strewn slope into a saddle between two hills. The oppressive darkness grew deeper once the fingernail wedge of moon slipped below the hills.

At the bottom, Frank got out and scouted around, played the dimming beam of the flashlight over the road.

"Maybe found us a place," he said, climbing back in.

They went forward slowly, stopped after fifty yards or so. Frank risked turning on the parking lights, and a surprisingly bright orange glow revealed a rocky but navigable region to the right of the trail. Frank gunned the engine and the truck lurched up a rocky shoulder, weaving past boulders and weedy hummocks and depressions.

"Don't know if this is smart or not," he said. "If this doesn't work out, we could get trapped in here."

"Anything else we can do?"

Frank tapped the fuel gauge. "What we can't do is wander around these hills all night, trying to keep one step ahead of them. I would've got gas in Quiode that night, but we left in kind of a hurry."

"Got an extra gun?"

"Nope."

"Figures," she said.

"Why? You know how to use one?"

"Just . . . point it and pull the trigger right?"

"Uh-huh."

The truck surged over loose rocks, wheels spinning. A low ridge of black basalt forced Frank to the left, where they reached a rocky formation forty yards from the road.

"End of the line," Frank said. He switched off the parking lights and killed the engine.

"Think we're far enough off the trail?"

"It wouldn't be in daylight, but now . . . Who knows? We'll just have to wait and see." He climbed out.

Some of the day's warmth still lingered in the air but the night was starting to cool. Suki put on one of Frank's shirts. Frank listened intently to the night. He heard a distant chirr of crickets, nothing more. Hills rose up around them, black and craggy, limned against the stars.

Suki came up beside him. "What about the money?"

"What about it?"

"Maybe we should like, I dunno, hide it somewhere. Just in case."

"Maybe." Hell, there wasn't much else they could do. It was better than letting Mutt and Jeff get their paws on over four hundred thousand dollars if things didn't work out.

Frank slung the canvas tarp over the side of the camper facing the trail, trying to cover its chromed surfaces. Might help, might not. He retrieved his money from the camper. In the dying glow of the flashlight, they tramped into the darkness beyond the truck. Suki's thongs flapped, shirt billowing on her, sleeves rolled up. She carried her duffel bag. Frank had given her a dark blue knit cap and told her to tuck her hair into it. Even in that darkness he'd been able to make out the platinum ghost of her hair.

Fifty feet from the truck he pried a large rock partway out of the ground, jammed his bag into the depression and shoved the rock back in place. Ten paces away they hid Suki's bag, piling a low cairn of stones over it.

Back at the truck, Frank checked his revolver in the glow of the dome light. He stuffed the gun in a jacket pocket and extinguished the light.

"Now what?" Suki asked.

Frank shrugged, a useless gesture in the dark. "Now we wait, see what happens."

"That offer of a beer still stand?"

"Water'd be better."

"Anything. I feel like I swallowed talcum."

With water and a bag of cookies, they sat on an outcrop of rock ten yards from the camper.

"What's Mink look like?" Frank asked, biting into an Oreo.

"Kinda thin," she said. "About five ten, hundred and forty pounds is all. Spooky gray eyes, like smoke. Nice smile—one he can turn off like a light. I never saw anybody who could do that before, not like Mink. If he wants, he can be the scariest sonofabitch I ever saw. Most of the time he's just this good-lookin' guy, nice face, nice clothes. If you didn't look at his eyes, you'd trust him with anything. Then, all of a sudden—*boom*, he's a devil or something."

"His eyes and his smile. That's what makes him so scary?"

For a moment she was silent. "It's more than that. Maybe it's his attitude, how he thinks. And the way he knows how to fight."

"Fight, how?"

"I dunno. Something Chinese, like in a movie. There was this guy working for Mink back in March, Jimmy Lynch. Like Mote an' Jersey. Jimmy stole some of Mink's money just before we left Pittsburgh. So in the house we'd rented—Mink always stays in some kinda big old house wherever we go, usually in a neighborhood where lawyers and types like that fix up places for offices. In Pittsburgh we had this big white house with green trim, two stories, big basement. Klein and Penrod Investment Group, that's what Mink's company was called there.

"Anyway, in the basement of this house, Mink and Jimmy had a fight. Jimmy didn't want to. It wasn't that kind of a fight. It was sorta . . . staged, like a kind of demonstration. Mink told all the guys to come and watch—ordered them to, really. I had to go down too. Mink wanted me to, and you got to do what Mink says. His mother came down, but she likes that kind of thing, I could tell. She thinks her boy's really something. Jimmy was tall, like six four. Maybe weighed two hundred twenty pounds. Real mean, but you could tell he was nervous anyway, the way his eyes kept looking all around.

"So Mink strips to the waist and takes off his shoes and asks if Jimmy's ready. Jimmy nods his head yes, sorta slow, and puts up his hands like a boxer. Then Mink comes in, kinda gliding, and hits him in the face so fast I didn't hardly even see it. Broke Jimmy's nose, I guess. There was blood all over, and Jimmy wipes his face and just stares at the blood on his hands. Mink backs away, tells Jimmy now he's gonna break his leg. I mean, he *tells* him what he's gonna do, like Jimmy can't do nothing to stop him, and then he comes in close and falls on his side real sudden and kicks Jimmy's knee. It sounded like someone breaking a chicken bone. Jimmy fell on the floor, screaming. Mink got up and kicked him in the head, kind of a funny kick with his heel, and Jimmy got real quiet. Mink told a couple of the guys to carry Jimmy out of there, then he took me back upstairs. Told me that's what happens when the hired help does him wrong."

"Very nice," Frank said, listening to the deep quiet of the night. "This Jimmy guy . . . he die, or what?"

"I dunno. Want another cookie?"

"Uh-uh."

"So anyway, that's Mink. Jimmy was a lot taller, heavier, pretty tough too, and still Mink knew he could take him easy. *Knew* it."

"That's confidence for you."

"Mink's got plenty of that, all right."

"And you went and tattooed that snake's forehead."

"Pretty dumb, huh?"

"Starting to look that way." He mixed some dirt and water and smeared mud on his face, put some on hers too.

They were quiet for a while, then she said, "Last night when I was kinda drunk—"

"Kinda?"

She laughed softly. "Okay, totally. I told you Mink never made love to me, didn't I?"

"I'm surprised you remember."

"I tell you any more than that?"

"You said you called him Minky."

"Yeah, he doesn't like that. I didn't do it very much. That all?"

"You didn't get around to telling me why he didn't make the effort, if that's what you're wondering. Why? Did you want him to?"

"I couldn't of stopped him if he wanted to, but he never did. But you want to hear something freaky?"

"Go ahead, shock me."

"You're makin' fun. So, okay, get this, you want to hear crazy. We'd been sleeping together in the same bed ever since this . . . gang of his, or whatever you call it, left Des Moines. We had this really weird relationship. We never did anything, and I never, you know, saw him hard. Like I was just some kind of . . . *jewelry* or something when we'd go out to dinner, him showing me off. You wouldn't believe some of the outfits he made me wear.

"So in Wichita we had this place, same kind of big house with lots of rooms, and I woke up one night. It was real late and Mink wasn't there with me, so I got up, kinda hungry, wondering where he was. He wasn't in the bathroom we had, so I—"

"You saw Mink break some guy's leg," Frank said, "might've even killed him, and still you stuck around?"

"I never found out what happened to Jimmy. Mink was treating me okay, buying me all these expensive clothes—"

"You knew he was a crook by then, didn't you?" There was an edge in Frank's voice.

"Yeah, and I know you're a crook, too. Looks like my life is all about crooks, everywhere I go."

Frank said nothing for ten or fifteen seconds. "Guess I deserved that. Sorry."

"Look, I never said I was real smart or wise or anything. I made a lot of mistakes, okay? Sometimes you just do something and it takes a while to know how bad it is and to figure out what you're gonna do about it. I was seventeen when I met Simon Voorhees, Frank. He was like some kind of a god or something to me that first month or two."

"Okay, I understand."

"Take your time, Frank. Don't bust nothin', okay?" She drew in a breath, let it out. "Anyway, our room was on the second floor of this big house. Mink likes places with lotsa rooms and more than one story. In Seattle we had three floors and a basement. So like I said, Mink was gone and I went out into the hall. It was dark. I heard noises coming from Charlotte's room, voices and breathing, like someone was doing exercises."

"Guess what that was," Frank said.

"Yeah, guess. Go ahead an' try."

"Mink and Charlotte?"

"Nope. The door wasn't locked, so I pushed it open a few inches and in a mirror I saw Mink without any clothes on, and these two naked girls, twelve or thirteen years old, almost no boobs at all, were all over Mink, touching and licking. He was tied with big silk-looking scarves to two hooks in the ceiling and a couple in the floor, kinda spread-eagled."

"Sounds like the man's got a problem."

"No kiddin', but get this. Charlotte was in a chair, watching the whole thing."

"Watching?"

"Yeah. Had all her clothes on and everything. Just sitting there, watching. She's thin as a stick, no boobs or ass, flaming red hair that's dyed, has a cigarette in her hand all the time. She was smoking, hardly blinking, eyes like some kinda bird that eats dead things."

"Jesus."

"I figure Charlotte goes out and finds these super-young girls somewhere for Mink, or maybe Danny does. Then she ties Mink up like that and turns the girls loose on him. And then she just sits there and watches, like she was watching TV or something. I don't guess it happens very often, though. Otherwise I'd have found out a lot sooner."

"After that, why'd you stick around?"

"Think I wanted to? I didn't, believe me, but Mink or Mote was always around. Mote was sorta my bodyguard, but I think he was really supposed to make sure I didn't run off. Sometimes Jersey'd look after me, and there was a black guy called Isaac and a jerk named Benny. So I never acted like I wanted to. I was pretty sure Mink'd hurt me if he caught me trying to run off. Besides, I never had any money of my own. I was like a prisoner there."

"So when the opportunity came up, you flew?"

"You bet. Took a while, but I finally managed to get the hell out of there. For a couple of months I was scared for my life, sleeping in the same bed with Mink like that. It made my skin crawl, thinking about him with those two girls, but I never said anything. I'd rather die than have him—"

Frank touched her arm. "Quiet."

A new sound in the night. An engine, laboring uphill. A few minutes later headlights threw shifting shadows over the rocks out by the trail, where Frank had turned off.

Slowly, the sound of the engine grew louder.

16

"Okay," Isaac said to Mote, "say you're in this rowboat that's floating in a swimming pool an'—"

"Christ up a rope, Iz!"

"—an' in the boat you've got this big rock. So then you put the rock into the water and it sinks. What happens to the water level in the *pool*? Does it go up or down or stay the same?"

"Howthefuck'dIknow?"

"You got to think, that's how."

"What with?" Jersey said, eyes searching the darkness to either side. "C'mon, Izzy, leave'm—hey!"

"Hey what?"

Jersey hit the brakes. "I just seen something."

"What? Where?"

"Back there." Jersey began to bounce the truck backward in reverse. "Something didn't look right."

"I didn't see nothing."

"That's 'cause you had your gums flappin', that's why. See?" He stopped and pointed. "Over there."

"I still don't see nothin'," Mote said.

Jersey put the truck in gear and swung it around, lights bouncing, glaring into the darkness off the trail.

"Look," Isaac said. "What's that over there?"

•   •   •

Blinding lights swung almost directly at them. Frank pulled Suki down behind the rocks and the two of them waited, barely breathing. The glare shone on the canvas-draped camper. Stark black shadows writhed over the ground.

The engine noise drew closer, then stopped. The lights went out and doors opened, slammed shut.

"Christ!" Frank exclaimed softly. "Here we go."

"What d'you want me to do?" Suki said in a frightened whisper.

"Stay here, keep down, and keep quiet. Make yourself small and don't move."

"What're you gonna do?"

"Don't know yet. Just stay put." He crept off into the darkness.

"Great," she breathed.

•   •   •

Blackness was a substance that coated the night like tar.

"Why'n't you put the headlights on, Jers?" Mote said.

"Keep quiet," Jersey whispered. "How 'bout I put on the lights and you go walk out there, take a bullet, huh?"

"Well, shit," Isaac said. "*This* ain't no good. I can't see a fuckin' thing."

"Maybe, but it's all we got," Jersey responded, crouched down by the side of the truck.

"Gimme my bullets, Jers," Mote whined.

"I'd rather stomp rattlesnakes barefoot."

"*Jers!*"

Jersey ignored him. In a low voice he said, "What we'll do is me an' Mote'll go down there to the right of the camper, real slow and quiet. What you do, Izzy, is hang back a minute or two then come in quiet, keepin' off to the left. You got that natural midnight color, might come in handy."

"What about my bullets?" Mote said.

"Shut up!" Jersey hissed. He grabbed the front of Mote's shirt. "Find a stick or throw rocks, Mote. If someone comes near you, you kin deck 'em, okay? But I don't want you using that goddamn gun. It's too fuckin' dark out here."

Jersey pulled his own gun and Isaac did the same. "Just be sure of what you're shootin' at," Isaac warned softly.

"Yeah. You too. Stay wide left, huh?"

Mote and Jersey crept off in the direction of the camper.

•   •   •

Frank crouched by the right front wheel of the truck, listening to the soft breath of the night.

Too late now to tell anyone, himself included, that this wasn't his fight. It'd become his fight when he'd followed those two clowns out of that bar in Quiode, and maybe even before that, back when he'd come across Suki sitting on the Trans Am in the desert. Since then, events had rolled over him like an avalanche. He'd figured her for trouble then, and trouble she was—trouble was dogging her heels like a black shadow. Dumb shit like him would get mixed up in it as natural as a giant sloth would wander off and get stuck in a tar pit.

What would Fanny say about *this*?

He had his .357 out, uncocked. Stars blazed overhead. Frank couldn't make out anything where the sound of the engine had stopped, not even moving shadows.

He and Suki could've just abandoned the truck and taken off cross-country with the money, hiked on down to Route 401 in maybe a day or so—if she'd had decent shoes, and if they could've been guaranteed that the first car or truck to come along wouldn't be Mote and Jersey's.

If, if, if. What was happening now was the result of all those ifs that hadn't panned out.

He could crawl under the truck. Be harder to spot under there, but then he'd lose his mobility. If one of them had a flashlight, that'd be the end of the game. And if he nailed one of them from under there with his gun, the other might do the same to him.

He had on blue jeans and a blue denim jacket, which made him all but invisible in the night. The darkness was filled with an electric tension. The thing to do, of course, was to wait it out, not move at all, let it all come to him. In the absence of light, sound or movement were the only things that might give away his position, or that of his enemies.

So he waited.

•   •   •

Crouched low, Jersey stuck out a foot, transferred his weight to it slowly, pulled his trailing foot after. His legs burned with the effort. Sweat made the grip of his gun slippery. He wiped his hand on his shirt.

Mote was somewhere off to his right—making a bunch of noise, but Mote was a fuckin' moose. Whether he knew it or not, he was acting as a decoy for Jersey. Trouble was, he was moving too fast for Jersey to keep up and still be as quiet as those goddamn Ninja books had said you could.

Jersey'd pored through some of the magazines Mink'd left lying around. Karate tournaments, uniforms, Tae Kwon Do (*Tae*: feet; *Kwon*: hands; *Do*: mind), kung fu and Ninja shit, lotsa Ninja shit. Tell you how to crawl up someone's asshole, light a candle and have a look around, leave without the guy ever knowing. Jersey'd thumbed through a couple of articles like that, hadn't really grasped what he'd seen, but it didn't look to him as if it'd work very well. Even so, he'd read a few articles and it had to have done him some good, right?

Something scraped in the dark, and suddenly Jersey was aware that he had no way of knowing who'd made the noise, Mote or that big sonofabitch who'd saved Suki. Or even Suki herself, who they weren't supposed to hurt even a little bit.

"Shit," he breathed. This wasn't working out the way he'd thought it would. A bead of sweat rolled into his right eye and he blinked it away.

Maybe what they should've done, to keep it simple, was spread out in the darkness around the camper, keep Suki and this guy boxed in, and wait till morning, take them then.

Too late now, though.

•   •   •

Frank heard a noise to his right, a scrape of leather on rock. He kept perfectly still, saw a shift of blackness in the night, darkness moving, gliding closer.

He could shoot, but then what? In Korea he'd maybe killed a guy or two, he didn't know. He'd sprayed a bunch of bamboo one morning with a machine gun while his company had scrambled for cover across a road that'd been churned to mud, but he'd never found out if he'd punched anyone's clock with it. War was like that. Imprecise, messy.

Now he could take a shot, but if he killed some guy he would probably regret it the rest of his life. And if he took the shot, would the guy's buddy see the muzzle flash and drop him? Worse, he didn't know for certain that this was really Mutt or Jeff. It could be some guy out camping. Frank didn't think so, but it could be, and he sure as shit didn't want to shoot some sorry bastard who'd taken off from behind his desk in some accounting office in Albuquerque and was acting like a complete idiot up here in the hills.

Too much was going on inside his head. Frank waited. The shadow drew nearer, and Frank wound himself up slowly, tensing. Whoever it was, the guy was a fool, standing up most of the way as he crept closer, visible as a drifting umbra, obscuring stars near the horizon. Too bad if this was some dipshit accountant without a brain; the guy was going to have a bad night. Closer now, his face was a pale luminosity. Frank squatted by the truck, a compact ball, waiting. Good thing he had smeared his own face with mud.

If the guy kept on like he was, he'd run right into Frank. Five feet away. Now three. Still hadn't seen him.

Two feet. Frank twisted and drove his right fist into the guy's midsection with all his strength. Air *woof*ed out of the guy's lungs, and he doubled over, sinking to his knees. Frank slammed the barrel of his gun against the side of the man's head. The guy crumpled to the ground.

A voice came out of the darkness. "Mote, that you?"

Confirming their identities. Good.

Frank grunted. "Yuh." Trying to imitate the voice of that big guy he'd decked outside Belinda's in Quiode. Also trying to get a fix on this genius, probably Jersey, who was out there calling for Mote.

"Where are you?" the guy whispered hoarsely, as if Mote could hear him but Frank couldn't. As if Mote would answer—but maybe the dumb sonofabitch would.

Frank grunted again and began edging cautiously around the back of the camper where the roll of canvas hung off the roof. He peered around the corner. His hands had started to shake from all the adrenaline flooding his system.

More silence. Then a scuffle of dirt, a moving darkness ten feet away, couched low.

Frank cocked his gun and said, "Hold it!" His aim felt unsteady. Suddenly ten feet looked like a hundred.

The shadow froze for an instant, began to twist.

"You're one second from dying, friend," Frank said. "Drop the gun, *now*." He didn't actually know if the guy had a gun, but it seemed likely. Couldn't hurt to tell him to drop it.

Something heavy clunked to the ground.

"Don't move," Frank said. "Don't even twitch." He crept out from behind the camper toward the shadowy form.

"Face down and spread 'em," Frank ordered roughly. "Do it! *Move!*"

The guy flopped down, still not saying anything. Frank put his knee in the small of the guy's back, eased the hammer down on his gun, then cocked it again, right behind the guy's ear so he'd know where it was and where it was aimed.

"Call your friend in," he said softly. He groped around in the dark, found the gun the guy had dropped, and put it in a pocket of his jacket.

"What friend? Thought you already got 'im."

"Not him, the other one." He was fishing, but, hell, it might give him something.

"What other one?"

Frank considered that. "What I'm going to do is turn on a light. If I see anyone else out there, you're dead, understand? If I see anyone at all, I pull this trigger then deal with them, but you won't know anything about that, not with your brains all over the place. Now, one last time: is anyone else out there?"

A pause. "No, man. There was just us two."

"Okay, make like a crab. Scoot on over this way, on your belly. Keep your arms and legs spread wide." Frank tugged the collar of the man's T-shirt, guiding him.

"Watch that gun, huh?"

"Just don't forget where it's aimed, ace."

They inched over rocks and hard-scrabble weeds, the guy grunting, working hard.

Frank opened the door of the cab. The dome light came on. Lying on the ground at his feet was Skinny: Jersey. In the cone of light Frank saw Muscles, out cold on the ground with his face in the dirt.

"Suki," Frank called.

Nothing.

"What're you doin' this for?" Jersey asked. "I got money. How 'bout I give you money? Lots of it."

"Shut up. Suki, c'mon in. I got 'em."

He heard a scuffling sound in the night: her thongs flapping as she came toward him on the opposite side of the truck.

"Suki?"

Light spilled out the truck's windows all around. A weak glow illuminated the ground for fifty feet to either side. Frank kept his gun on Jersey, muzzle pressed against the back of Jersey's head.

Suki came around the rear of the camper. A black guy with a gun jammed against her right temple was behind her, his left arm hooked around her neck.

"She dies if you even blink, hero," the black said. "Your move. What's it gonna be?"

Frank stared, frozen in a crouch over Jersey. The black guy's eyes were on his. Cold eyes.

"What's it gonna be?" the guy said again. "She dies, then I got this corpse to hide behind while I send you home to Jesus."

Frank stood slowly, letting the gun hang at his side.

"Drop it."

Frank dropped it, feeling empty. Hell with it, he'd lived a lot of years already. Maybe Suki would survive this. If he shot Jersey, both he and Suki would likely be dead three seconds later.

Suki's eyes were wide, frightened.

"Step back," the black guy said. "Slowly. Keep your hands where I kin see 'em."

Frank moved away from Jersey.

Jersey bounded to his feet, snatched up Frank's .357 from the dirt.

"Sit," the black ordered, his gun still against Suki's head.

Frank sat.

Jersey kicked him in the head and Frank went over on his side, a sudden roaring in his ears. The toe of Jersey's boot caught him on the cheek and he felt the bones in his neck creak. Dirt filled his mouth. Lights and shadows whirled. A foot slammed into his ribs. Frank rolled, tried to get away, but the boot hammered him again, and again, again. Frank tried to roll out of it, tried to cover up, and again the boot crunched into his side, Jersey breathing hard.

"That's enough Jers," a voice said. "Remember what the Dragon Lady said."

"Fuck that bitch."

The boot plowed into Frank's ribs again, and he felt something give. Pain ripped through his body. From a distance he heard Suki scream. The boot caught him full in the face and all the lights went out.

17

Half a dozen ants roamed the slopes and canyons of Frank's face, feasting where blood hadn't yet dried. Another experimented with the dark cavern of his nose, clinging precariously to the rim where moist, warm air shuttled softly in and out. Yet another explored the tunnel of his left ear, biting intermittently.

Frank snorted, then gasped at the pain that tore through his side. The ants began to scurry for cover.

He opened his eyes and stared out at the bright yellow sun, just beginning its climb into the morning sky. Dark brown silhouettes of mountains rose up in his vision. Rocks and weeds bit into his right cheek.

He struggled to sit up, found that he could move but movement produced pain, even as small a thing as blinking. Something moved in his ear. He dug it out with a finger, dragging out tattered pieces of the explorer. Grit filled his mouth. He leaned over and spat feebly, the effort unleashing new pain in his mouth and ribs.

Suki.

He looked around. The world spun and wobbled softly, as if imprinted on a soap bubble.

"Suki?" the word was just a whisper.

"*Suki?*" Pain ripped through his torso at the increased effort. No one answered.

His truck and camper were still there, but something was wrong with the way all of it was sitting. He wasn't sure what it was, but it wasn't right.

His head was a bell, ringing, aching savagely. He got to his feet, breathing in short gasps. He prodded his ribs gingerly and winced. His face felt huge, raw. One eye, the left, was swollen shut.

But his legs seemed all right. He could walk. Each step sent needles of pain shooting through his side as he shuffled toward the camper.

"Suki?"

The silence of the hills was unbroken. No voices, no distant sound of engines. Nothing.

Open cans of beer lay strewn about. The two coolers were on their sides, empty, lids torn off. Bottles of Jack Daniel's had been smashed against the side of the truck.

He reached up to open the camper door before realizing it was eight inches low. He walked around the truck like an octogenarian, hugging his left side, staring at the four flat tires.

"Shit," he said weakly, wincing at the flare of pain the word caused him. He probed his ribs gently again, deciding they probably weren't broken, just tender as hell. Maybe a little sprung.

He opened the camper door and stared at the mess inside. Mutt and Jeff and that black guy had trashed it, torn out the radio and ripped doors off cabinets, shredded his clothing and slung catsup and mustard and Quaker State motor oil over the debris.

Suki was gone.

Unless they'd killed her and left her outside somewhere, but that seemed unlikely. Mink would have reserved that sort of pleasure for himself.

Even so, Frank walked around, looking. This was a good place for murder, although they hadn't killed him. He remembered Jersey's gun. He'd put it in a pocket of his jacket. Gone now. And Jersey's knife. Jersey had that back again, too. Frank didn't find Suki, but the remains of the cairn of stones they'd used to hide her duffel bag were strewn around, the bag and money gone.

Frank searched for the place where his own money lay hidden. The hillside looked different in daylight, but in time he located the rock. He grabbed it and tried to move it, but the effort made his ribs sing. Sitting behind the rock, he pushed with his feet until it shifted. He peered into the gap and felt a flood of relief at the sight of blue nylon. He pulled the bag out. All his money was there.

She hadn't sold him out in the hope that his money would make a difference. She'd managed to keep some presence of mind during her ordeal, whatever it had been.

If even part of what she'd told Frank about Simon Voorhees was true, though, Suki was in for a very, very bad time.

"Shit," Frank said, and this time he hardly noticed the jolt of pain that accompanied the oath.

•   •   •

He would've thought his body would eventually get tired and shut down nerves that were sending unending messages of pain to his brain. What was the point? He knew he'd been trashed, for chrissake. Being reminded over and over was pointless. Nothing he could do about it. But the pain just went on and on and on, no sign of letting up. Every step was anguish; every mile was an encyclopedia of hurt. He sucked in air in shallow gasps.

The foothills of the De Bacas went on forever. Except for needlegrass and occasional tufts of hackberry and sandbur, the country was as empty and inhospitable as the far side of the moon. The sun rose high in the sky, baking the land. Frank walked through the brassy, shimmering heat, hunched into his pain, each plodding step penance for all the mistakes he'd made the night before.

Not penance enough, however. Simon and Charlotte had their hands on Suki again. Nothing could make that right.

He'd wrapped a strip of canvas around his ribs. The bag of money hung from his right shoulder. A bit of torn sheet over his head and shoulders, held in place by a California Angels ball cap, gave him a dusky Arabic look. With every step he took, a can of beer thumped at his hip, riding in a pocket of his jacket, which was tied by its arms around his waist. The can was one of two he'd found that hadn't been emptied and tossed. He'd downed one early on and was hoarding the second, the only liquid he had for a long, hot walk.

Sweat had already removed most of the mud he'd smeared on his face the night before. His sleeves were grimy where he had wiped his face with them.

Frank estimated that he and Suki had been caught eighteen to twenty miles from Route 401. By ten that morning, three hours after he'd started out, he'd covered five of those miles. At least he'd had the sense not to set out cross-country, trying to reach the highway just ten miles away as the crow flies. The canyons and ravines would've eaten him up. In the next few hours the day would heat up another ten or fifteen degrees, probably top out up around a hundred.

Dust devils spun in the distance like miniature cyclones. Carrion eaters wheeled overhead in the bright blue sky.

Simon Voorhees. The name came swirling out of the mist of pain that clouded his mind. Age thirty-four. Called himself Mink and made up names for himself and his "investment companies" like other people put on new clothes. Liked little girls. Frank realized he knew a surprising amount about the guy.

Five-ten, hundred and forty pounds. Rented older two- or three-story houses in the sort of neighborhoods inhabited by lawyers and other professionals.

The Shreveport operation was folding. Mink and company were

setting up next in Reno.

Frank slowed.

Reno. Christ, Reno wasn't all that big a place. Maybe a quarter the size of Pittsburgh or Seattle, half as large as Shreveport.

A long shot all the same, not much chance that he could—hell, who was he tryin' to kid? Walking along, hurting, he'd known what he was going to do from the moment he'd discovered that Suki was gone. Known what he had to do. If Mink preferred run-down tenements and was headed for Harlem or the Bronx, Frank would still try to find Suki.

He owed her that, for some goddamned reason.

He realized he had one slim hope: Mutt and Jeff couldn't take Suki on a plane. They'd probably have to drive her to Reno, and it was likely they'd hold their speed down to keep from attracting the attention of the highway patrol.

Frank calculated distance and velocity. Five hundred miles to Flagstaff, two hundred more to Vegas, four hundred to Reno. Total of eleven hundred miles at, say, sixty miles an hour. Assuming they'd reached the highway between Quiode and Imogene by one o'clock that morning, they could be in Reno by seven this evening. Not likely they'd get there that fast, though. With stops for food and gas, restrooms, they'd more likely get there between nine and midnight, possibly later.

But those calculations assumed that they'd head for Reno, not Shreveport. Frank picked up a little speed, trying to ignore the pain in his ribs.

A sense of helplessness filled him, crawled around in his belly. He had no way of knowing which place they would head to, and if he picked the wrong one, Suki would be dead. Very likely she'd be dead either way. His chances of finding her were slim to none. That damn tattoo. If Suki was right about Simon, the demented son of a bitch would kill her for that alone, never mind the money.

But Frank had to pick one or the other, and from what Suki'd told him, Shreveport was pretty much shut down, the Reno operation just about ready to roll. If they'd scammed a bunch of people from their place in Shreveport, the police might be about to get wind of it. Not likely Mink would stick around to find out.

So, Reno. If he was wrong . . .

Jesus, a pair of sociopaths like Simon and Charlotte Voorhees with their hands on Suki. No telling what they'd do. Frank didn't even want to guess. But if Suki disappeared from the face of the earth, so would this Simon character, guaranteed. In a week, a month, a year. Longer, if it took longer. Sometime.

He could at least promise Suki that.

•   •   •

Suki said, "There's over three hundred thousand bucks in that bag, Jersey. Take me back to Mink and you've got to hand over all that money. But if you let me go you could take the money and live real nice somewhere, not have to work anymore. Sit on a beach with a beer and pretty girls all around."

The Toronado's air conditioner was dead. Jersey sat slumped in the passenger seat while Mote drove. Suki sat between them in the heat, barefoot, wearing her shorts and little yellow top. Benny and Isaac followed along behind in the Malibu.

"Shut up," Jersey said.

"It's not like stealin'. No cop'd ever come after you, you take that money. I'd go with you. We could go to South America, you an' me." She wrinkled her nose at the thought of her and Jersey.

He glanced at her boobs, then looked away. "Shut up."

"You scared, Jersey? Must be, 'cause I know you're not honest. Jesus, think what you could do with that much money. You *like* workin' for Mink? You won't ever get a chance like this again."

"I said shut up."

"Christ, so scared of Mink you'd rather kiss Charlotte's wrinkled old butt and be poor all your life, right?"

"Keep talkin' an' you're gonna get gagged, sweetmeat," he said.

"That'd look real nice, wouldn't it? Some cop passes us and there I am, wearing this gag."

"Tied up on the floor in back, there wouldn't be much for a cop to see. Or maybe you'd like to ride in the trunk."

"Christ, three hundred fifty *thousand* dollars, Jersey. You got any idea how much that is?"

"Shut *up*."

•   •   •

Frank came across the burned-out ruin of Mink's Trans Am at a quarter past one that afternoon. Another truck was there, both rear tires blown. Frank didn't mess with it, just kept on walking, past the washed-out gully that murdered cars and trucks, down the trail that wound through the stifling kiln of the valley toward the highway.

He drank the second beer at three o'clock. Maybe six miles left to go. He'd picked up a little speed, worrying about Suki. Fifteen feet away an anthill swarmed red, like a tiny volcano. A good-sized hill, good-sized ants. Die here and a man would disappear into that nest with its myriad tiny rooms, bit by infinitesimal bit, until nothing was left but bones and patches of hair.

In the distance, blue and gray mountains danced in the heat, hazy and insubstantial.

He trudged on, ribs aching. A piece of cartilage felt loose in his nose, and a place inside his cheek was raw. A few teeth were loose in their sockets; he could wiggle one with his tongue, so he tried to leave it alone.

Insects buzzed in the weeds.

This was a land that could kill you, eat you whole, bleach your bones, and forget you'd ever walked the earth.

•　•　•

They passed a sign on Interstate 40:

WINONA 12
FLAGSTAFF 28

"I gotta go," Suki said. "Bad."

Jersey was driving, Mote dozing, Suki wedged between them. Jersey didn't say anything, just kept on driving.

"I said, I gotta—"

"I heard what you said."

"Well?"

"Well what?"

"We gonna stop or what?"

"Sure. That'd be smart, wouldn't it? You yellin' your head off, locked in a toilet somewhere."

"We're gonna drive another six or seven hundred miles and no one's gonna pee? That's intelligent. How 'bout I go right here?"

"Yeah," Jersey said. "How 'bout you do that?" He slowed, turned the Olds onto a rough dirt road that angled north off the interstate. The Malibu followed. Mote stirred when the car started bumping.

"Where're we goin'?" Suki asked.

"Find you a patch of ground t' squirt."

"Out here?"

"Out here or you hold it, sweetmeat. Take your pick."

"Stop calling me sweetmeat."

"You look like sweetmeat to me. What d'you think, Mote?"

"Yuh, sweetmeat."

Suki looked at him. "What've you got, Mote, like one brain to move the lips, another one to wag the tail?"

Jersey laughed, and Mote gave Suki a sullen look. "What d'you mean?"

"Nothing. Forget it."

Ten minutes later they were back on the interstate, headed west. The men had pissed all over the place like cattle. Suki had secured the barest measure of privacy by asking them how they thought Mink'd like it, them staring at his girl without her bottoms on. They got pretty nervous about that. They didn't know for sure if she was still his girl or not, so they'd turned, reluctantly. Even so she'd hurried, almost couldn't pee at all at first, and there'd been no chance of escape, not out there, half a mile from the highway.

She hoped Frank would be all right. He'd have been fine if she hadn't come along, bringing all this trouble. Before they'd left the hills she'd knelt beside him and checked his breathing. He was pretty beat up, but at least he was alive.

Before she was handed over to Mink, she might try to do Jersey some damage, payback for what he'd done to Frank. She hoped the opportunity would come up. If he'd taken her up on her offer to run off to South America with him, she would've found a way to kill him.

Mink. And Charlotte. Even in this sweltering heat the thought of seeing those two again—after what she'd done to Mink—made goose bumps stand out on her arms.

18

The world began to blur and spin. Frank squinted, trying to make out the numerals on his watch. Five twenty-one. Hot air scorched his throat as he clumped past the gravel pit and out to the highway. It was empty. Some-alien-plague-had-wiped-out-all-humanity-and-he-was-the-last-one-left kind of empty.

He opened his bag, took out five twenties, and stuck them in a pocket. He ran a tongue over his parched lips as he stood beside the road, waiting, feeling the heat try to kill him.

Five minutes . . . ten . . .

Fifteen.

The sun seemed to halo in the sky, growing larger. Dark spots floated in Frank's vision.

One of the spots drew nearer, missing every so often on one cylinder, coming up the road toward him. Frank blinked, squinted, made out a rust-red pickup doing maybe fifty miles an hour.

He removed the piece of bed sheet that had protected his head, stuck out a thumb and held up the five twenties, showing green as the truck went past.

The truck rattled on by, dragging dust, then went into a skid as the driver locked up its tires. It backed up, weaving, engine whining. Frank shuffled forward to meet it.

"Ride?" the driver asked.

"Yeah." Frank's voice was little more than a croak.

"That yer thumb you had out?" He was completely bald, in his fifties, face and scalp burned to a dark bronze color by the sun. Pale bushy eyebrows, nicotine-stained teeth. A small ice chest sat on the seat beside him.

"Uh-huh," Frank said. "And this." He held out the bills.

"Climb on in."

Frank's ribs spat fire as he opened the door and climbed in. Without a word, the man took the money, shoved it in a pocket. The truck started up, accelerating lethargically in the direction of Quiode, its one bad cylinder making the cab shudder.

The driver glanced curiously at Frank. "Hot, ain' it?"

"Yeah."

"Too hot fer bein' out here."

"My truck broke down. Up in the hills."

"Yeah? Lucky I come along, huh? The name's Hew. Hewitt Hooker."

"Frank."

"Y'look a sight, Frank," Hew said. "Had some kinda accident up there too, didja?"

"Some trouble, yeah."

"Look like you could use somethin' to wet yer whistle. Hep y'self." He indicated the ice chest.

"Thanks." Frank opened the cooler, found a can of Mr. Pibb and three cans of 7-Up swimming in half-melted ice.

He took a 7-Up, popped the top. The liquid was cool fire in his throat, swelling his parched tissues. He sipped it slowly, trying to keep it down, let it work. From time to time Hew Hooker cut a glance at him.

"Know where I can charter a plane?" Frank asked.

Hooker stared at him. "Nowhere round here."

"I figured. Where's the nearest place?"

"I dunno. Roswell'd be it, I reckon."

"How far's that?"

"From Quiode? Sixty-eight mile."

Frank sipped from the can. "Fast road, here to there?"

"Pretty fast, yeah. Ain't a lot of traffic round these parts."

"You live in Quiode?"

"More'n twenty years. Evenin' cook over t' Belinda's."

"Tell you want, Hew. You let me phone the airport at Roswell from your place and wash up a bit, then figure out a way to get me to Roswell in an hour from Quiode, and I'll give you three hundred bucks. Ten more for every minute you shave off that hour."

Hooker eyed him. "Had your fill of this dry sonvabitchin' country, huh?"

"That offer includes you not asking a whole lot of questions."

"If that's how you want it. I know how t' zip my trap."

"That's good, 'cause I got another question for you."

"Yeah? Whazzat?"

"Know where I can get a gun?"

• • •

Mutt and Jeff hadn't killed him, so all that was left now was borrowed time. Hooker was using that up at a hundred twenty-five miles an hour, hunched over the steering wheel of Belinda Maxwell's son's Kelly green '72 Camaro with the 350-cubic-inch engine and gray primer spots, sheepskin seat covers and fuzzy dice swaying from the rearview mirror.

"Quentin Maxwell's doin' ninety days over at the county jail in Carrizozo," Hooker said. "Good name for a jailbird, huh? Quentin? Reckon he won't mind we borra his wheels, blow the engine out a mite." He patted the dash as they chased the Camaro's shadow eastward on Route 401.

Frank turned the German Astra M600 pistol over in his hands and stared at the Waffenamt acceptance stamp, a small seal that also bore the date of manufacture: 1939. He had no idea what the relic was actually worth or if it would fire, but Hooker had parted with it for six hundred fifty dollars. It came with six nine-millimeter rounds in the magazine from a box Hooker had bought over in Socorro back in '76.

From Hooker's trailer, Frank had gotten through to Castledyne

Aviation at Industrial Air Center in Roswell. A secretary by the name of Rose acted as an intermediary on an intercom between the office and the hangar where Chase Castledyne himself was servicing the landing gear of an old Beechcraft.

"You wanna go where?" Rose had asked.

"Reno. Leave in about an hour. Something fast."

"Yeah, hang on."

He'd hung on. Rose came back on the line, saying, "This just a drop?"

"A what?"

"One way?" she asked with a kind of weary patience. "No hold at the other end, or are you comin' back?"

"One way."

"Hang on." Pause. "Mr. Castledyne's got a Seneca three, get you to Reno in about five and a half hours for thirty-two hundred bucks. He's got a Lear twenty-five waitin' on some guy wants to go to Chicago tomorrow morning, says you can have that for fifty-four fifty, get you there in maybe two, two an' a half hours."

"I'll take the Lear."

"Yeah, waitaminute." Pause. "Mr. Castledyne says that'd be cash only on the Lear. No checks, no cards."

And no paper trail, Frank thought. "I'll take it."

"Uh, okay. What's the name on this?"

"Wiley. Frank Wiley."

•   •   •

Through Castledyne Aviation's double-pane windows the little Lear 25 looked like a ballerina at an Arkansas square dance, pale blue elegance sitting on the cracked concrete in the heat outside, twin turbines already spooling up.

"Who's in her now?" Frank asked, hunched over slightly. He'd started to stiffen up on the drive from Quiode, but the pain in his ribs was easing some. The walk out of the hills in the heat had hurt, but it had kept him loosened up for most of the day.

"Copilot," said Chase Castledyne. He was a likely enough specimen in his blue flight suit, fortyish, a hank of ginger-colored hair falling across his forehead. He examined Frank's ruined face without comment. "FAA regs."

"Okay," Frank replied. "How soon can we get going?"

"Soon's you show me fifty-four hundred an' fifty dollars."

"Got a bathroom I can use?"

Castledyne pointed. Rose was looking at Frank too, not saying a word, paperwork piled high on a cluttered desk, green pencil stuck behind one ear, poking out of frizzy black hair.

"Back in a minute."

In the bathroom Frank peeled fifty-five bills off a stack of hundreds, splashed water on his face, stared at the damage in the mirror. Left eye puffed almost shut, a raw patch on his right cheek, a week's worth of gray stubble on his cheeks and chin. General blackguardly dishevelment. Nice.

Back in the office he handed the wad to Castledyne. The pilot quickly counted it out in the airy rumble of the room's air-conditioning. Frank didn't blame him for being careful.

He handed Frank two twenties and a ten, change. "Okay, Mr. Wiley. This business or pleasure?"

"Pleasure."

Castledyne gave him a look, then said, "Let's do it."

They crossed the scalded tarmac, heat waves boiling up off the weedy flatness of taxiways and runways, and climbed a few steps into the plane.

Castledyne folded the steps and seated the door. "Way it works," he said, smiling easier now, "is this little baby'll eat your money about as fast as you could comfortably peel dollar bills off a roll and stuff 'em into a mason jar."

"Get us to Reno pretty quick though, huh?"

Castledyne's eyes met Frank's. "I got the message, Mr. Wiley. You're a man who takes his pleasure pretty serious. Get yourself comfortable. We'll be up in a few minutes. There's a bar in back that covers the basics. Help yourself."

"Thanks."

Frank got a can of Coke, lowered himself with a groan into a seat of maroon crushed velvet, strapped in, leaned back, and closed his eyes.

Christ, this was crazy.

He tried to still his thoughts. Inside, a river moved deep and quiet, sluggishly churning up a load of debris: she was just eighteen, he was fifty-four, they had shared a bed, Fanny was gone, Suki had tattooed a psycho named Mink, blew up his car, Frank hadn't been to Reno in ten years, Rio was fulla bugs. Bunch of loose stuff, roiling around in there.

Four minutes later they shot down the runway and lifted off at a hundred fifteen miles an hour, climbing steeply toward the north into the hazy heat. Frank looked down; a green Camaro rolled northward on U.S. 285. Hooker down there, pockets stuffed with the four hundred twenty dollars Frank had handed him for getting him to the airport in Roswell in just forty-eight minutes.

They banked left, climbing. The De Baca Mountains already coming up ahead and to the left, sere and empty. Place was hell on tires.

Local time was 7:18 p.m.

•   •   •

"Three Big Macs," Mote said. "Two large fries—"

Jersey stared at him. "Christ, we could buy a condo in Hawaii for what this's gonna fuckin' cost!"

"I'm *hungry*, Jers."

"Yeah, Christ, what else?" Jersey had parked in a remote unshaded corner of a McDonald's in Las Vegas. Benny and Isaac had pulled up alongside in the Malibu. Isaac stood beside the Chevy, arms folded.

"You got the two fries?" Mote asked. "Two *large* fries?"

"Yeah, yeah, c'mon."

"Okay. Couple choc'lit shakes, large Coke, and a coupla those pie things."

"Jesus H. Christ." Jersey glared at Suki. "How 'bout you?"

"Whopper with cheese, small Coke."

"That all?"

"Yeah."

Jersey started off, came back a few seconds later, face red, fists clenched. "This's a goddamn *McDonald's*, sweetmeat. What the fuck you askin' for a goddamn *Whopper* for?"

She smiled at him. "You upset, Jersey?"

"Yeah, I'm upset—"

"Guy's throwin' away three hundred fifty *thousand* dollars," she said, looking at Mote. "Guess he's got a right to be upset. Ain't that right, apeman?"

Mote said, "I dunno—"

"Shut up," Jersey snarled.

"I'll have what Mote has," Suki said.

Jersey's face turned a fiercer shade of red. "Do that sweetmeat, I'll cram every fuckin' pickle and sesame seed down your throat, you don't eat it."

"So get me one of those McTunas or McWhales or whatever a fish thing is called. A McFishwich maybe, and a small Coke."

Muttering under his breath, Jersey strode off, Isaac in his wake, grinning. Benny, already thinning on top at the age of twenty-four, hung around by the driver's side of the Toronado, helping make sure Suki stayed put, doing deep knee bends to limber up his legs.

Suki turned to Mote, who smelled like a goat. "What would *you* do with three hundred thousand dollars, oaf?"

"I'm not supposta listen t' you."

"Three hundred *thousand*."

"You heard what Jers tole me. You talk t' me or scream or somethin', I got to shut you up."

"You wouldn't hit a girl, would you?"

"Yeah." He nodded. "Jers said do it, so I'd do it. You jest set still there an' be quiet, okay?"

• • •

Jersey shut his eyes for a moment, then dialed the Reno number, got through on the fifth ring.

"Tell me," the viper's voice answered.

Maybe he *would* take the three hundred grand and split. "We're in Vegas," he said. "Everything's cool."

"The girl's still with you?"

Wouldn't be very fuckin' cool if she wasn't, would it, Bitch? "Yeah. They been doing a lot of road work on the highway between here and Flagstaff, Mrs. Voorhees, an'—"

"*What* did you call me, Jersey?"

Jersey closed his eyes. *Shit*. "Uh, Mrs. Garrett—"

"Garrick, Jersey. Gar-*rick*. Is the name too long or too complex for you, Jersey?"

"No, ma'am."

"Is there any hope that you might remember it in the future, Jersey?"

"Yes, ma'am."

"Say it, Jersey. *Garrick*."

"Garrick."

"Wonderful. Very nice, Jersey. I know this is a bit challenging for you, but do you suppose it's possible we could use the name Garrick from this point forward?"

"Yes, ma'am."

"Okay, continue."

"Uh, that's all, ma'am. I was just reporting in, like you said."

"When do you think you'll arrive?"

"We're gonna leave Vegas soon." He checked his watch. "We oughta be up there maybe one, two in the morning."

"Fine. Now listen to me, Jersey. Are you listening *very* carefully,

Jersey?"

He ground his teeth. "Yes, ma'am."

"When you get to Reno, phone me. I'll have instructions for you on how to deliver the girl. Do you understand?"

"Yes, ma'am."

"Very well, Jersey."

The phone went dead in Jersey's hand. He slammed Ma Bell's equipment into its cradle, ignoring the scowl given to him by a monstrously obese woman in her twenties with buttocks the size of beach balls and thighs thicker than his chest. The bitch probably hadn't got change back from her dollar in over twenty fuckin' years.

• • •

Simon sat in the darkness of his room, eyes closed, resting, waiting. The door snicked open; Charlotte entered in a spill of light from the hallway. She shut the door quietly, crossed to the window overlooking Flint Street, and nudged the heavy curtain aside with a bony finger. A needle ray of late afternoon light fell on the crimson spread of Simon's bed like the eye of some malevolent god.

"Please don't smoke in here."

"Sorry," she said. She went to the adjoining bathroom and threw her cigarette into the toilet bowl, flushed it. Returning, she said, "It's a good house, isn't it, dear?"

"Yes, very good. Daniel did well this time." His voice was flat, however, betraying a certain lack of enthusiasm.

She sat in an armchair opposite him. "The advertisement was placed two days ago. On Friday."

"Which one?"

"For the new girl. Already there have been responses."

"I don't want another girl yet." A hard edge was in his voice. "I want Suki."

"I understand. Jersey says they'll be here sometime after midnight, darling, but we *must* look ahead. Suki will be but a fleeting thing."

His eyes glittered. "Not so fleeting, Mother."

She shivered, enjoying the sensation. "No, darling. Perhaps *fleeting* was not the appropriate word. Still, we must prepare. You'll be wanting a proper escort sometime."

"With *this?*" he replied harshly. The shadow of his hand moved over the shadow of his face, where the pale rectangle of the bandage hovered in the dimness of the room. "How can I go out with this?"

"It will mend."

"The scar will be visible six months from now. That quack, Pinnell, assured me of that."

"Only to those who know where to look. It'll cover with a bit of makeup, dear. And Dr. Pinnell is anything but a quack, Simon," she admonished. Into his silence she added, "Do you like your present, darling?"

"Present?"

"The *car*," she said, piqued. "It was meant to be a surprise. Daniel found one of the same color and everything."

"You should have asked. I'm tired of the Trans Am. I want a Ferrari, black with blue striping, dark plum interior. Something with a little class this time, not just heat."

She raised an eyebrow. "If you like, of course."

"Soon. Tomorrow."

She sighed, stood up. "Perhaps what you need is a little diversion. The hooks were installed yesterday. Would you like that, darling? I'm sure something could be arranged in the next day or two."

"It's too soon since the last time. Anyway, not until after Suki, Mother. I don't want to dilute that experience."

"Well, it's up to you, dear. I just hate to see you like this."

"All I need is Suki. Everything will be fine once Suki gets here."

"A few more hours. Just a few more hours, sweetheart." She slipped out the door with a faint rustle of silk.

19

The Lear banked to the left, bleeding off altitude. Frank Limosin peered out the window at the Sierra Nevadas. Even in mid-July, the higher peaks were still capped with snow. The sun dropped behind the mountains as the plane went down, backlighting the reddish-umber haze of forest fires burning in the west. The plane banked right as Castledyne held the tiny jet in a descending turn, flaps down.

Houses below, a vast shopping mall, roads crawling with toy

cars, then a field of scraggly weeds, a gray blur of concrete and the plane was down, rolling past a green-glassed flight operations tower that rippled in the desert heat.

They halted on an apron in front of a low building with a sign that read RENO FLYING SERVICE on the front.

The local time was 8:28 p.m. They'd crossed a time zone, gained an hour chasing the sun.

Castledyne came through the cockpit door and cranked open the fuselage hatch while the copilot made last-minute additions to the flight log. Castledyne stepped out into the heat and Frank followed. The two men hiked fifty yards to the building as a sleek National Guard F-4, sharklike in appearance, thundered down the runway and lifted off.

The night staff at Reno Flying Service stared curiously at Frank. He could only hope that his too-memorable face hadn't made the news up here, although his face had been changed some by Jersey's boots. It didn't seem likely that a truck robbery in L.A. would stir up much interest in Reno, but you never knew. Eight hundred grand was a lot of money. During the flight Frank had done what he could with his face, which wasn't much. His left eye was still caught in a puffy wink, and his white-stubbled cheeks gave him the look of an aging derelict. The Lear jet was an inexplicable contradiction.

"Mr. Wiley?" Frank turned. A secretary in a yellow dress was standing behind a counter, frowning at him. "There's a taxi waiting outside for you, sir."

"Yeah, thanks."

Frank shook Castledyne's hand. "Good service, thanks."

"Anytime."

Frank went outside. A Whittlesea cab was in the parking lot, engine running. He opened the front door, got in next to a middle-aged woman with drab brown hair, a mustache, big bulky breasts on a heavy frame. "You Wiley?" she asked.

"Yeah. Okay if I sit up front like this?"

"Suit yourself."

Her name was Shirley Budd. Her eyes fixed briefly on his face. She decided she'd seen worse. "Where to?"

"You got a place in town where lawyers hang out? What I mean is—"

"Lawyers, huh? You lookin' to get divorced?"

"No, what I want—"

"Can't say you look much like a legal corporation yourself. You aren't, are ya?"

"No."

"Good. Board of Trade'd be the place to go, if it wasn't Sunday, an' late."

"What's that?"

"Mouthpiece hangout. Fancy-ass waterin' hole."

"What I want," he said, "is to go to where lawyers have offices. Someplace with old refurbished houses, two or three stories, lots of rooms. Probably used to be old mansions."

"Think you'll catch one of 'em workin'?" Shirley gave him an astonished look.

"No." He offered no explanation. "This town got a place like that? Big houses, older, used by professionals?"

She pursed her lips and thought a moment. "Okay, that'd be up around the courthouse. Hill street, Flint, Court, Clay. And parts of Arlington and California. You wanna go up there?"

"Guess so. I'm in kind of a hurry though."

"Yah, sure." She put the car in drive and roared off. "How'd you lose the finger?"

"Korea," Frank said. "Commie machine gun bullet tore it clean off back in 'fifty-two. I looked around for it. Never did find it."

"Shame."

"Ruined a promising career as a concert pianist."

She stared at him a moment, then laughed.

They reached streets that grew progressively more crowded with traffic, hot streets with drivers who took off like jackrabbits then sat impatiently at the next traffic light. Dumb.

"Nice, huh?" Shirley said. "All this mess."

"You oughta try around L.A."

"Yeah? That where you're from?"

A mistake; he'd have to watch it. "Nope. Albuquerque. Been to L.A. a couple of times, though. Not my kinda place."

"It's comin'," she said.

"What's that?"

"L.A.'s problems," she replied, well-worn ferocity in her voice. "Traffic, drugs, crime, water shortage, street gangs, smog, gay punk-rock dimwits. Name anything you don't like about L.A. and it's on the way here. Lot of it is already."

He didn't respond, not wanting to encourage her. Woe and damnation was evidently this woman's forte. A little push and the conversation could turn into an avalanche.

Too late.

"This's a desert, right?" She shot him a quick glance. "Right. You think the goddamn planning commission's figured that out yet? *Hah!*" Her laugh was a derisive bray. "Not on your life! I've unplugged drain clogs with more intelligence than our planning commissioners. Or the goddamned city council. Developers've got the whole lot of 'em in their pockets. You get to talkin' water storage an' water rights with those snakes an' you learn the meaning of double-talk and bullshit, Mr. Wiley, you'll pardon my French. What's gonna happen is we're gonna have a five-year drought sometime and then the fur's gonna fly. Mark my words, people'll lose their jobs an' their homes an' there'll be graft-eaten officials hangin' from the trees in their own front yards. Serve 'em the hell right, too."

Her words washed over Frank. All he could do was tune her out and keep his eyes open for something familiar on the streets. Maybe that big ugly Toronado Mutt and Jeff were driving in Quiode. Already the hopelessness of the task was beginning to settle like a dark cloud in his brain. All these nameless streets, all this honk and hustle in the gathering gloom. And somewhere, perhaps not even in Reno, Suki might already have been delivered into Mink's hands.

Frank's chest felt tight at the thought.

". . . goddamn sticky fingers takin' money under the table while they smile an' tell you they're working like slaves in the public interest. Tell you what, Mr. Wiley, words is the devil's tool. Clever man kin say any damn thing he wants an' you can't never pin him down. Lies, half-truths, blather an' triple-talk; these folks are experts. They want something, nothin' like the will of the voters or the reality of livin' in the desert'll get in their way. They're like bulldozers. Get between them and the smell of money an' you better . . ."

Frank tried to visualize Mink, remembering what Suki'd said about him. And Charlotte Voorhees. There was that guy Mote, big and stupid-looking, and Jersey, skinny fellow with longish hair and small close-set eyes. Both of them with tattoos. And that black dude up in the hills. And some moon-faced guy called Danny.

If Mink was here, he'd have a new company with a new name, but Frank still wasn't sure how the operation worked, how it would look from outside on the street. It was unlikely that Mink would rent a big house somewhere and hang a sign out front that said G. F. LAYTON, INVESTMENTS, or whatever their name was this time.

". . . kickbacks, bribes, campaign contributions. Everyone runnin' around with their fingers twitchin' like maître d's in some snotty restaurant, smilin' out one side of their mouths while lyin' and sayin' 'Up yours, buddy,' out the other. So anyway, here we are. You want a shyster, tomorrow this place'll be crawlin' with 'em."

She pulled to the curb at the corner of a quiet street lined with aging two- and three-story houses. Tall trees stood dark and shaggy against a purple and red sky. Beyond the leafy veil, the luminous psychedelic glitter of casinos in the nearby gambling district was a visual roar: Flamingo Hilton, Circus Circus, the Virginian, Harrah's, Eldorado, half a dozen others.

Frank felt disoriented. How was he supposed to find Suki in all this?

"Drive me around," he said. "Slowly. Just wherever lawyers've got offices."

"It's your nickel. Really got a bug about lawyers, huh?"

"Guess so."

Gables, angles, cornices, columns, dense foliage and unkempt privet hedges, wrought iron, shingled roofs. All the accoutrements of small-city barristry. Lights glowed dimly behind a few windows. Shirley took him up one street, down another, circled slowly in the dark. The overall effect was one of general rattiness: too many run-down one-story shacks and weedy rubble-strewn lots standing side by side with brooding monstrosities that needed paint. Daylight was likely to reveal further shortcomings. Numerous signs out by the sidewalks announced the law offices of such-and-such and thus-and-so, along with those of CPAs, realty offices, marriage counselors, architects. For those who thought pain to be an essential ingredient in their "structural integration," there was even a certified rolfer. Not many people out walking. Frank didn't know if that was due to the day's residual heat or the neighborhood itself.

"That's it," Shirley said.

"One more time," Frank said. "I want to get to know the area better."

"Say, if you're a burglar, I could point out a couple of commissioners' homes to ya. Rich folks."

"Sorry, no."

She shrugged, took him around again. This time he paid more attention to street names, trying to create a map of the neighborhood in his mind.

"Again?" she asked, pulling to the curb outside an elderly lilac mansion with royal blue trim. It housed a graphic artist, a software designer, and a trio of attorneys.

"No, that'll do it."

"Comes to fourteen eighty-five altogether," she said.

He handed her a twenty. "Keep the change."

"Thanks. You wanna watch yourself in this neighborhood, Mr.

Wiley. 'Specially in the daytime." She cackled.

He got out and watched as she pulled away, turned right at the corner, disappeared.

Ribs aching, Frank stood on the sidewalk and considered his situation. He was armed with an old German pistol and he had just over seventy thousand dollars in cash in a small travel bag. He hadn't eaten in over twenty-four hours. He had no wheels, no place to stay, and he was in a city he didn't know well except for having been given a verbal tour of its corrupt officials courtesy of Shirley Budd. Not far away, police were uprooting entire counties, trying to find him, or so he imagined. Might not be literally true, but he was damn well wanted, probably couldn't withstand any sort of scrutiny by the local police. He looked like a recently-rolled wino in desperate need of a bath or delousing. Suki could be either practically under his nose in one of these old peeling monoliths or two thousand miles away. He had no way of knowing.

He couldn't do anything now but keep his eyes open and walk around, see what he could see. He toyed briefly with the idea of placing an anonymous call to the cops, seeing what he could stir up that way, but the only story he could tell was a lunatic's tale. He'd sound like a goddamn kook. Worse, the cops might send a few extra patrol cars into the area and end up hassling him, possibly finding his gun and money and picking him up. That wouldn't do Suki any damn good.

He began taking halting steps up Court Street, looking at every car and person in sight, trying to spot any subtle something that might ring a bell in his subconscious. Court Street crossed Arlington and climbed a low hill above the Truckee River. Frank walked past Clay Street to Lee, then over to Ridge and back down to Arlington. Across Arlington to Flint and Hill, up Hill to Liberty. Looking, listening.

Hopeless.

The thread leading eleven hundred miles from the De Baca Mountains of New Mexico to this old neighborhood in Nevada was too tenuous, too ethereal. It wasn't a waste of money, because Suki was worth it, but it was a wrenching, futile expenditure of hope.

But because Suki was worth it, and because hope was all he had left, Frank walked, keeping his eyes open, trying to stay alert, searching for that elusive gossamer filament that could be spun into thread and then into rope.

Just a filament would do. Anything at all.

But there was nothing.

20

"Yes?"

Not, *Tell me?* Jersey blinked. For an instant he thought he had the wrong number. The long drive had left his eyes grainy and red, his senses dulled. He wanted sleep.

"Mrs. Voor—Mrs. Gar . . . *rick?* That you, uh, ma'am?"

"Where *are* you, Jersey? Do you realize it's nearly two in the morning?"

"Yes, ma'am. We're in Reno, at some all-night place on, um, Wells Avenue, a couple blocks off the interstate."

"The girl is still with you, Jersey?"

Je-sus Christ. If she wasn't, Jersey would already be in Spain or Singapore or someplace, awaiting plastic surgery. "Yes, ma'am."

"Fine. Wait a moment."

Jersey heard paper rustling. She was probably reading a city map. In the Toronado, Mote was a hulking shadow behind a reflection of lights in the windshield, Suki beside him, Benny off taking a leak somewhere. Isaac was half-asleep in the Malibu, parked beside the Toronado.

"Are you there, Jersey?"

"Yes, ma'am."

"Okay. What you do is come south on Wells. Turn right on Fourth Street, then left on Arlington Avenue. Come across the river, turn left on Court Street, right on Flint. We're in the big off-white clapboard house on the left. It has third-story gabled attic windows and columns by the front doors."

"Yes, ma'am."

"You *do* know what gabled windows are, don't you, Jersey?"

Jersey picked his nose. "Yes, ma'am."

"Fine. Now I want you to listen very carefully to me, Jersey." Jersey let out a low growl. "Are you listening *very* carefully, Jersey?"

"Oh, yes, Mrs. Garrick."

She hesitated at his tone, then said, "I want you to bind and gag the girl before you bring her here. Do you understand?"

Christ on a Moped. Right here in the parking lot of an AM-PM Mini-Market and all-night gas station? "Yes, ma'am. Feet too?"

"Yes, Jersey. Bind her feet too."

"Yes, ma'am."

"Do it now."

The line went dead. Jersey went into the store, looked around, bought some nylon-filament strapping tape. It would have to do.

Back at the car, he told Mote to take off his T-shirt.

"What for?" Mote asked.

"Just do it, huh?"

"Yeah, sure Jers."

He took it off, revealing a chest like Schwarzenegger's. Son of a bitch'd been coldcocked twice in less than a week, so it was likely all that muscle was somehow feeding off what little was left of his brain.

Jersey tore the shirt in half.

"*Hey!*" Mote cried.

"Hey what?" Jersey tossed the remnant in Mote's lap.

Mote picked it up. "Goddamn, Jers. That was my fav'rit."

Jersey folded the rag several times. "Open wide," he said to Suki.

"Shit, Jersey, I won't scream, I promise. You don't gotta do that."

"I said open up, sweetmeat."

Suki screamed. Jersey'd been expecting it. He drove a fist into her belly, just enough to double her over and keep the scream from building. She gasped for air and he waited, watching, seeing if she was going to puke. When he saw that she wasn't, he forced the filthy rag into her mouth, wrapping tape across it and around her head several times.

He wrapped a few more sticky coils around her wrists and ankles, then backed the Olds out of the lot and turned left on Wells, the Malibu trailing. Mote kept Suki's head down in his lap, stroking her hair as if she were a kitten.

• • •

Frank walked up Court Street to Clay, up Clay to Ridge. The muscle cars turned the other way up Court Street, right on Flint, stopped in front of an oyster clapboard mansion that squatted in darkness, framed by half a dozen blighted elms.

Jersey got out, pushed open a raspy iron gate and went up a walkway to the front door. It opened before he got there. Mink stood beneath the heavy oak lintel, eyes bright, looking out at the car. "Where is she?"

"In the car," Jersey said. "Gagged an' tied like Mrs. Voor—Garrick said we should."

"Good. Excellent. Drive around back, to the left there. You and Mote carry her in through the back door. Keep the headlights off."

"Sure thing, Mink."

"Tell Benny and Isaac to stay put out there a while. I don't want a carnival in here. Tell them to watch the street."

"Yeah, okay."

Jersey guided the Olds up twin ribbons of cracked concrete to the rear of the house, deep in shadow beneath the trees. A garage stood apart from the house, double-hinged doors closed.

"Take her shoulders," Jersey said. "I got her feet."

Suki squirmed as Mote, bare-chested, hauled her headfirst out of the car. Jersey caught her feet. They clambered up three steps and through a door into a good-sized kitchen.

Yellow light leaked into the room from a hallway that ran into the depths of the house. Charlotte was limned darkly in its glow. Mink smiled at Suki as Mote stood her on her feet.

"Welcome home, Suki," he said. "We're going to have some fun, you and I. I'm sure you'll find it interesting."

• • •

Frank hiked along the buckled sidewalks of Ridge Street to Lee, then over to Court and down to Clay, where he stood on the corner, debating which way to turn next. Not that it mattered. He was shuffling down streets at random, trying to cover the entire neighborhood. It was all a crapshoot in a game that might've never come to town. He turned onto Clay and drifted back up to Ridge, thereby missing the pair of cars that rumbled down Court Street and swung right on Arlington, headed for the Rancho Sierra Motel on Fourth where a couple of rooms had been paid in advance by the week. Frank heard the heavy beat of horsepower, however, and he broke into a crippled run down Ridge, reaching Arlington as two loud cars crossed the bridge spanning the Truckee River and passed through a green light at First Street.

Not even much of a glimpse, really. Just a couple of muscle cars, out cruising. Even so, it had been a tantalizing moment. Frank breathed deeply, ribs throbbing, heart pounding, staring at the empty street that looped downward toward the western edge of the gambling district, casinos glittering in the night several blocks to the east.

This wasn't any good.

God, Suki. I'm so damn sorry.

• • •

Mink was crazy, insane, yet possessed of some sort of unimaginable control. Cold sweat formed at Suki's armpits. It would be better, she thought, to simply die, now, this instant.

The basement air was unpleasantly cool against her naked body. The only light came from a single bulb screwed into a white porcelain fixture in the ceiling. Cardboard cartons were stacked against one wall, otherwise the room was empty. Silver cobwebs fluttered in the corners.

"Knowledge, as they say, is power," Simon said, standing on a chair above her as he dumped crushed ice into a gallon bucket that hung from the joists of the mansion. "But certainly it's much more than that. It's also the wellspring of imagination, wouldn't you agree?" He smiled emptily down at her.

She lay spread-eagled on a thin mattress six feet from a stone wall, wrists and ankles securely bound with silk bands. Jersey's gag had been replaced with one that was more effective as well as more hygienic. With the new gag in place, she could barely grunt, much less respond to so philosophical a question. Several other silk bands had been looped around her inner thighs and rib cage, preventing all lateral movement of her belly.

"And," Mink continued, "imagination is the basis of fear, and *fear* is the primary source of the sort of unbounded agony of which the human mind is capable."

Suki stared at him, eyes wide. His bandage was off, exposing the still-angry wound of the graft on his forehead. Charlotte sat eight feet away in an overstuffed easy chair, smoking silently, watching with grackle's eyes as her adopted son made his preparations.

Simon stepped off the chair and crouched next to Suki. He looked into her eyes. "Wouldn't you therefore agree that knowledge is an essential ingredient of agony? Yes, I thought you might. For that reason I will explain what is about to happen, and I will tell you how you will react to it. I will give you all the *knowledge* you need to make this a most rewarding experience."

The bucket hung directly over Suki's midsection. A short length of glass tubing hung from an inch-long piece of rubber hose that protruded from the bottom of the bucket. A stopcock of the type used in chemical laboratories was fitted to the glass tube.

"The Chinese were masters at inducing agony," Simon said. "The so-called Chinese water torture is a case in point. Few of those raised in the West truly comprehend its power." He gazed upward, and

Suki's eyes followed. "The bucket holds ice water. Soon, drops will fall from the tiny spigot you see beneath it. Each drop will fall at a fixed rate at a specific location. In years past, this has generally been on a person's forehead, but to reflexively do what has been done before is to miss the point entirely. Perhaps," Simon said, standing, "in a while you will be able to tell me what that point is, Suki."

He reached up and turned the stopcock, catching the drip in a washcloth while he adjusted the flow to about four drops per minute.

"There," he said. "Shall we begin?"

He stood back. The next drop formed slowly at the end of the tiny valve, growing round and fat, catching the light. Suki watched it, mesmerized. It fell, landing with a hollow *thip* in the middle of her naked belly, three inches below her navel.

She blinked. A blood vessel in her neck began to throb.

"Cold, isn't it?" Simon asked. "And the height from which it falls greatly increases one's awareness of it, don't you think?" He watched as the next drop slowly filled, grew round and fat, trembling in an unseen current of air. It fell, splatting against Suki's belly with that same tiny, hollow *thip*.

"Notice how slowly each drop forms," Simon said, crouching intimately at her side. "If they come too often, one's mind tends to integrate the impact of each drop into a continuous experience. But if the drip is made sufficiently slow, the mind reaches a state of equilibrium between each drop in which each can be fully *anticipated*."

Thip.

"The brain then becomes an active participant in the process. A state of denial is achieved, continually disrupted. Like the very best sex, Suki dear, the very best pain occurs within the dark, uncharted pathways of the mind.

"On the other hand, too slow a drip would lack the same sort of significance. So *frequency* is important; moreover, the drip is ice water and it falls from a good height, giving it an impact that the mind finds meaningful. Observe . . ."

Thip.

He smiled at her, the smile of a cobra watching its poison work in its victim. "It *is* unpleasant, isn't it? Very cold and, as you will soon discover, very hard. Does that surprise you, Suki? That water can be hard, harder than stone, harder than diamond, harder than *life*?" He glanced upward, waited.

Thip.

For a moment, his eyes got bright. "One is incapable of fully comprehending this sort of torment without actually experiencing it for oneself. Intellectualizing is ineffective, while observation is just an abstraction of a different sort. Would it surprise you to learn that a little less than twenty-four hours ago I was lying where you are now?"

Her eyes widened.

Thip.

"It's true," Mink said. His voice was soft, soothing, almost dreamy, but his eyes had the empty stare of bullet holes in sheet metal. Charlotte's eyes were worse, her face pale and featureless behind a veil of blue-tinged smoke. Mink said, "Your suffering will be so much more real to me, Suki, as real as my own, because we will have shared this incredible experience. In less than ten hours I felt a scream building inside that I knew I would soon be unable to contain. I would have screamed, Suki, nor am I in the least bit ashamed to admit it. I watched with horror, absolute *horror*, as that unyielding—"

Thip.

"—globule formed above me, knowing, as few men on this earth will ever know, how it would explode upon me like a hideous devouring insect when it dropped. But *think*, Suki, it was not at the moment of impact that I felt the scream well up inside, but as it *formed.* Not at the moment of pain, but at the *anticipation* of pain. I think that's significant. Watch."

Above, the crystalline orb swelled, swelled . . .

Thip.

A tremor ran through her. Coolness touched her belly. Mink's face hovered nearby, pale madness in his eyes.

"Do you regret marking me, Suki? No? Yes? Wait and see? Oh, but I promise that you will, Suki. Whatever regret you might have at this moment is but the dimmest possible shadow to what you will feel, shall we say, eight hours from now."

Thip.

He stood. "I almost envy you," he said. "You will pass beyond even the distant shores that I have reached. You will know pain, Suki Flood, as few have ever known it. I don't particularly envy you the pain, but I do envy you the knowledge." He looked up at the droplet forming. "Would you like me to catch this next drop for you, my love?"

No . . . yes.

Thip.

Mink turned toward Charlotte. "Will you turn the music on

upstairs now, Mother? I think it's time."

"Of course, darling." She stood and went up the stairs without a backward glance at Suki, shoes tocking on the old wooden risers.

Thip.

Simon waited. Seconds passed.

Thip.

From upstairs came the faint sounds of music, jazz, Bix Beiderbecke and Paul Whiteman's Orchestra. "These old houses were built like fortresses," Simon said. "Screams down here are all but inaudible on the street outside, I know. With the stereo—"

Thip.

"—playing upstairs, it's quite impossible to hear anything that might take place down here. When you scream, Suki, I want to hear it. I want you to give full vent to your agony. I know you won't want to give me that, and I know you will do everything in your power not to, but you will all the same." He bent down and removed her gag.

Thip.

She tried to spit in his face, but her mouth was dry.

He smiled at her. "When you've had enough of the cold, my pet, you will ask me for the heat."

"Motherfucker." She spat at him again, still unable to work up any moisture. Her tongue was dry, slightly swollen. Even her teeth felt dry, like chips of porcelain.

Thip.

Charlotte appeared on the stairs, a wraith in dark silk. She stopped partway and looked down at them.

"You will ask for the heat," Mink said to Suki. "I promise you will. And when you ask, I will replace the ice water with boiling oil. *Oil*, Suki. Have you ever been spattered by hot grease? Sure you have. Each drop will destroy a hundred cells, eating into your guts in precisely the same place as the cold is now. The oil will drip upon you until you die. You might—"

Thip.

"—think you'll never ask for scalding oil, Suki, but that's only because you lack the imagination to know how the cold will affect you. You *will* ask. That is what is truly incredible about this … process. Inevitably, a time will come when you will scream out for change, *any* change—"

"I saw you with those girls, Mink. You're sick, and so's your crazy fucking mother." She shot a look at Charlotte and said to her, "I saw you in a chair, watching him—"

Thip.

"—with those young girls." She stared into Mink's dead eyes. "You two sick, disgusting perverts."

Simon raised an eyebrow at her.

"How old were they?" Suki asked. "Thirteen? Twelve?"

He said, "Do you have any idea how old *you* are, Suki. How jaded and ancient you've become? Do you realize how quickly innocence is corrupted on this vile planet, how quickly it is reduced to numbing, sexless cynicism?"

Thip.

She felt suddenly sickened by his presence, as if she would soon vomit. "You're a monster," she said, turning her head away so she wouldn't have to look at him.

He walked to the base of the stairs. "You *will* beg me for the oil, Suki. But first you will scream."

Thip.

"Concentrate now on just one thing, Suki. I won't return to distract you for a while. Your mind must attune itself to the rhythm of the water. Good-bye."

Footsteps sounded hollowly on the stairs. A door snicked shut above.

Thip.

Silence filled the room, a deathlike silence, full of dust and dark and age and rot. She would never scream. She would die before she gave Mink that terrible joy.

Overhead, the next drop grew swollen. Larger, larger . . .

Thip.

21

A purple glow revealed the contours of the mountains to the east. Stars faded overhead as royal blue brightened into day. Sunlight crept from the peaks of the Sierra Nevadas into the irregular bowl of the valley in which "the Biggest Little City in the World" inched year by year into the foothills like a kind of mutant fungus.

The night's chill burned off.

Frank's stomach growled. His mouth was dry and his ribs ached. He looked like a bum and felt like a bum, and like a bum he roamed the sidewalks restlessly, as if hoping for a handout or seeking a likely house to rob. One eye was still puffed to a slit. Even so, he wouldn't give up, wouldn't stray a few blocks outside his self-assigned beat to an all-night liquor store where he might get water or a can of Coke, maybe a bottle of orange juice. If he did, he might miss something and the thought of allowing the slightest hint of anything to escape his notice was intolerable. He didn't expect a parade of Voorheeses to come marching by.

Up Lee to Ridge, across Arlington to Hill, down to Court and then up Flint Street.

Music came faintly from a big off-white mansion to his left. Cab Calloway or Duke Ellington. One of those.

Up Flint Street to California Avenue, up California to Arlington; a brief tour of the immediate neighborhood south of California Avenue where he'd found a few more law offices, then back to Ridge.

A time would come when he would have to make a decision: continue the search, or quit. He didn't want to quit, but he realized the impossibility and futility of keeping this up indefinitely. He'd find her soon or not at all, and as the hours passed, the odds increased that Mutt and Jeff had taken her to Shreveport instead of Reno.

Despair welled up in him at the thought. He would continue his vigil at least another twenty-four hours before considering a search of Shreveport. Maybe Suki would survive that long in Mink's hands.

He would never forget her, though. And he would never allow Simon Voorhees to slip from his memory either. He was amazed at how quickly and thoroughly he'd become attached to Suki, cute little quirky girl who blew up cars.

•   •   •

Her breath came in short gasps. She closed her eyes, but saw the horrible globule forming anyway, growing fatter, heavier, an evil thing, ripening, near critical, falling . . .

Thip.

Her belly trembled under the impact. Her skin felt raw, half frozen. It seemed as if each drop were penetrating an inch into her skin. Her sides heaved. Her muscles stood out as she tried desperately to twist her body out from under the hideous drop, to make the next one fall in a different place, but the silken web held her immobile.

She opened her eyes. The next drop was half formed, as she'd known it would be, catching the light of that single bulb in a way that never varied. It swelled . . . grew larger . . .

A scream built up inside her. With effort, she forced it down. She'd never give him that. Never—

Thip.

She groaned, a low sound, full of agony.

"Yes."

The word was a mere breath, a sigh, as if the stones in the wall had whispered. She twisted her head, seeking its source. Simon stood in the shadows to her right. She hadn't heard him come down. Or maybe another staircase led down into the basement. The chamber was certainly large enough. Her mind seized upon meaningless thoughts like a drowning woman clutching at flotsam.

Simon took a step forward. He was naked, hard.

"Your first groan, Suki," he said. "Four hours, twenty minutes. You're—"

Thip.

"—doing very well, darling."

"Mink . . ." His name was airless on her lips.

He cocked his head, smiled. "What's that I hear in your voice, Suki? Could it be remorse?"

"Fuck you," she said, hating the clogged sound that issued from her throat.

"Really? We will see if you're still capable of uttering so tiresome a sentiment in a few more hours, Suki Flood."

Thip.

He stood over her, turgid, wiry, eyes glowing, yet oddly moribund. "If you will take back those hateful words, I will catch the next drop for you. Would you like that, dearest?"

Yes, yes, yes, yes, yes—

"No, you asshole motherfucker," she hissed. "I love this."

He gazed fondly down at her. "My, aren't you tough? That is good, Suki. *Very* good. This sort of . . . experience works best on the tough ones. When they break, and they *always* do, they break—"

Thip.

"—so *completely*, my love. When hammered, tough rocks often shatter. You will do everything I have said you will do, and more."

She stared up at him, numb with pain and hatred. Overhead, the next drop swelled. She realized that talking with anyone, even Simon Voorhees, was a relief, a diversion from the relentless hammering of the icy drops.

Simon turned away. At the base of the stairs he stopped. "Perhaps you are beginning to understand the wonderful, terrible patience of water, Suki." He began to climb.

"Mink . . ."

He looked down at her. "Yes, Suki?"

"Don't go," she whispered. Tears formed in her eyes.

Thip.

"What did you say, dearest?"

Her lips quivered. "Nothing."

"Until later, then." He went up. The door closed.

Silence.

The next drop filled, grew fatter, fatter . . .

She felt the scream, deep inside, wanting to come out, wanting to shatter the next terrible drop to atoms.

Thip.

• • •

Frank Limosin bought three prepackaged sandwiches and a can of Coke and bottled water at Dumar's Liquor Store on Center Street, three blocks east of Hill. If he collapsed in the street from dehydration or hunger, he wouldn't be of any use to anyone. Wolfing a stale tuna sandwich, he hurried back as fast as his hurting ribs would allow.

A parade of status cars had begun to arrive at a little before eight that morning, Audis and Porsches, Mercedes and Cadillacs. A quiet influx of glossy machinery. Lawyers and other professionals emerged from the softly purring metallic shells in business suits, many of them carrying attaché cases.

The day heated up. The sidewalks began to bake under the bright morning sun. Cicadas started their crazed electric song in the straw-colored weeds.

Frank stood on the corner of Court and Arlington. A red Trans Am rolled toward him along Court Street. Frank stared, a roast beef sandwich held motionless an inch from his mouth. A pudgy, baby-faced man sat behind the wheel, wearing wire-rimmed glasses and a dark suit. Suddenly Frank didn't know what to do. His vision seemed to dim. He froze, trying to absorb every detail, madly evaluating his options, most of which were insane, beyond reason. The car was new, spotless. A temporary license had been taped to a window.

The car turned south at the corner, rumbled away up Arlington.

Danny. Suki had told him there was a guy called Daniel, Danny something, who was sort of a business manager for Simon Voorhees. Kinda moonfaced, wore glasses.

Moonfaced, baby-faced . . .

Oh, Jesus.

His mind spun as he watched the Trans Am roll away up Arlington, headed toward California Avenue.

Couldn't chase it. The guy might see him, and that would give the game away. And what the hell could he do if he caught it, even at the light? Which was damned unlikely in his present condition. The guy might be any of half a million other moonfaced guys in North America.

But in a brand new red Trans Am, in Reno, in the kind of neighborhoods Mink was partial to, about forty years old, wearing glasses? Suki had said Danny was about forty. Mink had lost one Trans Am. Maybe he'd bought another. He was the sort who might.

Frank mopped sweat from his brow with his sleeve. He gazed up Court Street. The car had come from that direction. But from where, exactly? Some guy cruising through, or had this Mink character really set up shop in a big old house up that way?

Frank knew the streets by heart now. Court and Ridge and Liberty ran east-west, with Flint and Hill running north and south between them. Pickard was just a block-long alley.

The guy had come along Court. When he returned, if he did, chances were he'd come back the same way. Frank tried to remember exactly where he'd first seen the Trans Am. Not too far up the street; the image was engraved in his mind. He hadn't seen it turn onto Court from one of the side streets.

He walked up Court and stood at the first intersection, looking up

Flint Street. It was quiet, dozy, hot. Same general shabby look as the rest of the neighborhood. Big off-white, dingy clapboard mansion in the middle of the block with gables, columns, casement windows, ivy climbing partway up the north wall, a wrought-iron fence around the front yard, set between brick pillars. A collection of lilac trees and catalpa in the front yard, tall elms at the sides and in back, steeply pitched roof. Jazz music had been coming from the place since a little before dawn. Did that mean anything? To the left of the mansion was a low, single-story house with scaling paint, broken windows, and other signs of abandonment. To the right was a two-story house of blond brick, the offices of a pair of attorneys and some kind of a paralegal outfit. As he watched, a woman in a blue summer suit came out, eased into a little Toyota MR2, drove off.

Frank hiked down to the next corner, Hill Street, and scrutinized the street carefully. Two old mansions on the west side, one on the east. One empty yard of weeds and dirt. A house with peeling paint, lawns dried brown in patches, everything slightly grayed out.

The thing to do, Frank decided, was position himself midway between Flint and Hill, wait for the Trans Am to return, see which street it turned up, or if it pulled into a place on Court Street itself.

He couldn't think of any other way to handle it.

• • •

Thip.
Thip.
Thip.
The next horrible drop grew bloated, hung, fell.
Thip.
Her groan was a watery gurgle of raw agony, shattering every nerve. The long lean muscles of her legs stood out as she writhed helplessly in her silken web.

"Yes," Mink whispered.

"Mink?" Her eyes fluttered, trying to find him.

"I'm here, Suki. Over here."

"I'm . . . I'm s-sorry, Mink," she said, voice wrenched, cords standing out in her neck.

Thip.

"Aaa-agg."

"Are you *really* sorry, Suki? Truly?"

"Aaagh . . . Yes, yes." Tears rolled from her eyes. "Please, no more. Please, I can't . . ."

"It's been nine hours and ten minutes. You're amazingly strong.

Isn't she strong, Mother?"

Suki's eyes shifted. Wreathed in cigarette smoke, Charlotte sat in the easy chair, silent, intense, watching with empty grackle's eyes. The chair had been pulled back into the shadows. Suki, lost in pain, hadn't even smelled the smoke.

"Why don't you scream, Suki?" Simon suggested.

No.

Thip.

Her belly rippled under the impact of the falling glacier, muscles spasming.

"Oh, God!" she breathed, body arched. "Oh, my *Gooood!*"

"Yes," Simon said. "Yessss. Pain has stripped away your cynicism, has it not? Do you feel the innocence of your agony, the childlike purity to which you have returned?"

Her eyes refused to focus. Above her, he was a fractured figure, gently stroking himself. Charlotte watched. Insane.

"S-Simon—"

"What is it, Suki?"

Thip.

Her mind clenched. Agony reverberated within the ragged fabric of her brain. "Aaaa . . . aaaagh."

"Scream, Suki," he whispered.

Something was already screaming inside her, had been screaming throughout eternity, an insane shriek that threatened to shatter the world. Spittle ran from the corners of her mouth and down her jaw.

"Shall I catch the next drop, Suki?"

"Yes. Oh, God, *yes!*"

"Here it comes, dearest. I'll get it, I'll—"

Thip.

"I'm so sorry," he said. "I missed."

"You . . . bastard," she hissed weakly, then she began to cry, wet sobbing gasps that wracked her body.

"You look so cold," Mink said. "Do you want the heat?" he asked softly. "Do you want the boiling oil, Suki darling? Wouldn't the heat feel nice?"

Yes.

No. Oh, God, *no!*

Thip.

She bit back a soul-rending shriek, gagging.

"It will take a while to set up the oil. Fifteen minutes, perhaps. Would you like that, Suki? Fifteen minutes in which the drops will cease?"

Yes. Yes, yes, yes, yes.

"Scream for me, Suki Flood. Scream for me, then ask for the heat and I will give it to you."

Thip.

"Aaanaaghhh." Her eyes bulged with pain, the whites bloodshot.

"So close," he whispered soothingly. "So *very* close. Soon you can have the heat. Soon. And then the torture will begin in earnest. Boiling oil will hurt so very much more as it eats down into your guts, Suki, but even so, you will ask for it, *beg* for it, I promise."

The next drop swelled.

"Can you stand this for—"

Thip.

"—another hour, my love. Another day, another *week?*"

His words were bullets, ripping bloody tunnels through her brain. Another hour? The next few drops would surely destroy her, but another day, another *week?*

Thip.

She screamed, a tremendous blood-curdling shriek of utter agony, and Simon stroked harder, spurting warm semen over her belly as she writhed. The next horrible drop began to expand.

Charlotte watched a minute longer, then went upstairs to change the CD on the stereo. She was growing weary of Cootie Williams and his "growling" trumpet.

• • •

A midnight blue Ferrari rolled up Court Street, turned onto Flint. For a moment Frank didn't react. All his concentration was on the reappearance of the red Trans Am.

Suddenly he broke into a lurching run.

Jesus.

By the time he reached the corner, the Ferrari had pulled into the crumbling driveway beside the mansion from which the sounds of jazz still issued. A man with a round face and wire-rimmed glasses got out and, without knocking, used a key to enter the house through the front door.

Indecision was a bloated monster in Frank's mind. What was this? What had he seen? A harmless-looking guy who drove off in a Trans Am and returned in a Ferrari. Right city, right neighborhood. Maybe. An implied scent of money with a capital M. No lawyer's shingle in front of the mansion, no sign of any kind.

An inexorable logic took over, logic with its own truth, its own dark gravity pulling him to a place far beyond any code of law. He couldn't afford not to act, to take more time to gather a greater preponderance of evidence. If this was the right place, then either it was already too late or Suki needed him *now*. And if it wasn't the right place, then it wasn't. As best he could, he would extricate himself from the brouhaha that must inevitably follow and try to make his way to Shreveport, see what he could turn up there.

There wasn't anything else he could do.

He reached into his bag and pulled out the nine-millimeter German Astra, tucked it into the waistband of his jeans, concealed by the denim jacket but where he could reach it quickly. Perhaps the pistol would actually fire if he had to use it. The night before, he'd built a packet of money for just the kind of situation before him now, a brick of twenties with a couple of hundreds on the outside. It looked like something worth having. He slipped it partway up his left sleeve.

He wandered down Flint Street, same side of the street as the mansion, eyes wary, heart beginning to pound as if he were seventeen again, in high school and on his first date with a busty blonde who'd given off signals that she might be willing.

Had Mutt and Jeff told Mink what he looked like? Perhaps the two were inside the house now, watching through a slit in one of those darkly curtained windows as Frank ambled foolishly up the sidewalk. No muscle cars were in sight. Did that mean anything?

Frank's palms were damp. Distant traffic sounds came from the neighboring streets. Nothing was moving on Flint.

He reached the iron fence that separated the mansion from the moldering bungalow next to it, plodded along for another fifty feet, then stopped at the mansion's gate. He opened it, stooped as if to pick up something from the ground, let the money brick slip down into his hand. He stared at it, looked doubtfully up the street then at the house. Without further delay he trudged up a concrete walkway to the porch steps, climbed stolidly, and leaned on the doorbell.

His breath came in tense puffs though parted lips. He waited, rang the bell again, keeping the worst side of his face turned from the peephole in the door.

A deadbolt was thrown from within. A two-inch gap appeared between the door and the frame.

"Yes," a woman asked. She had a smoker's gravelly voice. Frank caught a glimpse of red hair, a wizened face.

Charlotte Voorhees had red hair. Frank tried not to stare. Was it her? *Was it?* Coincidences were starting to pile up.

"Uh, yuh," Frank said. "I found this in your front yard out by the gate, ma'am. Didn't know whose it was." He held up the money brick, fanned its leaves. "Thought maybe I oughta ask."

The woman pulled the door open a few more inches, gave his face a look and a frown, then reached for the money. Her hair was definitely red. A dead look was in her faded blue eyes.

Frank pulled the money back. "Is this yours, ma'am?"

"Yes, thank you very much. You want a little reward, I expect?" The door opened wider, the sounds of Thelonious Monk and his jazz piano leaking out in greater volume.

Frank grabbed the old crone by the throat with his left hand and stepped swiftly inside, forcing her back, pulling his gun. She scrabbled at him, reaching for his eyes, and he spun her around, arm clamped around her spindly neck.

"Simon!" she shrieked. Frank tightened his arm around her windpipe, choking off her cry.

Simon! Frank's heart leapt. He crouched, dragging the writhing witch down with him.

Too many coincidences. One too many.

The woman kicked at the floor. Her arms flailed as she struggled for air, bony blue-veined fingers hooked into claws trying to rake his arm.

"Where's the girl?" Frank hissed in her ear. He eased up on her throat. "Where's Suki?"

Charlotte attempted to scream.

"Christ!" Frank choked off her squawk and rapped the back of her head with the butt of the Astra, harder than necessary. She went limp in his arms.

The moonfaced guy came into the room with a sandwich in one hand. Frank leveled the gun at him from a distance of twelve feet. "C'mere, sport."

The man hesitated, about to run.

"Run or yell, you're dead," Frank said. "Get over here."

The man took a few hesitant steps toward him. A faint scream came from somewhere in the house.

Suki!

Frank tossed Charlotte's limp body against a wall, tore across the room in a lineman's rush, slammed the guy up against a doorjamb, and jammed the muzzle of the gun into the softness between his throat and chin.

"Where's the girl?"

"Downstairs," Danny gasped, blinking. "In the basement." The impact had knocked his glasses off. His myopic eyes were wide with fear. He'd dropped his sandwich.

"*Show* me," Frank said. "*Now*."

The sound of "Light Blue" filled the room, Thelonious ripping up the keyboard as Danny led Frank from the room and down a dim hallway. He stopped at a heavy oak door with raised panels.

"Down there," he said.

A muffled scream came from behind the door, full-throated and raw, barely recognizable as human. The hair on Frank's neck and head stood up.

He slammed the Astra against Danny's head, hard, lowered him gently to the floor to keep from making noise. A moment of sudden silence came over the house, then Chick Corea took his turn at the ivories, hammering out "Sundance."

Frank opened the door. A dark wooden staircase led down into gloom. Frank went down quickly, leading with his gun. Partway down, he was momentarily stunned by what he saw: Suki, naked, tied to the floor, writhing, breathing in hoarse gasps. A naked man stood at her side, turning slowly.

"Mother?" the man said. Whipcord muscles stood out on his body. His buttocks were pale, hard, hairless.

Frank aimed the Astra at him, came down a few more steps in a crouch. "Don't even breathe, asshole," he said.

With shocking speed, the guy leapt at Suki, placed a hand on her throat.

"Believe it or not," he said, "I can kill her even if you pull that trigger."

Frank came down the remaining steps, keeping the gun on the guy's chest. "I believe it."

"Well, then. Looks like we've got us a standoff here."

"Frank?" The word was half cry, half groan. It sounded bubbly, as if she were drowning.

"I'm here, Suki."

Thip.

Suki screamed again. "*Fraaaaaaaank! Oh, God, oh Jesus, make it stop, Frank! Make it stop!*"

Frank's blood went cold. His hands started to shake. He took a step closer.

"Stay back," Mink warned.

Frank stopped. "You call this a standoff?" *What in the name of Christ . . .?* The setup was weird. He couldn't figure out what was happening to Suki while he kept his eyes on Mink.

"Looks like it, doesn't it?"

Thip.

Suki gasped. Spittle bubbled at her lips. Her eyes were like frosted glass, staring blindly up at Frank. "*Frank! Oh, God, Frank, make it STOP!*"

"I'm not leaving," Frank said.

"Then she's dead, old man."

"What's her life worth, like that? I don't have a fuckin' thing to lose, you pile of mucus. She's all that's keeping you alive right now. She dies, you die. That's a fact."

Simon's eyebrows lifted a millimeter. "Who *are* you?"

Thip.

Suki's entire body shuddered. She moaned, thick and low. Finally Frank saw the bucket overhead, had an idea of what was going on. He stopped six feet from Mink.

"Question is, do *you* want to live, motherfucker?" Frank's voice shook. "If you're not face down on the floor by the time the next drop falls, you get a bullet in the head and that's an absolute promise. You're that many seconds away from eternity." He came another foot closer, gun steady in a two-fisted combat grip, aimed at the livid red scar on Simon's forehead.

Something in his voice got through. Or perhaps it was the gun's implacable dead eye gaping at Simon, as implacable and dead as Simon's own. Or Frank's finger, tight on the trigger.

For an instant Simon hesitated. He glanced up at the drop forming above Suki's belly, then dropped quickly to the floor, not far from a wall made of smooth stones set in concrete.

Frank caught the next drop in his hand.

Suki began to cry, a wet blubbering sound filled with madness. Frank tore the bucket from the ceiling and slung it across the room, icy slush spraying the floor as the bucket clattered into a dark corner.

Simon twitched.

"Uh-uh," Frank said. He aimed the gun at Mink's face from a distance of three feet. "Face down, nose against the floor, eyes front right now or die."

Suki sobbed weakly.

Mink slowly turned his head until his nose just touched the cold gray concrete. Frank crouched another few inches and pounded a fist into the back of Mink's head, slamming his face into the concrete. Stunned, Mink tried to come off the floor at him, snakelike and wiry. Frank caught Mink's face in an open hand and slammed the back of his head into the rock wall. The sound was that of coconut on marble. Mink's eyes rolled up in his head and he slumped to the floor, out.

Frank spoke to Suki as he untied her. She cried, an aching sound that wrenched his heart. An angry red spot low on her belly showed where the water had dripped. Freed from the silken web, Suki curled into a ball on her side, folded over the wound. For a moment Frank held her, his hands and heart clumsy, breathing unevenly. She was a rag doll, shivering, sobbing.

Frank stared at Mink, trying to understand what kind of a mad dog the guy was. How could evil come to so sharp a focus? The world did not deserve this.

He wanted to kill the guy, but found that he couldn't. Logic demanded it, as did justice, but logic and justice and the sick rage bubbling inside him weren't sufficient. He wished for an instant, for just one second, that he was capable of cold-blooded, well-deserved murder, but he wasn't.

Suddenly all he wanted was to get Suki and himself out of that house, away from the slimy evil things that inhabited the place. The gray walls were like the lining of a demon's stomach, trying to digest them, even now sucking them inch by inch down some unimaginable maw into absolute blackness.

"Can you walk?" Frank asked.

She was barely conscious, jackknifed on her side, still moaning, still in the grip of the horror she'd endured.

Grating agony shot through Frank's ribs as he lifted Suki into his arms and climbed the stairs. Beads of sweat stood out on his brow. He stooped momentarily over Danny's inert form and fumbled in the guy's pockets for the Ferrari's keys.

Charlotte was lying in the foyer where Frank had left her. He kicked her in the face as he stepped over her slack body because he couldn't help himself, and because her evil was as inexplicable and vile as that of her stepson's. He tore a curtain from one of the front windows, bundled Suki in it, and carried her out the door.

Coleman Hawkins's lively tenor sax followed them out into the hot afternoon sunshine.

22

Suki mumbled something.

Frank could barely hear the papery sound of her voice in the rush of air over the Ferrari's hull.

"What?" He leaned closer.

"Did you kill 'im?" Her eyes were closed, face pale. Her voice was a tattered wisp from all the screaming she'd done.

"No."

"Why not?"

"Christ, Suki. I couldn't."

Translucent flakes of spittle crusted her lips and chin. Her head lolled against the headrest. "I could've."

"I know."

She was silent for a moment. "That me I smell?"

"Both of us, I think."

A spasm of some kind seized her, doubled her over. She groaned miserably, teeth clenched.

"You gonna be all right?"

"I look all right?"

"Gorgeous." Cocooned in mauve polyester and cotton with ruffles all over and a tieback dragging on the floor. Tangled strands of hair covered her streaky face.

Her eyes were still shut. "If I die, my name's Flood. Suki Flood."

"You're not gonna die."

"Flood, as in too much water, Frank. That's my real name. I just want you to know."

"Anne Flood?"

"Used to be, yeah. Suki, now."

"You're not gonna die," he repeated.

Her eyes stayed shut. They weren't up to focusing yet. "I wanted to," she said. "He isn't human."

"I know."

"If you'd killed him, it wouldn't've been murder. It would've been like . . ." She paused, groping for an elusive idea. "Like public service or something."

They passed the Mount Rose turnoff and continued down U.S. 395 toward Carson City, capital of Nevada, now twenty miles away. Frank didn't want to head west, into California. Anyway, Auburn or Sacramento were too far to go with Suki in her condition. North and east of Reno was just desert wasteland, hopeless.

He wasn't yet sure what he was doing, driving around in a stolen car worth as much as a house, with a more or less naked teenage girl beside him who looked as if she'd barely survived the sinking of the *Titanic*. He wasn't likely to be mistaken for the Prince of Wales himself. They had to get cleaned up before any major moves could be contemplated, and he wanted to ditch the Ferrari as soon as he could. Suki needed a place to lie down and rest, soon, but first there were these technical difficulties to be taken care of.

"I want to kill him, Frank."

"I know."

"I'm serious."

•   •   •

"Oh, Christ, Vi, what'd he do to you?"

In his pain, Mink had inadvertently called his stepmother by her real name, Violet, breaking the one cardinal rule they had agreed upon right from the start. Violet and De Witt Schlenker had become Charlotte and Simon Voorhees five years ago, Paul Schlenker having had the good sense to run, to escape, years before that. In all that time neither of them had once slipped and called the other by his or her real name, until this moment.

But no harm came of it; no one was around to hear. Danny was still out cold in the hallway. The house was empty, quiet but for "Tiger Rag" being performed over and over by the self-proclaimed creator of jazz itself, Jelly Roll Morton.

Yet the old way quickly reasserted itself, and Simon lifted the battered face of his stepmother into his lap and cradled her on his naked thighs, crooning her assumed name almost soundlessly, over and over: "Charlotte, Charlotte."

Her patrician nose was cocked at an odd angle. Blood coated her lips and chin. Her thin hair was matted into sticky clumps by clotted blood. Air wheezed in and out of her thin body.

A bloody smear had formed on the wall where Simon leaned his head. Blood still oozed from his crushed nose.

"We will kill him, Mother," Simon promised in the dead quiet of the house. "Her too. We will kill them both."

. . .

The woman in the clothing store approached him warily, as if she realized she'd made a mistake in not calling the police when he first walked into Amy's Clothes Rack.

"May I help you?" she asked, but her tone was as if she'd asked him what in the name of our Lord and Savior Jesus Christ he was doing there. She hadn't seen him pull the Ferrari into a distant corner of the lot. She'd never had a "street person" wander in out of the heat to check out women's apparel before.

"So sorry about my appearance," he said, giving the clerk a Cyclopean stare, one eye still slightly puffed from the beating Jersey had given him. "I'm looking for an outfit for my, um, my daughter."

She looked him over doubtfully. The brute stank. The daughter ploy stank too, always did. "Daughter" translated to girlfriend, and that meant he was cheating on a wife, except this troglodyte could hardly be expected to have either.

"What did you have in mind, exactly?" She wouldn't, couldn't, address him as sir.

"The works. Pants of some kind, I guess. A shirt, bra, panties. Guess you don't sell shoes here, huh?" He gazed around the place.

She frowned. Business wasn't usually conducted this way. The gargoyle added nothing to the ambience of the place, which wasn't all that swank to begin with. It was just as well that this was a typically slow Monday afternoon.

"How old?"

"Huh?"

"Your daughter. How old is she?"

"Eighteen." He wanted to hurry this along, but didn't know how. Suki had told him she'd be all right, but how could he be sure? With dried spit crusted on her chin, she looked like a person on death's doorstep. He had to get her cleaned up and looking presentable, and soon.

"Size?"

"Uh, I don't know."

They never did. Men had some sort of a disease or lacked a critical part of their brain that was able to turn the female figure into the abstraction known as size. Men were so involved with *function*. It wasn't that Eileen Pengelly of Amy's Clothes was a particularly deep or gifted thinker, but she wasn't *unaware*, and she'd seen this kind of thing often enough over the years to have had her awareness congeal into words: men were brutes, period. Glandular heathens who operated on an entirely different plane than women. And now a new and not unexpected bit of information impressed itself on Eileen: street rabble, like the rest of God's ill-bred creations, came without that necessary refinement in the cortical fold.

But they got past that stumbling block with the usual estimates of height and weight and, the brute's face turning a nice plum color—which served him right—a not very useful description of bust size. Eileen had never before dealt with the descriptor "kind of a good handful each," but what could be more functional than that? A good mouthful? She wordlessly translated this mish-mash narrative into a 34B cup. He'd guessed her weight at one twenty, and the gargoyle didn't have particularly big hands, so a 34B seemed likely, although a 34-C was entirely possible. If this guy was in fact a nascent cross-dresser of some kind he was going to be in for a hell of a surprise, since he was a good 46 or 48B. It'd been a while since she'd seen a chest like that on a man. Shoulders too.

Tan pleated slacks, yellow shirt, white cotton panties, white bra. The brute lacked all imagination, but it was only to be expected. What she didn't expect was that so evidently destitute a soul, when presented with a bill for a hundred ten dollars and forty-four cents, would casually reach into one of those grubby voids and produce two hundred-dollar bills that didn't look counterfeit. She took them from a hand on which part of a finger was missing.

Frank saw her hesitate at the sight. He tried to resist, couldn't. "Lost it in a knife fight down Tijuana way," he said. "Nineteen and fifty-eight, it was. Makes it harder to floss."

She looked appalled. "Thank you for your business," she said, handing him his change and the bag. But she still couldn't call him sir and she didn't ask him to come back soon, either.

He walked back to the car. Suki was asleep. She'd wiped her mouth and was looking slightly better. Not a lot, but some. She roused groggily when he opened the door and got in.

"Get me somethin' pretty?" she asked in a whispery voice.

"Christ, I dunno. You tell me."

She had to get dressed before they ran into a cop who might wonder at a naked girl in a Ferrari. Frank found a side street that had been abandoned to the blazing heat. Beyond a tall cinderblock wall covered in graffiti, an apartment complex sweltered in the afternoon sun. Countless air conditioners emitted a restless insectile drone. Frank opened Suki's door and got her sitting with her feet out on the sidewalk. He unwrapped her from the curtain and held it around her loosely as she got out of the car stiffly, painfully, stood, and worked her way into the newly purchased panties.

Two boys, maybe fourteen years old, came rolling toward them on skateboards, going fast, wheels double-clacking on the expansion grooves of the sidewalk.

"Better hurry," Frank suggested.

"Fuck 'em," Suki said, in no mood for modesty. The boys tore on by, catching a brief flash of boob when the curtain slipped, one of the kids saying, "Oh, man, too cool. You see that?" They kept going, though, sent packing by Frank's dark glower.

Suki couldn't hook her bra. She turned her back to Frank and he fumbled with it, got it connected. She hiked up her pants, put arms into sleeves of the shirt, fastened the buttons with trembling fingers.

"Lookin' good," Frank offered.

"Like hell. I feel like a well-dressed stiff."

Frank couldn't argue the point. Her face needed a washcloth and her hair was a wreck.

Suki sank back onto the seat, wincing.

"Can you walk?" Frank asked.

"A little, I guess. Why?"

"We've got to dump this car somewhere soon. It'd draw attention if I had to carry you around afterward though."

"I can walk."

"You sure?"

She managed a tiny reassuring smile. "Yeah."

He drove to Carson Street. Suki asked him to pull into a supermarket parking lot and buy her a gallon jug of drinking water, a comb and brush, a pair of thongs, a sack of sugar, a dishcloth.

"Sugar? What for?"

"I'm hungry, Frank. I'm not really in the mood to answer a bunch of questions, okay?"

"Sure, fine."

Frank bought the items she'd asked for and a few of his own. He sloshed water on the dishcloth for her and she washed her face, rinsed out her mouth, drank some. Frank wet his beard and spread shaving cream on it. Using the rearview mirror, he shaved with a pair of Bic razors, using one until it began to pull, finishing with the second.

"Better," she said, looking at him. "Almost human."

"You too."

"Thanks so much, Mr. Limosin."

"Better just call me Frank."

"Yeah, all right."

As they tooled up Carson Street, she combed out her hair. Frank grew increasingly antsy to ditch the Ferrari.

He passed a Denny's restaurant and turned right at the next side street, went up two blocks, turned right again, parked in front of an old stucco house with a waist-high Cyclone fence protecting a dried-out lawn overrun with weeds.

They got out. Suki opened the bag of sugar with shaking hands. She unscrewed the gas cap, dumped two pounds of C&H into the gas tank.

Frank watched, not bothering to say anything. If there was some quick and easy way to convert the Ferrari into cash, he'd have done it, but his forte was unarmed robbery, not car theft or selling stolen property. He would just get into trouble trying to unload the car in a strange town. At least she hadn't set the sonofabitch on fire.

She capped the tank and poured what was left of the water over the cap and the car's body to wash away all trace of the sugar.

Frank wiped prints from the car as best he could, and left the key in the ignition. He put the German gun in a pocket then steadied Suki as she took faltering steps toward the Denny's. She didn't look too bad though, just a bit hollow around the eyes. Inside the restaurant, she went straight to the ladies' room while Frank called the local Greyhound bus station. Reunited, they sat at a booth in the back. Exhaustion showed in Suki's eyes, but beyond that she was looking almost like her old self again.

"Hungry?" Frank asked.

"Ugh, no. Maybe some tea." Suddenly she looked at him. "Jesus Christ, you forgot to get the money, didn't you?"

"Money?"

She leaned forward. "My *money*, Frank. The three hundred fifty thousand. It was probably there in the house somewhere."

He stared at her. "I was in kind of a hurry, trying to get you out of there."

"Goddammit." Her eyes flashed. "That sick fucker's got all that money again."

"Keep your voice down."

"Shit," she said. "I was rich."

"Now all you've got is your life."

A softer look filled her eyes. "Yeah, thanks. I didn't thank you yet, did I?"

"No hurry. You're still hurting." He leaned back, tired, gestured toward the phones. "Couple of buses a day leave for Vegas. Or Salt Lake City."

"So?"

He gave her a curious look. "Buses go west too, but California doesn't appeal to me right now. In case you forgot, I've got trouble out that way."

"What makes you think I want to go anywhere?"

"Christ, what's that supposed to mean?"

"I'm stayin'. That plain enough?"

He glowered at her. "What for? The money's not worth it. Hell, you couldn't get it anyway."

"It's not the money. It's Mink."

"You *crazy*?"

A fierce, determined, wounded look came over her face. In a low voice she said, "I *screamed*, Frank. He said I would, he *told* me I would, and I made up my mind I'd never give him the satisfaction, but I did anyway because it was so horrible and it hurt so bad I wanted to die. I never thought *anything* could hurt like that. I wanted to *die*, Frank. He was going to kill me like that. If you hadn't come along, I would've died—him watching, listening to me scream. Her too. Charlotte. I can't just walk away from that like nothing happened."

"No one's askin' you to."

"You are. You sure are. If I leave, Mink gets away with it, maybe kills someone like he was gonna kill me. I want to stop him, Frank. I want to hurt him."

"How?"

"I don't know how. I've got to think. Just I know I can't go off somewhere and forget about what he did to me."

"Christ, Suki—"

A waitress came over, slim from the waist up, flat-chested, large butt, with small eyes and stringy, lifeless hair. She cast envious looks at Suki as Frank ordered tea and a toasted cheese sandwich.

After she left, Suki said, "How'd you find me, anyway? I still almost can't believe it."

He gave her a brief account of the dry walk out of the De Bacas, the wild ride with Hooker to Roswell, Lear flight to Reno.

Their waitress arrived with crockery rattling in her pale fingers, left again, mouth pouty. No one would ever look at her the way they looked at Suki.

Frank told Suki how he'd found the neighborhood, how he'd walked the streets for hours before dawn, then into the morning, then seen Danny leave in the Trans Am, return two hours later in the Ferrari.

"I take back anything I ever said about you bein' dumb," Suki said solemnly, dunking her tea bag.

"You said that about me?"

"I think so. Maybe." She sipped her tea and a new spasm took her. Her face drained of color and her body shuddered.

"You all right?"

"I guess. I told you, Frank, that son of a bitch just about killed me. My stomach hurts and my brain still feels all kinda crookedy."

"I'm not surprised."

She wrinkled her nose, gave him a look.

"What?"

"That . . . smell. You don't smell it?"

"It's us. I told you, it's been a bad couple of days for both of us."

"Jesus, I'm surprised they don't throw us out of here."

"I think our waitress'd like to. Look, messing around with this Mink guy is a goddamned lousy idea."

"I know. I'm gonna anyway. I'm too tired to talk about it right now, though. What I really want is a shower. And a place to conk out for a while. I don't feel all that good."

He didn't want to argue about it, not there. Time enough later to talk her out of it. He stood up. "I'll call us a cab, get us a motel room somewhere, away from here."

"A motel room?" She smiled, actually managed to bat her eyes at him. He couldn't believe it—after all she'd been through she could still joke around.

"Jesus," he said, then headed for a pay phone in back.

23

The drop grew larger. It glistened like a wet eye, growing bigger, plumper, heavier . . . until . . .

Thip.

Suki screamed.

Frank came out of bed like a derailing Amtrak, tangled in the sheets. Light from streetlamps filtered through the curtains of the Oasis Motel, room 109. Suki was sitting up, shaking. The scream still lingered in the room.

Frank sat on the edge of her bed and put an arm around her. The Astra was on a nightstand between the two beds.

"You okay?" he asked.

"Yeah. Just a bad dream."

"Musta been a dandy."

"I was back in that house, in the basement, and . . . and ice water was dripping on my stomach again."

"Jesus," Frank murmured.

She turned toward him, put her arms around him. Her hair had a fresh scent, like strawberries. She clung to him for a while, then lifted the blankets and said, "Get in, okay?" She scooted over in the queen-size bed, looking at him. "Please."

He crawled in, wearing only his underwear. She put an arm across his chest and snuggled against him. "Thank you."

"Don't mention it. Gorgeous women are always askin' me to do things like this."

She punched his arm. A minute later she was asleep again, and Frank was left staring at blobs of light crawling over the ceiling as traffic passed by on Carson Street. Suki wasn't wearing anything, not a stitch, but Frank was almost used to that by now. Fanny too.

After ten minutes of meandering, clouded thought, feeling Suki warm against his side, breath soft against his cheek, Frank's breathing slowed and he dropped off too.

• • •

Waking with dawn light at the window, Frank felt Suki's hand wrapped lightly around an erection so stiff it was almost painful, but she wasn't awake yet so he gently extricated himself from her grasp.

She woke up in mid-extraction. Smiled sleepily at him and opened her fist. "I was dreamin' 'bout this giant boa constrictor," she said.

He was fifty-four years old, and he didn't have an answer to that. What Fanny had called it, of all the damnfool things, was his "Henry." "Henry up tonight?" she'd ask when the kids were into their early teens and had eager, questing ears. She sometimes called lovemaking "pokin' Henry," when she was in a frisky mood. Lots of variations on the theme.

"What that is, Frank, is a big snake."

"I know what a goddamn boa constrictor is."

"Hey, look, it's morning already."

"Ten after seven, actually." He swung his legs over the edge of the bed and planted his feet solidly on the floor, fervently wishing that the evidence of his longing for her would subside more quickly than it was.

"I'm starved," Suki said.

"Got no right to be. You haven't eaten in how long now? Day and a half, two days?"

She stuck her tongue out at him and crawled slowly off the end of the bed. She stood with a soulful groan. "God, it's like everything's busted."

Didn't look busted to Frank. She looked good, too good. But she had a red spot on her belly like a rash where the water had drilled her. Dim orange light came through the curtains, enhancing her tan. She slowly arched her back, "ooching" and "aahing" and "eeeping" as she twisted and turned, testing muscles that had been strained to the breaking point by her ordeal. Whatever internal messages her body was sending her, she still looked good to Frank, still looked like an Iowa beauty queen. A whole lot better than yesterday, which wasn't helping him any with his immediate problem.

After a long, lazy shower, she eased into bra and panties, slacks and shirt, pushed her feet into thongs. Frank wore new jeans and a short-sleeve shirt still creased with fold marks where it'd come straight out of a J.C. Penney package. His old clothes were wadded in a dumpster behind the motel.

"Breakfast?" Suki asked.

"After."

"After what?"

"After you tell me yesterday's talk was just talk, that you're not thinking about going after this Mink guy anymore."

Her eyes flashed. "No way."

"Jesus. That's a no-win situation there, you know that?"

"All my life I'll remember what he did to me. I'll never forget it, and you want me to just walk away from it."

"Alive, yes. I want that very much. I'm sorry for being such an asshole about it, though."

"I'm gonna be careful."

"Great. Want to tell me what the big plan is?"

"I haven't got one yet. But I will."

"Even greater."

Tears shone in her eyes. She sat on a bed, hands in her lap. "I want to hurt him, Frank. I want to hurt him like he hurt me. I've *got* to."

"You can't." He sat on the opposite bed, facing her. "Some things just aren't possible."

"Why not?"

"For one thing, you're not crazy. I don't think you've got the stomach for it. At least I hope you don't."

"I've got the stomach."

"You could tie this guy down, torture him, listen to him scream. You could do that?"

She was silent a long moment, looking down at her hands. "If someone else did it to him, I'd be glad. Maybe I wouldn't want to watch or anything, but I'd be glad, just knowin'."

"That's not the same thing as doing, not by a mile."

A tear rolled down her cheek. "Then *what*, Frank? What am I supposed to *do*?"

"Call it a learning experience, move on—"

"No! I can't, I *can't*! Don't you understand? He tried to take me apart. He tried to rip apart my goddamn *brain!*"

She began to sob.

"Hey, Jesus, honey, don't . . ." His words dried up. Don't what? Don't cry? No reason to cry, just 'cause this psychotic son of a bitch tied you down, tortured you, almost killed you.

Damn good reason to get out of town, though. Good reason to keep out of his way in the future, too.

"It didn't happen to you," she said, not looking at him. "It didn't happen to you, so you don't know what it was like."

"Yeah, but, *Jesus*, Suki—"

"I didn't tell you everything. He told me . . . he said he was going to use the heat."

"The heat?"

"Boiling oil, Frank. When I couldn't stand the cold any more, he was going to drip hot oil on me. He said he'd use it when I asked him to, not before. He told me it'd hurt an awful lot more than the water, but that I'd end up begging him for it anyway, just to have a change. I thought I'd never ask for that because that was just *crazy*, but I was about to. I was almost ready. I was going out of my mind. He was going to drip boiling oil on me till I died. He was going to fuckin' *cook* me, Frank. The son of a bitch was going to cook my guts, one drop at a time. How long would I have lasted like that? A day, two? Maybe a whole goddamn *week?* And I was gonna ask for it. That's what he did to me. If you hadn't come along, that's how I was gonna die."

Christ.

Jesus H. Christ.

Mink was a monster, or worse. His mother too. Which made the idea of hauling ass all the more sensible, the sooner the better. Frank told her so.

Suki shook her head. "I can't."

Frank stood up, fished around in his pocket, handed her five twenties and a couple hundreds, turned away.

"What's this for?"

"You're on your own," he said curtly. "You want to play patty-cake with a rabid dog, do it alone. I'm gone."

She raised her eyes, hurt.

He said, "I'm real sorry this creep hurt you so bad, but I've got enough to worry about without going after some homicidal maniac. I wish you luck, though." He opened the door, walked out.

He stood in the early morning sun. The day was still cool, but cloudless. It would be another scorcher. Which damn well figured; this was the goddamned desert.

The door opened behind him. Suki came out and slipped an arm through his.

"Okay, how 'bout we put the police on him, Frank? Turn him in. We could find out stuff about his operation in Reno and when we know enough, we could tell the police, let them handle it. That'd be safe, wouldn't it? Huh?"

"Aw, shit."

• • •

Multi-layered defense. In every city since the Louisville scare the operation had been built around a system of layered defenses.

Take Reno, for example. There was the house, the Citadel, in which Simon and Charlotte lived, and from which the yacks made their calls. It was important to have the men and women who actually made the fraudulent sales pitches in close contact at all times, in the fold. The house had been rented by a Mr. Cyrus Greenwold, acting as a proxy for the New Chance Agency, an aspiring job-placement firm with a newly-acquired business license in Washoe County. Daniel Turpin, Mink's right-hand man, had used the Greenwold ID, just one of a dozen he might have used. A bank of eight phones had been installed by Nevada Bell for the New Chance Agency without anyone raising an eyebrow.

New Chance would generate no revenue, however. The agency was a shell, nothing but a name under which property had been leased and phones installed. Employees of J. Alan Morrow & Associates, a second bogus firm, would actually staff the phones and solicit investors. J. Alan Morrow had been created by the ever-capable Daniel Turpin using the name Frederick W. Lowe. A two-room office in a business complex on East Second Street had been leased to J. Alan Morrow for a period of one year. This was nothing but an address to satisfy banks and other such entities. Other than Turpin's moonfaced visage, no connection whatever existed between J. Alan Morrow & Associates and New Chance. The judicious use of local law firms acting as subagents for the firms rendered the connection even more tenuous.

An apartment was rented in the name of Chester Fine, yet another of Turpin's alter egos. Three blocks off Kietzke Lane in the Woodridge complex, the apartment would be the dropping-off point for a "blind" courier, hired locally, whose only job was to load the contents of six private post office boxes into bags, one for each yack employed by J. Alan Morrow & Associates, and take them to the apartment via a meandering, predetermined route. That the route was not altered might've been a weakness, except that the courier was followed discreetly by Benny, Isaac, and Jersey, each in his own vehicle on a rotating basis to keep the courier from knowing he was being followed, and to ensure that the courier wasn't being followed by a third party, like the police. The courier would make the run on Mondays, Wednesdays, and Fridays at four p.m. If the courier was tailed by anyone, anyone at all, a radio message would be sent, warning a woman by the name of Anna Hoyt to leave the Woodridge apartment immediately, also causing Mink's entire operation to fold up and be on its way out of town within fifteen minutes.

If the courier was clean, the mail, mostly checks made out to J. Alan Morrow, would arrive at the Woodridge apartment and be immediately scanned by the competent Miss Hoyt for electronic bugs that might have found their way into the flow. Upon passing that test, the mail would be taken to the Flint house via another circuitous route, passing again through a similar protective sieve of counter-surveillance by Benny, Isaac, and Jersey. At Flint Street, each piece would be opened and each check thoroughly scrutinized, examined under fluorescent light, and judged valid or invalid. It would then all be sorted, placed into one of ten manila envelopes, and returned to the Woodridge apartment.

The following day, or on Monday, in the case of Friday's take, another locally-hired girl would appear at the Woodridge apartment, pick up the manila envelopes and deliver them to yet another office, leased in the name of Paul R. Kline, civil engineer. The office, however, had no sign out front. It was, in fact, a nameless bin. Its secretary, another local hired by J. Alan Morrow & Associates, knew the name Paul Kline only as the person or entity from whom or from which J. Alan Morrow had sublet the office. Her only job was to answer the phone, turn aside anyone who might appear at Kline's door, read magazines, chew gum, display no imagination whatsoever, nor show any interest in Morrow's affairs, and to lock the office on Monday, Tuesday, and Thursday afternoons to deposit the delivered checks into each of ten accounts maintained by Morrow & Associates at banks all over the city. Her office was bugged. Any slight hint of interest in J. Alan Morrow's business affairs by the girl would result in her immediate dismissal.

Surveillance was maintained at each of these nodes, and during each transition between them. Simon and Charlotte and all the other principals involved monitored radios tuned to a little-used VHF frequency assigned to the U.S. Bureau of Land Management, listening for the single word "Redsnake," which would send them all fleeing to a previously agreed-upon location—a shopping mall in Sacramento, a hundred twenty miles west of Reno.

This scenario, which Mink and Charlotte had developed and refined over the years, was a finely-honed defense. The few strands that led back to the Citadel were tenuous, well-guarded, quickly and easily severed.

And now, the day after Suki and her rescuer made their escape, the defense came into play, without, however, the dreaded code word "Redsnake" being uttered, scattering them like so many leaves in a hurricane. Simon and Charlotte were in a suite at Bally's, Reno's largest and most anonymous hotel-casino, registered as George and Faye Eberhard. Before she left Sherman Oaks, California, and flew with her son to Reno for a long-awaited vacation, Faye had slipped on a wet tile floor and suffered a broken nose, poor thing, but she had decided not to cancel their trip on that account because George so desperately needed to escape the rat race for a while. Faye only told this story once, to a receptionist who feigned interest while typing their personal data into a computer, setting up their account at the hotel, but that was sufficient. No one at Bally's was aware that George Eberhard was otherwise known as Saul Garrick, the founder of New Chance Agency, or that he also had an apartment in Reno on Lakeside Drive, rented in the name of Reid Ferris. This last identity was in fact Simon's "real" identity in Reno, if Simon could be said to have so concrete a thing as an identity. Simon, the "real" Simon, was vapor, as insubstantial as fog. He had a driver's license in the name of Reid Ferris. The new Ferrari, now gone forever, had been purchased in that name.

As Dorothy Ferris, Reid's mother, Charlotte Voorhees was equally vaporous. The address Reid and Dorothy shared, their social security numbers, credit cards, even the modest bank account they held in common, could be used to track these two apparitions only into a gray and featureless void.

The vast web of subterfuge required to create these defenses—the apartment that had to be rented, couriers and secretaries hired, phone services installed, businesses and bank accounts set up—had kept Daniel Turpin hopping in the six weeks prior to Simon and Charlotte's move to Reno. Into each new city, Danny led the parade, Simon and Charlotte following in his wake. Once things were settled, Danny moved on. Next stop was Tampa, Florida, where Simon's traveling minstrel show would bleed retirees who flocked in droves to the comfort and safety of their Sunbelt condos. Danny's loyalty to the Voorheeses, his penchant for intrigue, his boundless energy and organizational acumen, accounted for his salary of $500,000 a year. A mere pittance, in that Simon and Charlotte had grossed something over ten million the previous year and were well on their way to surpassing that total this year. Daniel was due for a raise.

Charlotte stared silently out the west-facing window of their eighteenth-floor suite in Bally's, bony fingers exploring the bandage that covered her nose. Simon phoned the residence of Reid Ferris on Lakeside Drive and punched in the four-digit code to retrieve messages on the apartment's answering machine. There were but two, the first from a drunken woman screaming furiously into the phone, calling him Gus, telling him to get the hell back home *right now* 'cause she *knew* he was with that big-tit floozy again and he was the world's all-time rottenest son'vabish. The second message, considerably less addled, was left by Detective John Shroeder of the Washoe County Sheriff's Department. Shroeder informed Reid that his new Ferrari had been found abandoned in Carson City, blocking traffic on a main street, keys in the ignition, and the car had been towed to the Carson City Police Department's impound yard. And would Mr. Ferris please be so kind as to contact Detective Shroeder concerning the incident at his earliest convenience. The detective left a number.

Well, the Ferrari was a loss anyway, had been from the moment Suki and the guy who'd saved her took off in it. Mink had never even set eyes on it. Lost in that same instant was the Reid Ferris identity. Already Danny was slipping through the bureaucratic underground, creating another "official" identity for Simon, and one for Charlotte. He had a headache from yesterday's events, but seemed otherwise unhurt. A $50,000 bonus had aided his recovery.

Simon left the room, rode an elevator down to the lobby, and called Detective Shroeder on a pay phone. Charlotte was still staring out the window when he returned.

"They went to Carson City," Simon said.

She turned, waiting for more. Stranger, in her own way, than the boy she'd raised.

"Police found the car a few minutes after midnight last night. Lights on, doors open, right in the middle of the main drag. Witnesses said a couple of kids left it there, ran off. The engine was frozen. Sugar in the gas tank."

"Suki's work."

Simon nodded. "Or the old man's. What we may infer from all this is that they ditched the car in Carson, loaded the tank with sugar, and took off. Later, some kids found it and took it for a joyride. Not long into their little adventure the engine seized up." He paused. "Detective John Shroeder would very much appreciate it if Mr. Ferris would come in, file an official report on the stolen car, go through the whole nine yards, and then claim what's left of his vehicle."

Charlotte stared at him.

Simon shrugged. "Reid Ferris no longer exists." He picked up the phone, dialed the Rancho Sierra Motel on West Fourth Street, and asked for room 22.

• • •

Mote lay on the bed nearest the bathroom, shoes off, alleviating his boredom by trying to balance a half-full can of Coors on his forehead. Jersey stared at the television in a catatonic glaze. Some championship bowling tournament somewhere in Ohio on cable TV, this tall skinny dufus in glasses beating the tar out of last week's PBA champ, 209 to 167 in the eighth frame, PBA champ with four spaced strikes and two open-frame seven-ten splits. New skinny-ass champ this week, looked like. Guy's wife up there in the audience, squealing and clapping with every strike, already spending the first-place prize of $35,000, lips bunched up like little rosebuds, eyes bright.

The phone rang. Mote spasmed, drenching the front of his T-shirt with beer. "Shit, man," he yelped, lunging off the bed.

Jersey turned down the tube, picked up the phone. "Jersey."

Mink said, "We've got a lead on the girl."

"Where at?"

"Carson City."

Mote was still cussing. Jersey threw an ashtray at him, clipped him on the jaw with it. He turned away. "Yeah, okay, what d'you want us to do?"

"I want Benny, Isaac, and Mote on the roads south and east of Carson." A pause. A map rustled in the background. "Put Mote on U.S. Fifty, east. Benny and Isaac south, on Fifty west and Three-ninety-five."

"Yeah, sure. What about me?"

"I want you to nose around the bus station down there, talk to taxi drivers, see if you can get a line on where they might have gone."

"Yeah, okay, right away."

"Mrs. Garrick will coordinate the search from the Woodridge apartment. I trust you have the number?"

Jersey closed his eyes. Christ, the Bitch again. "Yeah."

"Make sure the others have it too. And Jersey . . ."

"Yeah?"

"I'll give a bounty of fifty thousand dollars to the man who brings Suki in. Twenty thousand more for that old guy she's with. Pass that along to the others, will you?"

"Sure, okay, Mr. Garrick."

"Get on it." Simon hung up. Kind of like his old lady, but not quite so difficult to talk to. The Bitch had a corncob up her wazoo, no doubt about it.

"That hurt, Jers," Mote said, rubbing his jaw. "Shouldn't throw stuff like that."

"Get your shoes on, bucko. We're rollin'."

24

"Whatcha lookin' for?" Suki asked.

Frank didn't look up. "Somethin' cheap, invisible."

"Invisible?"

"The kind of car you see, but don't see. Something you'd barely notice parked all alone in an empty lot. What we don't want is a goddamned Edsel."

"Edsel? What's that?"

Frank shook his head, ran a finger down a column of the folded newspaper. They sat in a coffee shop in the relative morning quiet of the Carson Horseshoe Club. Suki stared at a lighted board with eighty numbers on it, GAME 87 lit up on its side. A waitress drifted by and topped off Frank's coffee cup. Her eyes snagged momentarily on his missing finger.

"Lawn mower," he said. "Chicago, nineteen and sixty-eight. Damn thing got away from me." The girl smiled uncertainly, moved away.

Suki nudged him. "What's that?"

"What's what?"

"That." She pointed at the lighted board.

"Keno."

"What's that?"

"Gambling game."

"How's it work?"

"DamnifIknow." He pushed the paper over to her, rubbed his eyes. "Here, see if anything strikes your fancy."

She pushed it back. "Very goddamn hilarious."

"Huh?"

"You think that's funny?"

"Do I think what the hell's funny?"

"I can't read, Frank. You gotta know that by now." She looked away.

He stared at her. "You can't?"

"Pretty much."

He didn't know what to say.

"Don't look at me like that. I'm not a bug or anything. I can read 'See Spot run. Run, Spot, run. See Dick ball Jane. Ball Jane, Dick,'— that kinda stuff." Her cheeks were burning with color.

"Look, I didn't mean to—"

"Yeah, I know. It's not your fault." She'd withdrawn into a shell, mouth tight.

Now what? Frank thought. His foot was so far in his mouth he could taste argyle in back of his throat. What could he say? C-R-O-K she'd inscribed on Mink's forehead. Crook. Yeah, hell, he should've known. He should've at least guessed. Christ, up in the De Baca Mountains he'd even offered her a book.

"Look, I'm sorry."

"Sure."

"I should've known. I didn't, but I should've, so I'm sorry, okay?"

The intensity of her silence gave off fumes.

"Okay?"

She gave him a sidelong glance. "Think I'm dumb, right?"

"Nope."

"Well, I'm not."

"Jesus, I just said—"

"I can't read, and I can't change flat tires—well, maybe now I can—and there's lots of other things I can't do, but I'm not dumb, Frank."

"Gotcha."

"Just don't ever forget it."

"Never. Look, there's that goddamn keno board over there. I've seen those things for thirty years and never figured out how they work yet."

"Don't try to make me feel better, Frank. I dropped out of regular school in the sixth grade. They sent me to some kind of special place, but it just didn't work out. There was this old teacher there with gray hair who was always putting his arm around me and squeezing my shoulder in this special reading class, like he was trying to help me. He tried to feel up all the girls, not just me. You could tell he didn't like his job—thought everyone there was a moron. But some of them were smart, like me. Just . . . I don't know. Somehow we got left behind."

"You could take an adult class, learn to read. It's not too late."

"Maybe." She stared off at the keno board again.

He picked up the paper. "How 'bout this? 'Seventy-nine Dodge Omni, great condition, clean. Sunroof, mags, six hundred dollars."

"Mag wheels, sunroof, six hundred? It's a dog. Guy's lyin' like a rug."

"Probably. How about an 'eighty-two Ford Tempo GL, air, clean, thirty-seven fifty?"

She sipped her tea. "You lookin' to spend that much?"

"Guess not." He read another: "Here's a 'seventy-four Chevy Nova, V-six. Eight fifty. A goddamn Nova wouldn't attract attention in a phone booth."

She smiled. It looked good on her. "Pa had a Nova once," she said. "Piss yellow, ma called it. Really attractive color. I can't hardly remember what the darn thing looked like now."

"There, you see? That's what I mean by invisible."

"Go for it then."

He went to a bank of phones, sank a quarter, dialed the number.

An elderly woman answered. "Yeah?"

"About that car, the Nov—"

"Bobbiiiee, it's for you. Bob*biieeeeeeeee*!"

Frank waited, ear throbbing.

A man came on the line, in his forties by the sound of his voice. "Yeah?"

"Still got that Nova for sale?"

"Yep."

"How's it run?"

"Good. Got sixty-two thousand miles on 'er, but she's a runner."

"What color?"

"Christ, I dunno. Kind of a faded yellow. Got practically new tires on 'er though. Goodyears."

"Where're you at?"

"Pleasant Valley. South of Reno, Pagni Lane, just west of the fire station."

"Tell you what, Mr. . . . ."

"Curtis. Bob Curtis."

"I'll give you eleven hundred for it, Bob."

Silence. Then, "I was askin' eight-fifty. What's the deal here?"

"Two things. One, you drive it down to Carson City, be here inside an hour. Two, you leave the plates on it."

"One, I can do. Two, that's against the law."

"Plates are worth an extra two-fifty. You can tell 'em you forgot to take 'em off. They might fine you twenty bucks."

More silence. Then, "How do I find you?"

"Horseshoe Club, downtown. Know where that is?"

"Course. Lived here all my life."

"I'll be around back, holding a newspaper. Hair's kinda gray, short. I run a little on the large side, about two-thirty."

"I'll be there. Thirty minutes, 'bout."

• • •

By noon, Frank and Suki were in Reno, rolling along South Virginia Street in a Chevy Nova the approximate color of a clouded urine specimen. Minor rust damage and a dent in the passenger-side door, scrapes and dings too numerous to count, but its engine was in fair shape, and the transmission, and its seat cushions weren't too far gone. The radio was tuned to a country station, KBUL, FM 98. When Frank started up the car after giving Bob Curtis eleven one-hundred-dollar bills, Hank Williams was blowing the carbon out of his lungs singing "Lovesick Blues."

"Ever been to Reno?" Frank asked.

Suki shook her head. "Not before yesterday."

"So you don't actually know where this house of Mink's is, do you?"

She stared at him for a long moment. "Bet I could find it. Same way you did."

"That's what I'm afraid of. First thing we want to do is find a safe place to hole up. Then we have to quit looking so much like ourselves. Or maybe vice versa on those two."

"Say what?"

"Disguises," Frank said. "Your hair in particular. We have to do something about the way we look."

She frowned. "Maybe *I* could, but how're you gonna hide two hundred and sixty pounds?"

He feigned a hurt look. "Two-thirty, sugar."

She grinned. "Sugar. I like that."

"I'll think of something, about my weight."

"Frank?"

"Yeah?"

"I appreciate all this. Really. It's not something you have to do, and it's costin' money."

"Yeah? Well I still don't know what the hell we're doing here.

There's no goddamn profit in revenge. If things start to go south, I'll probably tie you up, dump you in the trunk, and haul ass. And keep you tied up in some out-of-the-way place till Mink moves on to some other city you don't know about and gets lost for good."

She gave him a big, bright smile. "You care, don't you?"

He looked over at her. "Oh, Jesus Christ."

"No, you really do, huh?"

"Don't go makin' some big deal out of nothin', okay?"

"Mountains out of molehills."

"Huh?"

"What you say is, 'Don't go making mountains out of molehills.' See, I'm not so dumb. Except what you said wasn't a molehill, it was more like . . . like Fuji or something."

"I said I'd tie you the hell up."

"Exactly."

"Might be the best idea I've had since I got out of the army back in fifty-four. A gag might not be a bad idea either."

"It shows you care, Frank. That's the thing." A smug look appeared on her face.

"I'll be goddamned—"

She put a hand on his arm. "Don't let it worry you, okay? Anyway, we *are* looking for a motel or something, aren't we?"

"Aw, Jesus."

•   •   •

"How do I look?" Suki did a turn for him, showing off her new outfit.

"Stunning." Frank sat on a bed in the Shamrock Motel on North Center Street, staring at her.

"Bet you say that to all the dumpy old broads."

"As many as'll listen, sure."

Suki posed for the mirror, fluffing the worn cotton dress they'd found at a Goodwill store for two dollars, tugging on a shoulder. She turned sideways to examine the way the foam rubber pads bulged her midsection, adding forty pounds to her frame and doubling the size of her breasts. The hem of the dress came below mid-calf, revealing five inches of oversized nylon hose that hung in soft, bagging folds around her ankles. Her feet were wedged into lumpy shoes they'd found at the same thrift store on Gentry Way. Dark glasses covered her eyes. She squinted at the mirror and adjusted the short gray René of Paris wig they'd picked up at Bellissima's on First Street, near the downtown casino area.

"How old you think I look?" she asked, whirling.

"Ninety-five, thereabouts."

"Seriously."

"Seriously, seventy, maybe seventy-five from a distance. Senile, too, with that hose squirreled down around your ankles like that. Just don't let anyone get a close look at your face or hands."

"Wait'll I lump on some pancake foundation, lighten my face, rub a little too much rouge on my cheeks, and put some eye shadow under my eyes. You won't recognize me."

"I don't now."

"I mean, it'll make me look even older."

"Hop to it. We've still got things to do today."

"In a minute. This isn't right." She unzipped the back of her dress, shrugged it off and let it fall to the carpet. She stood there in bra and panties and some kind of ugly spandex thing hacked off at the top and bottom, packed with foam rubber around her middle. "It itches," she said.

"Looks like it would."

She adjusted the foam, retied a tie, bent stiffly and pulled up her dress.

"Zip a girl up?" she said.

"A dotty old broad, you mean."

"Whatever I am, yeah. Hop to it."

He stood with difficulty, zipped her up, caught a glimpse of himself in the mirror. He stopped, fascinated at the sight of an old duffer staring back at him, totally bald, glasses with black frames, blue suit way out of style but who gave a shit? Not the old duffer. Gray suspenders. Weight about three-fifty, with all the foam padding. If you couldn't get smaller, the only thing left was to get bigger. He looked bloated, an oil drum with arms and legs. Still had good-sized shoulders, but they didn't dominate the way they had before.

Suki rubbed the top of his head. "Miss the fuzz?"

"Yeah. Feels drafty up there."

"Well, you look like such an old sweetheart without it. Harmless, too. Probly feed pigeons in the park." She stood on tiptoe, pulled his head over, kissed him squarely in the middle of his naked dome.

"Shit," he said.

• • •

"Looks deserted," Suki said, disappointed.

"Looked that way when you were in the basement screaming, too."

"*Jesus, Frank!*"

He turned to her. "I just don't want you to forget what kind of dangerous slime you're screwing around with here."

"I know what Mink and his mother are."

"Good. Keep it in mind, huh?" He pushed a soiled homburg back a few inches on his head.

They were parked on Ridge Street in front of an architect's office, just west of the intersection of Ridge and Flint. From there they had an oblique view of the clapboard mansion, cooking in the heat. Sweat formed on Frank's brow. He mopped it away.

"Think they got scared, took off?" Suki asked.

"Don't talk to anyone either. Your voice doesn't jibe with your wrinkles."

"I'll try to remember. So, what do you think?"

"About what?"

She stared at him. "Christ, you gone senile too, Frank? Think they've run off?"

"Who knows? I would've. Maybe."

"Maybe?"

"From what you told me, this is a very expensive operation he's got goin' here. I guess he'd want to keep it going if he could."

"That's what I thought. Mink wouldn't want to run. He's not the type to—"

"Uh-oh."

"What? Oh, Jesus, Frank."

A taxi had pulled up and stopped in front of the old house. A man and woman got out. The man was slender; the woman was reed-thin with red hair.

"Jesus God," Suki said, voice quivering. "It's them."

"Okay, okay, calm down."

The two went up the walk, opened the front door, went inside. The taxi rolled away.

Suki trembled, staring at the old mansion.

"Guess that answers that," Frank said. "So, okay, here, remember this number. Eight four four, seven one one seven."

"What's that?"

"Real estate broker."

"Huh? Why?"

"Forgot the number already, haven't you?"

She hadn't. She reeled it off to him.

"Good," he said. "Old bat's short-term memory is still intact, anyway." He fired up the engine and pulled away.

• • •

"Meyer and Dunn Realty," said the voice.

"Yeah," Frank said. "I'm interested in that property on Ridge Street. You got a sign out front. Two-story red brick job, wisteria all over the front porch, trim needs paint."

"I'll connect you with Mrs. Meyer. Who may I say is calling, please?"

"Mr. Steven Wiley."

"Thank you. Please hold." Frank got a muted earful of George Gershwin's "I Got Plenty of Nuthin'."

"What'd they say?" Suki asked.

He clamped a hand over the mouthpiece. "I'm on hold. And old broads don't chew gum. At least they don't snap it like that. Swallow a denture, end up in a rest home somewhere, brain damaged."

She grinned, snapped her gum again. "You think?"

"This is Gloria Meyer, Mr. Wiley. How may I help you?"

"I'm interested in that place over on Ridge—"

"Oh, yes. The Pratt place. Beautiful, isn't it?"

"Guess it could be."

A brief pause to regroup. "Well, yes. It could use a little exterior work, but that's really a minor—"

"What I was wondering, is it available for rent or lease?"

"Yeeeess." She seemed hesitant. "In a manner of speaking. Depending on the use one intends to make of it."

"How's it zoned?"

"That's quite a complex question, Mr. Wiley. It's never been a place of business, so for business use the house may be grandfathered in under the old R-five zoning, which was multi-family dwelling and offices. R-five's been superseded, however—"

"But it's available for residential use?"

"Yeeeeess. However the owner is primarily interested in selling the property, not maintaining it as a rental. Therefore, no long-term lease is possible, and it isn't—"

"Wife and I wouldn't be needing a long-term deal."

"Well, in that case, it's possible something can be worked out."

"We'd like to look it over today," Frank said. "If that could be arranged."

"I've got . . . well, I suppose I could fit you in in, say, half an hour. Either that or tomorrow afternoon sometime."

"Half an hour would be dandy."

"Well, then, I'll see you at the property, Mr. Wiley."

"Bring papers," Frank said. "We might work something out this afternoon."

"Is there a reason for all this hurry, Mr. Wiley?"

"Yeah, the wife needs a nap."

Silence.

"Kidding," Frank said. "The wife and I just like old places, and the area, that's all. We've had enough of hotels."

•   •   •

Inside, the place was reasonably clean. Hardwood floors, a few scatter rugs here and there, no furniture. Casement windows with several cracked panes. Fireplace with a huge walnut mantel. The kitchen had a big double sink, expansive white tile counters, a view of a fenced yard and more flowering wisteria. Catalpa trees with long curving pods rustled in a breeze. Fragrant honeysuckle grew rampant up one side of the house. A basement, four bedrooms, three baths with old fixtures, big open living room. The place was dusty, battered and worn, but comfortable in spite of its wounds, filled with a palpable sense of history.

Frank stumped through the house on a cane, leaning on it heavily. Suki stayed in the background, looking out windows, fingering the curtains, stoop-shouldered, quiet, faking a little dumb-ass limp.

A window in one of the rear bedrooms gave a view of the front and south side of the clapboard mansion on Flint Street. Suki stood staring at the place for a long time. Dotty old broad.

Two thousand two hundred twenty-two dollars a month, Mrs. Meyer told them. Price not negotiable, so said the owner, Helen Pratt, an eccentric old biddy without a businesslike bone in her body, who wanted not a penny more than $2,222 a month, and not a penny less. Something to do with what a Tarot card reader had told her eight months ago, which had made it almost impossible to rent or sell the place. Purchase price would be $222,222, if they were interested.

$2,222. Frank tried not to wince. "Fine," he said in the grainy old voice he was cultivating. "We'll take it."

"I'll need the first month's rent in advance, and a fifty percent security deposit."

"Fine."

Gloria Meyer filled out a boilerplate rental agreement and gave Frank a startled look at the sight of the payment in cash. She handed Steven Wiley a receipt for $3333.00, a set of keys, and drove off in a charcoal-gray Mercedes 300E before the day had begun to cool off appreciably. The time was 4:16 p.m.

"Bought you a house," Frank groused, turning to Suki.

She gave his cheek a kiss that left a red smudge. "Treat me so good, snookie. Told you you were an old sweetheart, didn't I?"

"Shit," he said. "*Snookie?*"

25

Two birds with one stone. Simon found the economy of action agreeable.

He sat in the first-class section of United flight 516, bound for JFK airport in New York City with an hour layover in Denver, looking out at the dry brown mountains of Nevada as the 727 rolled along the taxiway toward the north end of the runway. Turn. Spool up, down. Then up again, and the big plane leapt forward, pressing him into the seat. Twenty-five seconds later, at a hundred twenty miles an hour, the wheels bumped off the runway and they were up. Reno sprawled below in the hot afternoon sun, the carcass of an eviscerated beast with its arteries and nerves exposed as it decayed in the heat.

Bird one: a freebie. Reid Ferris was on his way out of Reno. If the Ferrari investigation went anywhere at all, it would go to New York and turn to vapor. A Mr. Carl Sullivan would return, and Sullivan and Ferris had nothing whatever in common, including the airlines on which they traveled.

Bird two was the actual reason for the trip: cash was needed. Though the flight east was necessary, it was little hardship. Viewing his diamonds always gave Simon great pleasure. Five safe-deposit boxes in five banks under five assumed names. Forty-one million dollars in diamonds sat in those five boxes, discounting gains in the diamond market in the time since the stones had been purchased. Forty-five million was a conservative estimate of their present worth.

Soon they would have enough. Simon smiled, closed his eyes.

Enough for what? And what was enough? A pleasant, circular dyad to ponder, the basis for an absorbing soliloquy to while away a few unburdened minutes.

The French Riviera, Rio, Macao. No, too common. Skiing the Hohe Tauern in Austria, perhaps. Sampling twelve-year-olds in the more enlightened districts of Berlin. Yes, certainly. But what could be better than a quartet of *ten*-year-olds in the rackety, squalid depths of Katmandu, or a similar quartet of goatherder's offspring in the Tibetan city of Qagcaka? Or a minor death or two, here and there—something slow, exotic, unique. The world was an infinite playground for one with imagination, a fondness for experimentation, and the resources to indulge them. Wealth was the universal standard by which men were truly judged. Money, not character, was the key that flung open the world's doors. How much, though, was enough?

Ten-year-olds in Katmandu. A tremor ran through him at the thought. Perhaps another year, if that. He wasn't getting any younger. There was a time for all things, and Katmandu and Qagcaka were the songs of Lorelei in his blood.

Suki, though.

The reverie broke. Suki first. Suki was a loose cannon. She might still be dangerous. For safety's sake they needed money, a generous reserve of ready cash. Danny would soon leave for Florida to set up the Tampa operation. That would take a bundle. Fifty thousand to whoever brought Suki in; another twenty thousand if that old guy was captured too. Mink would need a new car, and the Reno operation might never bring in a dime. Moving expenses, new identities, money for bribes.

Trouble, really. That was all Suki had ever brought him. So they needed cash, and almost all of their money was tied up in diamonds. Mink had to go to New York even though his heart, his *soul*, was in Reno, hunting Suki.

But he'd be back in just over twenty-four hours. It'd be nice if Jersey and the others had captured her by then.

Because then . . .

Thip.

Suki screamed, muscles tearing . . .

Thip.

Screamed again, louder, voice shattering . . .

Thip.

And her mind was cracking, shrieks rupturing the tissues of her throat, entreating God, screaming at Him, which was a joke because there was no God, was no God, was no God, because if there was, if there was a capital-H Him, loving, benevolent and kind, how did one explain Simon Voorhees?

· · ·

Now what? Jersey thought.

The bus station hadn't panned out. Dinky little place, and the ticket girl at the counter hadn't seen anyone like Suki or that big old son of a bitch she was with.

Taxis had come through for him, though. But what the hell did you do with it? This old fart, must've been sixty years old, said he'd driven this older guy and a girl with nice tits and white-blond hair from a Denny's restaurant on Carson Street to a motel in the southern part of town, the Oasis Motel. That was yesterday, about four in the afternoon, maybe five.

So, okay, Jersey'd even taken the same cab, same driver, Denny's to the Oasis, gotten out, paid the $4.25, and what had it gotten him? Squat, that's what.

Owner of the Oasis remembered them, but so what? Room 109. How could you forget a sweet little piece like Suki, and with a guy who could be her father, too? Even showed Jersey the room for five bucks. Nothing. Maid had cleaned up, and Jersey'd even talked to her, chunky little rag pusher, used the Oasis guy to help cut through her Mex, and you think she'd know anything? Fuck no. What, you kiddin'?

No one even saw them leave the place.

Okay, then he'd gotten lucky. And so what? Found this *other* taxi driver, girl with braids and acne scars, couldn't've been over twenty-four, said she took them from a gas station a block or two from the Oasis just that morning to the middle of town, left them off on a corner, right by the Carson Nugget, biggest gambling place in town. Good. Think they'd go in?

Hell no. Had to go into the goddamn Horseshoe Club up the street, which cost Jersey another hour, tracking them down. But he'd done it, managed to get hold of some skinny waitress who was going off duty, no boobs, pretty good legs though, pale as new ice, and she'd said, yeah, they were in that morning, saw 'em leave but she didn't see which way or how, or where.

And that was it. Dead cold trail after that. A glacier was what it'd become. They walked out of the club and wandered right off the edge of the world. He'd been good, he'd even been lucky, and what it all amounted to was shit.

"Tell me."

Fuck you all to hell and that tell-me shit, too. "It's Jersey. Ma'am."

"Yes, Jersey."

He told her what he'd done, what he'd found. Nothing.

"What does all that suggest to you, Jersey?"

That they didn't want to walk anywhere. That they got hungry and sleepy, just like other folks. "I don't know."

"Does it suggest to you that they aren't in a big hurry to leave the area, Jersey?"

"Maybe." Yeah, that'd sorta been bugging him. Way back in his mind, of course, but yeah. It was him, he'd've had that friggin' Ferrari screaming through Nebraska by now.

"It may mean they're still around. You've done very well so far, Jersey. Will you keep digging a while longer?"

Like she was giving him a choice. Oh, shit, yeah, Mrs. Voorhees. I'd like nothing better. "Yes, ma'am."

"Now listen carefully to me Jersey. Are you lis—"

Jersey whacked the phone against the wall.

"Christ, Jersey! What was that?"

"Dropped the phone, Mrs. Vo—Gar*rick*. Sorry."

She coughed, roiling a gummy wad of phlegm in her throat. "Are you listening *very* carefully to me, Jersey?"

"Yes, ma'am."

"I'm going to send Mote down to help you. I want you to tell me exactly where he can meet you."

Jersey made arrangements. Mote would be a big fuckin' help down here. Mote had the same capacity for intelligent and creative thought as a moth batting itself against a porch light. He'd be one whopping big goddamn help, yessiree. Send 'im on down.

She hung up. No preamble, just *click*.

Fuck all this chase-after-Suki shit, Jersey thought. He went into a bar downtown, ordered a Wild Turkey, double, and chased that with another, and one more. Lots of money for Wild Turkey, and the dough wasn't even his, either.

Job had to be worth something, right?

26

The lady at the county clerk's office in Reno, fictitious business names division, had a decidedly equine mien, one of those long, thin faces with a stretched jaw. Kind of like a starved Clydesdale, Frank thought, not intending to be unkind. An unfortunate masculine face with mule's eyes, horn-rimmed bifocals hanging from her neck on a chain of beaded glass. Wisps of gray at her temples. Flat-chested. Gnarled fingers tipped with synthetic heliotrope nails.

You'd think this stolid guardian of the portal of public inquiry would delight in rolling out a carpet of red tape, revel in trotting out every roadblock available to the superintendent of records of a bloated bureaucracy, relish the all-encompassing "No," point one of those crooked phalanges toward the door and say, "Try corporations, downstairs," where another vassal of the administrative merry-go-round would, with secret joy, continue the process ad infinitum.

But, not so, not so.

What she wanted was to please Steven Wiley. Evident in every gesture she made, every word she spoke, was that Miss Evelyn Snoke—*Miss*, not Ms. or Mrs.—wanted to please the portly Steven Wiley in every possible way, such ministrations to include whatever a delicate reddening of the Morgan features might imply.

Her eyes strayed, landed on his finger. "Meat cleaver," he offered with a faint apology. "Connecticut, nineteen and fifty-five. Sold it for one twenty-nine a pound. Used to be a butcher, in my younger days."

"Oh, my," Miss Snoke said, mouth twitching in an indecisive smile. "Does it hurt?

"Not in twenty-five years and more," he assured her. "Although I frequently anticipate rain. What I wonder, Evelyn—if I may be permitted to call you Evelyn?"

But of course. But of *course*. And nothing would do but that she should call him Steven. And lean a little closer on the counter, the better to serve him.

"What I'm wondering, Evelyn, is how a person might obtain a

list of businesses that have been granted licenses to operate in the city or county in the past two months."

"Yes," she said. "I mean, that's quite simple, really. Are you certain you mean *all* businesses though? There's no specific one you have in mind? That *would* be simpler." And she did so want to be helpful.

"No, nothing specific. A general listing of some kind is what I'm after. Might that be arranged?"

"Of course, Steven." Her mule eyes searched his face. "Are you in business, then?"

"Thinking of it."

"Would it be, ah, prying to ask what kind of business?"

"Finance," he said vaguely. "Investments."

Another little flare of interest behind those dobbin eyes. She tapped several keys on a computer terminal on the counter, waited a few seconds, tapped a bit more, waited, asked, "What dates are you interested in again?"

"Let's say, middle of May until the first week of July. Something like that."

Tap. Taptaptaptap. Frank turned, looked toward the door, saw Suki lurking about, stoop-shouldered and gimpy. He waved her off, turned back toward Evelyn and her taptapping.

"Oh, my," she said. "There's been one hundred sixty-two licenses issued in that time. Are you sure you want a listing of them all?"

"Quite sure," Frank said, and Evelyn taptapped, and in a room behind her a dot matrix printer sprang into action like a forty-pound mosquito. A few minutes later it stopped. Evelyn smiled at Frank and went into the room, came back a moment later carrying a folded sheaf of computer paper with track holes along the sides.

She consulted her computer screen and said, "There's a six dollar and eighty cent charge for this, Steven, but I imagine I could . . . that is, I'm sure I could just—"

"Certainly not," Frank said. He dug seven dollars out of his wallet, waited as she opened a drawer and handed him two dimes change. He tucked the printout under an arm, took his cane in the other, and said, "You've been most helpful, Evelyn. Many thanks."

She wanted to do more, clearly she did, but, alas, it was not to be. Frank stumped toward the door, gave her one last smile before leaving, then went out.

"What'd you get?" Suki asked on the sidewalk.

"Jesus, you sound about eighteen years old, Mrs. Wiley."

"Sorry. No one's listening though. What'd you get in there? Get her phone number?"

"Thought she was going to stamp it on my hand, but no."

"So, what *did* you get?"

"Keys, roadmaps, ciphers, secrets. Let's go home, have a look."

· · ·

On a secondhand mattress in an upper bedroom of the "Pratt" place they had spread a couple of sleeping bags, zipped together at Suki's insistence. A card table and two folding chairs were in a corner, beneath one of the ugliest floor lamps Frank had ever seen. Such was the sum total of their furniture in the house.

A Tasco eighty-millimeter refracting telescope stood on a tripod in the southeast corner of the bedroom, aimed at the Voorheeses's mansion; so much power that they could just about see the mesh of the window screens over there. Too much power, so they used a low-power eyepiece, forty times magnification, supplementing it with 7x40 Zeiss binoculars.

Suki slipped out of her dress and the spandex iron maiden into something more comfortable in the heat: shorts and another little bandeau, this one black, not much different than the outfit she'd been wearing up in the De Bacas. She kept her face on, however, in case they had to go out with little notice. Frank found the contrast between her face and figure a bit disconcerting.

He opened the printout on the card table and sat down, still in his blimp suit, sans coat. The gun was on the table, close at hand. He flipped through pages idly to get a sense of what he'd paid $6.80 for while Suki stared at Mink's mansion, first through the binoculars, then with the Tasco.

"Nothing," she said.

"When it comes, it'll come fast, be over in an instant."

"When what comes?"

"Whatever. Someone comin' or goin'. These people aren't the types to stand around gabbing on their front lawn."

"You got that right. This's boring, though."

"So I've heard. Over and over."

She made a face at him. "How's that look over there?"

Frank started on page one. Entries were in chronological order, beginning on May sixteenth.

"Clair's Donut Shoppe," he read. "Got a lot of other information here too, but that's the business name."

"Not Mink's style, that one."

"Didn't think so. How about Northern Nevada Urologic?"

"What's a urologic?"

"Piss doctor."

"No way."

"Joyner Automotive?"

"It's gotta sound *financial*, Frank. Got anything with 'Associates' or 'Investment Group' or 'Ventures' in it?"

His finger slowly traversed the page. "How 'bout this? Ranier and Son Marketing."

"Could be. Better mark it."

A pause. "Wheeler, Sloan, and Dietrich. CPA outfit."

"I dunno, maybe. They weren't ever CPAs though."

"I'll flag it anyway. How about J. Alan Morrow and Associates?"

"Mark it."

"New Chance Agency."

"What's that?"

"Job placement service of some kind."

"Don't think so."

Pause. "Strauser Investments."

"See, you're catchin' on."

"Thanks, kiddo."

In half an hour he had nineteen possibles, another twelve maybes. The house was dim, quiet, airless, hot. Musty, too.

"How're you doing?" he asked.

"Bad. Bored silly. Nothin's happening."

"Put your good dress on, Tilly. We're goin' dancin'."

She stared at him. "What?"

"I'm done here. Let's start checking out a few of these places, see what we come up with."

It was the only way he could see to unravel Mink's organization. Get a little poop here, a dram of information there, scrounge around until the weight of evidence seemed like enough to send to the district attorney's office—anonymously. That might be a catch, anonymity, but Frank thought they could get around that by writing a reasonably literate letter explaining that if the DA didn't follow up on it and nail these jokers, the office might find itself up a creek, especially if the information was also sent to the local newspaper. They could tell the DA about Mink's other operations too, where and when. Tell them they had a real tiger by the tail this time if they wanted it, make the DA look good in the next election, get them some national exposure.

Might work, might not. It was a crapshoot, same as everything else in life, except without a big payoff, other than Suki's peace of mind. At times, Frank wondered what he was doing, staying mixed up in her problems like this. But he didn't wonder for long, didn't probe too deeply, because somewhere in those depths he might find an answer waiting to bite him. Hard to get past the fact that she was still only eighteen. *And* curvy and beautiful.

So he watched as Suki popped out of her bandeau, pulled on her baggy nylons, then wrestled into the bodice, wriggled into the gray-green dress, adjusted her wig, and pushed her feet into the old black shoes. She looked at him with a senile simper on her face.

"Terrific," he said. "A real classy dame."

"Sweet-talker. See what it gets ya."

They went outside, into the furnace of the day. The garage stood at the side of the house. He swung open the doors, backed the car out, shoved the car door open for Tilly. She got in, moving stiffly, seventy-odd years old.

Two things were certain: first, she made one godawful strange-looking old broad; and second, until they had at least the name of Simon's latest operation, they had nothing. Nothing at all.

•   •   •

Ranier & Son Marketing was five guys in suits and a couple of harried secretaries. A going concern, complete with bills and ulcers.

Wheeler, Sloan, and Dietrich were CPAs, all women; Gail, Kathy, and Celeste. They looked a little hungry when he and Suki walked into their office, eager, but their desks weren't empty and a computer was humming on each desk, so Frank thought it unlikely that they were starving. They seemed serious enough, businesslike, subtly aggressive in their neatly tailored suits.

On to J. Alan Morrow & Associates, over on East Second Street. A weedy-looking row of offices in a dismal green stucco building, dark windows facing an asphalt parking lot that shimmered in the heat. The parking area looked like a tar pit, potentially lethal, but Frank pulled the Nova up in a slot anyway. Got out with Suki and looked for suite seven. The gun was in a pocket; no telling what they might run into, fooling around like this.

Suite seven was right next to six, which figured, but it was locked up tight and no sign was out front or on the door. Frank stuck his nose to the glass, cupped his hands around his eyes and peered inside. The room was dark. An empty expanse of beige carpet, blank walls, stray wires snaking across the floor. A cardboard box stood against one wall.

"Nothing," Frank said, backing away.

"So it's a possible."

"Yeah, I guess. Not sure how, though."

"How about we ask around?"

Frank shrugged. "Give it a try." He went to the door of the next suite over, careful to use his cane and move slowly, like he really was carrying around that extra hundred pounds.

On the door of suite six Frank saw: DAVE YBARRA, M.S.E.E., M.B.A., B.S. COMP SCI. He tried the door. It was locked, but a few seconds later it rattled, opened, and a sallow man, obese, twenty-eight years old, with tiny features in the middle of a large face peered out. His forehead was a great curved dome, pale and smooth as glass. His belly hung well over his belt.

"Yes?"

Frank pointed. "I was wondering about your neighbor next door in suite seven. Thought I'd find J. Alan Morrow over there."

"C'mon in. Too hot outside."

Ybarra ushered them into his cave, piled high with boxes labeled cryptically, a long table that held old computer parts, slippery stacks of glossy computer magazines on the floor. Dishevelment, disorder, dirt. Clutter, confusion, chaos. McDonald's bags, Burger King detritus, Wendy's cups, smoke in the air and butts in a cheap ashtray that served only as a target, having long since overflowed. Something purple had congealed on the carpet in a corner, like raspberry epoxy.

Ybarra stuck out a pudgy white hand. "Dave. Computer nerd."

Frank shook the hand. "Steve Wiley. Computer illiterate."

Dave the Programmer grinned. "That's what keeps me in Fritos." He dropped into a chair, jiggled unhealthily. Before him was an amber screen, filled with indecipherable gibberish. A pair of jogging shoes were rotting on his feet. His shirttail was pulled out.

"So, you're wonderin' 'bout my neighbor?" He picked up a Bonnie Hubbard orange juice can with a spoon in it. He held it up, grinned. "Lunch," he said. "Whole months' worth of vitamin C." The concentrate was slush, still half frozen.

"Yeah. J. Alan Morrow. You know 'em?"

"Nope. Whadda they do?"

"Not sure, exactly. I was hoping to find out. I find myself in need of an investment counselor."

"Wish I could say the same." Ybarra peered past Frank at Suki, who was looking as senile as ever, not saying a word. "Sorry I can't help you, though. Don't think they've moved in yet, next door."

"No one's been around?"

"Not that I've seen."

Dead end, as he'd thought. Frank couldn't think of anything else to ask. "Well, thanks anyway," he said.

"Hey, no problem. You get a monster in your software, I'm the man who can help. Dave Ybarra. Spread the word."

Frank and Suki went outside.

"Still a possible," she said.

"Yeah, but we don't know, one way or the other."

•   •   •

"Now where'd that sonuvabuck go?" Ybarra asked, pursing his lips. Asked himself because there wasn't anyone else to ask, but it was good to have someone to talk things over with and you always had yourself. Never really alone, because you were always there with yourself. Computer logic, he'd found, had elements in common with masturbation. He was a good listener—when he was the one talking. Never knew one better; couldn't ask for more reliable company—

"Ah-hah! There you are. Two hundred bucks, right there." He pulled a Post-it off the side of an empty file cabinet, which had been stuck there along with a patchwork of other Post-its. The cabinet was empty because he could never find time to organize it, or anything else. One of the reasons Crista'd left him, but only one of dozens. Too many things Crista wanted, so what was the point in dealing with any of 'em?

He dialed the first number.

It rang.

Rang and rang and rang. "Out to lunch, Davey boy. Everyone's out to lunch."

He took another bite of slushy orange juice, spiking his blood sugar, and dialed the alternate number. It rang and rang and—

"Tell me."

Dave stared at the phone, scrunched his eyebrows. *Tell me?* What was that supposed to mean? Took him a moment to finally say "Peachtree," like he'd been told. Just that one word. Stupid, James Bondian, but that guy with the granny glasses said do it and—

"Mr. Ybarra?"

Hey, it worked. Old broad knew his name and everything. "Yeah," he said. "That's me."

"You have some information for me?"

"I guess. I mean, I just had a visit, some people lookin' for that Morrow outfit next door."

"What did these people look like, Mr. Ybarra?"

Her voice was a rasp. Harsh and to the point. This was one old termagant he didn't want calling him by his first name. Mr. Ybarra was just fine, forget Dave. "Some old guy, bald, run well over three hundred pounds, and an old lady, his wife or mother or something."

"How tall was the woman?"

"Kinda tall. 'Bout as tall as the guy. Five-seven, five-eight, something like that. Kinda stooped-looking."

"They're not still there, are they?"

"No. They drove off."

"What kind of a car were they driving, Mr. Ybarra?"

"Chevy Nova, kinda old and beat-up. Pale yellow. License seven seven three, XVN, five."

"You're sure about the license?"

"Yeah. The guy who told me to call you said I should try to get a license if anyone came nosing around."

"Describe the woman further, please."

"Well, she didn't say anything. Just let the old guy do all the talking. Gray hair, old dress, walked with kind of a limp. Wore dark glasses. Oh, and her nylons didn't fit. Hung down around her ankles, kinda."

"Did that seem at all strange to you, Mr. Ybarra?"

"Christ, you oughta see my grandmoth—A little, yeah, but I've seen 'em like that before, they get old, start losin' it."

"What color dress?"

"Dishwater, old soup. Kinda gray-green. It was old."

"Did you get a look at her hands?"

What was this? "No. She stayed behind the old guy pretty much."

"And him, what was he like?"

Big, bald, old, round, Dave told the woman. Used a cane. Blue suit, suspenders, some sort of old hat, maybe a derby.

"You've been most helpful, Mr. Ybarra."

"This guy told me I'd get two hundred—"

"That will be taken care of within the hour, Mr. Ybarra. In the meantime, will you please continue to keep an eye out?"

"Yeah, sure."

Click.

For a moment Dave the Programmer sat staring at the receiver in his hand, then he set it back in its cradle.

Weird, he thought. World was a weird damn place, fulla weirdos.

Like himself, he thought happily, and went back to spooning melted orange juice concentrate into his mouth.

27

The phone rang.

"Tell me," Charlotte said.

Jersey reported in, telling the Dragon-Bitch he hadn't found anything more yet and—

"Listen carefully to me, Jersey," she broke in. "Are you list—"

Crack!

Damn that clumsy oaf! *"Jersey!"*

"Yes, ma'am?"

"Do you have a firm grip on the phone now, Jersey?"

"Yes, ma'am."

"And in addition to that firm grip, are you listening *very* carefully to me, Jersey?"

"Yes, ma'am."

"The girl is here in Reno. I just found out—never mind how, it isn't important. The important thing is for you and Mote to get up here immediately. Is that perfectly clear?"

"Yes, ma'am."

She stubbed out a cigarette. "I've already told Benny and Isaac. They phoned in from Bridgeport half an hour ago. What I want is for you to come to the house. Is that understood?"

"Yes, ma'am."

She hung up. Whirled, just as her mind seemed to whirl, and pressed her bony fingers unconsciously to the splint that had replaced the bandage and the intranasal packing. The girl was still in Reno. Who would have thought the creature was so witless? Who would *ever* have guessed?

And, of course, that could mean only one thing, only one. Simon would be so pleased.

She phoned for a taxi, wiped the receiver and anything else she might have touched, took one final look around before locking up the apartment. This place would never be used as an intermediate drop for the money as intended. There would be no money now, not from Reno, not with the girl still around. Ybarra's phone call had effectively terminated the Reno operation.

Simon was due back at 6:17 p.m., not quite two hours from then. Fidgeting, waiting for the taxi to arrive, Charlotte lit up yet another Vantage cigarette with her gold Dunhill lighter.

•   •   •

"How much money you got?" Isaac asked.

"I dunno," Benny said. "Couple grand, I guess. Why?"

"I've got 'bout the same." Actually, he had a good deal more than that, nearly six thousand, but Benny had no idea he had that much, and Isaac was no fool. He squinted at the road thoughtfully, back in the direction of Reno.

"So?" Benny said.

"So, we've got wheels and a little bread. What say we split?"

"What for?"

"I've had enough of this shit, haven't you? Anyway, it's gettin' bad. You don't feel it? Some guy comes in, beats the shit outta Mink. Thought nobody could do that."

"The guy had a gun, Izzy."

"That's Mink's story. You believe everything Mink tells you? Anyway, it don't matter. What I'm thinkin' is maybe now's a good time to get out, go on down L.A. way."

"Money's been good," Benny said, conviction ebbing away like a Bay of Fundy tide. Benny was never one to stand firm in a breeze.

"Been good, yeah. How much longer, though?"

Benny shrugged.

Isaac said, "These people're *crazy*, Ben. No tellin' what they'll do next. Time to move on, check out the action elsewhere."

Benny shrugged again. "You want, I'm in. We gonna call the Dragon, let 'er know?"

"Christ. What d'you think?"

They got in the Malibu and took off, headed south instead of north. L.A. was just seven hours away. Good town, L.A., if you had money. And, Isaac reflected, it shouldn't take him long to figure out a way to get Benny's cash away from him and strike out on his own.

•   •   •

Mink knew diamonds. It didn't make sense not to know what you were dealing with when you had forty million invested in so subtle a commodity, when the smallest flaw or discoloration could mean thousands of dollars, even hundreds of thousands in a big rock.

But he hadn't thought that the VVS1 8.17-carat marquise would bring in as much as it had, or that Manny Herrmann would locate a buyer for such a stone so quickly. Manny was one of the best in New York City, however. His contacts in the market were like the root system of a giant sequoia. His partner, a thin, blind Jew named Hillel Weiss, spent virtually his entire existence on the phone in a back corner. The instrument was like an excrescence of his ear. Questions never ran to the personal with Manny; transactions were invariably hassle free. If they hadn't been, Simon would have taken his business elsewhere. Duane Chafee, Simon's alter ego during his dealings with the diamond broker, was not a minor player in the market.

Simon had been looking to turn an even million, but he would have settled for as little as nine hundred thousand—sorting through stones in the four-to-six-carat range lacked the precision of summing bank notes. But Hillel Weiss had made one phone call, just one, and twenty minutes later the big marquise had gone for a pleasantly ridiculous price.

Now Mink was sitting in a Deluxe cab on his way to the Flint Street house with $1,640,000 in a small suitcase on his lap. All hundred-dollar bills, some new, most old, just under forty pounds of paper. With Manny, there was never a problem with cash. Manny shuffled a third of a billion dollars' worth of diamonds a year. He could look at a diamond, four and a half carats, and in ten seconds, no more than twenty, say something like "Fifty-two five," then go on to the next. But he'd paused appreciatively at the sight of the big marquise for just a moment, a connoisseur transfixed by the stone's cold beauty. In no time at all, he had a firm offer of $1,125,000 by the Boston broker of a Mrs. Pendergast. On the transaction, Manny took $28,125, two and a half percent. The rest had ended up in Simon's briefcase, along with what Manny had given him for the rest of the stones.

The taxi pulled up at the Citadel and Simon got out, paid the driver, tipped him two dollars, and went into the house.

"She's here," Charlotte said. "In Reno."

A peculiar glow filled Simon's eyes. "Where?"

"Around, darling. Around. Mr. Ybarra phoned. It appears that the little fool is prying into our affairs."

"Tell me everything."

• • •

She told him everything, which wasn't much and which was all the world. Suki was nosing around with this guy she'd picked up somewhere in Texas or New Mexico, the same guy Jersey had kicked the crap out of up in the hills, so the old guy could take quite a bit of punishment and seemed unusually resourceful, all things considered. Amazing how he'd found Suki out here in Reno, and so quickly, too. It told Mink something about the man. That he'd bothered told Mink even more.

Yellow Chevy Nova, complete with license number. Suki now wore a gray wig and had been seen in a drab green dress. The old guy was bald, and very fat. Which would be a disguise, of course.

"You know why she's doing this?" Charlotte said.

"She's trying to find out what she can about our operation. She hopes to make trouble, and even though she cannot, she doesn't know that yet."

"Mote and Jersey are back. Benny and Isaac aren't. It's been over five hours. They may be gone."

Mink stood at an upstairs window, looking down at the street through a partly-open curtain. "Perhaps. It's happened before. I feel her out there, Mother. I *sense* her, don't you? Don't *you?*" His hands hung quietly at his sides.

"Yes, darling."

"She's close. So very close."

• • •

"I see him," Suki said, unaware that she was whispering. "Jesus, Frank, it's like he's right here in the room."

She had the Tasco on sixty power. Simon, a hundred twenty yards away, appeared to be six feet away, like he could reach out and grab her. The slanting afternoon sunlight cast shadows across his face.

"Trade you," Frank said.

He handed her the binoculars, then bent over the telescope and brought the image into focus. "Doesn't look much like a homicidal maniac, does he?"

"Not at first."

"Makes our job a little harder, though."

"I still want him, Frank."

"Yeah, I know."

• • •

Dressed only in an *orosu*, Mink danced. Now fast, now slow, always in control, always with perfect balance, feet in perfect contact with the basement floor. The *orosu*, a Japanese thong similar to the *mawashi* worn by Sumo wrestlers, was a coarse white cotton cloth that looped between his legs and tied at the waist, clothing his crotch while leaving his buttocks exposed, his movements free.

He lashed out with a foot, landed in a defensive crouch that was utterly without motion, wiry, unassailable.

"She knows about this house," Charlotte said, watching Mink unwind from his trip. "She will come around, don't you think?"

"If she's doing what we think she is, yes. Inevitably. The old guy was here. Even now, they may be watching the place."

"Jersey has a new car. And a haircut and a suit, off the rack, of course, but the fool looks surprisingly presentable. I've given him instructions to patrol the neighborhood and watch for a yellow Nova, or an old man and a woman matching their descriptions."

Mink's body twisted slowly on the floor, his shadow following, fingers curled into a kind of wedge. "I hope his car is something less visible this time."

"A Buick Century, I believe. Several years old. I told him never to bring it here to the house."

A blur of sudden motion. Mink's fingers stopped a quarter inch from the light bulb. His body was arched, muscles etched.

"Good," he said.

"Even so, she knows him. If she sees him driving around the neighborhood dressed like that, she might guess that we're on to her."

"We need someone new."

"A precaution I've already considered, darling. Danny is seeking a suitable replacement to take over Jersey's task."

"When that's done, I want to talk to Jersey. And Danny. I have one final job for him before he leaves for Tampa. And I want the yacks to come in tomorrow, Mother. If Suki is watching, we must keep up appearances."

"I'll see that it's done."

"Where's Mote?" A lunge, a deadly flurry of hands, then an elbow driven into an imagined face, driving shattered bone into a brain, followed by stillness, evaluation.

"Driving around the city, looking. I thought it best to keep him occupied, and even a fool may have luck. He reports in every few hours. I trust even Mote is capable of identifying a yellow Nova and checking license plates."

"Presumably, though it might strain his limits."

"How much longer will you be, dear?"

"Several hours. New York is still with me. It clings."

She turned away.

When she left him, he was standing on the toes of one foot, the other foot fully six and a half feet off the floor, hands held in a praying mantis position in front of his body.

28

The following day, Thursday, Suki looked out the window with binoculars. "There goes Mote again," she said. "In the Toronado. Keeps comin' and goin'. I wonder where Jersey is."

"My, aren't you a pretty sight?" Frank said, hitching up his pants, hooking up the suspenders.

She was dumpy, gray, busty, half-senile again. She followed the Toronado with the binoculars until it went around a corner, then she turned and smiled, face larded with pancake and rouge.

"Really know how to talk it up to the ladies, don'tcha?"

"Comes naturally. Words just bubble up. You gonna put on shoes, or are you adding a new dimension to your act?"

"Damn things hurt, Frank."

"Can't do much about it here. Let's get movin', huh."

"I'm coming, I'm coming." She paused, tilted her head and looked at him. "Funny. I said the same thing last night, didn't I?"

"Aw, Jesus."

She smiled. "When your face gets all red like that, so does that shiny bowling ball head of yours, you know that?"

"Bowling ball?"

"Uh-huh."

"C'mon," he said grumpily. "Crawford and Bell Securities is next on the list. Let's get to it."

• • •

The Century could move all right, not like the Toronado but it was okay. The Toronado could just get up and haul ass, which is what this road called for, but the Century just sort of rolled along the empty highway through the hot empty desert, which is what cars did in the hands of little frosty-haired old ladies, but was barely enough to keep Darby Etchemendy, otherwise known as Jersey, awake.

Etchemendy was bad enough, but *Darby*? The name was a bad joke, the name of a great-grandfather who owned a drygoods store up in Vermont, back in the day when a name like Darby wasn't automatic grounds for a fistfight. He'd been running from that name ever since the fourth grade. So he'd called himself Jersey. Grew up . . . where else? . . . in Newark. He hadn't been in New Jersey in ten years.

It was billed as "The Loneliest Highway in America," Highway 50 was. Not until you got east of Fallon, though. Until then it was just a flat and roomy run. East of Fallon, east of Frenchman, really, was where you started to learn what Highway 50 was all about. The ribbon of baked asphalt cut through a sun-charred expanse of grayish barren wasteland. Thirty-six empty miles beyond Frenchman was Cold Spring, which had been named by someone hallucinating as the sun vulcanized significant parts of his brain. Another forty-nine empty miles to Austin, quaint and useless, then fifty-six even emptier miles to Eureka.

Jersey got a sandwich and a beer at Eureka. Then another beer, and another, then backtracked a couple of miles to the junction of 50 and 278, turned north, then found that all that talk about Highway 50 was bullshit because here was 278, eighty-eight miles of molten desolation that made 50 look good by comparison, and if your car failed you here, Jackson, you were outta luck.

Jersey got out the topographical maps he'd purchased at Ken's Mountaineering off Mill Street in Reno. All those contour lines— Mote'd think it was a game, maybe a maze, see if you could figure how to get Fido back into his doghouse.

Mink had asked Jersey to find him a place where people rarely go, someplace so remote that you could fire a howitzer and no one would hear a thing.

You want desert or trees or what? Jersey'd asked.

Mink said he wanted desert, someplace hot.

Out-of-the-way-hot, Jersey'd said, and Mink had commended him on his perceptiveness.

Well, just look at the map. West was nothing. West was trees and California, all that mess. South wasn't any good, not if you wanted real desert, open empty desert. That left north and east, and north wasn't all that bad, really, once you got past Nixon, and it got even better once you got past Gerlach, but when some stretch of highway is dubbed "The Loneliest Highway in America" by *Life* magazine, you just had to pay attention.

But *then*, look up north of Eureka, at the Sulphur Spring Range, right next to that big alkali flat. That had to be lonely. That had to be seriously out-of-the-way hot.

Was, too. Thirty-two miles up that road and all you could see was nothing at all. A grim and airless drive on the face of the moon. Tinderbox, sage, yarrow and gumweed, rocks and rocks and rocks.

Up ahead, a kind of pass looped over a low ridge. At the top, a barely-visible dirt track wandered along the ridge and dropped out of sight. Jersey slowed the car, stopped dead right in the middle of the road, and who gave a shit? Road was as empty as the Sahara for miles in either direction.

He backed up, turned off 278, took the Buick along the ridge and down a slope, headed east. Path didn't look as if it'd been used in twenty years, but the desert changes slowly and it didn't matter if it'd been forty years since anyone had been down this way, the trail would still remain. Down around the back of a low hill, along a flat, up over another rise, a low place between hills of the Sulphur Spring Range, down again, and there was the southern tip of that alkali flat, a vast, hot, colorless plain. Desolate hot, too.

Jersey stopped the car at the edge of the flat, leery of the sand. Get stuck here and you'd walk out. He'd had his fill of that in New Mexico. Get stuck here and maybe if you were lucky the crows and bugs wouldn't strip your carcass on that road back there before someone came along. Why anyone would want to drive from Eureka to Carlin was beyond him. Why anyone would want to end up at either of those places was another mystery.

Scary place, this.

So empty. Like you were the last one left on a planet razed by nuclear holocaust and you were gonna die because there wasn't any food or water left and this was it, man, just this glassy scoured emptiness and a bunch of bugs waiting for you to drop so they could strip your bones.

No breeze, no nothing. The air was so hot and still that Jersey imagined himself standing in one place and suffocating in his own personal cloud of carbon dioxide.

Howitzer, hell. You could set off a small atomic bomb here and not disturb jack shit.

He located the alkali flat on the map, judged his position in relation to the hills, and marked an X where he stood. He got back in the car and damn near couldn't figure out how to get back to the highway again. Panic popped and sizzled in his head as he lost the trail, found it, lost it again. An hour later, with the smell of newly-splintered sage thick in the air around the alkali-crusted Buick, Route 278 appeared ahead. Jersey gazed back at the dusty rolling hills.

It was everything Mink wanted, and more. Jersey found he didn't even want to know why Mink wanted such a place.

Some things were better not to know.

•   •   •

William Kohler & Associates was a bust. Bill Kohler himself was a dapper man in his fifties, five foot two, enormous eyebrows, big ears, as tireless and full of energy as a bumble bee. His associates, an eclectic crew of three, were in the business of buying and selling mortgages, working off commissions with some outfit back east.

"Where now?" Suki asked, looking wilted. Her pancake seemed about to melt right off her face.

"Argosy Planning Group," Frank said. "Financial planners of some kind."

"Super."

"How about we get something to eat, first?"

"Fine, anything. You pick a place, okay? I'm dead."

The streets threw off an acrid smell of softening asphalt in the heat. Road construction had made traversing the city an adventure. Major thoroughfares had been cut down to single lanes in which traffic moved sluggishly past black stinking machines that roared and sprayed foul-smelling oil.

They'd learned to avoid Kietzke Lane whenever possible, but Kietzke was home to many of the city's fast-food places, so Frank turned off Mill onto Death Row, as he and Suki now called it, and crawled southward, headed for a Burger King he'd seen earlier.

•   •   •

What to do? What to *do*?

Mote's fingers were sweaty on the wheel. Salt stung his eyes.

What would Jersey do, huh? If Jersey was here he could tell him, but—shit! Did that make sense? If Jersey was here, Mote wouldn't . . . uh, wouldn't hafta ask, 'cause Jersey'd just do whatever he was gonna do, right?

But do *what*?

Mote shut down the engine. He sat in the oven-like Toronado in a parking lot behind a Chevron station across Kietzke Lane from the Burger King where that yellow Nova had gone in, just a few minutes ago.

They hadn't seen him. Couldn'ta seen him, because he was just comin' out of Vassar Street when they turned into the BK. So he'd turned right onto Kietzke while they parked, come back around into the parking lot of that fish food place and went behind the Chevron station, and here he was.

Maybe it was them. This old fat dude and a broad got out, went into the BK. Old folks. They moved old too. Reminded Mote of his grandfolks, back about ten years ago.

Mink had said they looked old now, but, shit, *that* old?

Green dress. Yeah, Mink said Suki might be wearing an old kinda green dress. Said the old guy was bald, but the guy over there'd been wearing a hat, so how was he supposed to know if the guy was bald or not?

Still. Might be them anyway, even with the hat.

At the thought of that fifty thousand bucks Mink said he'd give to anyone who found Suki, Mote's hands grew damp.

Jesus.

Fifty *Kay*, Jersey'd called it. Why he called it Kay, Mote didn't have any goddamn idea. Grand, he understood. Fifty big ones, fifty thousand. But fifty *Kay*?

Now what? Jesus.

Dimly, he perceived that he could call the house, get Mink on over here. Except he wasn't really all that sure exactly where he was, didn't think he could tell Mink how to get here. Besides, Mink might not get here in time. And, just as dimly, he perceived that following the yellow Nova in his air-scooped Toronado might not work out real good either. All it would take is a quick look in the rearview mirror and, poof, they'd be gone. Suki had sat in the Toronado all the way from New Mexico.

What to do?

They hadn't come out yet. Good. Maybe they'd sit there a while and eat.

But what to fuckin' *do*?

He flexed his arm, admired the way his muscles bulged, the way his veins popped up, just like Arnold's . . .

Didn't help though. Didn't help at *all*.

He felt panic building. He had to get out of the car, had to do *something*.

He got out and stood there looking around. Wheels. Had to have wheels. Had to follow Suki when she left the BK, and couldn't do it in the Olds. Thing was too loud an', an' . . .

Wheels. Where?

Kietzke was clogged, smelly, hot. Traffic moving slow. He could just rip some door open, yank some pencil-neck asshole out into the street, take his wheels. Like in the movies.

No, couldn't.

And here came along a taxi. Some old broad in back, mouth flappin' like crazy, but it gave Mote something he'd had only rarely before in his life and that was an idea, an actual, honest-to-god idea.

He waited at the intersection, using a telephone pole to shield himself from the windows of the BK. Waited as the light changed, turned red on Kietzke, green on Vassar, and traffic began to pile up.

Mote ran across Vassar Street against the light and began walking south on Kietzke, looking into cars. Guy in a big brown Caddy, no good. Two broads and five kids in a station wagon, no good. Pickup with three Mexicans, no good at *all*. A teenage kid in an old Toyota junker, and that was good, that was just about perfect.

He knocked on the window. Kid cut him a look, pimply little pinhead sitting there in his air-conditioning and loud music, stereo worth more than the car. Mote could hear it beating at the windows.

The kid ignored him.

"Hey!"

The kid inched the car forward, but there was no place to go.

Another idea. Mote got money out of his wallet. He had lots of money. He got out three hundreds, pounded on the window again and held the money up.

The music faded. The window slid down an inch.

"Yeah, man, what you want?" the kid asked.

"I need a ride, bad."

The kid stared at the money, licked his lips. "Where to?"

"I gotta follow this car.'

"What car?"

"Over in the BK over there."

"The what?"

Kid was an idiot. "The BK. Y'know, the Burger King 'cross the street."

The traffic began to move.

"What for?" the kid asked. The Mexicans up ahead began to roll.

"You want the money or not?" Mote shouted. "This here's a lotta money, dude." The car behind them honked.

The kid reached over, unlocked the door. Mote hopped in and the Toyota leapt forward.

The kid looked at him, at his muscles. Mote smiled. He liked it when people looked at him like that, like they were scared of what he might do, knew they couldn't keep him from hurting them if he wanted to. It's what he liked best. He flexed an arm, made a muscle for the kid.

"What car?" the kid asked, nervous now.

"In the BK over there. Yellow Nova, kinda beat up."

"Okay, I see it."

But there wasn't any way to get over there, not with the street torn all to shit and graders pushing gravel in the next lane over, so the kid hugged the Mexicans' bumper up to Automotive Way, then tore around the block back to Vassar, stopped at the light.

"How much you gonna give me?" the kid asked.

Now Mote wasn't sure. Three hundred? Did he want to give the kid all that? But he wanted the pinhead to stay interested and he wanted him to do it right, follow the Nova carefully, not lose Suki or anything.

"Tell you what," he said, handing over one of the bills. "I'll give you a hunnerd now. You stay behind the Nova as long as it takes, till I say, an' don't lose 'em an' don't let 'em see you followin', an' I'll give you two hunnerd more."

"These guy's you're after, they drive fast or what?"

"Prob'ly not. They're just old folks."

"What're you, like some kinda private eye or something?"

Mote liked that idea, liked it a lot. "Yeah, that's right. Like Mannix on TV," he said. "You ever see Mannix?"

"Never heard of it."

Figured. Figured, the pinhead wouldn't know Mannix. Mote was thirty-three. He'd been fuckin' *raised* on Mannix. Mannix was the best, him and Peggy.

The light changed. The kid drove straight across, bumped over Kietzke's torn-up cattle track and slipped into the parking lot of the Carl's Jr. roast beef place on the corner, right next to the BK, parked beside a big green dumpster. Mote peered around the dumpster, saw the Nova still sitting there, baking in the heat. Thank Jesus.

"I was goin' to my buddy's house," the kid said, a whine edging into his voice.

"He gonna give you three hunnerd bucks?"

"Uh, no."

"Now you're gonna make some easy money. Which'd you rather

do?"

Kid didn't answer.

Pinhead.

• • •

By 3:48, Danny Turpin was on a United Flight to San Francisco with $225,000 in his bag. Good, untraceable cash. In Turpin's line of work it wasn't advisable to leave a paper trail. Cash was clean, especially when you had your choice of a dozen aliases. If William G. Ridgeway's plan, Bold $troke, ever came to fruition, they'd be out of business—fast. But there was blessed little chance of that. Right-wingers'd all scream bloody murder about some communist plot, Ku Klux Klan'd dynamite the White House, and the Mafia would blow away half of Congress.

From Frisco he'd go to Atlanta, then catch a flight to Tampa. In a month, possibly a little more, Tampa would be ready for Mink and the yacks to move in, begin making money again. Too bad the Reno thing hadn't worked out. He'd done some of his best work in Reno.

Last order of business before he left was buying that nice little Jamboree motor home for Mink. He'd paid cash, a stack of hundreds, $42,575.28, bought it at Camino Camper in the name of Carl Sullivan, Mink's latest Reno identity. Mink didn't say why he wanted it, just that he wanted a nice one, comfortable, but not too big.

Other than unloading bank accounts, you never really had to shut a town down. When you took off you just looked in all the closets, real and metaphorical, then hauled ass. Like he was doing now. Catch a plane or get in your car and go, let the rental properties, leases, post office boxes, bank accounts, and all the bureaucratic bullshit sort itself out. It always did, one way or another, although at times Danny imagined the municipal wheels locking up and tossing dozens of pale drones through the municipal windshield.

One thing Danny didn't do was think too long or hard about the sounds that had come out of the basement of that big old house. Do that and you might feel sort of bad, and if you got to feeling too bad you could end up blowing half a million a year doing something about it. Mink had his life and Danny had his. If Danny didn't approve . . . well, he wasn't paid to do that. His job description didn't include approving or disapproving of anything Mink did.

He was just the setup man, nothing more, flying off to Tampa to set things up. Again.

29

"Jesus," Mote said. "Lookit that."

"Look at what?" the kid asked.

"No, don't stop!" Mote yelled. "Keep on goin'!"

The kid gunned it and the Toyota shot down Ridge Street, past Flint.

"Go 'round the block," Mote said. "Go on past where they just went in. Fast."

The kid, Rick Bonoli, did as he was told, and they raced south on Hill, back around to Arlington, then up Ridge again.

The old guy and the old woman—Mote still couldn't see her as Suki—were just going into a house on the corner. The yellow car was nowhere in sight.

"Okay," Mote said. "Take me back to where we first met an' I'll give you the rest of the money."

He didn't want to, knew he could scare the crap out of the kid easy, but he gave him the two bills anyway when they got back to Kietzke and Vassar. All the thinking he'd done that day had stimulated a mostly-dormant part of his brain, made him craftier, and the idea occurred to him, still dimly but there, that if he cheated the kid the kid might come nosing around the house Suki and the guy had gone in, and Mink might not be happy if he did that. So Rick drove off rich and Mote got back in the Toronado and made his way across town to the Citadel. First thing the Bitch said when he walked in was, "Where've you *been*, Mote? It's been hours since you last reported in." Her and Mink both standing there, looking at him. And Mote, heart pounding, said, "I found 'em, Mink. I found Suki."

The two just stared at him.

· · ·

It was frustrating in the extreme. There was the house over there—the Citadel, Mink called it—and still she and Frank didn't know the name of Mink's business, didn't have much of anything they could go to the district attorney with. The yacks had all come in that morning, casually dressed young men and women that Suki knew from Louisiana and before, but it wasn't likely that money had come in yet and that crimes had been committed, nothing prosecutable, so this cat-and-mouse game would have to continue a while longer.

J. Alan Morrow & Associates and Silver Sage Investment Group were currently the two most likely choices for Mink's phony business in Reno. She and Frank still hadn't checked them all out. Tomorrow was Saturday, though, so they could rest a couple of days, even if they didn't really want to.

Suki lay on her back on the sleeping bag, wearing nothing but panties, the sticky layer of pancake freshly scrubbed from her face.

She could feel the house over there, Mink and Charlotte roaming its hallway, Mink doing that scary killing dance of his, all silent and controlled, breaking imaginary bones. More than that, though, she could feel the malevolence of his spirit, like noxious gas venting from a bloated corpse. The devil had his implements, and Mink was one of his worst.

Maybe this wasn't so smart, like Frank said, staying here in Reno, but what else could she do?

Frank wandered into the room. "Cheer up."

"Who says I'm not cheerful."

"Your face."

"What's to be all cheery about?"

"You're young, alive, beautiful. That's not so bad. Once this is over, you've got your whole life ahead of you."

She rose up on an elbow. "Doin' what?"

"Doing whatever." He sat down at the card table, began to flip through the computer printout again.

"What about you, Frank?"

"I've got my own load to haul."

"That trucker talk?" She sat up. "Why'd you do it? You never said. I can't imagine you ripping off a whole truck like that. I can't imagine you stealing anything."

"It's sort of complicated."

"We've got time. Tell me."

He sighed. "You really want to hear?"

"Yeah, and I really need a shower, too. How 'bout we do both? Together."

"Christ, give my old heart a break, huh?"

"C'mon." She stood up, long muscles rippling in the washed-out light coming through the curtained windows. She took his hand and pulled him toward the door. "You're not that frail."

"Who says?"

"Me." She stepped out of her panties. "*I* say."

•   •   •

Mote pointed out the window. "That house, right over there."

"Are you sure, Mote?" Charlotte asked, eyes narrow. "Are you very, *very* sure?"

"Sure, I'm sure. I followed 'em like, I dunno, three hours. Got a look at their license up close lotsa times. Seven seven three-XVN-five. I seen 'em park at that house there, seen 'em go inside an' everything."

"It has a certain daring logic," Mink said, and Mote gave him a hopeful look, not at all sure what 'daring logic' meant.

"Of course it does," Charlotte agreed. "But there simply cannot be any mistake about this, Simon. None at all."

"So bold," Mink said softly. "So wonderfully angry."

Charlotte drew on her cigarette. "So foolish," she said, the words riding a cloud of smoke.

Mink turned to Mote. "You did very well today."

"Do I get that, uh, that fifty Kay?"

"What we'll do is check out the house. If Suki is there, you'll get the money."

"I found *him* too, din't I? That guy? I get the money for him too, like you said?"

"Yes, Mote," Mink said. "If he's there, you get the money for him too. Now why don't you go back to the motel, take a shower and a nap or something?"

"Uh, I hadta give that kid three hunnerd bucks."

Mink peeled off five hundred dollars and gave it to him. Mote left, humming happily.

"It's coming together," Mink said. "It's happening."

"As we knew it would, in time," Charlotte responded, lighting a new Vantage from the butt of the old. "But what I find incredible is that Mote, of all people, found her. Do you really intend to give that—that hopeless *churl*, seventy thousand dollars?"

"He's had his moment in the sun, Mother. I rather think not."

"I positively shudder to think what that dimwit would do with so much money."

Jersey knocked on the back door and came in, interrupting them. "That Mote I seen leavin'?" he asked.

"Yes," Mink said. "Did you find us a place?"

"The best." Jersey spread a map on a table and explained the dotted lines and the X, told Mink what it looked like out there, 288 miles east of Reno.

It was good, Mink saw. It was very, very good.

•   •   •

"I knew this secretary at J. K. Lomax," Frank said. "JKL, on the sides of the trucks. We called the company 'Jeckle'."

"Yeah? Just how well'd you know this secretary?" Suki lathered his chest, giving him one of those smiles of hers.

"Not *that* well, kiddo. And you don't have to do that. I'm perfectly capable of washing myself."

"I want to. That all right? So you knew this secretary at this Jeckle company. That's pretty exciting, Frank. What happened after that?"

He squinted at her. Water drummed on his shoulders. Suki stood eye to eye with him in the big shower stall, one of the finer features of the house, caressing him with soapy hands.

"Nell Henderson. Guess her name must've been Eleanor or something. Anyway, she's about sixty years old and what you might call a bit hippy, maybe more than just hippy, always into chocolates and whatever else moved through the office."

"What you're sayin' is, you weren't interested."

"Nell was one of the good ones," Frank said. "Still is, I guess. Always pleasant to be around, good-humored. Anyway, she's got an inside track on just about everything that goes on in the place and she doesn't always agree with the way they do business."

"What? They're crooked?" Her hands drifted lower.

"Uh, no. Not to their customers. They turn out a good product. What they sometimes do though, is they lay off employees who're older, like me, people who're getting close to having their retirement vested. I didn't start working for Lomax until about five years ago."

"Is it legal, them doin' that?"

"No, but legal considerations have never stopped crooks yet. At JKL, what happens is they fire you for something that doesn't have anything to do with your age. In my case, Nell said a dock foreman by the name of Tug Winders was all set to testify that I'd knowingly signed a manifest for a long load."

"What's that?"

A truckload of stock bigger than what shows on the shipping manifest. In my case, long by some forty-six hundred dollars."

"So you could sell the extra somewhere, right?"

"That's the general idea."

"Did you?"

"Hell no. Tell you what did happen though, four or five months back. I caught Winders—*oof!*"

Suki smiled. He was aroused and she'd jangled his circuits with firm, slippery hands.

"Jesus," he said.

"You were sayin'?"

"Winders," he said hoarsely.

"What about Winders, Frank?"

"Christ, girl!"

"We're havin' a lot of trouble gettin' this Winders thing out." She crouched and began lathering his legs. He took a deep breath.

"I got to work late one day. Car battery was dead when I headed out that morning. I went out on the loading dock at midmorning and didn't see anyone, so I went around back and caught Winders loading this box into the back of a pickup. Standard small inside diameter bearings—I could tell from the box. Driver looked nervous as hell, but Winders just calmly told me to go on back to the dispatch office and he'd be with me in a minute. When he got back his eyes had a look in them, like what did I think I'd seen and how much did I know and was I likely to say anything. That kind of look.

"He was stealing, of course. Must've been seven, eight thousand dollars' worth of bearings. Four months later the son of a bitch was gonna accuse *me* of taking off with a long load. He was covering up his thefts by putting them off on others. No doubt he could back it up with paperwork—dock and weight records, everything. Winder's a sly sonofabitch."

Suki stood up, handed him the soap. "Here, make yourself useful. I got these tits need scrubbin'."

"Aw, Jesus."

"Sorry to put you out, Frank. Get busy, huh."

He lathered her up and began working on her boobs.

"Slow down, Frank. I'm not a car. Go slowly, okay? Take your time." She pushed her chest out at him.

She was soft and firm, pliable, nipples hard. She threw her head back, eyes closed. "That's nice," she breathed. "Don't stop. So, there was that Winders thing goin' on."

"Well, yeah. Uh, so Nell took me aside one day, said she'd heard these two front-office guys talking, said they were gonna can me. She told me they were gonna pink-notice me in two weeks. The bastards weren't going to accuse me of anything, just let me go quietly. She said it was a rotten deal, that she didn't believe for one minute I'd done what they said I did and it sure was funny that they didn't do it right off, if they were so certain I'd stolen from the company.

"But of course they knew I hadn't. Just that by getting rid of me before I was vested, the bottom line would look a little better for the management types—are you listening to any of this?" Her nipples were like pebbles against his palms. Her eyes were still closed.

"Sure, Frank. Just don't stop, okay?"

"Jesus. Anyway, that's why I did it. Wasn't right, I know, but Fanny was dead and I was all alone, kids grown up, if you could call 'em that, and these college boys in the offices with the windows and carpet and golf trophies were about to trash what little retirement I'd managed to accumulate at Lomax. I've been stepped on before, but never by such cowardly slime, so I decided to fix up my own damn retirement."

"You coulda gone to prison, Frank." Her eyes were still closed, face relaxed and drifting.

"Maybe it wasn't the brightest thing I've ever done, but I didn't want to fight it in court. It would've taken years, and there wasn't anything to fight anyway. They would've said they fired me for stealing. Can't fight that. Like fighting vapor, just these suited slimes hiding behind walnut desks. I was a liability to them, a greasy trucker who had a few years of hauling left in him and then years of bleeding them, drawing his pension.

"So Nell told me what they were up to, and I started visiting a bunch of these sleazy places, bars mostly, and—"

Suki pressed herself against him, moving slowly, soap making their bodies slick. "Um-hmm," she said.

"Christ . . . an' I talked to this one scroungy character who put me in touch with another one who knew this guy who was willing to deal."

Suki gently bit his ear.

"Girl, you're lookin' to get roughed up some."

"Uh-huh. Might be what I want. Last I heard, you were gettin' in touch with some scroungy characters."

"Actually, I'm having trouble getting air in my lungs."

"Sweet talker."

Frank took a deep breath. "Guy told me if I delivered a truck he'd give me two thousand bucks plus ten percent of the manifest value of the small general-purpose bearings and three percent on the special-order stuff. Hard to unload turbine bearings for anything like their true value. The guy said he'd have to go through some other guy he knew, everyone gettin' a cut.

"Anyway, me an' this other driver were on a run up to a big distribution center in Sacramento. I'd been on trips with him before. Cliff Tabert, young guy, just twenty-six, probably never in his life got to shower like this with a girl like you."

"That's tough."

"Yeah. We stopped at a truck stop just outside Bakersfield, a hundred or so miles out of L.A., went in for coffee. I told Cliff I was going to the head, then slipped out, got back in the truck and took off west, through Greenacres then up north to Shafter where this other guy was waiting for me. Drove the rig into a big shed south of town and we figured out what he owed me according to the manifest. Then I caught a bus to L.A. and another one out to Palmdale, just in case, bought the truck and the camper and headed east."

"To New Mexico."

"Yeah."

"Lucky for me. I'd probably still be stuck out there if you hadn't come along."

"Probably." He didn't tell her what she'd look like if she'd been out there another three days.

"We clean enough now, you think?" she asked.

"For what?"

She smiled. "What d'you think? I'm all worked up."

"Aw, Jesus."

"And afterward I want dinner, Frank. A real dinner somewhere. I'm hungry."

"Christ."

30

This was where they would come out, if they came out at all—a door at the side of the house near the unattached garage, just off the kitchen. If they were out, this is the way they would come in.

Night had fallen. Mink stood in the shadow of a big Spartan juniper, twelve feet tall, dressed in a BDU SWAT uniform, a flat-black cotton utility suit with a martial-arts look to it that blended invisibly with the darkness. Black T-shirt, bare feet. Around his waist was an Airborne belt with a buckle that was also a three-inch carbon steel knife. Several lengths of black nylon cord were in his pockets.

Lights were on in the house. Several upstairs windows were pale luminous rectangles. No sound came from inside.

Were they inside? Would they come out?

Questions that had no relevance, quests for certainty that might be asked by someone in the Western world. Questions that grasped at assurance, that denied *inevitability*.

If they came out, he would take them here. If they stayed inside, he would take them there. Either way he would take them. The where and when didn't matter, so the question had no meaning.

Very Zen, it was.

Spider's mind. Empty, patient, asleep-alert.

Waiting for the inevitable.

Waiting.

Waiting.

• • •

"C'mon," she said. "Get up."

"I'm whupped."

"I know. I whupped you. But now I'm hungry and you oughta respect that."

"I'm having trouble breathing, much less respecting."

She pulled him to a sitting position on the sleeping bags. It's that bald head of yours, isn't it? Makes you think you're old."

"I *am* old," he groaned. "Somethin' you don't get."

"Bull-oney." She pulled harder, got him standing upright. She was wearing panties, still topless.

"Is that English?"

"Sorta. We'll begin with your shorts. It's kinda like changing a tire. A bunch of little tasks. Do 'em all in the right order, don't leave any out, and you're dressed. Here, put these on. Legs go through these holes here. Okay, now the other leg. Real good, Frank."

"I'm dyin', you're laughin'."

"You'll feel better with food in you."

He clung to a wall for support. "We're not dressing up in our bladder suits again, are we?"

"I'm sick of that. Let's go someplace out of town where it's safe. Like regular people for a change."

"Like father-daughter, huh?"

She made a face. "Not *that* regular."

"Think I oughta shave my head again before we go?"

"Let's just let 'em think you're a punker, okay? All that fuzz growing crazy wild up there."

"Yeah, let's."

• • •

Waiting was not unpleasant. Waiting was a state of mind in which one merely *was*. Inert, but ready. Coiled . . . waiting . . .

Deadly, knowing he was deadly. Invincible, and knowing that too. Knowing the advantage was all his for this next encounter: surprise, eyes adjusted to the dark, and most of all, technique and training—terms that did little justice to the weapon he'd become. Much more than a collection of techniques, his training was an entire philosophy, every muscle and neuron of his body responsive to inner commands that resulted in specific effects on the outer world. Those who didn't understand, found those effects irresistible, deadly. His thoughtways were focused and calm. He was a weapon.

And what this weapon wanted was Suki.

Suki beneath the boiling-oil drip.

Suki pleading.

Suki screaming.

Suki dying.

From inside the house came a thump, footsteps, people coming. The spider grew awake-alert.

Voices. A light inside. More voices from within. Then the scrape of a doorknob turning, the whispery rasp of a door beginning to open, and now the question that had no meaning had its inconsequential answer.

"Still warm out," Suki said, voice hushed.

"Got clouds up there tonight," the old guy said. "They keep the heat in."

"Funny, I thought clouds made it cold."

"Not in the desert, not in summer."

The door closed. *Click*. The spider tensed.

Two steps down to a concrete walk that led past the side of the house, past the big juniper. Shadows moving.

Simon glided forward and out.

"Boo," he said softly.

They turned, still night-blind, staring at the empty nothingness of the night, and Simon spun effortlessly, in control, and the nothingness took the old guy first, clipped him under the chin with a foot like a blade and the guy didn't make a sound, not a grunt, just fell back like a tree and landed on the ground as the girl stared, stared, didn't yet know what was going on, it'd happened so fast. Then she began to scream. The spider took her in the solar plexus with the same foot, so easy, so easy, and she couldn't scream, couldn't even breathe, blind agony in her eyes, and then Mink had her by the hair, forcing her head up and back, and he said, whispering in her ear, "Remember the heat, Suki. You've felt the cold, now you will feel the heat."

She tried to scream, tried to empty her paralyzed lungs in one final effort, but he flicked his fingers against the side of her head, just so, and she crumpled to the ground next to the man.

So easy it was. Didn't take ten seconds. These were not people who understood the essential nature of violence, that at its very best it really wasn't violent at all. These were not people who commanded respect.

These were flies.

And now they would die. Slowly, slowly, slowly.

31

Watching Mote, Jersey snarled inwardly. As Jersey turned from Ridge Street onto Flint, Mote kept his eyes averted from the house on the corner where Suki was holed up. Didn't even want to look at it, as if Suki would know if he even peeked at it. Jersey couldn't believe Mote found the girl. Mote, of all people. Like a caveman banging two rocks together and, *boom*, there's a bust of Lincoln or something. Worse, if Mote's happy burbling had any merit, Mink told Mote he was going to give him seventy thousand goddamned dollars. Worst of all, it looked as if Jersey, who'd been out running around in the desert on one of Mink's useless errands at the time, wasn't going to see squat from it, not one freakin' nickel.

Morning sun fell on the corner house, an old place that needed paint, like many of the houses in the neighborhood.

"Right there," Mote whispered, pointing—like Suki and the old fart could hear him from fifty yards, right through the windows of the car as they went by. "They wuz right there, Jers."

Jersey growled again, deep in his throat. Imagine, Suki hiding right under Mink's nose like that! The girl had balls. Stupid, though, her hanging around. He thought about all the money he'd given back to Mink. Maybe Suki'd been right, he should've run with it. And her.

He pulled the Buick into the drive at the Citadel, went around back and parked. He and Mote clumped up the back stairs and into the house.

The place was silent, deserted. Eight-thirty in the morning and it was like a tomb or something. Jersey's skin prickled.

They went through the place. Nothing. Mink and his crazy Bitch-mother were gone. All their clothing had been cleared out too, so they probably weren't coming back.

"Christ," Jersey breathed.

"Now what, Jers? Think I'm gonna get my seventy Kay?"

"Shut up, Mote."

On a kitchen counter, Jersey found two manila envelopes, one labeled MOTE, the other JERSEY.

He tore open the one with his name on it and read the note that fell out, ignoring the money that fell out too.

> *Jersey:*
> *Your services, and those of Mote, will no longer be required. For services rendered, here is $10,000. Consider it termination pay. Mote has been given $5,000. Calm him, Jersey. Make him see that this way is better than any other.*
>
> *And do not make the mistake of thinking that any part of your future lies with us.*
> *Charlotte*

"What's this mean?" Mote asked, handing his note to Jersey. It was similar, but shorter.

"Means we're unemployed." Jersey stuffed his money into a jacket pocket.

"Five Kay. All I got was five lousy Kay, Jers. How 'bout you?"

"Same."

"He said he was gonna give me *seventy* Kay."

"Forget it, Mote." Jersey turned away. He went out the door into the morning heat, telling Mote how lucky they both were that it had ended this way, this simply, all things considered. It'd been one hell of a ride while it lasted. Trouble was, nothing lasts forever.

Finally, he and the Bitch were quits.

32

A delicate purple-blue translucency limned the mountains, first sign of the approaching dawn. Pretty, Frank thought. Spectacular, in its own quiet way. Just when you think the desert is beyond redemption, it surprises you, puts on a show like this. The world was alive with unexpected beauty. He hadn't seen enough of it, not yet. He didn't want to die.

Overhead, stars still twinkled, just beginning to fade. In the dim light, Frank couldn't see for any great distance, but he sensed a vast openness all around.

"Sit," Mink commanded.

Frank sat. His hands were tied at his sides to a rope around his waist, and what little resistance he'd put up was met with pain, directed against Suki. It had happened once that night, and once had been enough, that one sharp shriek of agony.

Frank's jaw ached where Mink had kicked him eight hours ago. Even though he'd slept for a few hours in the motor home, he felt exhausted, eyes grainy.

Before leaving Reno, Mink had tied a single loop of nylon cord around Frank's neck, knotted in back at the base of his skull. Now Mink secured the two trailing ends of the line to a canopy strut at the east side of the motor home. Mink was good with knots, knew just what he was doing, and Frank wasn't any Harry Houdini. His hands were held immobile at either side of his waist. He couldn't get them together to work on the knots. Mink went back inside the motor home and Frank explored his bonds, found no weaknesses at all. He finally gave up when his fingers began to cramp.

The sky brightened from purple-blue to royal blue. No lights were visible out there in the desert, no sound reached Frank's ears. He'd never before seen such an expanse of dead flat nothingness. Miles and miles of it.

Mink came outside, stood beside Frank and sipped a cup of something that threw off tendrils of steam. A patch of light shone on the ground from a window of the RV.

Frank shivered.

Charlotte Voorhees moved about inside, clattering dishes. From time to time Frank caught a whiff of tobacco smoke. Suki was in there too, also bound, but Simon had gagged her to keep her from spitting. Charlotte had objected to Suki's way of showing disrespect.

"Restful, isn't it? Simon said mildly.

Frank said nothing.

"Pity to disturb all this with screams." Simon gazed out at the emptiness. "But that's life, isn't it? This world was never meant to be a happy place."

•   •   •

The sun rose above the hills. The air warmed. Simon went down to the alkali flat sixty feet away, and wandered about for half an hour. He strolled a quarter mile north along the edge of the flat then returned. A tracery of pink stood out on his forehead where Suki had tattooed him.

Mink untied Frank from the motor home, told him to stand. Frank's wrists remained tied. The ends of the nylon cord trailed from his neck down his back.

"Can I trust you?" Simon asked.

"What do you mean?"

"I'm going to move the RV over there." Mink pointed. "If you want, you can walk on over, meet us there. How would that suit you?"

"You gotta be nuts."

Mink smiled. "It'd save me some trouble. I thought maybe you'd like to stretch your legs a bit."

Frank didn't bother asking what would happen if he tried to run. Suki would get hurt, bad, and Frank wouldn't make it a quarter mile before Mink would be on him.

"Why move? What's over there?"

"Anthill," Mink replied casually. "Big one. I'm going to feed you to it."

Frank felt the color drain out of his face. "Jesus, you're really certifiable, aren't you?"

"Merely curious. Anthills have always fascinated me. All that instinctual, genetically-encoded activity. Out here, alone like this, this is a wonderful opportunity to watch a big hill at work. I don't know when I'll get another chance. Start walking."

Frank moved off a few paces. Simon watched, then got into the Jamboree and started the engine. Frank kept walking, trying to think, trying to keep his mind from giving up, shutting down. It was important to keep exploring options, but under the circumstances he found it difficult, forcing his legs to carry him downslope through scraggly sage toward the inhuman fate that awaited him.

I'm going to feed you to it.

So cold-blooded a statement, said in such a matter-of-fact voice. It didn't seem possible that Mink had a soul. He was a monstrous void in the universe, a subhuman portal into Hell.

Frank felt like a prisoner who'd been told to aid in his own execution. If only he could start a fire, maybe it'd flare out of control and attract attention. But he had no way of starting one, and the sage was too thinly distributed for a fire to spread effectively. He could try to run, of course, but the gently sloping plain was empty. There was no place to run to, no place to hide. And even if he could somehow save himself, Suki was still in Mink's hands.

Other options? Damn few. He could try to bite Mink. Knock the guy down, try to get on top, bite him, try for the throat, the jugular. If he got close enough, he would give it a try.

The Jamboree swayed over the sage, down toward the edge of the vast, shimmering alkali flat, heat mirages already spreading pools of nonexistent water over its surface, obscuring its distant northern extremity.

Frank followed, flexing the muscles in his legs. They were going to die anyway, so he might as well try to kick Mink in the groin or the knee, then kick him to death. What difference did it make now if Mink threatened to hurt Suki, or him? Quick deaths were preferable to the horrors Mink had chosen for them. Mink was rapidly losing his leverage.

Ants. Frank remembered that anthill he'd seen while walking out of the De Bacas. Hungry, swarming, energetic little bastards. It wasn't the thought of being bitten that made his knees feel like jelly, but the idea of being carted, bit by tiny bit, into the ground. He'd come across that anthill in the De Bacas how long ago? Last Sunday, five days ago. Jesus. Monday before that he'd stolen the truck and its cargo. Curious, how life moved along so damn fast.

His ribs still weren't a hundred percent, but they didn't bother him too much anymore. Just a twinge now and then. He could maybe get off a good kick at Mink. Worth a try. Anything was, now.

The motor home halted at the edge of the playa. Mink and Charlotte came out. Mink unfurled the canopy to provide shade over a flat patch of ground that overlooked the miles-long flat. He watched as Frank drew near.

"Nice walk?" he asked conversationally.

"Very."

Frank swing a foot at Mink's groin, hard. Mink took a half-step sideways and gently lifted Frank's foot. Frank landed on his back in the dirt. His ribs flared.

"Telegraphed it," Mink said, backing off a step. "Eyes, the set of your back leg, everything. Too slow, too clumsy, but I can't say I blame you, old man, so I'll let that one go. Look over there. That's what I'm going to feed you to."

A mound almost two feet high and eight feet across was twenty yards away, just beyond the edge of the flat. Its crown was somehow blurry, a shifting, dusty-raspberry color. It took Frank a moment to realize that the almost-liquid stirring was a swarm of ants, already on the move.

Hair lifted on the back of his neck.

"First things first," Mink said. "Get over here by the RV and sit down like you did before. I've got things to do and I don't want to worry about you."

Frank was still on his back. "How 'bout you make me."

Mink smiled. An almost sleepy look came over his face. "As you wish."

He took a step closer and Frank raised his legs, pulling them back, readying himself to lash out in a kick. Another step and Mink was within range. Frank kicked, trying for a kneecap, and Mink easily caught his right foot in both hands, heel and toe, and twisted. Frank cried out and flipped over on his stomach, hands still tied to the nylon rope around his waist. Mink leapt on him and grabbed the loose ends of the cord tied around Frank's neck. He pulled Frank's head up.

The noose cut off Frank's air.

"Let that be the end of your foolishness, old man," Mink said softly in Frank's ear. "If you persist, I will twist wire so tightly around your ankles that your feet will gangrene. I have heard the process is most unpleasant. If you like, we can delay your time with the ants for a day or two while your feet rot off your legs."

He stood and said, "Sit over here."

Frank got to his feet awkwardly and sat where Mink indicated. There was no point in further resistance, not yet. Mink tied Frank to the canopy strut as before, using the neck noose, then checked the ropes at Frank's wrists.

"Preparations," he said. He gave Frank a wink. "So much to do and, happily, so much time in which to do it."

He gathered four steel stakes, two feet long each, pointed at one end, with a loop at the other. He hammered them into the sand of the alkali flat in a rough square, seven feet on a side. As he worked, Charlotte came out and watched silently, drawing on a cigarette, arms folded across her skinny chest. Her nose was deeply discolored by a bruise.

Mink returned and went into the Jamboree. He came out with Suki struggling in his arms, bound hand and foot, still gagged. He set her on her feet in the shade of the canopy.

"Soon you will feel the heat, my love. Do you remember our previous discussion?"

Charlotte turned, watched as Mink used a pair of scissors to cut Suki's clothing from her body. Snip, snip, right up the front of the shirt she'd put on to go out to dinner the night before. He didn't bother with the buttons. Suki's eyes were wide, staring. The scissors slashed, and the shirt opened at the throat, fell open in front. Mink began cutting up her sleeves. He started low and moved up over her shoulders to her neck. Suki's wrists had been bound to her waist the same as Frank's. Mink pulled the shredded shirt off her and tossed it aside. Suki stood there in jeans and a bra, shivering, lips puffed out around the heavy gag.

Mink cut the bra off her then began to shear off her jeans, cutting upward from her ankles. Charlotte stood a few feet away, staring out at the expanse of dead alkali.

Snip, and the waistband parted. Mink crouched before her and started on the other leg. Suki fell suddenly, landed hard on her back, kicked Mink in the face. He twisted sideways to avoid the brunt of her kick, rolling away as Suki spun on her back and kicked Charlotte in the shins.

The old woman shrieked and fell howling to the ground.

Frank watched. There was nothing he could do, no way he could help Suki take advantage of the situation.

And . . . it was already over.

Mink grabbed Suki's feet and flipped her onto her belly, same as he'd done to Frank. He grabbed her hair, lifted her head, and pressed fingers into the side of her throat. In less than five seconds, she went limp in his arms.

Mink stared at Frank, an angry scrape showing on his left cheek, dirt and a bit of blood. He touched it, smiled. "Ornery little barbwire bitch, isn't she?"

He helped Charlotte to her feet and up into the Jamboree. He came back out and cut away the rest of Suki's clothing, picked her up, carried her naked to the stakes he'd driven into the sand. She regained consciousness halfway there, bucking with all her strength, bending at the waist, lunging madly in his arms, screaming through the gag. Simon wasn't a big guy. Suki was a handful even for him, but he got her over to the stakes and dropped her on the sand.

He had to knock her out again to get her tied to the stakes, spread-eagled in the sun, thirty feet from the anthill. She came to as he was tying the last arm, her left. She tried to fight him again, still gagged, but he had little difficulty holding her arm down, tying her wrist to the last stake.

He removed her gag.

"You *fucker!*" she screamed. "You horrible sick slimy son of a bitch! You're gonna rot in hell, Mink. You're gonna *rot!*"

"Do tell," he said. He turned away.

Huge red ants roamed the sand, a few whose foraging took them as far away as Suki. Mink poured a ring of Quaker State motor oil around Suki. Ants reached the barrier and turned away. Mink stepped on the few that were caught inside the ring, crushing them into the sand.

Mink returned to the motor home and crouched in front of Frank. "Now things get interesting," he said. "You see, you're going to dig a hole for me—well, actually, it's for you, but it means I'll have to untie your hands and give you a shovel, a potential weapon, and that means you'll have a wealth of ideas about how to use it against me."

"Never," Frank said.

Mink smiled, went into the Jamboree, came out with a .22 revolver. "I may be wrong, but I have the impression that you and Suki actually have feelings for one another. That seems unlikely, but there it is. I understand your interest in her. She's young and beautiful and relatively witless, a rather nice combination. But any reciprocal feelings on her part seem quite preposterous." He shrugged. "But that's irrelevant, isn't it? What's important is that I'm not certain to what extent you can be trusted to care about her welfare under these conditions. So here's how it'll work: you pull any stunts while you're digging and I will remove her nipples with a razor. Shall I show you the razor, old man? Do you believe I have one?"

"I believe you."

"Very good. In fact, I have several. And do you believe I'd use it in the manner specified?"

"I believe you're capable of anything, yes."

Mink smiled. "I am, yes. Still, I can't rely on you to care about Suki's pain, so the gun is additional insurance. If you try anything, I will gut shoot you in the intestines. It's just a little twenty-two, so it won't kill you, but the pain would be tremendous, especially hours and hours afterward. Do you understand?"

Frank said nothing.

Mink's fingers lashed out, struck a nerve in Frank's arm that drew an involuntary cry of pain from his throat. He'd never felt pain like that before, couldn't believe a mere tap near his elbow could do that to him. His vision went white for several seconds, then returned. His eyes filled with tears.

"Do you understand, old man? Answer."

"Yes."

"Very good. It's unlikely that we will ever become friends, but I promise you that before this day is done we will understand one another perfectly. When I ask questions, you *will* answer."

Charlotte came out, looking frail. She had a glass of orange juice in one hand. Mink unfolded a lawn chair for her and she sat down slowly. She was silent and evil. The air around her seemed miasmic, almost chilled. She didn't look at Frank as she sipped her drink.

"Now," Mink said to Frank, "here's the drill. I'm going to tie your feet, leaving about six inches of slack between them. Then I'll untie your neck and we will walk down to the anthill. When we get there, I will free your hands. Think we can manage all that without Suki losing her nipples, old man?"

"Yes."

"Good. Let's give it a try, shall we?"

Mink tied his ankles using a length of nylon rope, untied his neck, told him to stand. Frank got to his feet. Mink picked up the shovel, then motioned Frank forward.

Frank could manage nothing more than a ungainly shuffle. The temperature was in the high seventies, climbing rapidly. It would be a hundred before the day was done. Where Suki lay on the sand, the air temperature might reach a hundred forty.

"Stop," Mink said.

Frank stopped, twelve feet from the hole in the top of the anthill. It was teeming with mindless, scurrying scavengers. Forty feet away lay the skeleton of a bird, picked clean, along with the scattered empty shells of countless insects.

Mink stood behind him and cut the ropes holding Frank's wrists, then stepped back. He tossed the shovel at Frank's feet, pulled the revolver and backed away twenty feet.

"Remember what I told you, old man."

Frank bent over stiffly and picked up the shovel.

"Begin," Mink said. "Not too wide. Say, two feet in diameter and a little over three feet deep." His dead eyes gazed at Frank. "Do you wonder why, old man?"

Frank knew. "Not particularly," he said.

"When you're finished, I'll bend your legs at the knees and tie your calves back to your thighs, slide you in, and bury you up to your chin. When the ants find you, well, we'll see what happens. They ought to go wild, finding a big hunk of meat like you within reach."

33

Red ants half an inch long stumbled around. As Frank worked, he dumped sand on those that came close. Mink had warned him not to throw his tailings on the central hill. Doing so didn't seem like a terrific idea anyway—getting the nest all stirred up, maybe getting the ants hungrier, worked up, *aware* of him in some way—

Ridiculous. His mind was simply churning, trying to deny the demonic thing Mink had planned for him. When Mink put him in the hole, the ants would do what they were going to do, and it wouldn't matter what he did or didn't do now to provoke them.

He tried not to think about it, tried not to visualize his head resting on the sand as if decapitated, easy prey for the scavenging ants, Mink watching with clinical detachment as the army first explored this miraculous intrusion, then went to work, covering his head until his flesh was barely visible beneath the swarm, burrowing into him like tiny miners with their tough scissoring mandibles . . .

He looked over at Suki. The sun was hot, blazing down on her. She lay ten yards away with her eyes closed, not saying anything, not moving. Sweat glistened on her body. Naked like that, she looked so horribly vulnerable.

Hell, she *was* vulnerable.

Mink and Charlotte sat in the shade of the motor home on lawn chairs with drinks in their hands. They couldn't be human. Nothing Suki had told him about those two had prepared him for these black, suppurating horrors.

Eight inches beneath the surface, the sand was dark, still damp from whenever the last thunderstorm had come through. The sides of the hole held firm as he dug. Too bad.

A rivulet of salty sweat ran into Frank's left eye. He blinked it away. The sun beat down on his shaven head. His scalp was already starting to burn. If it blistered, it would give the ants a good place to start . . .

Jesus, quit with that, will you?

The hole was nearly waist deep. He'd had to climb down into it to keep digging. He had less than a foot to go.

Mink walked over with the gun. He stood twenty-five feet away as they went through their charade again.

"Toss the shovel behind you, old man."

Frank judged the distance between himself and Mink. Too far. Reluctantly, he dropped the shovel behind him.

"Get out of the hole and step away to your right."

Frank got out, shuffled away.

"Sit."

Frank sat on the sand. Mink came closer, gun on Frank, and peered into the hole.

"I get the feeling you're not working as quickly as you might," Mink said, smiling faintly.

Frank said nothing. It was true. He had no desire to hurry this along. He'd hoped the hole would collapse, but the sand had just the right moisture content to keep from falling in on itself. It was hard-packed, having sat and settled for countless years. Left undisturbed for another forty million years, it would become sedimentary rock.

"Continue," Mink said, backing away.

Frank retrieved the shovel and got back in the hole, his own grave. When the ants were done, his bones would fold up and collapse into the hole. Sand would blow over the alkali flat and bury him. In a few years, this would all look exactly as it had before he'd begun to dig.

Mink crouched on his heels twenty feet away, observing Frank's labors.

"Know how much this is costing, old man?"

"How much what is costing?"

"All this." He swept a hand at the desert, including Frank and Suki in the gesture.

"Twenty-five bucks?"

Mink chuckled. "Man's got a sense of humor. I like that. You're tough, old guy. I'll give you that."

"Maybe you'd like to try your luck. Just the two of us, one on one."

Mink flicked away an intruding ant. "Actually, that's what I have in mind. Before I put you in the ground, I want you softened up a bit, but not too much. I want you conscious, aware. However, I digress. What these experiments are costing, in round numbers, is about two and a half million dollars."

"Too bad."

"Isn't it, though? The amazing thing is, not only can I afford it, but it's worth it. I haven't had a real vacation in years, always on the go. You know how it is: work, work, work." He smiled. "Certainly I haven't had any time off as interesting as this. You see, my line of work involves a great deal of stress."

"Running scams on old people. Keeping one step ahead of the law. You're a real hardworkin' guy, full of that old Protestant work ethic."

Mink smiled. "Suki's been telling tales, I see."

Suki spoke up. "Until forever, Mink, even after you die, worms will crawl in and out of your brain and your rotten, horrible heart."

Mink's eyes never left Frank. "In your own way, Suki girl, you're as bad as I."

"Nothing on earth is as bad as you, except your crazy psycho-bitch mother."

Mink's smile faltered.

Touched a nerve there, Frank thought.

"So," Mink said to Frank, "this is costing a bundle. Few people can visualize so much money, so let me put it in perspective for you. Two point five million dollars, arranged as a stack of one-dollar bills, would make a pile well over a thousand feet high. How about that?"

Frank dug. There was nothing to say, nothing to be gained by exchanging madness with a madman.

"As you're being consumed, old man, I wonder if you'll spare a moment to appreciate the cost."

If not for Suki, and the hope that Mink might yet leave some tiny opening, make some tiny slip, Frank would already have thrown the shovel in a futile attempt to split Mink's skull. Failing that, he would charge him in a hopeless shuffle. A bullet might kill him, deny Mink the pleasure of watching him die beneath that voracious, churning swarm.

But, not yet. What had Mink said about softening him up before putting him in the ground? Was there any hope in that? Exactly what had he meant by it?

"Where'd the money come from, old man?"

"Huh?"

"Sixty-six thousand dollars, give or take. It was in the house where I found you two."

"Know how you empty out your pockets when you get home, accumulate a bunch of spare change? Well, after thirty years of that, I ended up with quite a pile."

Mink chuckled again. "Doesn't really matter, does it?" He sent another ant scurrying away with a flick of a finger. "Sixty-six grand is an entirely insignificant sum."

He stood up, began circling the anthill from a distance of perhaps fifteen feet, observing it, keeping an eye on Frank as he ambled along.

"Fascinating, isn't it?" he said. "Consider, if you will, this coming exercise from the ants' perspective. Word is somehow passed that a rather large quantity of raw material has been discovered, not far from the nest." He stopped on the far side of the hill from Frank, out of reach. "It's alive, this raw material is, still moving, and perhaps that's a consideration, but it's essentially defenseless. So, alive or not, the workers begin to hack away at it because it's important to get as much of it as possible into the nest in as short a time as possible. No doubt that's one of nature's axioms of survival out here.

"It takes a while, but eventually the raw material stops yelling and thrashing and becomes an inert decomposing mass, infinitely intriguing to our little friends. A vast pile of drying tubes and gristle and meat all waiting to be nipped into tiny portions and hustled down into the ground. Every so often a pocket of something particularly savory is discovered, thyroid, liver, pancreas, and a renewed flurry of excitement ripples through the nest . . ."

Frank tried not to listen to the pustulant conversation, but it was hard—impossible, really. The image was too real, too awful to be denied. It would happen very much as Mink described it, if not in its particulars then in broad outline. The colony wouldn't devour him in anger, but as a simple matter of survival. Without a doubt, he would be the greatest discovery in the history of the nest—

Mink had said something and was looking at him.

"What?" Frank said.

"I asked if you'd care to estimate your approximate value in dollars per pound at this moment."

Jesus, don't listen. Mink was just trying to get to him, trying to play games with his head. What he could maybe do is use the shovel to slice through the rope holding his feet together, try to get an edge on Mink if he got careless and moved closer.

"Over five thousand dollars a pound," Mink said. "Assuming, that is, you are worth half of the two and a half million you and Suki are costing us. But that's fair, since all men are created equal"—Frank rammed the blade of the shovel into the rope between his ankles—"which makes her worth twice as much as you, per pound. In fact, she's worth a great deal more to me than that, and if you try one more time to cut that rope with the shovel, Suki will lose her left breast and I will force feed it to you, understood?"

Frank held the shovel motionless before him.

"Dig," Mink commanded.

Frank took another scoop of wet sand. The hole was deep enough that it was difficult to remove more than a third of a shovelful at a time. The sand came out dark and heavy, drying quickly in the sun where he slung it out on the ground.

Mink moved around the anthill, crossing over to where Suki lay. He said a few words that Frank didn't catch.

"Fuck you." Suki's response rang out clear and strong.

She was still fighting. Frank's heart felt heavy, filled with a terrible sadness.

Another partial shovelful.

And another.

The day was cloudless, the air still. Heat refractions corrugated the desert, causing it to shimmer in the distance. Ants sped across the sand, hunting.

Could he risk another try at the rope? The first slice had frayed it slightly, but not much, and could he hit it in exactly the same place again? If Mink caught him at it, would he do to Suki what he said he'd do? Perhaps. He was crazy enough.

Risk it?

No, not yet.

He tossed another few pounds of damp sand onto the alkali and glanced over at the motor home. Mink was there with his mother, watching him. Psycho bitch, silent and sullen, crazy as a loon, but she wasn't raving crazy, just crazy crazy, able to watch all this and accept it, agree with it, perhaps enjoy it. How had God managed to pair up those two, assuming He had anything to do with that kind of thing? What a colossal, cosmic blunder that had been. The two of them made Manson and Dahmer look like guys with mild antisocial tendencies, nothing remarkable, nothing serious.

"I'm sorry, Frank," Suki called out to him.

"It's all right," he answered. What else could he say?

"God will punish him."

"I know."

Fifty feet away, Mink chuckled. Frank felt the absolute darkness in the sound.

Twenty minutes later Mink decided the hole was deep enough. Things started to happen faster then.

34

Mink knelt beside her. Ice clinked against the sides of the glass as he held it to her lips. Even though Suki knew it would be better not to drink, to die as quickly as possible, knew that whatever Mink was going to do to her would be easier to endure if she were dehydrated, she lifted her head a few inches and drank thirstily.

She wasn't yet ready to die.

She turned her head. Frank sat in the shade of the motor home again. He'd been tied by his neck to something at the side of the vehicle, hands bound again.

"More?" Mink asked her.

"No."

"We'll see." He strode back to the Jamboree, returned with another glass.

She drank all of that one too.

"See?" Mink said. "You didn't mean no."

Her eyes hated him, loathed him, stared at him venomously, tried to kill him. Please, God, split open the earth and drag this worm back down to Hell!

"Soon we will begin," Mink said. He crouched beside her stroking her hair. "Do you remember what I told you about the heat, Suki?"

She arched upward, spat into his face.

He wiped his cheek. "Extremely hot oil," he said. "The outcome of this little experiment will be twofold. First, the physical impact of each drop will be much greater than it was with the cold, no doubt accelerating the destruction of your mind. The second result will be a bit less interesting, but unavoidable. The oil will cook you, my love. Just your guts, of course. To tell the truth, I don't know which will ultimately cause your death, but we will find out, won't we?"

"My God, Mink, how can you *do* such horrible things?" She hadn't wanted to say it, hadn't wanted to say anything, but it just came blurting out.

He smiled. "Ask any quack psychologist, Suki, my love. I was scarred by an unhappy childhood. I wasn't permitted to play with others, to become skilled at social interactions. I was laughed at, introverted, shy. I'm seething with latent hostility, acting out feelings of aggression against a father who gave me none of the love I so desperately craved, then deserted me at a tender age. Girls didn't like me as an adolescent. I didn't date. I had no real friends. I was lonely, frustrated, and made the butt of cruel jokes. Choose one or several."

He stood up.

"Please," she said. "Please . . . don't."

"If at any time you have the urge to scream, do not hesitate to do so. I chose this place with you in mind." He walked away.

She trembled, told herself she would never scream—but this time she knew she would. She pulled at the ropes holding her wrists, felt no give in them. The stakes were driven in too deep.

Mink returned with a medieval-looking apparatus—a wooden arm connected to a heavy plank base. Two hooks were at one end of the arm. He set it on the sand beside her, the arm suspended a foot above her midsection. A heavy bucket of sand held the base in place.

"See what I made for you," he said.

She didn't want to look, couldn't help it though. Mink's face was calm as he worked, tranquil insanity and empty death moving around inside his eyes.

"Please don't do this, Mink. Please."

As if he hadn't heard, he swung the arm of the contrivance to a spot a few inches below her navel.

Then he went away.

•   •   •

Mink emerged from the motor home dressed only in some kind of a loincloth. Frank stared. Mink's feet were bare, his buttocks naked. Sinewy muscles rippled in his legs. His rib cage showed. The coarsely-woven cloth, knotted at either side of his waist, covered only his groin.

"It's called an *orosu*," Mink said. "Any number of garments worn throughout the world are similar in design, but the *orosu* is unique. It originated in sixteenth-century Japan, specifically in the Oki Gunto archipelago in the Sea of Japan, off Honshu. Only those skilled in hand-to-hand combat were permitted to wear it, and then only within the walls of the temple-schools known as *kishoki*. My use of it is a bit of a bastardization though. You see, my specific discipline is an offshoot of what you would probably call kung fu, practiced only in the mountainous Xinjiang Province of China. It's quite an exotic hybrid, nothing at all like the form of self-defense that evolved in the Oki Guntos of Japan."

"You look very sweet in it anyway," Frank said. "Quite the fashionably dressed child molester."

Mink smiled. "I will enjoy tearing you down, Frank. May I call you Frank? You're a bit overly self-righteous for my taste. You and I are going to engage in that hand-to-hand you expressed an interest in a while ago. My 'kung fu' against your lumbering, uneducated, street-brawling style. It's been a while since I've had an opportunity to practice my art against an opponent fighting for his life. And, as I said earlier, I want you softened up before I put you in the ground."

"Try it, asshole. Nothing would suit me better."

"Good. Bravado, I like that. Hang onto that thought. You know what's in store for you, of course, and you have an idea of how Suki will die if you should lose. I went into detail about how the ants will consume you for a reason, Frank. I want you motivated. I want you to pull no punches, to do your very best to win. I like a challenge, and I especially like it that you challenged *me*. I hope you won't make it too easy. I would find that disappointing."

"Just so long as you untie me, asshole."

"Oh, I will, Frank. As soon as Suki begins her ordeal. I want to be certain you'll do your very best to kill me."

"Count on it."

Mink smiled. "I am."

Charlotte came out of the Jamboree smoking a cigarette, wearing black silk slacks and a red blouse with short sleeves and a high collar. Dark glasses protected her eyes.

"When?" she asked. Her voice shook. It sounded empty to Frank, hollow, as if she were in pain.

"Soon, Mother. Very soon now."

"I want the gun, Simon, just in case."

"There's no need."

"All the same, I intend to keep it with me."

•   •   •

Mink and Charlotte came toward her. Mink carried a thermos encircled by wire bands with loops in them. A curious attachment was at the top. Suki trembled.

Mink crouched beside her and placed the thermos upside down on the hooks of the wooden arm over her belly.

"You will note," he said, "that I have positioned you in such a way that you will be able to watch Frank as the ants swarm over him and eat him. Perhaps you will find that an interesting diversion from your own woes. It might help."

"You . . . bastard."

"Making fun of my unhappy childhood, darling?"

"There *is* a God, Mink. You'll see. You can't do this."

"I'll believe in God when He stops me. Until then, all there is is what happens."

He placed a sponge on her belly. "Don't move, Suki." He twisted a tiny glass valve at the top of the thermos. Pale yellow oil dripped onto the sponge. Slower. Slower.

Thip . . . Thip . . .

Thip . . .

Thip.

Mink wrapped a bit of fiberglass insulation around the valve and stem, then stuck the back of his hand into the drip. The next drop landed on his flesh. He closed his eyes and shivered, smiled.

"Stings, Suki. It's ready. Are you?"

"My *God*, Mink. Please, please, don't. Please, I'm sorry I hurt you, I didn't mean—"

He took his hand away, and the sponge.

Thip.

Her body tensed when the fiery drop hit her belly. Lean muscles stood out like rawhide strips.

"Oh my God," she breathed.

"Yes, Suki. Yes, darling. Tell me of your pain."

No. She wouldn't scream, not ever. The insulation hid the drop as it formed. This time she couldn't see it, couldn't tell when the next one hung bloated and—

Thip.

She growled, gritted her teeth, writhed on the sand, held in place by ropes at wrists and ankles.

Mink stood up. "Mother will keep you company for a while, Suki. Tell Mother of your pain." He walked away. Charlotte Voorhees stood above her with the gun in her hand.

Please, God, kill him, kill her . . .

Thip.

• • •

Mink cut the noose from around Frank's neck. Frank got slowly to his feet.

"Walk," Mink said. "Out there."

Feet still loosely bound, Frank shuffled out to a flat sandy area between Suki and the motor home.

"Stop."

Frank turned and faced Mink. Charlotte stood on the far side of Suki, gun dangling from her fist. Suki moaned.

Blind rage threatened to overwhelm Frank, but blind rage wasn't what he needed right now. He took a few deep breaths.

Mink moved behind him with a knife. Suddenly the ropes that held his wrists came free. Frank massaged his wrists and worked his arms, pulled off the remnants of rope.

"I'll leave it to you to free your ankles, old man. Then we'll see how motivated you are." Mink moved off a dozen feet and began to move around, loosening up.

Suki cried out.

Crazy, Frank thought. Madness.

He had to win. *Had* to. He outweighed this skinny fucker by close to a hundred pounds, and that Bruce Lee kung fu shit was just that: shit. Guy was limber, though. Standing on one leg, the other stuck damn near straight up in the air, calf touching his ear.

Frank remembered what Suki had told him about Mink, how the guy was fast, real fast. Frank wondered how fast he'd be with his eyes full of this alkaline grit.

He sat on the ground and untied the knots at his ankles. A weak feeling spilled through him as Suki groaned again, louder this time. Frank's belly was empty, hollowed out by Suki's pain. He didn't care as much about what would happen to him if he didn't beat Mink as he cared about Suki. He cared about her, a lot.

Twenty feet away, Charlotte watched him with dead eyes. Mink spun gracefully, without effort, hands doing weird things—all just shit. In a real down-home brawl, kung fu was just a bunch of crap.

The rope came free. Frank got slowly to his feet. In his right fist he had a handful of sand.

"Ready?" Mink said.

Frank nodded. Could he reach Charlotte before Mink took him down, or before she put a bullet in him? Would it do any good if he did? Maybe—if he could get his hands on that gun.

"Your move, old man," Mink said, eyes locked on his. "You're the one with the gripe, remember?"

No good. Mink was between him and Charlotte. Frank would never get to her without going past Mink.

He tried circling.

Still no good. As Frank moved, Mink shifted with him, keeping himself between Frank and Charlotte. His muscles were stringy but well-defined, tough-looking. The *orosu* was a considerably less ridiculous garment now than when Mink had first appeared in it.

Mink smiled, hands swaying. Frank took a step closer.

Another step. Frank held up his fists like a boxer. From four feet away he threw out an experimental fist, not really trying to hit Mink. Mink didn't duck, didn't flinch, didn't even lose his predatory little smile.

Frank threw the fist again, whipping the sand into Mink's face. Suddenly Mink pinwheeled, a spinning blur, and a naked foot caught Frank beside the ear. A single bright light exploded inside his head.

He was on the ground, on his face before he was aware of having fallen. Bitter sand flecked his lips. He was dazed, the sand close, a gray blur in his vision.

Frank rolled suddenly, panicked at the thought of Mink pouncing on him. But Mink was near Suki, dancing, not coming for him, waiting for him to get back on his feet.

Frank took his time.

Suki sobbed. Not loud, but it got Frank to his feet. He couldn't reach her. Mink was right there, in his path again.

"What this is," Mink said, "is *Kha Xih*. Kung fu is really just a distant relative, and nowhere near as interesting. I doubt that half a dozen in the West practice Kha Xih with any regularity."

Frank approached cautiously.

"Now I'm going to break your nose, old man," Mink said. "See if you can stop me."

Frank covered up, guarding his face. But Mink might also be setting him up, so Frank was wary for an attack elsewhere. Mink glided up and Frank dropped way down and lunged for him, trying for a shot to his groin or to get an arm around Mink's waist. Mink danced to one side and grabbed Frank's wrist, gave it a gentle twist. Pain shot up Frank's left forearm all the way to his shoulder. He almost screamed. He went down, rolling in the sand, and again the foot came out of nowhere and cracked against the side of his nose.

The pain was excruciating. Frank landed on his back. His eyes filled with water and suddenly there were several Minks, fractured, dancing around.

"The wrist hold is called *chong jhu xih*," Mink said. "The broken nose is painful, is it not?"

It was, very. Blood bubbled down Frank's throat.

Suki cried out. Frank staggered again to his feet, blood from his nose drenching the front of his shirt.

• • •

Thip.

Suki heaved against the ropes. The pain of the oil was huge, like fire on her belly.

Charlotte stood impassively above her, to Suki's left, watching her boy battle Frank beneath the hot desert sun.

That was hopeless. Mink was too good. Frank was on his feet again, but his nose was bleeding badly and he looked stunned.

Thip.

Suki sobbed thickly. Such an ugly, demented way to die.

Please God, Jesus, help me, help Frank. *Help us!*

Her body gleamed with sweat, every fiber standing out as she strained at the ropes—and the stake holding her right leg in place shifted, a quarter of an inch.

• • •

"Next," Mink said, "I will break one of your ribs. Unlike the wrist hold I used to defend against that barroom stunt of yours, you should expect a blow. *Kwan du xih*, this is called. There are many variations, however."

Frank's wrist still hurt. His nose was seething agony and something inside seemed loose, the cartilage torn. But the biggest hurt of all was that Mink had told him he was going to break one of Frank's ribs, and Frank felt powerless to stop him.

Still, he had to try. If only he could get his hands on the bastard's skinny neck. Mink was fast and strong, but he wasn't what you'd call powerful. He had a long neck, not all that thick. One good hard twist and that'd be that.

Mink glided forward, danced, spun, and Frank expected the foot again. He threw up his hands to block it, but the foot didn't come. A hand slapped his face—so fast he never saw it coming—then his balance was off and he stumbled to his left. Mink's elbow cracked into his side, hard, and Frank felt a lower rib on his left side go.

He fell to the sand, barely able to draw a breath. Five seconds. Mink had told him he was going to break a rib, and five seconds later it was done. Maybe this kung fu stuff wasn't a bunch of shit after all.

"You disappoint me, old man. I expected better from you than this."

Suki cried out again, a terrible sound, full of agony. How many drops had fallen on her? Dozens. It took all Frank had to get his knees under him and stagger again to his feet.

This wasn't any good. He couldn't touch the guy, couldn't so much as lay a finger on him.

"Last demonstration," Mink said. "You're going to like this one."

Frank faced Mink. He saw Suki behind the guy, writhing on the ground, sobbing.

"It's called *xian jian xih*, a paralyzing strike to a specific nerve in the thigh. Quite difficult to do properly, I might add. You will be unable to use that leg for some time afterward, I'm sorry to say, so this will conclude our little session. The nerve is in the center of the thigh, a few inches above the knee. I will strike your right leg, so be prepared to defend in that area."

Frank could only draw shallow breaths. There was no hope in this, but he gathered himself to meet Mink's attack as best he could.

•   •   •

Thip.

Suki's entire body tightened in agony, tendons creaking, and the stake that held her right leg gave another half inch. She had a few precious inches of freedom now.

Her scalded belly was on fire. She lunged one more time against her restraints, felt the stake give another half inch. She pushed it outward with her ankle, then tried to work it from one side to the other. Some freedom there, but not much. Charlotte stood near, inside the oil barrier that was keeping the ants away, gun hanging from one blue-veined hand. Her eyes shone as she watched her boy, her pride and joy, as he took down the man who had broken her nose.

Thip.

Suki cried out involuntarily. Her muscles went rigid. The stake holding her right leg moved upward half an inch. She pushed outward, tried to lift up. It was stuck. She drew the stake toward her then hammered it away, in and out, in and out, working it, using her other limbs for leverage.

She tried to lift again, and the stake slid upward another quarter of an inch.

Thip.

Pain filled her and she sobbed again, tears coursing down her cheeks. In, out, in, out. Now up, and the stake was looser. It came up several inches. In, out. Now up, and suddenly the stake ripped free. Without thinking, Suki threw her leg upward in a hard, slashing arc, body twisting, the metal rod whipping awkwardly at her ankle. Charlotte glanced down at her just as the stake glinted in the sunlight, surprise just beginning to contort her features, when the stake hit her shoulder and slammed into the side of her head.

With a shriek, Charlotte staggered and pinwheeled down, red hair flying in her face. She fell close to Suki's left hand. Suki's fingers closed on her hair.

Her grip tightened like iron.

• • •

Mink closed on Frank. Out of the corner of his eye, Frank saw sudden movement where Suki lay on the sand.

Charlotte shrieked.

Mink's hands were already in motion, too late to stop, but they faltered a fraction of a second when his mother cried out. A wedge of fingers slammed into Frank's thigh just as Frank's fingers closed on Mink's wrist.

Frank squeezed. His right leg collapsed and he fell to one knee, but his grip tightened, strengthened by years of exercise, squeezing tennis balls. In all those years on the road, he'd never gripped anything with such intensity. Ropy muscles stood out in his forearm.

Mink's bones came apart. Where the radius and the ulna join the wrist, the radius tore loose and ground against the ulna. Mink screamed. He'd never felt pain like that before, a white-hot shriek of agony that exploded in his brain. Frank got hold of the same wrist in his other hand and instinctively dropped to the ground and rolled over and over, a barroom move, twisting all the joints, winding up Mink's arm. Mink's humerus ripped out of its shoulder socket then his elbow came apart. In an instant the arm was useless, limp, all the major bones unglued, twisted out of their joints, tendons tearing, his arm nothing but an appendage attached to the howling beast whose flesh was reduced to screaming agony.

• • •

Charlotte thrashed. Suki's grip tightened. The gun lay in the sand a foot from Suki's face, pointed at her eyes, but that didn't matter. All that mattered was that her fingers were knotted in Charlotte's hair and the bitch was face down in the sand.

Like a hydraulic ram, Suki's wrist crushed downward. She got leverage from the stake holding her wrist, and she shoved the deadly harridan's face into the ground.

Charlotte screamed, inhaled. Alkaline grit rattled down her throat and into her lungs. She coughed, inhaled more grit. Her skinny arms hammered the sand. Her fingers, formed into claws, tore at Suki's arms as she tried desperately to crawl forward and rip at Suki's eyes.

Her left hand landed on the gun, knocked it away a few inches, then her fingers scrabbled for it, groping blindly.

•   •   •

Frank rolled over and over on the sand, clinging to Mink's wrist. A gagging wail erupted from Mink's throat, and still Frank rolled, destroying the arm, paralyzing Mink's brain with pain. Mink flopped in the sand as Frank rolled, twisting the mutilated arm. Tendons in Mink's arm tore loose, blood vessels twisted shut. The mad dog clung to his arm and rolled, not letting Mink pull loose, strike back, nothing, until nothing remained except pain beyond imagining, and, finally, not even that as Mink's world slipped into a place of silky dark.

•   •   •

Charlotte screeched, inhaled, coughed. She hacked abjectly as dust and grit filled her mouth. Suki shoved her face deeper into the alkali. Tendons stood out on Suki's arms, her face flushed with effort. Down and down and down, kill the bitch, kill her, *kill* her, and—

"Die," she breathed, panting. "*Die*, you fuckin' witch!"

Charlotte's fingers found the gun. Suki shifted her elbow and mashed the muzzle into the sand.

Down, down, *down*. Strands of Charlotte's hair popped in Suki's fingers. Bury her, *crush* her, face down, down, the witch's nose deep in the sand. For an instant Charlotte's face came up, tongue crusted with sand, then Suki mashed her face back down. Again Charlotte got her face up half an inch. Simon!" she cried, an inhuman, gritty sound, then her face was back in the sand. Her finger found the trigger of the gun, jerked, and an explosion blew sand over Suki's face. Charlotte's chest heaved. A spasm wracked her, then another, weaker. Her nails raked furrows in the sand then her arms slowly went slack, fingers beginning to twitch.

Down and down and down, Suki's arm burned like it was on fire and now the burn was good, pure, and if she had to do this for all eternity she would this was good this was God's fire clean and honest, her fingers like steel wires burning, burning as she forced the viper's head down and down and down and down and—

"Enough."

She didn't hear, couldn't hear. There was nothing in the universe but her fingers in this horror's stringy hair, muscles burning, burning, burning—

"Christ, Suki, that's enough."

Something forced her fingers apart, pried them one by one from the loathsome thing in her grasp.

Her fingers tightened. "*No!*" she screamed. "*No!*"

"She's dead, Suki. She's dead." The voice, coming to her from some unimaginable height, wasn't Charlotte's, wasn't Mink's. Her eyes opened and Frank was there, on his side beside her. Frank, with blood oozing from his nose, eyes bloodshot. Frank, not Mink. Frank. Mink was fifteen feet away, crumpled strangely on the ground, lying very, very still.

"Oh, God," Suki wailed. She opened her fingers, turned her head away from Charlotte, and began to cry.

35

"Vi," Mink sobbed. "Oh, *Violet . . .*"

He lay on the sand, ankles tightly bound, his one good arm lashed to his waist and thigh. Frank had rigged a lawn chair and a bed sheet to provide him with some shade, which was more than he deserved. Charlotte lay face down on the sand where Suki had suffocated her ninety minutes ago.

"Mother," Mink wailed.

"*I'll have you killed!*" he shrieked suddenly. "Both of you. I've got money. I will hunt you down and stake you to an anthill with your mouths wired open and your eyelids cut off!" His voice drilled into the quiet of the afternoon. The windows and doors of the motor home were open, allowing a faint breeze to drift through.

Outside, Mink started sobbing again.

Suki wore nothing but a towel wrapped around her hips. Mink had ruined her clothing and she couldn't bear the thought of wearing anything that had belonged to him or his mother. A blister several inches in diameter was on her stomach, two inches below her navel. Frank had rummaged through the Jamboree and found a first-aid kit. He'd rubbed ointment onto a piece of gauze and gently taped it over her wound. She sat with her feet up, nursing a bottle of mineral water.

Frank's nose throbbed and his broken rib pulsed with every beat of his heart. He'd removed his bloody shirt.

"I need a doctor for this arm!" Mink yelled.

It had taken most of an hour before Frank's right leg was able to support his full weight, but it was still shaky. On a table within easy reach was Charlotte's gun.

While hobbling around, trying to find a first-aid kit, Frank had come across a black-enameled safe hidden away in a closet next to the toilet, a Fidelity model 40—most likely the same one Suki had opened in Louisiana. No telling what was in it. Maybe later, when she felt up to it, she could give it a try.

A map on the driver's console gave Frank a good idea of where they were: central Nevada, around the Sulphur Spring Range, thirty or so miles north of Eureka. An X on the map marked the spot.

"Violet," Mink moaned. "Vi." With sudden fury he shouted, "You killed her. You killed my Mother! I'll hunt you both to the ends of the earth!"

"We gotta listen to that?" Suki asked.

"How's the stomach?"

"It's been better. Guess I'll live though."

"*I'll carve out your eyes!*" Mink screamed. "*If it takes all the money I've got and all the rest of my life, I will find you!*"

Frank looked at Suki. He felt sick. "He means it."

"Shit, Frank, I know that. When Mink talks about hurting people or killing them, he means it."

Frank got slowly to his feet. Dark folds of skin sagged beneath his eyes. "Stay put awhile, okay?"

"Why? What're you gonna do?"

His voice was suddenly tight. "Just stay the hell inside, all right?"

"Jesus, all right!"

Frank went outside. He trudged over to Charlotte's body. Mink tracked him with his eyes. Frank grabbed one of Charlotte's arms.

"What're you doing?" Mink snarled.

Frank dragged the hideous old crone toward the pit he'd dug that morning, the hole that was to have been a hellish death and his grave. His broken rib felt like a knife was twisting in there.

"What're you doing? *Put her down!*"

Charlotte's heels dug grooves in the alkali. She weighed no more than ninety-five pounds. Her flesh was hot and dry, scaly. Rigor had already begun to set in.

Frank stood at the edge of the hole, staring down. Head first or feet first? The hole was two feet across, three and a half deep, a weird little shaft in the sand.

"No!" Mink screamed. "The ants'll get her in there!"

Frank looked at Mink. "At least they'll get her dead, not alive." He dragged her across the hole until her head and shoulders tilted in, then he let her slide in headfirst.

Mink went crazy. "*Whatever it takes!*" he screamed. "*No matter where you go, I'll find you!*"

A kind of sadness filled Frank. He hadn't asked for this kind of responsibility, didn't want to be the one to do it, but it had to be done and there was no one else to shoulder the burden. He wouldn't let Suki do it, even if she wanted to. And she would. No way could he allow that to happen, or even to give her a say in the matter.

Hugging his ribs, he walked over to Mink, looked down at him. Mink's arm was dark, a brown-black color, already rotting and dead. No one could save it now. The flesh was bloated, twisted from the shoulder down, veins and arteries kinked shut. Mink was on his back, breathing shallowly. His eyes were pits.

"Whatever it takes," he hissed.

Frank grabbed an end of the nylon cord he'd tied around Mink's ankles.

"What're you doing?" Mink said.

Frank pulled. Mink slid across the sand, his ruined arm trailing behind like a rag above his head. Mink screamed in sudden agony and Frank willed himself not to hear, not to feel, not to think. He got no joy from Mink's pain, but he had to do what he had to do and this was the only way to do it.

Mink's shrieks filled Frank's brain. It would have been a blessing if Mink had simply passed out, but he didn't.

They approached the hole. Mink lifted his head to see where they were going.

"What're you *doing?*" he cried. "Oh, Jesus Christ, no, *you can't! You can't!*"

Frank hurried now, not wanting this, not knowing what else to do. If it was just him he might risk it—but it was Suki too.

It had to be done.

"*NO!*" Mink screamed.

Headfirst into the hole. Mink ended up with Charlotte's black lips kissing his cheek. His neck was bent forward, chin against his chest, legs reaching almost all the way to the surface. His ruined arm was wrapped impossibly around the back of his head.

Frank picked up the shovel.

"No," Simon Voorhees said, staring up at him. "Don't, please. I don't want to die." His eyes were shiny.

"No one does, pal. Too bad you never understood that."

He threw in a shovelful of sand.

Mink sputtered. "Don't, *please*—"

Another shovelful.

Mink coughed.

Another shovelful went in. Frank didn't look. Another, another, working quickly now, ignoring the pain in his ribs, breathing hard, and Frank didn't see Mink's legs begin to kick, beating against the sides of the hole, his body bucking as his head went under and the ancient sand filled his nostrils and poured into his gaping mouth, no longer able to scream.

Frank shoveled madly, frantically, scooping sand into the hole, sweat pouring off his body beneath the hot sun, ribs burning, the sand gritty on the shovel, plopping heavily into the hole, Frank's breath hoarse, ants stumbling around, Mink's feet gone now as the hole was almost full, only the toes of one of Charlotte's feet still showing, and then they were gone and nothing was left but a place in the desert where sand had been disturbed, not far from a giant thriving anthill.

"God keep you both," Frank whispered over the grave.

The words seemed ambiguous enough.

36

Sun sparkled on the water, glittered on the sand across the road, Avenida Vieira Souto, reflected off bronzed bodies lying lotioned on the beach. Ever-present samba music filled the tropical air around the café.

A beautiful mulata waitress, skin the color of café au lait, leaned closer and said something in Portuguese, then paused at the sight of Frank's missing fingertip.

"Tell her I lost it in an elevator in London," Frank said. "Nineteen and sixty-one. Door closed on my finger and took it straight up to the fourteenth floor. Back then they had lousy safety devices on some of those old lifts over there."

Suki glanced up from the book she was reading. "Christ, Frank, she doesn't want to know what happened to that old finger of yours."

" 'Course she does."

"What she *asked*, was if you want another *chopinho*."

Cold draft beer. "Tell her no, I want a *batida*, and tell her about the finger, too."

Suki hesitated.

"Go on, tell her."

In halting Portuguese, Suki spoke to the girl, a native of the city known as a Carioca.

The girl looked at Frank, smiled, and went away.

"See, what'd I tell you?" Frank said.

"What I told her was they let you out the first Tuesday of every month, and you're harmless and sweet in spite of how you look."

"Jesus." He shook his head.

It was March, hot. They'd survived Rio's famous Carnival, barely, and now the city's *avenidas* were merely raucous. Suki sat across the tiny table from him, dressed in a batik print dress, beneath which Frank knew she was wearing some sort of a micro-thong bikini that wasn't much better than wearing nothing at all.

Ipanema Beach, right next to the Garden of Allah beside the canal separating Ipanema from Leblon. To their left was a stretch of sand where many of the women were lying topless in the sun, Copacabana Beach beyond that, past Ponta do Arpoador, while to the right, two kilometers away, rising fifteen hundred feet above them, was Pedra Dois Irmãos, its shantytown debris visible among the trees.

No bugs, that was the amazing thing. Well, a few, but none that really bothered him. They kept the wandering spiders pretty much out in the jungle. Frank had taken to Rio like a duck to lingonberry sauce. Rio was different, exotic—nothing he couldn't get used to except for the Portuguese, which he figured was just screwed-up Spanish. Suki was acting as their interpreter, picking up the lingo like a champ. Learning to read English, too, and Frank was finding that he wasn't too bad a teacher.

She'd opened Mink's safe in the Jamboree and there'd been $1,463,900 in there and a key to a safe deposit box. Even now, just thinking about the sight of all that money made his scalp tingle. They'd used some of it to set him up as Frank Wiley—social security, driver's license, passport, the whole nine yards—got her fixed up as

Suki Flood, then flown to Georgetown on the Caymans where they'd set up his-and-hers accounts, $700,000 each, then gone on to Rio with over $40,000 stuffed in their jeans. They still had the safe deposit key, but didn't have any idea what to do with it or where the box was.

At an interest rate of 4.8 percent, each of them was making $33,600 a year. Frank didn't know how they were going to spend that much, and they weren't, so the Cayman money was growing. For now they lived dutch, in a nice apartment off Rua Barata Ribeiro, and Frank hadn't asked her how long she was going to stick around before getting on with the rest of her life, and really didn't want to know.

What to do, that was each day's question. But there was always something. One thing he would try someday was deep-sea fishing. Tuna, marlin, maybe dorado—but for that you had to go out forty miles, out by the continental shelf. That could wait a while. Far as he knew, the fish weren't going anywhere.

Suki stood up and let her dress slip down around her ankles. She stepped out of it, set it on her chair. The bikini was even smaller than Frank remembered. From the back, she looked entirely naked.

"Christ, you're gonna cause a riot," he said.

"Sweet-talker. I'm just gonna get my feet wet. Watch my stuff, okay?"

"I'm watching your stuff right now. So's everyone else."

She made a face at him, turned away, then turned back. "How the hell *did* you lose that goddamn finger, Frank? I've heard so many stories my head is spinning."

"Nineteen and fifty-two," he said. "Korea. I stepped out of this helicopter just south of Pyongyang and felt this big draft. So I wet my finger and stuck it up to see which way the wind was blowing and, pow! off the sonofabitch came. Turns out it was a *down*draft and I shouldn't've—"

"Oh, my God." Suki walked away, toward the water.

He watched her go. It was quite a sight.

Rob Leininger is the multi-genre author of 14 novels (as of this writing). He was taught electronics in the U.S. Navy, worked on shipboard radios and radar on two cruisers. "Wintered-over" at McMurdo Station in Antarctica where the temperature reached 77 degrees below zero. He received a bachelor of science degree in mechanical engineering at the University of Nevada in Reno and worked on "black" projects for the defense industry. He took graduate-level courses in mathematics and taught high school math in Reno for twelve years. Currently he lives in Northwestern Montana with his wife and three spoiled dogs.

NOVELS BY ROB LEININGER

Killing Suki Flood—a thriller. Optioned many times for a movie, and still under option.

Sunspot—a "science thriller." Published by Avon Books in 1991 as *Black Sun*, it has been extensively revised and retitled.

Richter Ten—another "science thriller," and a love story. An enormous earthquake (not the San Andreas) threatens the Pacific Coast of the U.S.

The Tenderfoot—an unusual western. Brains vs. Brawn.

Gumshoe—a mystery, nominated for a Shamus Award by the PI Writers of America. An IRS agent abandons the shakedown of taxpayers to become Reno's newest private detective.

Gumshoe for Two—The Mort Angel Saga continues.

Gumshoe on the Loose

Gumshoe Rock

Gumshoe in the Dark

Gumshoe Gone

Gumshoe Outlaw (pub date to be announced)

January Cold Kill—a mystery written in the first person as a 29-year-old gorgeous woman. (Which Leininger is not.)

Maxwell's Demon—a boy with a "gift" that makes him the "most dangerous person on the planet" according to the CIA.

Nicholas Phree and the Emerald of Bool—"a children's story written for adults." Really. See Leininger's website (below).

Olongapo Liberty—a novel about the most infamous liberty port of the Vietnam War. Based on the "real" navy, this one is not for the squeamish. Language is raw. Even the tattoos are ugly.

www.robleininger.com

Made in the USA
Columbia, SC
11 January 2022

54113053R10148